Lynsay Sands

Falling for the Highlander

AVONBOOKS

An Imprint of HarperCollins*Publishers*

Excerpt from *Immortal Unchained* copyright © 2017 by Lynsay Sands.

First Avon Books mass market printing: February 2017
First Avon Books hardcover printing: January 2017

ISBN 978-0-06-267330-5

17 18 19 20 21 LSC 10 9 8 7 6 5 4 3 2 1

Falling for the Highlander

Chapter 1

"They're here!"

Murine glanced up sharply from the message she was writing as her maid entered the room. She waited until Beth closed the bedchamber door before asking, "Did ye find out who they are?"

"Nay." The brunette looked vexed. "None o' the maids or the lasses in the kitchen seem to ken, or if they do they're no' telling me."

"Oh," Murine said with disappointment, then shook her head and returned her gaze to the message she'd been writing. Mouth tightening, she signed her name to the bottom. "It matters not. They're Scots. Surely their trip home will take them past the Buchanans or the Drummonds and they will deliver this for me." Biting her lip, she began to wave the parchment about to dry it and added, "I ha'e a couple coins left I can give them fer their trouble."

"Most like they'll pocket the coins, say they'll deliver it and toss it away as soon as they've left Danvries," Beth said unhappily. "I do no' ken why ye just do no' send one o' yer brother's men with the message."

"I have sent three that way and got no response," Murine reminded her grimly. Mouth flattening with displeasure, she admitted, "I begin to suspect Montrose is not sending them at all."

"But why would he do that?"

"'Tis hard to say with my brother," Murine muttered unhappily. "He's a . . . difficult man."

Beth snorted. "He's a selfish, greedy cur, hell-bent on wagering his life away and yours with it. But I see no reason for him no' to send yer messages to yer friends."

"Neither do I," Murine admitted unhappily. "But if he did send them, then . . ." She bit her lip, unwilling to give voice to her biggest fear. If Montrose had sent her messages, then Saidh, Jo and Edith just weren't bothering to answer.

That thought was a troubling one and made her worry that she had said or done something when last they were together to upset them all. Murine had wracked her brain trying to sort out what that might be, but could think of nothing. She'd then switched to wondering if perhaps her brother wasn't sending them as he assured her he would. She couldn't imagine why, but was actually beginning to hope that was the case. It was certainly preferable to thinking her three best friends had turned their backs on her for some reason.

"It should be dry enough now," she muttered and quickly rolled, then sealed the parchment.

"How are ye going to get it to the Scots without yer brother seeing?" Beth asked worriedly as she stood up.

"I heard Montrose ordering Cook to be sure he has lots of food and drink on hand when the Scots get here," Murine explained as she slid the parchment up her sleeve and checked to be sure that it was concealed and wasn't being crushed. "I shall slip the message to one of the men when Montrose is distracted with eating."

"Yer brother is offering food and drink to someone?" Beth asked dryly. "I never thought to see the like. The bastard's so cheap I'd think he'd choke on the offer."

"I expect he's hoping to fill them with ale or whiskey to make them more amenable to accepting credit rather than demanding payment for the horses he wants," Murine said, satisfied that the parchment would be fine up her sleeve.

"Aye, well, Lord knows he has no' the coin to actually buy them. He's already gambled away all of his own money, and your dower to boot," Beth said bitterly.

"Aye," Murine agreed wearily. It was not a subject she cared to contemplate. She'd been horrified when she'd learned that bit of news. She'd thought her situation dire enough when she'd had a dower but no betrothed, but without dower, it would be impossible to find anyone willing to marry her. It now looked like she would live out her days here at Danvries as an old maid, dependent on her selfish brother, and that was only if he didn't tire of her presence and send her off to the Abbey to become a nun.

Pushing that depressing thought from her mind, she brushed the wrinkles out of her gown, straightened her shoulders and headed for the door. "Come. We will sit by the fire in the great hall until they come in. Then once the food arrives, we will use that as an excuse to join the table and slip my message to one of the men."

"I'D BEEN TOLD YOUR ANIMALS WERE SUPERIOR AND THEY certainly are that."

Dougall waited patiently as Montrose Danvries ran a hand down the mare's side and then circled the horse, examining every inch of her.

Lord Danvries next moved on to the stallion and gave him the same attention, examining his withers and legs, sides and head just as thoroughly. His expression was a combination of wonder and appreciation when he paused at the beast's head. Rubbing one hand down the stallion's nose, he murmured, "Exactly what I was hoping for."

"If they meet yer expectations, perhaps we should discuss payment," Dougall suggested.

Danvries stiffened, several expressions flickering across his face. Settling on a wide, fake smile, the man turned away toward the keep. "Come. Let us go inside for beverages."

"I told ye," Conran muttered, stepping up beside Dougall. "The bastard has no' the coin. He lost it all in that last wager with his king."

Dougall sighed at his brother's words, recognizing satisfaction amidst the irritation in the younger man's tone. Conran had always liked saying *I told ye so*.

"Come along, gentlemen," Danvries said without looking back. "There is much to discuss."

Mouth tightening, Dougall glared at the man's retreating back. Danvries should have tossed him a bag of coins, and bid him on his way. The only time the buyer wanted to "discuss" matters was when he didn't have the coin, or wanted to talk down the price. Dougall was not one to be talked down. Despite knowing this was a great waste of time, though, he waved away his brother's further mutterings and trailed the Englishman out of the stables and toward the keep. He didn't need to look around to know that Conran, Geordie and Alick were following. It had been a long journey here and they were all thirsty. The least Danvries could do was see them fed and watered before they took their beasts and headed home to Scotland.

"He'll try to cheat ye," Conran warned, on Dougall's heels. "Bloody English bastards. Most o' them'd sell their mother for a coin."

"Nah," their younger brother, Geordie, put in behind them. "It's their daughters they sell. The old women wouldn't be worth a coin. They're too bitter from years living with the English bastards to be worth anything. The daughters, though, are usually sweet and pretty and have not yet grown bitter. Get 'em away young enough and they're almost as good as a Scottish lass. Almost," he repeated, stressing the point.

"Lord Danvries has neither a mother nor a daughter, so I'm sure that's no' a worry," Dougall muttered impatiently.

"He has a sister though," Conran pointed out. When Dougall glanced to him with surprise, he nodded. "An old maid left to whither on the vine thanks to Lord Danvries wagering away her dower."

"He wagered away her dower?" Geordie asked with surprise when Dougall didn't comment.

"Is that even allowed?" Alick added with a frown.

"From what I heard, he was named her guardian in the father's will so had control over it," Conran said with a shrug.

Dougall shook his head and they all fell silent as they trailed Danvries into the great hall and noted the people milling about.

There were soldiers at the table enjoying their noon repast, servants bustling about cleaning, and a lady seated by the fire. Dougall's gaze slid over the woman in passing, and then almost immediately moved back to her. She was young. Not in the first blush of youth, but perhaps twenty or so and still retaining some of its dew. Dougall guessed she must be Danvries's bride. If so, he was a damned lucky man, for she seemed to glow as brightly as the fire in that dim great hall. Her gown was a pale rose color with white trim on a shapely figure, and her hair was a halo of golden tresses that poured over her shoulders and down her back. She was peering down at some needlework she was stitching, but when Danvries called for ale, she glanced over briefly and Dougall's attention turned to her face. Heart-shaped lips, large doe eyes and a straight little nose all worked together in an oval face to make her one of the most striking women he'd ever seen. Danvries was definitely a lucky man.

"Come sit."

Dougall dragged his eyes from the vision by the fire, suddenly aware that he'd stopped walking and the Englishman was now at the great hall table while he was still just inside the door with his brothers at his back. Danvries was eyeing him with a tinge of amusement that suggested he was used to men ogling his wife.

Forcing himself to move again, Dougall led the men to the table and settled on the bench where Danvries indicated, noting that it left him with a clear view of the woman by the fire.

Women, he corrected himself, for a dark-haired maid accompanied the blonde, working diligently over her own stitching. But the lady's beauty seemed to cast the maid into shadow; he'd hardly noticed her ere this.

"My sister," Danvries said quietly.

Sister? The word echoed in Dougall's mind, and he felt a sense of relief he didn't really understand. She definitely wasn't the withered old maid Conran had described, but what did it matter to him if she was Danvries's wife or sister? It didn't, he assured himself, and turned determinedly to his host, pausing as he noted that the man was eyeing the woman with something like speculation in his eyes. He frowned over that and then said, "About payment fer the horses . . . ?"

"Ah, yes," Danvries offered a somewhat tight smile and said, "Your horses are, of course, every bit the quality animals I'd been led to expect. Lord Hainsworth did not oversell them when he told me about your abilities at breeding quality mares and stallions."

Dougall nodded, waiting for the *but*.

"Howbeit," Danvries began and Dougall just restrained himself from rolling his eyes. *But, howbeit* . . . However the man chose to phrase it, it was a *but*.

"Howbeit?" Dougall prodded when Danvries hesitated.

"Well, I had the money here ready for you, but a bit of bad luck came my way."

The wager with the king, Dougall thought dryly. That hadn't been bad luck, it had been stupidity. The English king always won at wagers, and had backed La Bête at jousting, a smart move. Danvries betting against La Bête when the warrior had never ever lost . . . well, that was sheer stupidity. It wasn't Dougall's problem, though, except that it meant he'd made this trip for naught.

Sighing, he stood with a nod. "So ye do no' want the horses now."

"Nay, nay, I want them," Danvries said quickly, catching his arm as the men rose to stand as well. When Dougall turned his eyes to the hand on his arm, Danvries immediately released him. "Sorry. Sit, sit. I do want the horses. Of course, I do."

"Ye just can no' pay fer them," Dougall suggested dryly, still standing.

"Nay. I mean, aye. Aye, I can," Danvries corrected himself quickly. "Of course I can."

When Dougall remained standing and merely waited, Danvries muttered a bit irritably, "Do sit down so we can discuss this. I am getting a crick in my neck looking up at you."

Dougall didn't think there was much to discuss. Either he could pay for the horses or he couldn't. However, a young maid had arrived with the ale, so he settled back on the bench. His brothers were quick to drop back in their seats as well. It had been a long dusty ride here. He'd give Danvries until he'd finished his ale, but unless the man could come up with the coin, he was leaving . . . and taking his horses with him.

Nodding his thanks to the young maid, Dougall took a drink of his ale, his eyes wandering back to the blonde by the fire. She and her maid were chattering quietly now and casting glances toward the table.

"I'm sure it will only take me a couple of weeks to get your coin," Danvries announced, drawing his attention again.

The man's words were abrupt and overloud, a sign of anxiety, Dougall thought and wasn't surprised. He nodded slowly. "I can hold them fer ye fer a couple weeks. Ye can come collect them when ye have the coin. But if the month ends and ye have no' arrived, I can no' promise—"

"Nay, nay, nay," Danvries cut in. "You do not understand. I need them now. I cannot be without a horse. I—"

"What happened to yer horse?" Dougall interrupted.

Danvries dropped his gaze and looked away, a frown curving his lips. It was Conran who leaned close to Dougall and murmured, "Part o' the wager."

Dougall sighed. The man was gambling his life away. Shaking his head, he said, "Ye will no' be without a horse. I saw a good thirty in the stables, and—"

"They belong to my men, not me," Danvries said stiffly, and then added, "I need a horse. A lord without a horse is like a king without a country."

"A sale without payment is no' a sale at all," Dougall countered with little sympathy. It was hard to feel sorry for someone who had willfully and foolishly gambled away his horse and his wealth. Danvries had been one of the wealthiest estates in England under this man's grandfather, and then he had died and Danvries had inherited. Dougall had heard rumors the man was running through his inheritance with poor spending and worse bets, but had paid it little heed. His brother had apparently paid more attention.

"There will be payment. It will just take me a little bit of time to get the coin together," Danvries said pleadingly. "Surely you can extend me credit for a bit of time?"

Dougall eyed the man, and then glanced to his sister. She was staring down at her stitching, but unmoving. He suspected she was listening and briefly considered extending Danvries the credit he requested for her sake. The man wasn't just buying a stallion for himself. Dougall suspected the mare was for the sister. Obviously Danvries had also lost her horse in the wager and it seemed a shame that she would suffer for his bad habits. But in the end, Dougall shook his head. He never extended credit. He insisted on payment ere handing over any horseflesh and didn't like the idea of changing that now. Especially not with a man who had gambled himself so deep that Dougall suspected he wouldn't be able to pull himself back out.

"I do no' extend credit," he said calmly and stood.

"Wait." Danvries grabbed his arm again, desperation on his face. He then glanced wildly around, obviously seeking something to trade or to convince Dougall to give him credit. Dougall's stomach rolled over when the man's eyes landed on his sister and stayed there. Surely he wouldn't—

"My sister."

Dougall's eyes narrowed.

"Leave the horses and take her with you," Danvries said.

"I'm no' in the market fer a wife at the moment," Dougall said dryly.

"I did not say you had to marry her," Danvries countered at once.

Dougall glowered at the man and then deliberately misunderstood his offer in the hopes that he would rethink and recant it. "Are ye suggesting I keep her as a marker? A hostage until ye pay fer the horses?"

Danvries hesitated, his eyes on his sister, and then he turned back, determination on his face. "Or you could keep her in place of payment. Until you think you have got your value for the horses. Of course, you would have to return her eventually."

Dougall's gaze shifted to the women by the fire as a gasp slipped from the blonde. She had been looking over her shoulder toward them with horror, but quickly jerked her face away now. If he'd been tempted by Danvries's offer, and if Dougall was honest with himself, the idea of having this woman in his bed was a tempting one, the woman's reaction was enough to make him forget it. He had never forced a woman into his bed and didn't intend to start now.

He shifted his gaze back to Danvries, dislike rolling through him. The man cared so little for the lass that he'd sell her as a sexual slave in exchange for horses. It made it hard to believe that he was actually buying one of them for her. Now Dougall suspected it was for another woman, his betrothed perhaps, if he had one. All of which mattered little, he thought and said coldly, "Ye shame yer sister, yerself and me with the offer." Turning to his brothers, he added, "Our business here is done."

He needn't have bothered; Conran, Geordie and Alick were already getting to their feet.

WHEN THE SCOTS ALL STOOD TO LEAVE, MURINE RELEASED A little shudder of relief, and then drew in a deep breath. It was only then she realized that she'd been holding her breath ever since her brother had offered her to the Scot in exchange for horses. Her mind was still reeling from that event. She couldn't believe he'd done it. She and Montrose had not grown up together and, in fact, had spent very little time in each other's company until her father's death had left her in his care, so there was little in the way of affection between them. Still, he was her *brother* and she was his sister and charge, and the idea that he would offer her out like some lightskirt . . .

Murine swallowed and got stiffly to her feet, eager to escape the great hall and the possibility of having to deal with her brother after his monstrous action. She glanced to Beth to see that the other woman was already on her feet and ready to follow. Relieved, Murine hurried toward the stairs. They'd managed to mount the first few steps when she heard Montrose cry, "Nay. Please wait! If you will not—I can get you the coin."

Murine didn't slow, but she did glance around to see the leader of the Scots shake his head in disgust as he reached the great hall doors.

"By tonight!" Montrose added, sounding desperate. "Ye can enjoy a nice meal and a rest and I'll ha'e the coin by tonight."

Murine noted that the Scot stopped at the door and turned to eye Montrose as if he were a bug scuttling out from under a rock. When his gaze then slid to where she and Beth had been seated, she hurried up the last few steps in case he glanced around in search of her. Murine didn't look again until she'd reached the safety of the shadowy upper landing, then she slowed and turned to have a good look at the men below. It was something she hadn't really been able to do until now. While seated by the fire in the great hall, she'd only dared cast quick, furtive glances at the visitors. Now, however, she examined each of the Scots in turn.

They were all tall and strong with dark hair, but Murine

found her eye returning to the one who appeared to be their leader. She couldn't have said why. They were all good-looking men, but for some reason she found him the most compelling. He was obviously angry and disgusted by her brother's proposition, but then all of the men appeared to be. However, when he'd looked toward the fire for her just now, there had been something else in his eyes. Not pity, but simple concern and perhaps sympathy.

"I can get you the coin by tonight. Tomorrow morn at the latest," Montrose repeated, drawing Murine's reluctant gaze away from the leader of the Scots and back to her brother as he added, "My neighbor and friend, Muller, has always had an eye for my sister. He'll give me the coin for the chance to spend time with her."

Murine actually had to cover her mouth to stifle the cry that wanted to slip out. Offering her up to these men for horses was bad enough, but offering her to Muller for coin? Her stomach turned over violently at the suggestion. The Scot had been kind and chivalrous enough to refuse the offer. Muller would not. He would jump at the chance and would not care whether she was even willing. She would be no better than a—

"I'll no' be a party to yer turning yer *lady* sister into a whore."

Murine winced as he said the word she was thinking.

"Coin or no coin, the horses are no longer fer sale to ye," the Scot added coldly.

When he then turned on his heel and walked out of the keep with his men hard on his heels, Murine almost wished she could give chase and go with them. Instead, she whirled and caught Beth's arm to rush her down the hall to her room. She had to get out of there, and quickly. Montrose would waste no time setting his plan into action and she needed to be far away from here when Muller arrived to claim his prize.

Once in her room, Murine paused and glanced around wildly before turning to Beth and ordering, "Fetch me an empty sack from the kitchens, please. But do no' let anyone see ye take it."

Beth nodded and was gone almost before the last word was spoken. Murine immediately hurried to the chests against the bedchamber wall to begin sorting through her belongings, trying to decide what she should take and what she could not. Traveling light seemed the smartest option. A spare gown, a spare shift, coins . . .

Her mouth tightened at that thought. All she had were the few coins she'd intended to give to the Scots for taking her message. She would be delivering that message herself now, and would need those coins.

By the time Beth returned, Murine had chosen the few things she would take with her. She'd even rolled her gown and shift in preparation of packing them away.

The maid handed over the sack she'd gone to fetch. Her gaze then slid over the few belongings on the bed and she frowned. "Ye're fleeing?"

"Aye," Murine said grimly.

Beth hesitated and then asked worriedly, "Are ye sure this is the right thing to do, m'lady?"

Murine's lips tightened and she merely nodded as she stuffed the rolled-up gown into the sack the woman had pinched from the kitchens.

"But 'tis dangerous to travel at the best o' times, e'en with a large party. A woman alone . . ." Beth shook her head at the very thought. "Could we no' send a message to Lady Joan, or Lady Saidh instead? I'm sure one o' them would send an escort fer ye."

"Montrose is probably down there writing up his offer to Muller as we speak," Murine said grimly. "If I do no' leave now, I shall no doubt be ruined by nightfall."

"But, m'lady," Beth said, tears in her eyes. "Ye can no' travel alone. Ye could be killed by bandits . . . or worse."

Murine stilled briefly at the words, thinking of her brothers Colin and Peter who had been killed on a trip two years earlier, but then shook her head and shoved a linen shift into the bag.

"There are some things worse than death, Beth. And staying here where I will be sold off by me own brother . . ." She shook her head bitterly. "Thank ye, I think I'll take me chances on the road."

Beth was silent for a moment, her expression conflicted, and then raised her shoulders and said stolidly, "Then I'll come with ye."

Murine hesitated, briefly tempted by the offer, but shook her head on a sigh. "Nay, ye'll not. Ye'll stay here."

"But—"

"I need ye to stay here and help hide the fact I've left," Murine interrupted quickly.

Beth closed her mouth on her unfinished protest and asked uncertainly, "How am I to do that?"

"Stay here in me room. If Montrose comes looking for me, claim I am sleeping and send him away," Murine said as she finished packing and closed the bag. She didn't really think that ruse would work. Mostly she was using it as an excuse to keep from taking the maid with her. Murine had little hope of actually managing this escape attempt. She suspected she'd be hunted down and brought back ere the first night ended, but if she did manage to get away . . . well, as Beth had said, the road was dangerous. It was one thing to risk her own life to try to preserve her honor. It was another thing entirely to risk Beth's life as well.

"Where will ye go?" Beth asked worriedly, following her to the door.

"I'll slip down the back stairs to the kitchens and then sneak around to get Henry and—"

"Nay, I mean, where will ye go once ye leave Danvries?" Beth interrupted.

"Oh." Murine breathed and then shrugged helplessly. "To Saidh. Buchanan is closest, I think, and she did say if I ever needed assistance to not hesitate to call on her. I am in definite need of assistance now."

"Aye, ye are," Beth agreed solemnly, and then reached out quickly to hug her. "Be careful m'lady, and pray stay safe."

"I will," Murine whispered, then pulled back and forced a smile. "I'll send fer ye . . . if I can."

"Oh, do no' worry about me. I'll be fine. Ye just take good care o' yerself," she said bravely, dashing away a tear.

Murine squeezed her arm gently, then opened her bedchamber door and peered cautiously out. Finding the hall empty, she slid out and rushed for the stairs.

"I CAN'T BELIEVE THE BASTARD TRIED TO SELL HIS SISTER FER a couple horses."

Dougall grimaced and glanced at his brother Conran at those bewildered words. After the debacle at Danvries, they had ridden to the village inn for a meal ere starting the long trek home. The conversation there had been focused on who they might sell the mare and stallion to now, and to wonder how they would find things at home. Not wanting to shame the sister in her own village, no one had even got near the topic of Danvries and his offer . . . until now as they left Danvries's land.

"Aye," Dougall acknowledged quietly.

"Ye do no' seem surprised."

"People rarely surprise me anymore," Dougall said grimly, and then added in a lighter tone, "The only thing that surprises me is that ye were kind enough no' to discuss it in the village and waited so long to bring up the subject."

"'Twas no' kindness," Conran denied quickly. "I just did no' want to ruin me meal. Was like to give me indigestion."

"Oh, aye, o' course it was," Dougall agreed with amusement. He knew that wasn't true. Conran just didn't like to appear soft. Although, Dougall thought, talking about it now was making his own lunch roll in his stomach.

"Ye ken that now the idea's occurred to him, he's going to sell her off to his friend fer coin," Conran said heavily.

"Aye. He'll use her to make what money he can to make up

fer his gambling," Dougall said with distaste, recalling the glowing woman.

"If she allows it," Conran said with a shrug. "Mayhap she'll refuse."

"Hmm." Dougall muttered, but thought she might not be given the choice. Danvries was obviously her guardian, although she was of marriageable age. "Why is she still unwed?"

Conran shrugged. "As I said, talk is he gambled away her dower."

"Aye, but how? It should have been protected," Dougall said with a frown. "And she should ha'e been betrothed as a child and collected long ere this."

"Mayhap her betrothed died," Conran suggested, and then added, "And I'm sure the king would have stepped in and no' allowed Danvries gambling away her dower . . . had he no' been the one who won the wager."

"So she'll ne'er marry," Dougall said thoughtfully.

"And be at the mercy of her brother all her days," Conran commented, shaking his own head.

"Dear God," Dougall breathed and almost felt bad that he'd turned down the man's offer. At least he would have been kind to her, and mayhap had things worked out . . . Well, he had grown quite wealthy through his horse breeding. The only reason he hadn't already purchased himself an estate was that their older brother, Aulay, had needed his aid raising their younger brothers and sister when their parents had died. A dower wasn't an absolute necessity in a wife for him. On the other hand, he didn't know the woman. She was pretty enough, but her brother was a weak man with a few bad habits, drinking and gambling among them. He also apparently had little in the way of moral fiber to him. For all Dougall knew, the same was true of her. But that gasp from her when her brother had offered her . . .

Dougall pushed away the memory. He had nothing to feel guilty about. He didn't even know the lass.

"'Tis a shame," Conran said quietly. "She's a lovely lass."

Dougall merely nodded. She was indeed lovely.

"She looked sweet and demure," Geordie commented from his other side when he remained silent.

"Aye, she did," Dougall said on a sigh. "Mayhap me refusal to sell him horses no matter whether he has the coin or no' will stop his plans."

"For now, maybe," Conran said dubiously. "Though I suspect he'll go ahead with it in hopes ye'll change yer mind when he presents the payment. On the other hand, he could buy horses elsewhere . . . were he to get the coin."

Not wanting to encourage this line of conversation, Dougall didn't comment. He had no desire to think the woman would still be sold off like a cheap lightskirt. Besides, he could see something on the path ahead and was distracted by trying to sort out what it was.

Noting his sudden stillness in the saddle, Conran glanced ahead and squinted. "It looks like someone on horseback, but . . ."

"But 'tis a very strange horse," Dougall murmured. It looked short and wide, a squat creature that moved with a somewhat awkward gait.

"Is that a cow he's riding?" Conran asked with amazement as they drew closer.

"A bull," Dougall corrected as the rider shifted and he spotted a horn poking up into view. "And if I'm no' mistaken, he is a she. That looks like a gown to me."

"Hmm," Alick murmured behind them. "A rose gown. Lady Danvries was wearing a rose gown."

"Aye, she was," Dougall agreed, and urged his horse to move more quickly.

"DAMN," MURINE BREATHED WHEN SHE HEARD THE APproaching horse. She'd spotted the men on horseback behind her just moments ago and had recognized them as the Scots

Montrose had been trying to buy horses from. It could have been worse. Montrose could have discovered that she'd fled and come after her, but this was bad enough. These were the men her brother had tried to sell her to and the embarrassment and shame of what he'd done was overwhelming. She'd really rather not have to face them again.

"M'lady."

Murine kept her gaze straight ahead, hoping that if she pretended not to hear him, the man might just leave her be and travel on.

"Lady Danvries," he said, a little more loudly and when she again didn't respond, commented, "Yer brother did no' bother to mention ye were deaf when he offered ye to me. I should ha'e guessed as much, though. He's obviously a cheat and a louse, so o' course he'd try to pass off a defective lass in exchange fer me high-quality beasts."

Gasping in outrage, Murine gave up her pretense and turned to glare at the man as she snapped, "I'm no' defective! And ye'd ha'e been lucky to ha'e me, I'm worth a hundred o' yer horses."

When his mouth quirked up on one side and one eyebrow rose high on his forehead, she realized what she'd said and quickly added, "Not that I'd ha'e agreed to such a shameful bargain." Turning forward again, she muttered, "Me brother has obviously lost his mind to sink so low."

"And so ye're running away before he offers ye to someone who is no' as honorable as meself and might accept?"

Murine's mouth flattened with displeasure. That was exactly what she was doing . . . or trying to do. But now she was fretting over the possibility that this man might somehow interfere and prevent her escape.

"Dougall."

Murine glanced around at that shout, her eyes widening when she saw that his men, who had been keeping back apace, were suddenly urging their mounts to catch them up.

"What is it, Conran?" Dougall asked with a frown.

"Riders," the man explained, glancing worriedly toward Murine. "And I'm thinking it's Danvries's men after the lady here, to take her back."

Cursing under her breath, Murine started to turn her bull toward the trees, intent on hiding, but found her way blocked by horses as the other men caught up and surrounded them.

"No time fer that, m'lady," Conran said sympathetically. "They're moving fast; ye would no' make cover."

"Then we shall have to be her cover," Dougall said grimly. "Surround her, and cover her hair and dress. I'll meet the riders."

Murine opened her mouth to protest, but then let out a startled gasp when a cap landed on her head.

"Tuck yer hair up, lass," someone said.

"And here, put this round ye to hide yer pretty gown," someone else said, dropping a plaid around her shoulders.

Murine didn't argue, but clumsily shoved her hair up in the cap, then clutched the plaid around herself and glanced about at the Scots and their horses. Her bull sat perhaps a hand lower than their mounts, which helped hide what the plaid didn't cover of her skirts, but there were only three of them now and the two riderless horses they'd hoped to sell to her brother.

"Mayhap we should . . ." Rather than finish the suggestion, someone suddenly tossed another plaid over her, this one covering her head as well. She then felt pressure on the back of her neck as someone silently urged her to press herself flat to the bull's back. Hoping it was enough, Murine ignored the fact that she found it difficult to breathe in this position with the heavy cloth over her, closed her eyes and began to pray.

DOUGALL MANAGED TO GET ABOUT TWENTY FEET BACK UP THE path before the oncoming English riders reached him. He hoped it was far enough away from the woman his men were trying to provide cover for, but there was little he could do if it wasn't. The choice then would be whether or not to fight for the lass. Dougall hadn't yet made up his mind on the matter. It wasn't the fact that there were twenty of them. He and his brothers were skilled fighters. They could easily beat twenty lazy, poorly trained English soldiers. But he wasn't sure if Lady Danvries was worth fighting, and killing, over. If she was anything like her brother, she definitely wasn't . . . and really, this was none of his business. He supposed he'd have to play it by ear.

"Did Danvries find coin fer the horses, after all?" he asked lightly by way of greeting once the riders had stopped.

"Nay." The man in the lead glanced past him to his brothers and then back. "We are looking for Lord Danvries's sister. She went out for a ride and has not yet returned. Her brother grows concerned."

"A ride ye say?" Dougall asked, feigning surprise. "Are ye sure? I understood she was without a mount. 'Sides, she was sitting in the hall when we arrived and 'tis sure I am that she went above stairs ere we left."

"Aye." The man frowned and glanced back the way he'd come. "I gather she left after you and your men, and we did not pass her ere encountering you. She must have gone another way."

"That would make sense," Dougall agreed and he supposed it did make sense if you didn't know that he and his brothers had stopped for a meal ere leaving Danvries land.

The man nodded, and spun his horse back the way he'd come with a brusque "Good journey to ye."

"And to ye," Dougall said cheerfully and grinned as he watched the English soldier lead his men away. He hadn't even had to lie. Gad, the English were stupid. Of course, now he had to deal with the woman, he acknowledged, his smile fading.

Ah well. Dougall shook his head and turned to ride back to his own men.

"Lookin' fer the lass, were they?" Conran asked as the men eased aside to allow Dougall to move his horse up beside the woman's bull.

"Aye." Dougall glanced toward Lady Danvries, expecting her to thank him for his aid. But she proved she was English by refusing to even acknowledge his presence. The woman was still huddled low on her cow, the plaid covering her.

Scowling, he tugged the plaid off her, and then leaned quickly to the side to catch the woman when she started to tumble from the back of her beast.

"Well," Conran breathed with disgust when Dougall pulled her unconscious body across his horse to peer at her. "It looks like she's gone and died on us. That could cause trouble with the English."

"Nah, 'tis a faint," Dougall said, but then had to tear his gaze from her pale face to her chest just to make sure she was breathing. She was, but shallowly.

"It can no' be a faint," Alick protested at once, standing in the saddle and craning his head to try to get a look at the woman. "If the lass is brave enough to run away on her own, she's hardly the type to faint o'er a little scare like this."

"Unless it was no' courage that had her running away," Conran pointed out.

"What else would it be?" Alick asked with a scowl.

"She could be lacking the sense God gives most," Geordie suggested.

"Or she could be a few men short o' an army," Alick added reluctantly.

"This lass is no' daft," Conran snapped. "Nor is she witless. The two o' ye ought to be ashamed to suggest it."

"Well, why do ye think she's fainted then?"

Conran eyed her briefly and then said, "Well, now, mayhap she's ailing. 'Tis obvious her brother cares little for her well-being. Mayhap she's taken ill."

"And mayhap," Dougall said, shifting the woman to a more comfortable position on his lap, "Ye should stop acting like a bunch o' old women so we can continue on with our journey."

Conran raised his eyebrows. "Are we takin' her with us then?"

"Well, we can hardly leave her here by the side o' the road in her state, can we?" he pointed out with exasperation. "We'll carry her with us until she wakes."

"And then what?" Conran asked, eyes narrowed.

"And then we'll ask where she's heading and if 'tis on our way, we shall escort her there," he decided with a small frown. The woman was turning out to be a bit of trouble and he wasn't happy about that.

"And if where she is going is no' on our way?" Conran asked. "Or what if we've carried her right past where she was headed?"

"Then we'll deal with that at the time," Dougall said with forced patience, and then added irritably, "Right now, I'd jest be well pleased if ye'd get yer arses in gear and yer horses moving."

"All right, no need to holler," Conran said soothingly. "'Tis obvious the lass has set ye aback." He glanced around and then asked, "What about her cow?"

Grimacing, Dougall glanced at the beast and shrugged. "Leave it behind. It'll most like return to the keep. Then mayhap they'll think she took a tumble and'll waste days searching Danvries's woods fer her."

"But then she'll have naught to ride when she regains her wits," Conran pointed out.

"Then she'll have to ride with me, will she no'?" he asked dryly.

"Aye, but what if her travels lead her away from us. She can hardly follow her own plans with no beast to ride."

"'Tis a cow, Conran," he pointed out with disgust. "No one with all their faculties would ride a cow anyway." Sighing impatiently, he shook his head. "I shall supply her with a horse. We've two spare with us right now anyway."

"Two fine beasts worth a pretty coin or two," Conran pointed out sharply. "Ye can no' be thinking—"

"I'm thinkin' I'm tired o' listening to ye bend me ear and am eager to be off," Dougall snapped. "Do what ye like with the cow, but we are continuing on now."

He put his heels to his mount, sending it into a gallop that had Lady Danvries bouncing around in his lap like a sack of wheat. Muttering under his breath, Dougall slowed the beast and rearranged her before setting out again. But he found himself glancing down repeatedly at the woman in his arms, wondering what she would have done had he agreed to the trade with her brother. Had she been offered and used thusly before? That thought hadn't occurred to him ere this and now that it had, it angered him for some reason. He grimly turned his attention to the path ahead and urged his mount to move faster. But he also tightened his hold on the woman to ensure she wasn't bounced out of his lap in the process.

Chapter 2

THE SOUNDS OF MALE LAUGHTER, TALKING AND MOVEMENT stirred Murine from sleep. Turning on her back, she inhaled a deep draught of air, relieved to be able to do so. It seemed like forever since she'd managed that. She'd woken half a dozen times throughout the day to find herself caught tight to a man's chest and unable to catch a deep breath. Each time it had caused panic to rush through her and that, combined with the lack of air, had sent her back into unconsciousness again. This time, however, she was no longer in the warm airless cocoon she'd woken to so many times before. In fact, she was a bit chilly, Murine noted with a frown, and opened her eyes to the night sky.

A loud burst of laughter caught her attention, and she turned her head on the ground to peer at the dark figures silhouetted against a small fire. The men were all large, and definitely Scots, she realized as she noted their dress. The men who had hidden her from her brother's soldiers, she guessed. Certainly, she was quite sure it had been their leader who had held her so tightly on his horse. She didn't think he'd deliberately been trying to squeeze the breath from her, and fortunately, she hadn't died as she'd feared more than once as she'd awoken only to find consciousness slipping away again, sucked from her by the lack of air.

The laughter died down, and Murine tore her glance from the men to peer about. She was lying in front of a large tree, its trunk at her back. Somewhere beyond it in the darkness, she could hear the unmistakable sounds of horses moving about, and of course before her were the men and their fire, but everywhere else seemed so dark she could have believed she'd gone blind. It was a cloudy night, obviously, the fire giving the only light, which was a pity, really, because she had a terrible need to relieve herself.

Grimacing, Murine cautiously sat up, and then eased to her feet, a little surprised to find she was a bit light-headed. But then she hadn't eaten since morning. Between that and being starved for breath all day, she supposed she shouldn't be surprised. Reaching out, she pressed a hand to the tree to steady herself until the worst of the light-headedness passed, then moved quietly and carefully into the darkness to her left, reaching out blindly with her hands as she went. She was pretty sure the horses were to her right, but it was easy to get confused in such utter darkness and she didn't want to stumble under the horses, give them a scare and end up trampled.

Much to her relief, rather than bumping up against the warm shoulder, flank or buttock of a horse, she came to a halt when her hand flattened itself against the bark of another tree. Murine let out a little breath and felt her way around the tree until the fire was out of sight. Unwilling to go further and get lost in the darkness, she then hitched up her gown and squatted where she stood, a little sigh slipping through her lips. It was followed by a startled shriek as something warm and wet nudged her nose and cheek. In the next moment, Murine toppled over on the ground.

THE MEN ALL FELL SILENT AS A SCREAM RENT THE NIGHT AIR. Dougall turned his head, instinctively seeking out Lady Danvries where he'd laid her at the base of the tree behind them. She was no longer there.

Cursing, he grabbed the cool end of a burning log from the fire and stood even as his brothers did. Using the log as a makeshift torch, he started toward the tree, walking around it in the direction he thought the scream had come from. Off to the left of the horses he thought, slowing as her voice came to him muffled through the darkness.

"Oh, Henry! Fer heaven's sake ye scared the wits from me. Leave off with yer silly kisses now and let me be."

Dougall came to a halt. Henry? Kisses? Did the lady Danvries have a lover she'd ridden off on her cow to meet? If so, the man must have followed them and waited until they were distracted to creep up to her. It seemed she was not as innocent as she looked, he thought and was unaccountably disappointed by the knowledge.

Mouth tightening, he started determinedly forward, only to stop a moment later as his torch lit up a scene he'd not soon forget. Lady Danvries lay on her side in the grass, fending off a cow who stood over her, trying to lick her face as if it were a tasty treat. Nay, a bull, he corrected himself dryly as he took note of the horns as the bull stopped trying to lash her with its large tongue and raised its glaring eyes to him.

"Looks like her bull followed us," Conran commented behind him with amusement and Dougall glanced around to see that all three of his brothers had followed him and were grinning at the sight Lady Danvries made.

"Oh, m'laird." Lady Danvries scrambled to her feet, clasping one horn of her bull to manage it, then quickly brushed down her skirts before facing him with a pained expression. "I was just . . ." She waved vaguely to the woods, and he thought she might be blushing, though it was hard to tell in this light.

"Rolling about on the ground with yer cow," he suggested, feeling a smile trying to tug his lips wide.

"Certainly not," she said with dignity. "Besides, Henry is a bull." She turned then to caress the beast's snout as if to soothe any insult he had taken from being called a cow. "I raised him from a bairn. He was small and the stable master did no' think he'd survive, but I took him into the castle and tended him meself and he is growing into a fine big beast."

"Are ye mocking us?" Conran asked suddenly, stepping up beside Dougall, irritation on his face.

Lady Danvries frowned slightly. "Nay. I really did raise him meself, and he really is a bull."

"No' about the bull, lass. With yer speech," Dougall said quietly, knowing what had caused Conran's query. He hadn't noticed until his brother asked the question, but the woman was speaking with a Scots brogue. Seeing her bewilderment, he explained, "Ye're English, but mimicking our speech, Lady Danvries."

Her eyes widened at the suggestion and she drew herself up proudly. "I'm no' English. And me name is no' Danvries. Montrose Danvries is me half brother. I'm Lady Murine Carmichael. Me father was Beathan, laird of clan Carmichael."

"Murine Carmichael?" Conran breathed as if she was one of the world's finest wonders, a sentiment Dougall completely understood as he realized just who he was staring at.

It was Alick who said, "Our Saidh's Murine?"

Murine glanced to him sharply. "Saidh Buchanan? Ye ken her?"

"Ken her?" Geordie echoed with amusement. "Aye, ye could say that."

"We're her brothers," Alick announced. "I'm Alick Buchanan, and these are me older brothers Geordie, Conran and Dougall."

"Oh," Murine breathed, relief pouring over her face. Her expression then turned to startled alarm, however, when Alick suddenly launched himself forward and grabbed her up in an exuberant hug that lifted her off the ground.

"Thank ye, thank ye, thank ye," he crooned happily, swinging her around.

"Leave off, Alick. Ye'll make her dizzy swinging her about like that," Geordie growled and then stepped up to take his place when Alick set her back down. He too hugged her, lifting her off the ground to do so, but he didn't swing her about. He merely lifted her up in his arms and probably squeezed the breath out of her as he rumbled, "Thank ye, lass. We can ne'er repay ye fer what ye did fer us."

"Oh," Murine repeated weakly, patting Geordie's back uncertainly and looking confused. She obviously had no idea what the men were thanking her for.

The moment Geordie set her carefully back on her feet, Conran stepped forward to take his place.

"Aye, thank ye," Conran said and gave her a hug as well, though his was more circumspect. He let her stay on her feet and just gave her a quick, hard hug. "Saidh told us what happened with that harpy who tried to kill Lady Sinclair."

"Oh!" Murine said with sudden understanding now as Conran released her. Waving away their thanks with one fluttering hand, she mumbled an embarrassed "'Twas nothing."

"'Twas no' nothing," Dougall growled, and rather than hug her, crossed his arms and glared at her for the very suggestion. "Ye saved both Lady Sinclair and our sister when the wench would ha'e killed them. 'Tis a debt we can ne'er repay."

"But ye already ha'e," Murine assured him solemnly. "Ye saved me from me brother's plans fer me. Ye've definitely repaid the debt."

"Nay, lass, ye saved yerself, escaping on that cow o' yers," Dougall pointed out with a frown, thinking now that they should have done the saving rather than leave Danvries, and forcing her to save herself. Certainly, they would have had they known who she was. Saidh had told them a lot about the woman standing before them. She hadn't just saved Saidh's life, she'd become a dear friend to her as well, and by their sister's accounts was a fine lady; smart, honorable and brave.

"Aye, all we did was hide ye from yer brother's men when they came looking," Conran pointed out with a frown.

"And we'll continue to do so, will we no', Dougall?" Alick said excitedly. Without waiting for a response, he continued, "Ye're safe with us lass. We'll no' let that bastard English half brother o' yers catch and sell ye off like a mare to the first comer."

Geordie grunted an agreement and assured her, "Yer worries are over. We'll keep ye safe, will we no', brother?"

When all three of his brothers turned to him expectantly, Dougall hesitated and frowned. If Danvries was her guardian, he could do with her as he liked. If he found her. The best they could do for her was get her somewhere she might be safe from him. The problem was, Dougall couldn't think of many places like that. A nunnery came to mind. If she took vows, she would be protected by the church, but it did seem a waste to see a lovely lass like Murine, who was not only pretty, but brave and, according to Saidh, clever, locked away in a church for the rest of her days.

"Dougall?" Conran prompted when he remained silent. "We'll keep her safe, will we no'?"

Blowing his breath out on a sigh, Dougall nodded reluctantly. He couldn't in good conscience see her return to Danvries. The man would just use her horribly to gain the coin he lost with his wagers. So they would have to do what they could. First he had a couple of questions he needed answered, though. "Where were ye planning on going when ye fled on yer cow? Do ye ha'e family who might offer refuge?"

"Henry is a bull, no' a cow," Murine repeated firmly, and caressed her cow's nose. The animal immediately tried to lick her hand as if it might be a tasty treat, and Murine smiled crookedly as she avoided the tongue. Glancing to him, she added solemnly, "Thank ye fer bringing him along too. I ken it must ha'e slowed ye down."

Dougall ignored the nudge Conran gave him and didn't mention that he'd ordered the bull left behind. The ornery beast had decided to follow them on its own. In truth, Dougall was rather impressed that it had been able to keep up. To prevent one of the men from admitting that, he shifted and gestured back the way they'd come. "Let us all go sit by the fire. Ye can tell us where ye were headed. We'll escort ye there safely."

"Aye," Alick said with a smile as he turned back toward the fire. "We owe ye that much and more fer saving our Saidh."

The men all started to head back to the fire, but Dougall

waited for Murine and arched an eyebrow when she didn't immediately follow them.

"I was just slipping away to attend to . . . er . . . personal needs," she finished demurely, and then scowled at the bull and added, "But was most rudely interrupted."

"Ah." Dougall said, and then frowned, unsure what to do. If he left, he took the light with him, and it didn't seem right to leave her standing here in the woods in the dark. On the other hand, she'd hardly appreciate his standing over her with a torch while she squatted in the bushes. Holding out the log, he asked, "Would ye like this?"

"Er . . ." Murine eyed the makeshift torch uncertainly, then stepped forward to take it, her eyes widening and her second hand rising to join the first as she felt its weight. It was rather a good-sized log, he supposed and wondered how she'd manage what she needed to do with both hands occupied holding the makeshift torch.

"Mayhap I should make ye a proper torch, one smaller, or longer that ye could plant in the ground and—"

"Nay," she interrupted and then offered a somewhat forced smile and added, "My need is rather pressing, m'laird. So, I'll make do," After a pause, she added, "If ye'd just like to return to the fire and leave me alone to get to it."

"Oh, aye." Dougall nodded and started to turn away, but when he realized he could see the men settling themselves around the fire, he turned back and suggested, "Ye may want to move a little further behind the tree there. Otherwise me brothers'll—"

"Aye," she interrupted, and with the torch so close to her face, this time there was no question that she was blushing.

Nodding, Dougall started to turn away again, only to pause and turn back in question when she cleared her throat.

"I . . . would ye mind . . . ?" She gestured to her amorous bull, who was presently licking at her arm through her gown, and Dougall had to bite back a smile.

Scowling instead, he walked over, caught the beast by the bulky collar around his neck and pulled at it. The bull was a stubborn cuss, and dug in, bracing his legs and refusing to move until his lady said, "Go on with ye, Henry. I'll be along in a moment."

Much to Dougall's amazement, the bull stopped resisting then and allowed Dougall to drag him away from his lady, as obedient as a dog. Shaking his head at the thought, Dougall led the beast back to the area behind his men, then paused, unsure what to do with the animal.

"He's probably hungry," Conran commented, glancing over his shoulder with a grin.

"Well then mayhap ye should feed him," Dougall growled.

Conran cocked an eyebrow, and then nodded and turned to look at Alick. He didn't have to say a word. The younger man got up with a sigh and moved around to take the bull's reins from Dougall. He was the one in charge of the horses when they traveled, after all. Releasing the reins, he moved to sit where he'd been ere they'd heard Murine scream. He immediately found himself struggling not to turn and look in the woman's direction to see if she'd taken his suggestion and moved to a spot where she was less likely to be seen.

"Murine Carmichael," Conran murmured and then shook his head. "And here I thought her English."

"Aye," Dougall said thoughtfully.

"She's a fine-looking woman," Conran added.

"Verra fine-looking." Geordie agreed with a grin. "Saidh ne'er mentioned that."

"'Tis good she got away from that bloody brother o' hers," Alick said grimly, returning to the fire. "It makes me blood boil that he'd try to sell her like that. 'Twas bad enough when I thought her an English lass, but a Scot? And the brave lass who saved our sister?" He shook his head with disgust.

"Hmm," Geordie muttered, his grin fading. "We shall ha'e to see to it that her brother does no' sell her off."

"And how do ye plan to ensure that?" Dougall asked quietly, finally speaking his worries aloud. "He is her brother, and guardian. If he finds her—"

"Then we'll ha'e to see he does no' find her," Alick said with a frown.

"We could hide her at Buchanan," Geordie suggested.

"He kens she and Saidh are friends," Dougall pointed out. "Buchanan is one o' the first places he will look when they do no' find her close to home. Especially since we were at Danvries when she went missing. In fact, his men may already be following us."

His brothers all frowned at this truth and then Alick pointed out, "Were she to marry, he would no longer be her guardian with any rights o'er her."

That thought had occurred to Dougall, but he gave a humorless laugh and asked, "Are ye planning to marry her then?"

"Mayhap I will," Alick responded, sitting up a little straighter, his chest puffing out. "Certainly, I'd rather wed her than see her returned to Danvries. And bedding her would no' be a hardship."

The last comment made Dougall scowl. Bedding her would definitely not be a hardship, but for some reason he didn't like the idea of Alick being the one to do it, but it was Geordie who said, "The devil ye will! I'm older than ye. If she needs marrying, I'll be the one to do it."

"Ye're only a year older," Alick snapped. "Besides, no doubt she'd prefer a handsome young man like me to a big brute like yerself."

"If by handsome and young ye mean puny, mayhap she would," Geordie growled. "But I'm thinking she'd pick a real man o'er a hairless youth any day."

"I said it first and if she needs marrying, I'm the one going to do it," Alick said firmly.

"The hell ye will!" Geordie snarled, standing up threateningly.

"Enough," Dougall snapped as Alick got to his feet with every appearance of intending on attacking Geordie. "I'll no' ha'e ye fighting o'er her like dogs with a bone. And I'll no ha'e ye shaming the lass with talk o' her brother's doings. So sit down and shut yerselves."

His brothers fell silent and reluctantly sat down again, but they continued to glare at each other and Dougall knew he could expect them to continue the argument at another time. It made him want to knock their heads together. Hell, he wanted to knock their heads together just for suggesting they would marry the lass, though he wasn't sure why. It would take care of their worry over her well-being and as far as he was concerned she *was* now their worry. After all, this was the lass who had saved Saidh's life. That was a debt they could never repay, and he knew every single one of his brothers would feel the same way. So why not let one of his brothers marry her and take care of the worry? It wasn't like he wanted to. Between his duties toward their eldest brother, Aulay, first and all he did with his horse breeding, Dougall hadn't got around to even contemplating marriage yet. That was a consideration for the future, when he'd eventually purchased a nice estate where he could concentrate on his breeding and take the time to start a family of his own. That had been the plan.

But now there was Murine and her difficulties and the fact that there was no way he could leave her to her brother's planned fate for her now that he knew who she was. Hell, he couldn't have done it and lived with his conscience after finding her on the road, fleeing on her cow. And that had been before he'd known who she was. On top of that, he was recalling how nicely she'd fit against him during the ride that day, and that she'd smelled as lovely as she looked. Dougall had found himself lowering his head to inhale her sweet scent several times that afternoon during the ride.

Cursing under his breath, he stared into the fire and wondered just how they could save the lass from the fate her brother would force on her. Could they? It would help if he knew if she had family to aid her. Someone to petition the king on her behalf to remove her from her brother's guardianship. But he wouldn't know that until Murine joined them to answer his questions. Which made him wonder . . . what the bloody hell was taking the woman so long? How much time did it take to have a piss and walk back to them?

Dougall scowled into the flames for a minute, then lifted his head, gave in to the urge and glanced quickly toward where he'd left her. He then frowned and stood up. Not only had she moved out of sight, but she'd moved altogether. At least, he couldn't see light, and the torch he'd left her should cast a glow he would see even from behind the tree.

"What's the matter?" Conran peered up at him from his seat, but didn't turn to look toward the woods, he noticed.

"Murine's gone," Dougall said grimly and bent to snatch up the end of another burning log sticking out of the fire.

"What?" Conran stood and turned to look. "Where the hell would she go?"

Dougall headed into the woods without responding and heard the others scrabbling to follow. This time more than one of them grabbed a log as well. He could tell that by the glow that surrounded him as he walked.

"Bloody, stupid . . ." Murine muttered to herself as she pushed through the bushes, grimacing as the branches caught at her hair and gown and scratched at her face. She could do nothing to prevent it. It took both her hands to manage the weight of the great heavy log Dougall Buchanan had given her as a torch.

It was her own fault, of course. The man had offered to fetch or make her a smaller one, but she had been so desperate to relieve herself at that point, she'd said nay. Now she still hadn't gone, was sure she was about to burst with the need, but was dragging herself through the woods in search of somewhere she could do it without starting a forest fire. She needed someplace she could set the bloody log down while she held her skirts and squatted, but so far everywhere she looked appeared to be covered with dry grass and leaves.

She pushed past another bush and nearly stumbled forward on her face as the woods gave way to a clearing. Managing to keep her feet under her without her hands to aid in the effort, Murine raised her makeshift torch and peered about. She then breathed out a relieved little breath as she spotted a large boulder in the center of the small clearing. It was perfect, she decided and strode forward to lay the log on the boulder.

Now that she was unhampered by holding the makeshift torch, Murine couldn't get to the business she'd come here for quickly enough. She had her skirts up and was squatting within seconds. But she didn't sigh her relief until she actually finished with the task without Henry's amorous assault or any other interruption. She'd learned her lesson last time.

Murine was just straightening and letting her skirts drop back into place when the light seemed to move and then suddenly went out. She froze briefly, then turned slowly toward the boulder where she'd left the log and stared into stygian darkness. It was only when she lowered her gaze that she saw the last glowing embers of what used to be her torch. The damned thing had rolled off the boulder, dousing its own flames before landing on the ground.

"Ah hell," she muttered, and then smacked herself for saying it and shook her head. She'd obviously spent too much time around her friend Saidh to be throwing curses about as she had today. Sighing, she hurried forward to grab the log and began blowing on it to try to bring the flame back to life. But even as she raised it the last glow died, leaving her unable to even see the log she was holding.

"Well, is no' that just perfect?" she groused, dropping the useless bit of wood and turning to peer about. She had no idea where she was or even in what direction the camp was. Biting her lip, she tried to orient herself. She'd set the log on the boulder and turned her back to it, facing the way she'd come. And then she'd turned around and rushed over to pick it up. Her back should have been to the direction she'd come from at that point. But then she'd dropped the wood and turned again.

Had she turned all the way around so that she should be pointed in the direction she wanted to go? Or had she only performed a half turn? And had she moved straight through the woods from the tree behind which she was mauled by Henry, or had she taken a slanted course?

Murine threw up her hands with exasperation. She didn't have a damned clue, and she couldn't hear the men's voices as she had when she'd started out. They had died abruptly, just before she'd pushed her way out into this clearing. She paused for a minute and cocked her head, hoping to hear their muffled voices and follow the sound back to camp, but heard nothing. Either they'd all gone to sleep or . . . well, she didn't know what else would silence them. Death maybe, she thought and imagined a band of silent marauders creeping up behind the Buchanans as they sat around the fire, and then slitting their throats so quickly they died without a sound.

A shiver went through her and Murine rubbed her arms and peered nervously around. One of those marauders could have followed her out here and be even now creeping through the darkness toward her, ready to slit her own throat.

Murine moved one hand to rub her neck now, her chin unconsciously tucking down to leave less of it exposed. But then, realizing what she was doing, she forced her hand away and her shoulders to rise.

"There's no one out there," she told herself firmly. "Ye just need to find yer way back to camp and all will be well."

At least she hoped it would be. In truth, she hadn't had much time to consider her situation. She presumed she was safe with Saidh's brothers and that they were looking after her . . . and Dougall had said something about her telling him where she was heading and that they'd escort her, but really she wasn't sure about that last part. Her mind had been firmly fixed on her personal needs at the time.

Muttering under her breath with disgust, Murine started walking straight ahead, her hands outstretched to feel for the bushes and branches she'd fought her way through to get to the clearing. It wasn't like she had much choice but to return to the men. Murine hadn't any idea where she was or in which direction she should ride to reach Scotland.

If they weren't already in Scotland, Murine considered as she stumbled through the brush, tugging on her gown when it got caught, and yanking her head away from the branches that seemed to be constantly grabbing at her hair. It would be a terrible shame if she was already in Scotland and rode the wrong way, taking herself back to England. Frankly, with the kind of luck she'd been having lately, there was a good chance of that exact thing happening.

Distracted by her thoughts, Murine was slow to realize the ground she was staring at had suddenly lightened a bit. She'd started to keep her head down to keep from being poked in the eyes by the branches snatching at her. She stared at the lightening ground blankly for a moment, her steps slowing, then raised her head quickly as she crashed into something. Something that grabbed her arm.

Murine stared up at the large shape looming before her. Light was coming from the side and behind it, casting it into rather horrific features. She opened her mouth, closed it, then simply felt herself falling as her vision dimmed and her world shrank to a small black dot.

SHOVING HIS LOG TOWARD CONRAN, DOUGALL CAUGHT THE woman as she sank toward the ground.

"Damn. She fainted again," Conran muttered.

"Saidh did mention this tendency o' hers." Dougall grunted as he scooped up Murine into his arms.

"Aye, but did she no' also say Joan had made her a tincture that seemed to be helping?" Conran commented with a frown, stepping back to make way as Dougall turned with his burden.

When Dougall merely shrugged, Geordie asked, "What the devil was she doing all the way out here?"

"I thought ye left yer log with her earlier," Conran pointed out as Dougall started back through the brush.

The comment made him pause and turn back. It had been unusually dry of late and an open flame left unattended could start a forest fire. "Could ye—"

"I'll take a look about," Conran assured him, then handed the log Dougall had been carrying to Geordie, the only one not carrying a log. "Ye and Alick head back with Dougall. I'll be along directly."

Turning, Dougall carried Murine back the way he'd come.

"Ye do no' think she's ailing, do ye?" Alick asked with concern. The younger man was nearly treading on Dougall's heals. He was also holding his burning log high to help light the way for Dougall. "I mean, Saidh did say Lady Sinclair's tincture was helping, but Murine was in a dead faint all afternoon as we rode, and just the sight o' us made her faint dead away again just now."

"Mayhap she needs to eat," Geordie suggested from behind. "If she left directly after we did, she'll ha'e missed the nooning meal, and the sup too."

"That does no' explain the first faint," Alick pointed out. "We had only jest eaten ourselves at that point."

"True," Geordie sounded like he was frowning. "Then mayhap she had trouble breathing under the plaid and that's why she fainted then."

"So ye're suggesting she fainted the first time because she could no' breathe, and the second time because she is faint with hunger?" Alick asked.

"Aye," Geordie agreed. "That or she's ailing."

"That is what I suggested to begin with," Alick pointed out with exasperation.

Dougall spotted the campfire ahead and began to move more swiftly, eager to get away from the arguing duo behind him. He had no idea why the woman had fainted this time. Saidh had said it happened when Murine got overexcited or got to her feet too quickly, but she'd already been on her feet, and there had been nothing to get excited about that he knew of. Although she had looked terrified just before fainting, he noted, and then shook his head. Despite knowing this was normal for Murine, he found it a bit disconcerting that she kept dropping as she did. She was likely to hurt herself if she kept it up. He wouldn't always be there to catch her.

Chapter 3

*M*URINE SIGHED SLEEPILY AND SNUGGLED INTO THE FURS surrounding her, then stiffened when those furs tightened around her in response. Waking up fully now, she opened her eyes and found herself staring at the white linen shirt she presently had her nose pressed to. Raising her eyes, she peered up at the bottom of a chin that was sprouting dark stubble.

Biting her lip, Murine took a deep breath and started to lever herself away from the man, but paused at the delightful scent that filled her nostrils. Whoever she was cuddled up to smelled quite lovely, sort of woodsy and spicy and . . . well, she couldn't identify the other scent she was inhaling, but it was very nice.

The chest in front of her vibrated against her breasts as a rumble of sound that could only be called a snore hit her ears and then the man rolled onto his back, taking her with him. Murine suddenly found herself lying on top of him, her chest plastered to his and her lower body splayed over his legs and something else that was rather hard and a bit uncomfortable against her stomach.

Holding her breath now, she raised her head a little to try to get a better look at just whom exactly she was lying on. For some reason she was actually relieved to find that it was Dougall Buchanan. For some reason she found herself trusting the man. Still, it was just wrong for her to be relieved that he was the man she was sleeping on. There was no male she should be happy to find herself sleeping on. She was an unmarried lass, after all, and this was completely inappropriate. Actually, it was also completely inappropriate for her to be traveling alone with the Buchanan men. In effect, if anyone found out about this, she would be ruined, but since she wasn't likely to marry, that mattered little. And at least she was only ruined in reputation, not in fact. Had she stayed at Danvries, Murine was quite sure she would have been well and truly ruined by Muller by now.

Murine sighed unhappily as she thought of Montrose's neighbor and dubious friend, Lord Muller. The man had been leering at her ever since Montrose had brought her to Danvries to live. He'd even tried to corner her a time or two and grope her. Thank goodness Saidh had taught her that move with her knee. She'd left him moaning on the floor as she'd rushed off to her room that night. Even so, Murine was sure Montrose was right and Muller would have jumped at the opportunity to pay a few coin to take what she was unwilling to give . . . and with Montrose's blessing, she thought bleakly. While they'd never been close, they were still half siblings and she would have expected he would feel at least some protectiveness toward her. Apparently not.

"Good morn."

Murine blinked away her thoughts and shifted her gaze back to the man she was lying on. Dougall was awake. At least his eyes were open, though in truth he was peering up at her rather sleepily. He looked much younger and very handsome without the stern expression he'd seemed to wear every time she saw him before this.

Pushing these irrelevant thoughts away, Murine forced a smile, cleared her throat and then said, "Good morn." Grimacing, she added a little tentatively, "Do ye think ye could let me go so that I can get up?"

One eyebrow rose on Dougall's face, and then he released her, opening his arms and spreading the plaid she'd mistaken for furs.

Smiling with relief, Murine immediately scrambled off him.

She then froze and gaped when she saw that it was his own plaid he'd wrapped around them, the one he'd been wearing yesterday, and that without it he was dressed only in a shirt that did not quite cover—

"Do no' faint!"

Murine glanced to his face at that roar and then abruptly turned her back on him. Her gaze slid over the other men, and she was much relieved to see that they were all still sleeping. Or at least they had been. They were beginning to stir now thanks to Dougall's roar.

Muttering that she would go take care of her morning ablutions, Murine rushed blindly away into the woods.

DOUGALL SIGHED AND THEN SHIFTED TO HIS KNEES, LAID OUT his plaid, and began to pleat it in preparation of putting it on. It had been chilly last night and Murine had been lying shivering where he'd set her when he started to bed down a few feet away. He'd tried to ignore it at first, but when her teeth had begun to chatter, he'd scooted closer to her and then drawn her into his plaid with him. She hadn't even stirred at the action, though her shivers had stopped and she'd cuddled into him with sweet little sighs. He, however, had lain there for a long time, very aware of her warm body against his, cuddling back against him, her bottom rubbing—

Cursing, Dougall finished donning his plaid and strode into the woods after the woman. He could hardly leave her wandering around by herself to faint without someone there to catch her. Besides, he didn't trust her not to get lost. Not that she seemed a featherhead, but the woman did have that tendency to faint and had apparently done so for some time. She'd no doubt hit her head a time or two and . . . well, it just seemed better to not take any chances.

Dougall soon realized he should have paid more attention to which direction she'd gone, or just wrapped his plaid around his waist and set out after her at once. The thickets here grew close together and were the devil to get through. On top of that, there was no way to tell which direction she'd gone. Cursing, he paused, propped his hands on his hips and then shouted, "Lady Carmichael!"

Birds went winging into the air on every side of him, but there was no answering call. A frown slowly creasing his forehead, he called out again, and then began to move. The damned woman had obviously fainted again and was no doubt lying unconscious somewhere, waiting to be rescued.

Shaking, his head, he called out again as he pushed his way through the trees.

MURINE DUCKED LOWER BEHIND THE BUSHES SHE WAS CROUCHING in as Dougall's voice sounded again and the man six feet in front of her turned to look in her direction at the sound. Part of her felt foolish for ducking behind the bushes as if she was a child playing hide-and-seek. Murine wasn't even sure why she had. She'd been moving through the woods in search of a likely place to relieve herself when her dress had got caught on a branch; she'd paused to tug at it, but instead of freeing her gown, the branch itself had snapped and stayed tangled in the gown. She'd noticed that when she'd started to walk and the damned thing had dragged behind her, pulling at her skirts. She'd ignored it at first, thinking it would drop away after a couple of steps. Instead it had caught between the branches of another bush a couple steps later and she'd been forced to stop and try to untangle herself.

That stopping had kept her from continuing forward and probably crashing right into the man now frowning in her direction, though she didn't think he could see her. He was just looking in the direction Buchanan's voice was coming from as he shouted her name again, sounding closer.

Murine had been tugging at her gown when the snapping of branches had drawn her attention and she'd peered forward to see something moving through the trees ahead. Giving up on her gown, Murine had instinctively ducked behind the bushes. She'd stared wide-eyed at the approaching darkness in the trees, fighting off a faint, and worrying that it might be a wild boar or some other such animal. A moment later she'd realized it was too tall to be a boar. A heartbeat after that she'd recognized that it was a man, but not one of the Buchanan brothers, and she'd instinctively stayed where she was, waiting for the man to move away before daring to continue on her way herself.

Murine did not have a great deal of travel experience. Most of her life had been spent at Carmichael, but she'd been on a handful of trips in her life and they had mostly seemed a bit tiring, boring and inconvenient . . . until the trip where her brothers had been killed by bandits in the night. She'd been nervous about traveling ever since. Of course, her last trip had not helped to relieve that nervousness. It had been when Montrose had collected her from Sinclair with the news that her father was dead. He'd spent most of their journey to England warning her not to travel far from camp on forays such as this one. He'd reinforced that warning by regaling her with horrible stories of what bandits might do to her, and had seemed to enjoy the telling. Since she'd already lost her brothers to such a raid on their party, she really hadn't needed his warning. Murine had no intention of drawing the attention of the man presently standing with head cocked, listening to the sounds of someone moving through the woods toward them.

When Dougall shouted again, sounding closer still, the man in front of her turned away and headed back in the direction he'd come. Murine watched until he was out of sight, and then straightened abruptly and was alarmed to find the world tilting in front of her. Dammit, she should not have stood so abruptly after such a scare, Murine thought as darkness began to crowd her vision. She thought she heard Dougall's voice behind her just as the light blinked out in her mind.

"WHAT THE DEVIL ARE YE PLAYING AT, LASS? WHY DID YE no'—?" Dougall broke off his tirade and caught Murine as she keeled over like a stack of hay bales piled too high. He'd just started to think he would have to go back and get his brothers to help him search the woods when he'd suddenly pushed through a set of bushes and found himself standing directly behind Murine. Irritation had immediately claimed him that she was not unconscious, but had apparently just chosen not to answer and he'd started in on berating her.

Now he peered blankly down at her pale face for a moment, then sighed in resignation and scooped her up. Dougall started to turn back the way he'd come with her then, but couldn't. Something was holding her fast to where he'd found her. A quick glance showed him the problem. Her gown was caught. Rather than set her down, Dougall shifted the hand under her legs to clutch at the material of her gown and gave it a good yank. The action immediately produced a tearing sound.

"Ah, hell," he muttered. Not only was the gown not free, but it had torn up the seam to nearly her hip. He hadn't gathered all the material, Dougall realized with a sigh. Shifting her in his arms, he re-gathered the material and gave it another yank, this time managing what he'd tried to do the first time. She was free. However, there was no way he was taking her back like that. The bottom half of her gown was hanging over his hands, leaving her hip and leg bare. His brothers were already fighting over Murine; he wasn't letting them see her like this.

Kneeling, Dougall set her down, and then shifted to examine the tear, lifting the material slightly and revealing the bottom of a shift and a long, shapely leg from just below the hips down.

"Aye, it's ripped," Dougall said aloud as if that might have been in question. He then just sat there for a moment, staring at what was revealed of her leg, and wondering if he'd go to hell if he lifted the bottom of her shift too for a quick peek of what it hid.

Probably, Dougall decided and knew he should be ashamed

of himself for even considering doing such a thing. And he was sure he would be just as soon as her naked leg was no longer blinding him to shame's presence in his heart. With that thought in mind, Dougall caught both flaps of the gown by the bottom corners and then quickly tied them together. It didn't really help much. The material now gathered at hip and ankle, but flapped open all the way between.

"Hmm," he muttered, eyeing the seam. If he just had a way to tie it halfway up, that might make the difference and cover her properly, Dougall thought, and retrieved his *sgian-dubh* from his belt to begin slicing at the cloth of her gown about halfway up her leg.

MURINE WOKE SLOWLY, SOMETHING TUGGING HER TO CON-sciousness like little hands pulling at her gown. She opened her eyes to see branches all around her. Frowning, she glanced downward, pausing when she recognized Dougall kneeling with his upper body bent over her lower body. She peered at him briefly with confusion, and then glanced farther down to see what he was doing. A squawk of dismay immediately slipped from her lips and she began to drag, and then scramble backward away from him. Murine didn't stop until her shoulders came up against what she thought must be a tree.

When Dougall simply stared after her with surprise and did not pursue her, Murine peered down at the tatters of cloth that had once been the skirt of her gown and asked with horror, "What ha'e ye done?"

"That's what I was about to ask."

Murine stiffened and then glanced to the side to see Conran standing halfway through a bush on the edge of the very tiny clearing Murine and Dougall occupied.

"Ye found her?"

"Is she a'right?"

Those two questions were accompanied by Geordie and Alick pushing their way through the bush on either side of

Conran. Both men came to an abrupt halt, though, as they took in the scene before them. Their eyes widened, then narrowed, and their fists clenched, but Conran put up a hand when they both started to move past him.

"Now lads, 'tis sure I am that Dougall can explain why he was tearing the clothes off o' Lady Murine here . . . a fine Scottish lass who bravely fled her home to preserve her virtue and who saved our sweet Saidh's life," he added grimly.

"I was no' tearing off her clothes," Dougall said with disgust, getting to his feet and putting his *sgian-dubh* away. "I was cutting up her gown."

Conran had to place a hand on the arms of both Geordie and Alick then to keep them in place. Once he was sure they would stay put, he turned back to Dougall and arched an eyebrow. "That is no' helping to convince us that ye ha'e Lady Murine's best interests at heart."

"Nay, I can see that," he said dryly. "And ye ken me well enough ye should know better. I'd ne'er abuse a woman under me care."

All three men seemed to look a little less ruffled at that, Murine noticed, and scowled at them for it. She then turned a glare onto Dougall and said sharply, "I, however, do no' ken ye and would appreciate an explanation as to why ye were cutting me gown to pieces, if ye do no' mind."

"Because I tore it and—by accident," he interrupted himself to add quickly when her anger turned to alarm again.

"I found ye just as ye fell into one o' yer faints. I caught ye ere ye hit the ground, but when I went to head back to camp, yer gown was caught," Dougall said, sounding almost resentful that he was having to explain at all.

Murine relaxed a little and nodded. Her gown *had* been caught.

"I gave it a tug thinking to free it, but instead . . ." He grimaced and gestured to the strips of her gown. "It split right up the seam to . . . well, verra high," he muttered, and then pointed out, "Well, I could no' take ye back to camp like that, could I?"

Apparently that was a rhetorical question, because Dougall didn't wait for an answer, but continued, "So I set ye down and tied the ends of each flap together. But yer gown still gaped from the ankle up, so I thought to fix it."

"By cutting it to pieces?" she asked with disbelief.

"Nay," he snapped. "I thought to slice a strip in the center on each side and tie it together too, but there still seemed a lot o' gaping in between, so I was making strips all along the seam, intending to tie it together all the way up."

Murine glanced down at the horizontal strips in her gown and shook her head sadly. It had been her favorite dress, made from the material Joan had given her back when they'd first met. Fingering the ragged strips, she said sadly, "If ye'd only just waited fer me to wake, I might ha'e been able to save the gown."

"Well, I could no' carry ye around like that," Dougall said with a frown. "And I could no' wait all day fer ye to wake up from yer faint either."

Murine stiffened and pointed out, "It would no' ha'e been all day, though, would it."

"Well, I did no' ken that," he muttered, shifting impatiently. "Yesterday ye stayed in yer first faint all afternoon, and yer second one all night."

"I did no'," she denied at once and got to her feet. Bending then, Murine began to tie the strips of cloth together as she explained, "I woke up several times on the journey here, but ye were squeezing me so tight I could no' get air and kept losing consciousness again."

"Ye did stay in yer faint last night, though," Conran pointed out quietly.

"Aye, well, I ha'e no' eaten since yester morn," she muttered without looking up from her task. "I do no' think I stayed in me faint so much as I just slept through the night from exhaustion and lack o' food."

"Well, there ye go!" Alick exclaimed. "That's why ye're fainting. Ye need to eat."

"We should get ye back to camp and feed ye then," Conran muttered and moved to her side to kneel and begin helping her with the ties. He was quickly joined by Geordie and Alick. Murine straightened to get out of the way and simply stared helplessly as the three men crowded around her side trying to tie the ties their brother had created.

"God's teeth!" Dougall muttered suddenly and strode over to urge them out of the way. He then scooped up Murine from the side with the strips so that the undamaged side of her gown faced out and turned to start through the underbrush.

"You're angry?" she asked curiously as she eyed his grim expression. It seemed obvious he was angry, and while it normally would have made her anxious to be carted about by an angry bear of a man, Murine found she wasn't at all afraid of him . . . and had no idea why.

She was puzzling over that when he said, "Aye."

Murine considered him briefly and then asked, "At me?"

"Aye."

She waited for the expected anxiety to appear, but it didn't. Murine still wasn't afraid of him. In fact, she felt completely safe in his arms, angry or not. It was quite a nice feeling. Murine had not felt safe in a long while. Realizing he was waiting for her response to his acknowledgment, she cleared her throat and asked, "Why?"

Dougall scowled and then said, "I do no' ken."

Murine blinked at the admission and then he added, "But it seems we've encountered nothing but trouble since riding through the gates at Danvries. First we had to hide ye to preserve yer virtue from yer skeevy brother, and then ye fainted so that we had to bring ye with us and . . . well, frankly, all ye've done is cause bother and strife among me brothers with yer weak fainting ways. Now ye've got them all acting like ladies' maids trying to dress ye in the woods."

"I did no' ask fer their help," she pointed out with quiet dignity.

"Ye did no' ha'e to," he responded gruffly, and then asked, "Why are ye fainting so much? Saidh said Lady Sinclair had made a tincture that helped ye with that."

"Aye, she did," Murine agreed sadly.

"Did ye forget to pack it when ye fled?" Alick asked with concern.

Murine glanced over Dougall's shoulder with surprise to see that the other three men were directly behind them, following, and apparently listening to everything they'd said.

"That should ha'e been the first thing ye packed," Geordie assured her solemnly when she merely gaped at them. "Surely ye kenned escaping would be easier were ye no' keeling o'er like a lame goose e'ery other minute?"

"Aye, o' course I ken that," Murine said with irritation. "And I did no' bring any o' the tincture because I ha'e none left, I ran out two months ago."

"Could ye no' make some more, lass?" Conran asked with concern.

"I do no' ken how," Murine confessed unhappily. "Montrose arrived with the news that Father had died and we left Sinclair in such a rush that we all but forgot about the tincture until I was leaving. As Joan pressed the vial into me hands, she said she'd send me the recipe, but ne'er did. So when me supply started to dwindle I wrote asking her fer it, but . . ."

"But?" Alick prompted.

"She ne'er responded," Murine admitted unhappily.

"Well, that does no' seem right," Geordie muttered. "Ye saved the lass's life. The least she could do is respond to yer messages."

"Hmm." Conran muttered, and then asked, "Are ye sure yer message was delivered? I would no' put it past that brother o' yers to simply no' send the message. She may e'en ha'e written ye and he ne'er passed on the message to ye."

"That is what I am hoping," Murine admitted quietly. "It is me only hope really."

"Why is that?" Geordie asked.

"Because Jo and Saidh both said if I were e'er in need, I should come to them and they would do all they could to help me," she explained, and then added miserably, "Yet neither has responded to me messages. If they did no' mean it, then I am lost."

Dougall slowed to peer down at her face. "Ye wrote Saidh as well?"

"Aye," Murine murmured, looking uncomfortable. "Yet she did no' respond either."

"Because she did no' get it," he assured her.

"Aye," Conran agreed, moving up beside them to meet her gaze. "There has been no messenger from Danvries, ever, that I ken of. At least not ere we left to deliver horses to Lord Brummel in southern England a couple weeks back," he added. "When did ye send yer message to Saidh?"

"I sent one just a couple weeks past, but sent three others ere that, the first back in the spring when we arrived at Danvries. Just to let her ken we'd arrived safely and see how she was making out at MacDonnell," she admitted.

"Then yer brother must be stopping the messages from being delivered," Dougall said quietly. "Because I'm fair certain none reached her."

"Oh, thank goodness," Murine breathed and had to blink away the tears of relief suddenly crowding her eyes.

"Ye thought the lasses were ignoring yer messages," Dougall said solemnly and Murine glanced to him, surprised by his understanding. The man might look like a big brute with his height and all his muscle, but he obviously understood people for all that.

"Aye," she said softly. "I think that possibility upset me more than anything else that was happening. I ha'e never had friends like Joan, Saidh and Edith before and feared mayhap I'd somehow offended them or . . ." She shrugged helplessly, but then waved that worry away and admitted, "But I could no' think how I might ha'e done so. And then I began to suspect that Montrose was preventing the messages from being sent."

"Aye, he must ha'e been," Alick assured her as they left the woods and entered the clearing where they'd camped. "We would ken if a messenger had reached Buchanan."

"If nothing else, Aulay would ha'e mentioned it, and we certainly would ha'e kenned when he sent the message on with one o' our men to MacDonnell," Geordie added as Dougall paused to set her on a boulder by the now dead fire they'd built the night before.

"Oh, I did send the first message to MacDonnell," Murine assured them quickly as Dougall straightened. "I thought Saidh might spend a week or two there at least. It was only after that I sent them to Buchanan." Tilting her head to peer up at the men now surrounding her in a half circle, all still standing, she asked curiously, "How long did she end up staying at MacDonnell with yer cousin?"

"She's still there," Alick announced with a grin.

Murine blinked in surprise at this news. It had been more than six months since they had stopped at MacDonnell on their way to England and left Saidh to comfort her cousin Fenella MacDonnell on the death of her husband. Despite having just learned her father was dead, or perhaps because of it, Murine had wanted to stop and pay her respects to the man's mother, her own aunt by marriage, as well as her cousin's wife, Fenella, on the way home. Fortunately, Montrose had been more than happy to have an excuse to stop and spend the night in a castle, drinking someone else's ale and eating someone else's food rather than suffering their own meager supplies in a rough camp. He'd agreed to Saidh's accompanying them. They'd stopped at MacDonnell for a night before continuing on without her. Murine had expected Saidh to stay a week or perhaps two and then send for her brothers to collect her. She hadn't expected her friend to still be there all these months later.

"Is Lady Fenella still refusing to leave her room?" she asked with concern.

"Fenella's dead," Dougall announced solemnly.

"What?" Murine gaped at him. "How?"

"Stabbed." The word was as blunt as a rock and hit her just as hard.

"Oh dear," Murine breathed with dismay, and then her eyes widened as she recalled that Lady Tilda MacDonnell, the deceased Allen's mother, had been sure that his bride, Fenella, had had something to do with his death. Good Lord, if her aunt Tilda had killed Saidh's cousin in retribution—"Lady Tilda did no'—?"

"Aye," Dougall interrupted.

"Oh dear," Murine breathed again, amazed that Saidh had not written her with such news herself. Montrose must be blocking incoming messages as well, she decided and then sighed and asked, "What has the king done about Lady Tilda?"

"Nothing," Dougall said abruptly.

It was Conran who said, "He did no' ha'e to. She's dead too."

Murine's eyes widened. "How—?"

"A fall," Dougall said abruptly.

"From the bell tower," Conran added helpfully and nodded when she gaped at him.

Murine shook her head slowly, absorbing all of this, and then frowned and asked, "But if Fenella and Lady Tilda are both dead, why is Saidh still at MacDonnell?"

"She lives there now," Geordie explained.

"She married Greer. The new MacDonnell laird," Alick added helpfully.

Murine hadn't needed the added explanation. She'd met the new laird of MacDonnell, Allen's cousin Greer, when they'd stopped at MacDonnell. Truth be told, while she was surprised at this news, she wasn't as surprised as she might have been had she not seen the two together. Murine had sensed something strange and powerful between the two at the time. She'd even mentioned it to Saidh and warned her to take care. It seemed she needn't have bothered. Things had worked out for the pair. At least, she hoped they had, Murine thought and asked, "Is she happy?"

"Disgustingly so," Alick assured her with a smile.

"They are perfect together," Geordie added, grinning widely.

"Aye, they are," Conran agreed with a small smile of his own.

Dougall merely nodded in agreement.

"Well, that is wonderful. I am happy fer her," Murine said, and she was. She was very pleased that her friend had found a husband and was so happy with him. She was also a bit envious. Murine didn't want to be, but she was and couldn't help it. Her situation was so dire . . .

"Where were ye headed on yer cow?" Dougall asked suddenly, bringing up the subject she'd been happy to avoid last night in her need to relieve herself. With her fainting, they'd never returned to that question. Until now, and Murine wasn't too pleased to have it crop up again. She was rather embarrassed at having to admit the truth, but there was really nothing else to do, so she admitted, "I planned to ride to Buchanan to see Saidh. Not to stay for long," she added quickly lest they think she'd planned to just move in and settle them with her burden. "I thought mayhap if Saidh and I, and mayhap even Joan and Edith, put our heads together we might figure a way out of the mess me life has become."

When the men were silent, she added, "There is the church, o' course. I could take the veil. But I ne'er imagined that would be me future. I was betrothed, me future settled. I was supposed to marry and ha'e children and . . ." She let her words trail off helplessly. All her hopes and expectations for the future were crumbling around her and Murine just didn't know what to do or where to turn.

"Ye're saying ye *were* betrothed then?" Dougall asked when she fell silent.

"Oh, aye," Murine smiled crookedly. "To a fine young man. He was ever so handsome and good."

"What happened?" Conran asked curiously.

"He died on the way to collect me some three years ago," Murine said, lowering her head unhappily. That had actually been the first of all the tragedies to strike and knock her life off the course she'd always expected it to take. Waving her depressing thoughts away, she went on, "Anyway, I may yet ha'e to take the veil, but I am hoping Saidh and the others can help me find another solution. Mayhap a nice old laird who would no' mind a bride with no dower, or—"

Geordie took a step closer and then said, "Ye could—"

"If ye plan to feed her as ye mentioned, ye'd best get to hunting, else we'll be camping here again tonight," Dougall interrupted sharply.

Geordie scowled at him briefly for interrupting whatever he'd been about to suggest, but Dougall's expression was cold and grim and held a wealth of warning. After a moment the man turned to Murine and said, "He's right, I suppose. I'll catch a fine pheasant or hare fer ye to feast on and we'll talk of this while ye eat."

"I'll help him hunt," Conran decided. "If we catch three or four pheasants we can clean and cook them all up and eat in the saddle at nooning to make up fer the time we're losing here."

When Dougall nodded approval, Conran slipped off after Geordie. Dougall then turned his gaze to Alick and said, "We'll need more wood fer the fire to cook the meat."

Alick hesitated, but then nodded and moved off, leaving Murine alone with Dougall. He watched until all the men had left camp, then turned to peer at Murine.

"We'll ride to Buchanan to drop off yer cow and the horses yer brother did no' buy, then escort ye on to MacDonnell so ye can see Saidh," he assured her solemnly. "If the two o' ye then want to continue on to Sinclair to include Lady Joan, and stop to collect Edith on the way, we'll see to that too."

"Thank ye," Murine breathed with relief and just barely refrained from hugging him for the generosity and kindness he was showing in his willingness to help her. She had hoped they would see her to Buchanan, but she hadn't even allowed herself to hope that he would offer to take her to MacDonnell and then on to Sinclair. Dougall was a good man, she thought and beamed a smile at him as just the possibility of talking to Saidh shifted a great weight of worry from her shoulders.

Surely Saidh could help her come up with a solution to her problem? And if she couldn't, then with Joan and Edith's help they definitely would think of some way to keep her safe from her brother's clutches. Something that did not include giving up her life to God and never having the children she'd always imagined would fill her life.

"Rest now," Dougall suggested gruffly. "'Twill be a while ere the boys return with their catch and then it still has to be cooked."

Murine smiled at him widely and shifted to lie down by the remains of last night's fire. She didn't close her eyes at once and go to sleep, though; instead she watched him putter around the camp gathering twigs to start a new fire with. Saidh had spoken often about her brothers, claiming they were, every one of them, fine men with good heads on their shoulders and true hearts. Murine was much relieved to find it so. Dougall was a good man.

His brothers were, too, of course, she added quickly in her thoughts. But it was Dougall she found herself most often looking to. She would have liked a husband like him. In fact, Murine began to think he would be a husband any woman would be happy with. Unfortunately, he wasn't in the market for a wife just now, she reminded herself, recalling his words in her brother's great hall.

Sighing, she closed her eyes to rest.

Chapter 4

$\mathcal{D}$OUGALL CAME AWAKE WITH A START AND OPENED HIS EYES to find all three of his brothers staring back at him. Geordie was glowering, Alick looked like someone had stolen his pudding, and Conran was grinning like a fool. Scowling at the trio, Dougall arched an eyebrow. "What's about?"

"Nothing," Conran assured him solemnly, and then grinned wider and added, "I was just commenting to Geordie and Alick on how sweet the pair o' ye look cuddled up like ye are."

Dougall stilled at the words. Anger tried to flicker to life somewhere low in his belly at the teasing, but confusion was making that impossible.

"What the de'il are ye talking about?" he demanded in a growl, and then followed Conran's gaze down to see that Murine sat beside him. Really, she was almost on top of him, cuddled against his side, one leg thrown over both of his where they lay stretched out before him. One of her little fisted hands rested low on his stomach, and her head nestled on his chest. Her mouth was open and she was drooling all over his tartan.

Worse yet, in his sleep he'd curled his arm around her back and his hand was curved around the outside of her breast, his fingers resting across the globe as if it was his to touch. As he noted that, his fingers tightened instinctively and Murine moaned and then closed her mouth and shifted against him. She next frowned and began to make smacking sounds that suggested her mouth was either dry or was filled with an unpleasant taste. Perhaps both, he thought distractedly as he felt her nipple pebble under his fingers through the cloth of her gown. His cock twitched in response and began to harden just as she opened her eyes to peer sleepily up at him.

Dougall stared into the clear sky blue of her eyes and thought that a man could easily get lost in their cerulean depths.

A loud throat clearing from Conran brought Dougall back to their situation, and he quickly released Murine and straightened, allowing his arm to drop away.

Still half asleep, Murine was slower to stir, but did straighten after a moment and peer about trying to get her bearings. The moment she was off his chest, Dougall crossed his arms and scowled at Conran, who was still grinning like a fool.

"Is the food done?" he demanded impatiently. That was what they'd been waiting for when his lack of sleep had caught up to him and he'd dozed off leaning against the log by the fire. The men had returned to camp by then, Geordie with three plump pheasants, Conran with two rabbits, and Alick with wood and a third rabbit he'd managed to scare up. Their arrival had woken Murine from her rest and she'd sat up to congratulate them on their fine catch.

Dougall had watched idly, stifling yawns as the men had cleaned and skewered the birds and beasts to set over the fire. They'd all then settled in to wait for them to cook, the men talking quietly. Murine had started out seated on the log beside him, but then had shifted to settle on the grass so that she could lean back against the log. Tired after his restless night, he'd thought it a good idea and had shifted to sit on the ground next to her . . . and that's the last thing Dougall recalled, except that Murine had begun to nod off beside him just before his own eyes had begun to droop. He had no recollection of how they'd ended up cuddled together with his arm around her. That must have happened after he'd fallen asleep, Dougall decided.

"Aye. It should be ready now, I'd think," Conran announced, still looking damned amused.

Dougall glowered at the man, and then turned that expression on Murine and ordered, "Eat."

Much to his satisfaction, she didn't have to be told twice, but shifted closer to the fire as Conran removed the skewered pheasant from the flames and offered it to her. His satisfaction began to fade though when he saw how tiny a serving of meat she took. Before he could comment, however, Conran said kindly, "Ye'd best take more than that, lass."

"Oh no. This is enough fer me," she assured him with a smile.

Conran stared at her with bemusement for a minute, and then shook his head. "Nonsense, ye've no eaten since yester morn. Take more."

"Oh, nay, I . . ." Murine let her voice trail away in resignation as Conran piled more meat on the scrap of cloth she'd been given to use for a trencher. It had been Geordie's idea. After starting the fire, he'd retrieved the cloth from his bag and given it to her to use when the food was ready. It was just a clean spare bit of linen, yet Murine had reacted as if she'd been presented with the finest jewels, beaming with pleasure and thanking him profusely for his thoughtfulness.

Her reaction had made Dougall angry. Little things like that were telling, and what that had told him was that wee, brave Murine was not used to even the smallest consideration. It made him wonder about her past and what life had been like for her before her father had died and her brother had gained guardianship over her.

"Dougall?"

Drawn from his thoughts, he saw that Conran had turned the skewer his way, offering him food. Dougall shook his head. He wasn't much for eating in the mornings. None of them was. Usually they'd have risen, taken care of personal matters, and mounted up to head out. They might have an apple or something else in the saddle mid-morning, but none of them tended to eat first thing, so he wasn't surprised when Conran next offered the meat to Geordie and Alick and they both refused. Bypassing the chance to eat as well, Conran set the skewer to the side of the fire before resetting himself. They all then simply sat to watch Murine eat.

She was very slow about it, pinching off the tiniest bit of meat and then ducking her head as she popped it in her mouth. It seemed to take forever for her to finish the small serving she'd accepted.

Dougall wasn't surprised when the moment she did, Alick immediately took a skewer and offered it to her, saying, "Rabbit?"

"Oh, nay, thank ye," she said, softening the refusal with a smile as she finished the last bite of the small bit of food she'd taken.

"Some more pheasant then?" Geordie suggested, lifting it to offer to her with an encouraging smile.

"It was lovely, but nay. Thank ye," she murmured, neatly folding the used linen.

"Would ye prefer an apple then?" Alick suggested, tugging one from the bag that dangled from his belt. "I've one left. Ye can ha'e it."

"Thank ye, that's verra sweet," Murine's smile was beginning to look a bit forced. "But I've had me fill."

All three men stared at her blankly and then turned to Dougall as if he had the answer to some puzzle that confounded them.

He remained silent for a moment, considering all that Saidh had told them of Murine and what he'd seen so far and then said quietly, "I'm thinking mayhap 'tis no' a tincture ye need so much as to eat more, m'lady. Ye ha'e no' eaten enough to fill a bird and that after going a full day and night without. 'Tis no wonder ye tend to faint."

Murine blinked in surprise at the suggestion, apparently never having considered it before, and then she straightened her shoulders and turned back to glance at the meat cooling at the side of the fire. "Mayhap I will ha'e a bit more then."

Dougall nodded with satisfaction, but didn't stay to see how much she would have. Instead, he stood and left her with his brothers while he went to find a spot to relieve himself.

Once she had finished this serving, they would have to head out. Everything but the meat was packed away and ready to go, so they would just have to stow the meat in the cloth bag they carried for that purpose and they could be on their way. He'd already decided that Murine would be riding with him again today. And it was not just because he did not want to have to explain to Saidh how they'd let her friend and savior die on the journey to Buchanan. He wouldn't see that happen to her either. Despite knowing she was brave enough to take on a murderer on her own, and flee her brother on her ridiculous cow, there was just something about the lass that brought out the protective side of him. The problem was it appeared to be doing the same with his brothers, at least it was with Geordie and Alick. Conran didn't seem quite as affected, but their two younger brothers appeared to be very taken with Murine . . . which was a shame, because if the situation called for it and one of them had to marry her to save her from her brother, Dougall didn't think he could stand to see her with one of his brothers. He was coming around to the knowledge that he might want her for himself.

"SO, M'LADY, TELL US . . . HOW DID YER MOTHER END UP FIRST married to an English laird, and then to the Carmichael?"

Dougall glanced down at the top of Murine's head in front of him as she turned to peer at Conran, who rode beside them. Much to his relief, the question distracted her and she stopped shifting about in front of him. Despite her protests, he had made her ride with him again today. It had seemed the sensible thing to do. The way the woman constantly lost consciousness at the least upset, Dougall hadn't been willing to risk her toppling off that damned cow of hers should a squirrel run across her path. With the way things had been going, one of his brothers' horses would have trampled her under their hooves before they realized she'd fallen.

They had set out only moments ago, and yet Dougall was already regretting that decision. Riding with the woman awake was an entirely different prospect than riding with her asleep in his lap. Asleep, she'd snuggled up to him, warm and soft as a cuddly kitten. Awake, she had so far sat as stiff as a plank and constantly shifted about against him as if she couldn't find a comfortable spot. It was making it damned uncomfortable for him. There was nothing like a woman's body bouncing about against a man's groin to make sure he didn't relax and enjoy the ride.

"Well, I gather me mother's father and Lord Danvries's father were friends when younger and arranged the betrothal shortly after me mother was born. They were married when she was still quite young, fourteen I think."

"Aye, 'tis young." Conran nodded, and then added, "But I've heard o' younger lasses being married off and 'tis legal at twelve."

Murine merely nodded.

"Was her marriage to Danvries a happy one?" Geordie asked curiously, and Dougall scowled as he noted that his brother had crowded his horse up on his left to better hear. His mood was not improved when Murine shifted in front of him to turn to peer at him. He would not mind except that every time she moved, her sweet bottom rubbed against his—

"Mother ne'er spoke o' her first husband," Murine admitted quietly. "But Old Megs said Lord Danvries was a cruel, spoiled boy who treated me ma most shabbily."

"Old Megs?" Alick asked from behind them and Murine shifted again, this time turning sideways in his lap and clasping his shoulders to lift herself up enough to see behind them and smile at the other man.

Dougall ground his teeth together and tried to ignore how sweet her scent was, and the fact that she was climbing him like a tree . . . or a lover.

"She was me mother's lady's maid," Murine explained. "She went with Mother when she married Danvries and then returned to Scotland with her when she married me father."

"Ah. She would ken then," Conran said and Murine moved about again to peer at the man and nod.

"So she was married to the Englishman, had Montrose . . . and then what happened?" Geordie asked and Murine began to shift again even as Alick added, "Aye, how did she end up married to the Carmichael?"

Dougall clenched his hands on the reins as she moved about in his lap to peer at the other two men.

"Actually, she had two sons by Danvries. Montrose was the younger son. We had an older brother named William too, but he died shortly after me betrothed three years ago."

Dougall frowned at this news. To his mind, this Old Megs's description of the father as cruel and spoiled and treating her mother most shabbily, could also be applied as descriptions to Montrose Danvries and his treatment of Murine. He doubted the other brother had been any better. Apples rarely fell far from the tree they spawned from. Still, the bodies were beginning to add up. Her mother, her father, and her betrothed as well as her half brother in three years? 'Twas a lot of death in one family.

"As fer how me mother ended up married to me da, the Carmichael," Murine said now, and hearing the smile in her voice, Dougall dropped his gaze to see it mirrored on her face. He supposed that's why he was so shocked when she said, "Well, apparently he killed Lord Danvries and stole me mother."

Silence fell among the group and Dougall wasn't surprised. No doubt his brothers were not sure how they should respond and were wondering whether congratulations were in order, or they should pretend to be horrified.

Murine glanced from one man's face to another, taking in

their expressions, and then laughed. It was a tinkling sound that drew a reluctant smile even from Dougall.

"'Tis all right," she said. "'Twas no murder, 'twas at jousting."

"Oh," the men said as one, relaxing in their saddles.

"I gather Lord Danvries liked to joust and since his father still lived and was lord at Danvries, he was free to attend the tourneys as he liked so dragged me mother to several tournaments a year."

"And yer father?" Geordie asked.

"He was a laird, and claims he ne'er much liked jousting. His being there was an unusual occurrence, he rarely attended such events and it was just chance he was there that year at all." She paused and then admitted slowly, "He ne'er told me what brought him there that year." They were all silent for a moment and then she shrugged the worry away and continued, "At any rate, that is where he saw me mother for the first time. He arrived early, a couple days before the tourney began. Several others had as well, including me mother and Lord Danvries, and so their tents were close together."

She paused, smiling softly, and added, "Da once told me that he could still remember the first time he saw her. He was coming out o' his tent and she and her maid were walking past on the way to hers. He said he would ne'er forget his first sight o' her. She wore a blue gown the same bright color as the sky on a cloudless day, indeed, the same color as her eyes, and he said her hair shone brighter gold than the sun o'erhead. Da said she was the loveliest creature he'd e'er set eyes on and he fell a little bit in love with her on first sight."

Dougall scowled. Men did not go about saying flowery things like that, even if it was true. That was women talk.

"But then he learned she was a married lass and quickly turned his eyes elsewhere." Expression solemn, she added, "However, with their tents so close, he could no' help but see her again and again, and was often seated close to them at the nightly feasts."

"What about yer ma?" Geordie asked. "Did she notice him?"

"Aye. She said she noticed him that first night at the feast. That every time she looked about he seemed to be nearby and that he had the kindest eyes and the prettiest face."

"Aye, the Carmichael was a handsome de'il in his youth," Conran commented with a nod.

"Ye kenned me da?" Murine asked with surprise and Conran shook his head.

"'Tis more that I knew o' him," he said. "Da used to tell us many a tale that included him. According to him, yer da was a damned fine warrior, but held more fame fer his looks. They called him the Peacock. No' because he preened a lot or was vain, but just because he was so handsome," he assured her quickly, and then continued, "The story goes that lasses all o'er England and Scotland were trying to catch his eye and lure him to their beds. They were all heartbroken when instead his heart was caught by a wee injured bird with a broken wing." He smiled faintly and added, "I'd be guessing that bird was yer ma."

"Aye." Murine nodded solemnly.

"Why was she a wee injured bird with a broken wing?" Alick asked with a frown.

"Lord Danvries," Murine said with a grimaced. "Me da said that e'ery time he saw me mother at that tourney she seemed to ha'e a new bruise or injury and it made him wonder. He had no heard shouting or any untoward sounds from their tent to suggest Lord Danvries beat me mother, though, so he had begun to wonder if she was no' merely incredibly clumsy. But the second last day o' the tourney Da happened to return to his tent in the middle o' the morning to fetch something and arrived in time to see Lord Danvries drag me mother out o' their tent and head into the woods. He hesitated briefly, but then followed. However, his hesitation had put him behind enough that he lost them.

"Da was just debating returning to camp when he heard a

woman's distant screams. He followed the sounds, but then they stopped. He paused to listen, waiting for something to tell him which direction to go, and a moment later spotted Lord Danvries some twenty feet to his left, returning alone. Da waited for him to pass, then headed in the direction Lord Danvries had come from. After a bit he heard soft sobbing and followed that to where my mother lay in a small clearing. He said she was lying in the dirt; bloody, bruised and her gown in tatters."

"The bastard," Alick growled.

"Aye," Geordie agreed grimly.

Dougall nodded in agreement.

"Me da picked her up gentle as he could. There was a small brook nearby and he carried her there to clean away the blood and filth and check to see how bad her wounds were. Apparently, he said no' a word as he did it, but was e'er so gentle me ma knew he'd no' hurt her. He then scooped her up again and carried her back through the woods to the tents. Ma said he spoke gently to her the whole way, tellin' her she was safe, he'd no harm her, and indeed that no one would harm her again."

Alick sighed behind him like a love-struck lass and Dougall glanced over his shoulder to give his younger brother a glare meant to remind him he was a warrior. He glanced back quickly to Murine, however, when she continued her story.

"Ma thought he'd deliver her to Old Megs at the Danvries tent. Instead, he took her back to his own tent, tended her wounds and tucked her in his bed, then found Old Megs and gave her two messages, one was to be delivered to Lord Danvries and the other to the English king."

"The English king was there?" Geordie asked with surprise.

"Aye," Murine said solemnly. "Apparently he was fond of tournaments."

"Ne'er mind that old bastard. What happened?" Conran said impatiently.

Dougall saw Murine smile crookedly, and she continued.

"The king and Danvries arrived at the same time. Me da showed them both into the tent where me mother was resting. O' course, Lord Danvries was no' well pleased to find his wife in the Carmichael tent. He accused him o' raping and beating her and demanded a wager of battle."

"Wager of battle?" Alick murmured. "That's where they battle to decide guilt or innocence, is it no'?"

"Aye, I've heard it called trial by combat," Conran said quietly and then asked, "'Tis what yer da intended when he placed her in his bed and sent fer the king and Danvries, is it no'?"

Murine nodded. "He suspected that the reason Danvries dragged her out to the woods to beat and rape her was because he had no wish fer others to witness or overhear and ken how he treated her. He was quite sure Danvries would ne'er admit he'd injured his wife so badly in front of the king. Da also knew that few kenned o' his skill as a warrior, that instead all they seemed to talk about in reference to him was his looks. And since Danvries had settled past disputes by crying for wager of battle when he thought he could best his opponent, he was sure Danvries would try it again."

"Clever," Dougall murmured with true admiration, and his brothers all murmured in agreement.

"Obviously, yer da won the battle," Geordie said.

"Aye." Murine grinned. "But Da swears God lent a hand in that. They were to take three courses of jousting, and then exchange three blows and strokes with battle-axes, swords and daggers. They ne'er made it to the third course o' jousting. Da got in a hard blow to Danvries's chest on the second course. His lance shattered and a sliver flew into the eye o' Danvries's horse, piercing right though into his skull. The horse reared, toppling Danvries, and then trampled him, screaming in agony the whole while, ere falling dead on top o' him. When they got the horse off, Danvries was well and truly dead."

"Bloody hell," Alick breathed.

"Aye," Geordie agreed.

They were all silent for a minute and then Conran cleared his throat and said, "So then yer da wooed yer ma?"

Murine chuckled at the question. "Aye. If ye consider his returning to his tent, telling his men to gather everything and follow and then packing her up and carrying her off back to Carmichael wooing her." She smiled faintly. "Mother always said he wooed her as he nursed her back to health, and he was so sweet and gentle she began to trust him and agreed to wed him."

Her smile faded then, Dougall noted and understood why when she continued.

"They sent for William and Montrose then, but her first husband's father, the then Laird Danvries, refused to send them. He claimed they were his heirs and would be raised at Danvries. But the truth was he blamed her for his son's death and was punishing her by not letting her see her sons. That about broke Mother's heart, I think."

"But then she had you," Geordie pointed out. "I'm sure that helped soothe the ache."

"She had two boys and then me," Murine corrected and then admitted, "And, aye, I'm sure it helped, but she still missed Montrose and William. Fortunately, old Danvries died some ten years ago and William became laird. They came to visit Mother then and met me and my older brothers."

"Wait," Alick said with a frown. "Ye've two English half brothers and two full Scot brothers?"

Geordie added, "If ye've two Scottish brothers, why the de'il were ye sent to England when yer da died?"

"Colin and Peter died more than a year before me da did," she said quietly.

"How?" Geordie asked at once.

Murine fell silent and Dougall felt a tremble slip through her. "We were attacked on our way home from Sinclair. Both me brothers and half the soldiers who traveled with us died that night."

"Night?" Conran asked sharply. "Ye were attacked at night?"

"Aye. They crept up on us while we slept and had slit the throats of the guard and several of the sleeping men, including me brothers, before someone woke and cried the alarm. The remaining soldiers managed to fight them off, else we'd all be dead, I'm sure."

When Conran's gaze shifted his way, Dougall nodded solemnly, knowing what his brother was thinking. Bandits made traveling dangerous. They waited at passes and bridges, hiding to the sides and charging out to rob unsuspecting travelers on their approach. But they didn't usually follow a party, wait for them to fall asleep and then creep up to slit their throats. That sounded more like an assassination, murder *for* coin rather than murder in the hopes of gaining coin. It was a very slight difference, but with the number of people who had died in Murine's life of late, it was very, very suspicious.

"Who the de'il did that?" Alick said suddenly, apparently not suspecting what Dougall and Conran did, but then he was still young.

Murine shrugged helplessly. "We ne'er found out. Me father suspected they were mercenaries, hired to kill me brothers, and perhaps me. But he ne'er told me who he thought was behind it." She fell silent for a minute and then said wearily, "Losing me brothers on top o' losing William just the year before that . . ." She shook her head. "Me mother took it hard. She wouldn't eat and was always weeping, and then she became ill and she just did no' ha'e the will to fight it." Murine shrugged unhappily. "She died a month and a half after me brothers."

"Ye lost both brothers and yer ma and then yer da too in the span o' little more than two years?" Geordie asked with dismay.

"And yer half brother William died the year before yer other two brothers?" Alick pointed out as if she may have missed that fact.

"Aye," Murine said, and before he could ask, offered, "A riding accident."

"How long before that did yer betrothed die?" Dougall asked now.

"Just a month before William," Murine admitted.

"That's a muckle lot o' death fer one family to suffer in so short a time," Conran said grimly.

"Aye, too much," Dougall muttered and when she turned to glance at him in question, he asked, "How did yer da die?"

"He fell ill this past spring, just ere I was to visit Sinclair again. A chest complaint; fever, cough and a runny nose. It did no' seem that serious. Still, I almost did no' go because o' it, but he insisted, and he did seem to be improving so I went, but the day after Joan had her child, Montrose arrived at Sinclair. Father was dead, cousin Connor had inherited the title and Carmichael Castle, and Montrose had been named my guardian. I was to live with him in England."

"That's no' right," Geordie said grimly. "Who the de'il was this cousin Connor?"

"Aye, and why were ye left with nothing?" Alick asked and pointed out, "The English may no' leave lands and castles to their women, but we Scots do. If the clan supported ye, ye'd ha'e been clan leader."

Murine had turned her head sideways at Alick's question and Dougall saw sadness and disappointment cross her face, and then she bit her lip and turned her face forward before admitting, "Connor is the son o' me father's sister. She married the younger brother o' Laird Barclay and Connor was raised among the Barclay clan. I've ne'er met him."

"Yer da left Carmichael to a Barclay rather than his own daughter?" Geordie asked with dismay.

"Connor is only half Barclay," Murine corrected. "He is Carmichael by blood on his mother's side."

"Still," Alick said with a shake of the head. "He was raised at Barclay, with no ties to the Carmichael clan. Why the devil would yer father leave all to him and not you?"

Dougall was rather interested in the answer himself. It just didn't seem like something the Carmichael he'd heard of would do.

Murine lowered her head and plucked unhappily at one of the ties on her skirt as she admitted, "Montrose said 'tis because I am so weak. That with me constant fainting, Da did no' think the clan would back me as clan leader. He thought it best me cousin Connor take his place, and that 'twould be kinder for me to live in England and start afresh than to have to step aside and watch me cousin claim all I was too weak to gain."

Dougall noted the expressions on his brothers' faces and knew they reflected his own. Reluctant understanding. Aye, it might be hard to get the clan to rally behind a lass who so frequently dropped in a faint. Still, he felt the father could have and should have done better by her than to leave her in the hands of her half brother. Surely the man had known Montrose's nature? He must have. He'd never heard the Carmichael to be a stupid man. Hell, the story of how he gained his wife, Murine's mother, proved his intelligence. His leaving Murine to Montrose's less than tender mercies just didn't make sense.

"And o' course he was right," Murine said suddenly with a firmness that brooked no argument.

Dougall peered down at her solemnly. She sat stiff and still before him again, her head lifted and face turned forward so that she needn't look at anyone as she gave that lie. Her father's decision had obviously hurt her, but on top of all the other losses she'd suffered, he suspected that to her mind it was just one more blow among many that she'd had to endure the last couple of years.

"But—" Geordie began in protest, only to pause abruptly when Dougall turned a stern look his way.

"Enough talk. We left late and need to make up time," he

said grimly and then urged his horse to more speed, making talk impossible.

While he did want to make up time, Dougall's main concern was Murine and how this discussion upset her. She had suffered a great deal in a short time, and was ailing because of it. He suspected her fainting problem was completely due to her not eating enough. He also suspected that issue may have saved her life. Had she been healthy and hale enough to rule as clan leader, he was quite sure she too would have died in some unnatural manner. Either slain by roadside bandits, or a nasty fall. Because he suspected this cousin, Connor, might be behind the deaths. Certainly, he was the one who had gained from them.

Dougall's arms tightened around her as they rode, and not just to prevent her tumbling from the horse should she faint again. For some reason Dougall found himself with the most damnable urge to protect the lass; from her brother, from the pain of her father's decisions . . . hell, from the world at large. And he hadn't a clue why.

Chapter 5

"'Tis early to stop, is it no'?"

Dougall glanced down at the top of Murine's head at that comment as he turned his horse off the road and into a clearing. He then shifted his gaze to Conran when his brother urged his horse up beside them and agreed, "Aye. Should we no' continue on for another hour or so?"

"There will no' be a spot by the water in another hour or so," Dougall said mildly, although that wasn't completely true. He'd traveled this route many times delivering his horses and there were a couple some distance ahead, but none of them offered a waterfall to bathe under. His decision to stop here was because he fancied a nice dip in the water and thought Murine might too. She'd commented self-consciously about the lack of water at their last stop, and that she hoped she did not have a dirty face or something.

Noting the way Conran was eyeing him, he added, "The horses need water."

"We let them drink an hour or so ere stopping last night and then a couple o' times today," Conran pointed out mildly.

"Aye, but this way they can drink their fill," he responded firmly.

"Hmm," Conran murmured, and had the audacity to smile knowingly.

Dougall glowered at him for his trouble as he slid off his mount. He then turned to lift Murine down.

"Thank you." She almost whispered the words as he set her on the ground. She'd been as quiet as a mouse since their discussion of her family. But then, Dougall had kept up a steady pace to prevent conversation.

"Oh, how lovely!"

Dougall glanced around at that exclamation to see Murine at the water's edge, peering along the river to the right and even now moving in that direction. The sight made his eyes widen with alarm. He'd set her down beside him and turned to retrieve the bag with the cooked meat from his horse, expecting her to stay still and wait for him, but the woman had not stayed where he put her. Off she'd flitted like a butterfly, traipsing across the clearing to the water's edge where—should she have one of her fainting spells—she'd most like tumble into the river and drown before anyone could reach her.

"Ye chose well. She likes the spot," Conran commented, smiling after the woman like a simpleton.

"I did no' choose this spot fer her," Dougall lied to discourage teasing. "I told ye, I wanted to camp by water fer the horses."

"Oh . . . aye," Conran agreed with obvious disbelief, and then his expression grew somber. "Just . . ."

"What?" Dougall asked when he didn't continue.

Conran considered him briefly, seeming to have some kind of inner argument, and then he straightened his shoulders and advised, "Have a care with her."

Dougall narrowed his eyes. "What do ye mean?"

"I mean she's an unmarried lady without chaperone or even her lady's maid, and I ken ye're attracted to her."

Dougall considered denying the claim, but in the end just said a wary "So?"

"So I do no' blame ye fer wanting her; she's an attractive woman. But she's also a lady born who is depending on us to see her safely to Saidh and Lady Sinclair. Her hope is that they may come up with a way to save her from a brother who apparently thinks and treats her as little more than a lightskirt."

"I ken all o' that, Con," Dougall said dryly, annoyed at the lecture. "What's yer point?"

"I just think ye should step lightly," Conran said quietly. "Do no' follow yer instincts and unintentionally make her think ye see her as a lightskirt too." He didn't wait for a response, but moved to help Geordie and Alick set up camp.

Dougall watched him go, then turned to peer toward Murine, his heart sinking. He hadn't stopped here with the intent of seducing Murine, but as they'd ridden that day, his mind had wandered to this spot and he had found himself imagining certain scenarios once they reached the waterfall. Murine being as over pleased at his choosing the spot as she'd been at Geordie's giving her the linen. Of her giving him what started out as an appreciative hug, but turned into much more.

Closing his eyes, Dougall rubbed a hand wearily around the back of his neck. Whether he wanted to admit it or not, he really had intended on seducing her with kisses and caresses, of laying her in a clearing, stripping her clothes, kissing her protests away and taking her there in the grass. It had seemed an exciting and even beautiful thing when he'd imagined it, but now Conran's words made him feel as lowly as her brother. Murine was a lady, and a damned fine one at that. She had courage as she'd proven both when she'd saved his sister and when she'd fled her evil brother on that damned cow of hers. But she also had revealed intelligence and kindness to himself and his brothers. She deserved more than a roll in the grass by the side of a waterfall. He just couldn't treat her like the lightskirt her brother had tried to make her, Dougall thought with self-disgust. Especially when he had offered his escort and protection. So he would have to marry her to have her, or keep his hands off.

Oddly enough, the prospect of marrying Murine wasn't nearly as distressing now as it had been when his brothers had first suggested they would be willing to do it themselves. He could certainly do worse for a bride, and began to think he would never find better.

A little stunned by his own thoughts, Dougall started toward the woman, intending to catch up to her ere she fainted, fell in the water and drowned herself, removing the option of marriage before he could even decide if he wanted to do it. He had barely taken a step when she started to drop. Heart lurching, Dougall burst into a run, but slowed just before reaching her when he realized that she was crouching, not fainting.

Wondering what the devil she was doing, Dougall came to a halt behind her and peered over her shoulder. His eyes widened slightly when he saw the mess of baby rabbits huddled together.

She glanced over her shoulder and grinned at him. "Are they no' lovely?"

Dougall stared at her blankly and then pointed out, "They're rabbits."

"Aye, but just wee babes, and so soft. Feel it." She popped up and turned, holding out one of the wee beasties. When Dougall merely stared at the little ball of fur with dismay, she pressed it closer, nearly against his chest. "Go on. Feel how soft 'tis."

Dougall shook his head. "I do no' usually pet me dinner."

Murine snatched it back with alarm. "Ye're no' eating it."

"Nay, but we'll be eating one o' its older cousins shortly," he pointed out dryly and then nodded toward the nest where at least nine others nestled together, their eyes all closed. By his guess they were only a week to ten days old. "Ye'd best put it back, lass. 'Tis probably terrified and'll die from fright."

"It's no' terrified," she said, holding the ball of fur to her chest and smiling as she petted the animal.

"Still, its ma may no' take care o' it if she smells you on it," he pointed out.

Murine raised wide, alarmed eyes to him. "Nay!"

"Aye," he said with a shrug, and then suggested, "Put it back. Hopefully it'll rub up on the others and the smell o' its siblings will cover yer smell ere she returns."

When she hesitated, he almost expected her to refuse and insist on bringing the creature with her rather than risk it being abandoned by its mother. But after a moment, she heaved out a sigh and set the little ball of fur down in the center of its siblings. They all immediately shifted and jostled around until you couldn't tell which one she'd picked up. Apparently reassured that her smell should be eliminated or absorbed by them all, she then moved away from the nest and farther along the shore to peer at the water.

"'Tis a beautiful spot," she commented on a happy little sigh.

"Aye," Dougall agreed, following her. He then pointed along the river to the right where it curved out of sight. "There's a waterfall just around that bend. "

"Really?" she asked with interest, leaning out a bit as if she could crane her head far enough to see it. She couldn't, of course.

"Aye, 'twill offer privacy do ye wish to bathe there," he said, clasping his hands behind his back to keep from grabbing her arm to prevent her tumbling into the water. He just as quickly unclasped them and let his left hand hover near her arm to be prepared in case he did have to save her. When she didn't seem to notice and leaned even farther out, he gave in to his worry, caught her arm and turned to march her back to the horses. "But ye can attend to that later. Ye should eat now."

"But I'm no' hungry," Murine protested and his lips twitched. Honestly, she sounded like a child balking at being sent to her bed, he thought as she added, "Can I no' take a bath now?"

"Nay," he said, escorting her toward the fire his brothers were building. "Ye'll eat first, and this time ye'll no' get away with a couple bites. Ye'll eat proper and like it," he added firmly. The lass needed looking after and he was the man to do it, Dougall decided and when she didn't comment, was satisfied that it would be as he said.

"THIS IS NOT PRIVACY."

Dougall gave up scowling at the trees and turned to arch one irritated brow at the woman presently plaguing his life. Murine stood in the small clearing next to the waterfall, hands on hips, glaring at him as if he was the one being difficult. Him! When she was the one who would not do as he ordered and refused to eat until she'd bathed. She hadn't started to argue until they'd reached his brothers. She'd probably been thinking of what argument would best work, he thought. And find one she had. She'd claimed she could not possibly enjoy the delicious food with her own foul stench assaulting her nose. It would ruin her appetite.

Well, once she'd said that, Dougall's brothers had looked to him with alarm, a reaction he'd fully understood. Anything that threatened to take away her appetite was to be avoided, for they were sure that was the reason she kept fainting.

Dougall had given in and led her to the waterfall, intent on remaining in the clearing, near enough to rescue her should she faint and fall in. But it seemed she was taking issue with that as well.

He tried reasoning with her. "Ye can no' swim alone. 'Tis dangerous what with yer fainting all over the place."

"I do no' faint all the time," she said sharply. "I have fainted once since meeting ye."

Dougall raised his eyebrows in disbelief that she would make such a claim.

"All right, perhaps it has been twice," Murine said, blushing.

"Ye were in a faint all the afternoon through yesterday," he pointed out dryly.

"I was not. I told you I woke up several times while we were riding."

Dougall nodded. "And then fainted dead away again and again."

"I could no' *breathe*," she stressed impatiently, then shook her head with disgust. "This is stupid. All yer presence here does is make me uncomfortable. 'Tis no' as if ye would hear me drowning over the pounding water."

Dougall stiffened at the claim, recognizing the truth behind it. Lord knew they'd been practically yelling at each other to be heard over the rush of water.

"Very well," he acknowledged and promptly began to remove his sword and sporran.

"What are ye doing?" Murine asked warily.

"Undressing. Ye can no' swim alone. As ye pointed out I'd no' hear ye if ye faint and fall, so I shall swim with ye."

"Oh, nay!" she cried, rushing forward to catch his hands as Dougall reached to undo the pin that held his tartan in place. "I will no' swim naked with ye. Are ye mad?"

"Ye can wear yer shift," he said with a shrug, and then seeing her expression, asked with concern, "Surely ye packed another one in that bag o' yours?"

Murine bit her lip, but nodded. "Aye, I packed one."

"Good," he said, relaxing, and then pointed out, "Ye can change into it after ye bathe and leave the wet one to dry overnight. Both ye and yer shift'll be clean that way."

Murine grimaced, her shoulders drooping as she admitted, "I did pack one in the bag I brought with me, but my bag is missing. It must ha'e fallen off Henry as we traveled yesterday. I ha'e nothing else to wear."

"It didn't fall off," Dougall assured her. "I had Alick move it to the mare I brought yer brother."

"Oh." She looked so pleased and relieved at this news that Dougall didn't add that it had not been his own idea, but at Conran's suggestion.

Dougall glanced back the way they'd come as he considered the trek they would have to take to fetch her bag. The waterfall had been farther away from the clearing than he'd recalled, and the path through the woods to get here was overgrown, full of those damned thickets that seemed everywhere in this part of the country. They'd caught repeatedly at Murine's gown and slowed their walk to the point that Dougall had been ready to whisk her up in his arms to speed them along. Only Conran's little warning and the fact that she'd no doubt protest the action had held him back from doing so. He didn't care for the idea of making that trip again, twice, both to fetch her bag and then to bring it back, at least not with her hampering his speed.

Glancing back to Murine, he said, "If ye sit yerself down and promise to no' go in the water until I return, I'll go fetch yer bag fer ye."

"I promise," Murine said promptly, dropping to sit where she stood, a happy and excited smile claiming her lips.

The sight made Dougall pause. The lass was so damned beautiful when she smiled like that. Her full pink lips spread, her large blue eyes opened wider and a flush of color bloomed on her cheeks. She looked healthy and happy and so damned kissable.

That thought bringing him up short, Dougall scowled and turned abruptly.

"Stay out o' the water," he barked and then rushed from the clearing as if all the demons in hell were chasing him.

MURINE SMILED CROOKEDLY AS SHE WATCHED DOUGALL HEAD out along the path. The man acted all stern and grumpy, but truly he was kindhearted under the crustiness. She was quite sure few men would have returned for her bag as he was doing, and his obvious concern for her was sweet. If he were in the market for a wife . . .

Murine pushed the thought aside and turned to peer over the clearing. It had been hard work to get here in her destroyed gown, but was well worth the effort. She didn't think she'd ever seen a spot as lovely.

Smiling faintly, she plucked a blade of grass and twirled it between her fingers as she closed her eyes and raised her face to the sky. It was early enough that while the sun had started its downward journey, it was still shining brightly and she enjoyed its warm caress on her skin. In that beautiful spot, bathed in the sun's warm glow, she could almost forget her troubles and what a tangle her life had become.

Almost, Murine thought wryly as she lowered her head and opened her eyes again. That was when she spotted the figure in the woods. Murine had sat down facing Dougall, her back to the water, it left her a perfect view of the woods; otherwise she might never have seen whoever it was. She certainly hadn't heard anyone approach over the sound of the rushing water.

She got slowly to her feet and squinted at the shape she could just make out through the branches, trying to figure out who it was. Was it one of the Buchanan men looking for more game to cook? Or searching for wood? If so, why didn't they approach and say something? They must see her there looking at them.

Frowning, she took a step toward the woods.

"Ye were supposed to stay sitting. Ye promised."

Murine whirled at that barked comment to see Dougall returning with her bag in hand. The man was scowling at her for daring to get to her feet. Good Lord, while she appreciated his concern, he and his brothers all treated her like she was the frailest child in need of constant supervision, and Murine just wasn't used to such treatment. While her father had been concerned when she'd suddenly taken to fainting after her brothers' deaths, he'd been too distracted by her mother's failing health to hover. And certainly Montrose had never worried over her well-being. Having these men treat her like some weak, fragile creature was beginning to wear on her nerves.

"I did no' promise to stay sitting," Murine said mildly. "I promised no' to go in the water. Besides, I was just trying to sort out who—" She paused in her explanation as she turned toward where she'd spotted the figure in the woods and realized that whoever she'd seen through the trees was now gone. She frowned at the spot, and then shrugged and turned her attention back to Dougall as he paused in front of her.

"What were ye trying to sort out?" he asked, now looking into the woods as she had done a moment ago.

Murine just shook her head. She didn't want to get one of the brothers in trouble for spying on her, if they had even been doing that. They might have simply been out hunting wood, and stopped when they spotted her in the clearing.

"Thank ye." Murine took the bag he held.

"Ye're welcome," Dougall rumbled and then reached for the pin of his tartan.

Murine's eyes narrowed warily. "What are ye doing?"

"I told ye, ye can no' swim alone. Should ye faint—"

"But what will ye wear?" Murine asked, reaching up to cover his fingers and prevent his undoing the pin that she knew was the only thing holding his tartan in place. Once it was removed, the cloth would drop like a lady's dress, leaving him in only his shirt.

"Me shirt," he answered simply.

Recalling just how short his shirt was, Murine snatched her hands away and backed up, shaking her head violently. "I'll jest return to camp then," she said and turned toward the path they'd used to get here. "Ye go ahead and swim."

"What? Wait," he said, catching her arm as she started to turn away. "Ye were the one who insisted on bathing ere ye could eat."

"Aye, but I did no' expect ye'd join me, let alone that ye'd think to do so in nothing more than a shirt that barely covers yer treasures and is no doubt see-through when wet."

"Me treasures?" he queried with gentle amusement.

Murine flushed, but gave a weary shrug. "'Tis what Montrose calls his . . . treasures," she ended helplessly, and then added wryly, "The way he talks ye'd think they were made o' gold."

"He talks to ye o' such things?" Dougall asked with dismay.

"Nay," she said quickly, and then grimaced and admitted, "But when he's in his cups he brags about them to his men with little concern that I am present."

Dougall's mouth tightened and he said grimly, "He and I'll ha'e much to talk about when next we meet."

Murine's eyes widened and she swallowed down a sudden lump in her throat as she digested his words. She was touched that he was offended for her and wanted to confront her brother on her behalf. However, the truth was Murine was seriously hoping none of them ever encountered her brother again. In fact, shameful as it was to admit, she was rather hoping her poor luck when it came to family would strike again, this time taking her half brother from her. And that was not something she'd ever wished on anyone in her life ere this.

"I'll no' join ye in the water," Dougall said suddenly, drawing her attention back to the matter at hand. She was just relaxing when he added, "But I will ha'e to watch ye while ye're in the water."

"But—" she protested and he cut her off.

"'Tis the way it has to be, lass," Dougall said firmly, "Do ye faint, ye could drown."

Murine sighed with frustration. This damnable fainting was making her life such a bloody misery, and she was becoming convinced that it really was her own fault. She supposed she'd run herself a little ragged after her brothers died, first looking after her mother, and then her father when he fell ill. Like her mother, grief had stolen Murine's appetite, but unlike her mother she hadn't fallen ill, she'd merely begun to faint, and usually at the most inopportune times. Unfortunately, she hadn't regained her appetite since. She just couldn't seem to find an interest in food, or much of anything else really.

That wasn't completely true, Murine acknowledged. She'd perked up a bit while with Jo, Saidh and Edith, and had even begun to eat more again at Sinclair. But after her father's death and moving to England, Murine had lost interest in pretty much everything once more. The tincture Joan had made for her had worked to stave off the fainting fits, but once it had run out, she'd started fainting again.

"Ye can swim in yer shift and I shall just watch here from the shore," Dougall bargained. "That way, if ye run into trouble I will ken it."

Murine stared at him silently for a minute and briefly considered arguing, but doubted that would matter. This was probably the best offer she would receive. If she wanted to bathe, and she really did, then she would have to accept his watching her.

"Very well," she murmured with resignation.

Apparently, Dougall had expected an argument. At least he looked surprised by her easy capitulation, but then he nodded and gestured to the bag she held. "Then get to it. I'm hungry."

Grimacing, Murine turned and moved to the shore's edge. She quickly opened the bag and, after a bit of digging about inside, found and dragged out her clean shift and gown. She hung both over a nearby branch, and then turned and peered at him uncertainly. "There's no need fer ye to watch me undress. I'm no in the water yet. Could ye no' just turn yer back while I remove me gown and get into the water? I'll tell ye once it's proper fer ye to turn around."

IT WAS THE WORD *PROPER* THAT MADE DOUGALL CAVE IN THIS time. She was an untried lass. This couldn't be comfortable for her, and if it weren't for her propensity to faint at the drop of a dagger, he wouldn't be insisting on it. Giving a solemn nod, he turned his back and crossed his arms. "Yell when ye're in the water."

He then stood and listened for the sound of her disrobing. But as she'd pointed out, the sound of the water rushing over the falls made it impossible to hear anything.

"I'm in!"

Dougall started at the sudden bellow and turned sharply.

Murine smiled at him innocently from the water and shrugged. "Ye said to yell," she pointed out with a grin, then turned and moved toward the waterfall. Dougall knew from previous stops at this spot that the water she was moving through would be only up to her waist, yet it covered her from the neck down. She must be squatting in the water, he decided as she paused before the waterfall and hesitated. Reaching out, she stuck a hand in the rushing water to test its force, then moved under it before straightening to her full height.

Dougall caught his breath. He suspected she thought the foamy white water would act as a curtain, obscuring her from view, but it didn't. If anything, it seemed to frame her almost lovingly, highlighting the slight curves and hollows that her damp and now nearly see-through shift was hugging with adoration.

The woman was painfully thin, which wasn't a surprise after seeing how little she ate. But she was still gorgeous. He wouldn't deny that he'd like to see a little more meat on her, but even without it . . . Well, the erection stirring between his legs and pushing at the rough cloth of his tartan said it all. Murine was beautiful to him; her pale skin shone like alabaster under the water and dwindling sun. Her hair darkened to a burnished gold as it grew wet, and her nipples were round rosy patches showing through her wet shift. Patches he'd like to see without the gauzy wet material veiling them the little bit they did, he acknowledged and began to wonder once again what would have happened had he taken up Montrose's offer.

Most likely the same thing that had happened without his accepting it, he thought wryly. The wench would have fled the first chance she got and set out on her cow, but then she would have been fleeing from him as well as her brother.

His gaze dropped over her flat stomach and to her hips and Dougall frowned at the sight of her bones pressing against her skin. The lass really was terribly thin. He was surprised she hadn't fallen ill as her mother had. Fortunately, now that they knew, or suspected they knew what was causing the fainting, they could see to it she ate more. Perhaps it would help her regain her usual appetite and move her toward a more healthy weight.

Aye, he'd see to it that she ate more, Dougall decided and then his brow furrowed as he realized that if he delivered her to his sister as planned, he couldn't see to that at all. Between the group of them, his sister and the other two friends would surely come up with a way to save Murine from her brother. She wouldn't need him then. She'd be out of his life and away from his influence. The thought brought a scowl to his lips as he settled on the ground and grabbed up a piece of grass to chew on as he waited.

MURINE CLOSED HER EYES AND LOWERED HER HEAD, ENJOY-ing the pounding of the water on her back and shoulders. She was not used to sleeping on the cold, hard ground or riding for hours on end. The combination was leaving her back muscles sore. At least that's what she told herself, though if she were to be honest, she knew the aches and pains were probably more a result of holding herself so tensely when riding with Dougall today. She just hadn't been able to help herself. If she relaxed, her body curled into his, her back pressing against his chest, and that combined with having his arms around her had made her feel surrounded by him. His scent all she could smell, his breath stirring her hair . . .

Murine gave a little shiver that had nothing to do with the temperature of the water pouring over her. With her father being the clan chief and having two elder brothers, Murine had led a rather sheltered life. At twenty-one she hadn't even been kissed yet, but in Dougall's arms on his horse, pretty much in his lap, she . . . well, frankly, it had made her wonder what it would be like if he kissed her. It had made her wonder what it would be like to experience other things too, things from the marriage bed that she, Saidh and Edith had giggled over as Jo, their only married friend, had described them.

Frankly, Murine didn't know how to handle that. She was pretty sure she'd never get to experience any of the things she was thinking about. At least, not as a wife. Murine very much feared she was going to end up in a nunnery. She was hoping not to, that once she reached Saidh, they would travel on to Sinclair to see Jo and the three of them, or four of them if they could reach Edith and get her quickly to Sinclair, would be able to come up with an alternate plan. But she suspected the best they would be able to come up with was an ancient laird who needed a wife and didn't care about her not having a dower, or something of that ilk. That being the case, it wasn't likely she would ever experience the tingles and yearning she had felt seated before Dougall . . . which made it a kind of torture, as if fate were taunting her with all she would never have. So she'd avoided it by sitting as stiff as a log in front of him. Her lower back was now complaining.

Grimacing at the throbbing in her back, Murine bent and let her fingers dangle down toward her toes, allowing the water to pound on her lower spine where it would do the most good. The position made water rush down over her face, but her eyes were closed so she didn't care. Besides, the position gave her some respite and made it worth it. At least it did until she suddenly staggered under the water and realized that she was woozy. Cursing her stupidity, Murine quickly straightened, only to curse herself again as the abrupt action merely intensified her light-headedness and darkness began to close in.

Dammit, this was exactly why Dougall had insisted on watching over her and what she'd assured him wouldn't happen, Murine thought with irritation as she felt the familiar darkness of unconsciousness close in around her.

MURINE BLINKED HER EYES OPEN AND PEERED INTO THE SKY. It was early yet, but the sun was making its coming arrival known, its light creeping up on the horizon. It was just enough for her to make out the dark shapes of the men sleeping around the long-dead fire. They wouldn't wake for a bit yet and Murine almost closed her eyes and tried to slip back into sleep, but the nagging need to relieve herself prevented it. She had to go so terribly bad, a result of her not going last night before sleeping. It was something she'd refused to do because Dougall would have insisted on following her to keep her safe from herself and her propensity to faint.

The thought made her grimace with disgust. After losing consciousness under the waterfall, Murine had woken up at the water's edge with Dougall leaning over her. He'd saved her, of course, which she'd appreciated. However, she was less appreciative of his determination to stay by her side at all times and guard her like a mother hen. It had taken a lot of talking and pleading to get the man to turn his back long enough for Murine to don her fresh dry linen and a new gown, and then he'd made her talk the entire time she did it so that he could be sure she was still conscious.

Murine supposed it was the head wound she'd received when she'd fallen. Apparently her forehead had struck either a rocky outcropping or a boulder under the falls. Whatever the case, she'd woken to find she had a nasty lump and cut on her forehead and Dougall was washing blood from her face. A lot of blood. He had refused to leave her side ever since.

Rather than suffer his presence next to her as she attended to embarrassing personal tasks, she'd foregone them altogether. Now her body was letting her know it wasn't happy with that decision.

Moving slowly and cautiously to avoid waking the man sleeping just inches away, Murine got carefully to her feet and slipped into the woods, slowing with every step she took as she waited for her eyes to adjust. While it was starting to brighten in the clearing, the woods were still as dark as full night and if she didn't have such an urgent need, Murine might have turned back and waited for the sun to fully rise. But she continued cautiously forward. Dark as it was, Murine didn't think she had to go far. She'd just be quick about her business and get back before the men woke up.

She went about ten steps into the woods and quickly tended

her business, eyes darting nervously this way and that as she listened to the sounds of movement in the darkness surrounding her. It had seemed to be dead silent when she'd woken up, but now there was the crackle of branches and leaves as creatures moved about, and the sounds appeared to be drawing nearer to her.

Just nerves, Murine assured herself. It was rather spooky out here alone in the dark woods. She finished quickly and started to head back the way she'd come, then paused and spun around at the sound of a branch snapping. It had been loud in the silence, and startlingly near. Small woodland creatures wouldn't have made that sound. At least she didn't think so. Another sound caught her ear and she turned again, but couldn't make out anything in the black night surrounding her. When a rustle sounded on her other side, Murine's nerve broke and she bolted for camp. At least, she'd thought it was toward camp. It was only when she'd gone what she considered to be much more than ten feet without breaking out of the woods that she began to worry she'd got turned around and run in the wrong direction. When she heard the sound of rushing water growing in front of her, she knew for sure she had.

Stopping abruptly, Murine swung back the way she'd come and then cried out when something smashed into the side of her head.

Chapter 6

"DAMNED SILLY O' HER TO WANDER OFF ON HER OWN."

Dougall didn't respond to Conran's muttered words as they made their way through the thickets and trees in search of their lost charge. But he thoroughly agreed with him. Damned silly. Irresponsible even.

Dougall's heart had nearly dropped out of his chest when he'd woken to find Murine gone from the clearing. He'd started out in search of her, only to pause and return to wake his brothers to help him look. The sun had just been creeping over the horizon then and he knew the woods would be dark. He might need the help if the silly woman had gone off and fainted somewhere in the thickets. Besides, he didn't want a repeat of the last time this had happened. He wanted a witness if her gown somehow got all torn up.

"Is that the waterfall I'm hearing?" Conran asked with sudden alarm as the sound of rushing water reached them. "Ye're no' thinking she decided to bathe on her own, are ye? Dear God, she nearly drowned the last time and that was with ye there to keep an eye on her."

Dougall didn't need to be reminded of that. Murine had scared the life out of him when she'd suddenly dropped into the water under the falls. He'd launched himself to his feet and catapulted into the cold liquid after her without a single thought except for the desperate need to pull her out. Dougall couldn't recall the last time he'd been so scared . . . and he hadn't liked it. Just thinking about it made his heart race with fear even now. If she'd gone and drowned on him—

"She—what was that?" Conran interrupted himself to ask as a broken cry sounded ahead of them.

Dougall didn't respond, he was already charging forward. While the sun was lightening the sky in the clearing, it was still dark and gloomy in the woods. Dougall didn't find Murine so much as trip over her in his headlong rush. It sent him tumbling flat on his face, but he quickly pushed himself up and turned to crawl to her, even as he barked a warning to Conran so the other man didn't take the same tumble.

"Ye found her," Conran said with relief, reaching him as he began to run his hands quickly over her dark figure on the ground. Dougall was searching for injuries, but it wasn't until he slid a hand under her head to lift her to a sitting position that he felt the sticky dampness. Blood.

Cursing, he scooped her up in his arms and turned back the way they'd come.

"What's the matter? Is she all right?" Conran asked, tripping along beside him and craning his head to try to get a look, though Dougall couldn't guess why he was bothering. It was still too dim in the woods to see much other than her dark shape.

"Her head's bleeding again," Dougall growled.

"Did she hit it again or is that from last night's wound?" Conran asked with concern.

Dougall didn't bother responding. He didn't know, and wouldn't until he could see her better.

Conran must have realized that as well, because he didn't ask the question again and fell silent as they rushed back to camp.

The clearing was empty when they reached it. Geordie and Alick had headed out to help look for Murine, leaving the horses unguarded. Fortunately, they were still there and well. Dougall carried Murine past them to kneel beside the dead fire from the night before and examined her head. The light was much better in the clearing and he saw that while he'd felt blood at the back of her head, the wound was on the side.

"A new wound," Conran said with dismay, dropping to his haunches beside him.

"Aye," Dougall growled.

"Damn me, she knocked herself silly," Conran muttered with concern. "She must have fainted again and hit her head as she fell."

Mouth tightening, Dougall merely said, "Fetch me some water and a clean cloth. And whistle for Geordie and Alick so they know they can stop searching."

Conran nodded and rushed off, giving a piercing whistle as he went.

Catching at a corner of his tartan, Dougall raised it to wipe away some of the blood on the side of Murine's face. The lump forming on her temple was the size of a fist with a gash in the middle. It didn't look deep, but in his experience head wounds often bled worse than the same wound would elsewhere.

A soft moan drew his gaze from the lump forming at her temple to Murine's face as her eyes slowly blinked open. Her gaze was confused at first, and her eyebrows drew together as she peered at him.

"What happened?" she asked in a whisper and then winced and squeezed her eyes closed, her hands raising instinctively as she moaned, "Oh, my head."

"Pounding is it?" Dougall asked sympathetically, catching at her hands to keep her from touching the wound and no doubt increasing her pain.

"Aye," Murine breathed, squinting her eyes open to peer at him.

"Ye fainted again," Conran explained gently, drawing Dougall's attention to the fact that he'd returned.

"The water?" he asked with a frown when he saw that Conran's hands were empty.

"Alick is fetching it," Conran answered, and pointed out, "He's younger and faster on his feet so when he offered—"

Dougall waved away the rest of his explanation and nodded. Alick was faster, he acknowledged as Conran turned his attention back to Murine and said with concern, "Ye can no' go running off on yer own like that. One o' these times ye're like to kill yerself with all this head banging."

"Nay," Murine said with a frown.

"Aye, ye will," Conran assured her.

"Nay, I mean, I did no' faint," she explained, her voice barely above a whisper and then frowning as if trying to recall, added, "Something hit me in the head."

"Aye. We can see that," Dougall said dryly. "Probably a rock as ye fell."

"Nay," Murine repeated. "I was standing and something smashed into my head."

Conran looked dubious and glanced to Dougall, who just shook his head. He didn't think that likely either, but she was in no shape to argue with. Leaving it for now seemed the best bet.

"Ye do no' believe me?" she asked, sounding both wounded and annoyed at once.

Dougall shifted his gaze back to see that Murine was peering at him with disappointment.

"'Tis true," she insisted. "I was standing and I turned and something hit me in the head and then . . ." She shrugged helplessly. "It must have knocked me out."

"Could be ye turned into a branch," Conran said when Dougall remained silent. It was purely an effort to soothe the lass, Dougall was sure. His brother still looked dubious and Murine seemed to think so too, because she shifted fretfully, pushing out of his arms.

"I am telling ye I did no' faint. Someone hit me," she said shortly, struggling to her feet and pushing away Dougall's hands when he tried to steady her.

"What are ye doing, lass?" he asked with a frown, straightening as she did, his hands hovering in the air between them, ready to catch her if she fell.

"I . . ." Murine paused and frowned, obviously not knowing what she intended to do.

"Ye should sit, lass. Come, sit by the fire," Conran suggested gently, taking her arm to lead her the few steps to the fallen log by the now-dead fire.

Murine didn't push Conran away, Dougall noted, an odd sensation stirring in him. It was something that was a cross between irritation and pain, as if his feelings were hurt by the realization. Which was ridiculous. He didn't get hurt feelings.

"Someone really did hit me, Conran," Murine said earnestly as she settled on the log.

"I ken ye think that, lass. But could ye no' just be a bit confused after yer latest head wound?" Conran asked gently. "All o' us were sleeping until Dougall woke us to hunt fer ye. And it did no' take us but a minute to find ye after we heard ye cry out and there was no one near ye. Is it no' more likely that ye fainted and hit yer head as ye fell?"

"But—"

"Bloody hell! Are ye all right, m'lady?"

Dougall glanced to Geordie as he rushed into the clearing and straight to Murine, his gaze horrified as he took in the blood staining her face yet again. The wound was still bleeding and while blood had run back into her hair as she'd lain on the ground, it was now trailing down the side of her face and down along her neck in rivulets.

"Where the devil is Alick with that water?" Dougall snapped impatiently.

"Here!" his youngest brother called out, crashing into the clearing. Water slopped from a bucket he carried and he had another strip of clean linen in his other hand. He rushed to Murine, and no doubt would have commenced to cleaning her up, but Dougall stopped him with a hand on his chest and took the items from him. If anyone was cleaning her, it would be he.

"Oh, look, ye've ruined yer gown, m'lady," Geordie noted sympathetically as Dougall knelt next to Murine and dunked the clean linen in the water.

Wringing out the linen, Dougall glanced up to see that Murine had her chin tucked in as she tried to peer down to see what Geordie was talking about. The blood had trailed down her neck and begun to soak into the neckline of the gown she'd donned after her swim the day before. There was no way she could see the stain and her expression was vexed as she attempted to.

"'Tis just a wee bit o' blood on the neckline," Dougall assured her and then took her chin in hand and raised her head so that he could wipe the blood from her neck and prevent the stain growing any larger.

Murine was silent as he worked. But she drew in a hiss of breath when he then rinsed the cloth, wrung it out again and pressed it firmly to the still bleeding gash.

"I ha'e to stop the bleeding," he muttered, regretting causing her further pain but knowing it was necessary.

"O' course," Murine whispered.

"I'm thinking ye should stitch it up," Conran decided, kneeling next to him to eyeball the wound when Dougall took the cloth away and blood immediately began to trickle from it.

"Nay," Murine gasped, and then frowned and said shakily, "Surely putting pressure on it will be enough? 'Twill stop bleeding in a minute."

Dougall was of the mind that stitches might be necessary, but understood her dismay at the thought. Pressing on the wound was no doubt painful, but forcing a needle through the skin of her forehead again and again would be excruciating. Besides, he was not pleased at the thought of permanently scarring her so. As it was this gash would leave a mark, a thin line if she were lucky. With stitches it would look like a branch on her temple.

"We'll try pressure first," he decided.

Murine relaxed a little and offered a grateful smile.

Dougall smiled back, then glanced around to Alick. "If ye've more clean linen, fetch it. We'll need to wrap her head to keep her wound closed while we ride."

Alick nodded and moved to the horses to begin rooting around in the satchel hanging from his mount's saddle.

"Thank ye."

Dougall glanced back to Murine at those words to see that her expression had turned more tentative.

"I am sorry. I ken I've slowed ye down and been nothing but a bother. And I appreciate yer kindness in seeing me safely to Saidh," she said softly.

Dougall hardly heard the words, his attention caught by her lips as they moved. His mind was filling with thoughts that had nothing to do with what she was saying.

"'Tis all right, lass," Conran said when Dougall remained silent. "We're nearly to Buchanan now. In fact, we should arrive just in time for sup. We'll stay the night and take ye on to Mac-Donnell in the morning. It's only a half day's ride, so ye should be laughing about all o' this with Saidh by the nooning."

Dougall stiffened. Unless they were further delayed they should reach Buchanan well ere the sup tonight, and MacDonnell by noon the following day. Then this task would be completed and they would return home . . . leaving Murine behind. The thought did not please him and his voice was a bit rough with that displeasure when he said, "Ye should break yer fast."

"Oh, nay, I'm no' hungry," Murine said quickly.

"Then eat fer yer health," he said abruptly.

Murine hesitated, and then asked, "Are any o' ye going to eat?"

Dougall shook his head while his brothers all said nay and Murine raised her chin.

"Then—"

"But none o' us faints from a lack o' nourishment," Dougall interrupted her, knowing she was going to use their not eating as an excuse to refuse food herself.

Murine blew her breath out in resignation, but then rallied and said, "Fine. I'll eat. But could the rest o' ye no find something to occupy yerselves with other than staring at me? 'Tis most discomfiting." When she didn't get an immediate agreement, she added, "And takes me appetite away."

"I'll go check on the horses," Alick said at once.

"I wouldn't mind a quick swim ere we set out," Geordie decided.

"I'll join ye fer that swim," Conran announced and the three brothers immediately moved off, leaving them alone.

"What about you?" Murine asked when they were alone.

"I'm staying," he said simply, and then teased her gently, saying, "Someone has to make sure ye actually eat and do no' just claim ye did while we are gone."

Murine scowled at the suggestion.

"But I'll ha'e a bite or two with ye if it means ye'll eat more," he added.

"Deal," she said, brightening.

Chuckling for no reason he could understand, Dougall took her hand and raised it to press against the cloth he was still pressing against her forehead.

"Hold that firmly in place," he instructed, then stood and moved to the horses to collect the bag with the cooked meat in it. He had a couple of apples left in his own bag, and grabbed them as well as the leather flask of cider that hung from his horse's saddle, before returning.

Murine still held the cloth in place when he returned, and judging by the way she was wincing, she was pressing more firmly than was necessary in an effort to stop the bleeding and avoid getting stitched up. Dougall didn't comment on it, but merely began to set out the food.

"I did no' think about it, but I'm sorry if our not eating and watching ye eat made ye uncomfortable yester morn," he said quietly as she accepted the large serving of meat he offered her.

Murine smiled wryly. "Ye were no' so bad, but Alick and

Geordie were like a pair o' crows perched on the log. I kept think-ing they were about to swoop over and grab the food from me."

Dougall smiled faintly at the words. Now that she said it, he did see the resemblance between his memory of how they'd perched on the log, leaning forward, and a pair of interested crows. The truth was they had both been more interested in her than her food, but he didn't say as much.

They ate in silence for several moments, Dougall pleased to see she was making short work of the meat he'd given her. She was eating it quickly. He suspected that was so that she could get as much in as possible before her head told her she was full. He thought that was a good sign. Now that he had mentioned that the fainting might be due to her lack in eating, she appeared to want to correct it herself. If he was right, her fainting spells should end quickly and she would not need the tincture Joan had made for her, or its recipe. She'd return to the healthy young lass she'd been ere the troubles had hit her family. Healthy enough to be a wife and mother.

"So, ye've imagined yerself married and having a passel o' children?" he asked suddenly as he recalled her saying some-thing to that effect when she'd said she'd always expected to marry. He himself had always thought a half a dozen or more would be good. But then he'd grown up in a household with eight healthy children in it, so it seemed natural.

"Aye," Murine admitted. "But I think all girls probably do. We are usually betrothed in the cradle."

Dougall nodded. That was true. Pretty much every child born to nobility was betrothed quite young. Saidh had been as well. And like Murine's betrothed, Saidh's had died ere claim-ing her.

Murine smiled at him tentatively and commented, "Saidh once mentioned that while yer parents arranged betrothals fer her and Aulay, they never arranged them for the rest o' ye?"

Dougall nodded and then explained, "Ma wanted to but Da refused."

"Really?" Murine asked with wide eyes. "Why?"

"He always said it was hard to ken how a bairn would turn out and he did no' want to saddle any o' us with unpleasant, or amoral mates, or even ones whose personality did no' suit us," Dougall explained. "He wanted us to have a chance at happiness and choose our mates for ourselves as he had."

Murine's eyebrows rose at this, and she pointed out, "But Saidh was betrothed."

"Aye, and so was Aulay. Our mither insisted on it. Saidh because she was a lass, and Aulay because he was the eldest son and heir to the title," Dougall explained.

"And yet Saidh's betrothed died like mine and Aulay's—" She paused abruptly, looking uncertain, and Dougall immediately understood that Saidh had told her what had happened there and how angry they had all been about it, so was afraid to upset him with the subject.

"Aye, Aulay's betrothed refused to fulfill the contract when she saw the scar marring his face," he said grimly. "And she was no' kind about it either. She decried him as more monster than man."

Murine winced and nodded solemnly. "That was cruel."

"Aye," Dougall muttered. Just the memory of the woman's words and Aulay's pain made him want to hit someone. He forced himself to take a deep breath to calm that urge and then added, "She also said she'd gladly give up her dower fer breaking the betrothal, but she would no' marry him, she'd rather die or take the veil."

Murine gave a humorless laugh and pointed out, "And yet I would marry Aulay in a heartbeat rather than take the veil." Her yes widened suddenly and she said, "Oh, say! Do ye think he is in the market for a—"

"There are a few things I need to do ere we leave," Dougall interrupted sharply, getting to his feet. He didn't wait for her to say anything else, but strode abruptly out of the clearing, his mind a storm of emotion.

MURINE FROWNED SLIGHTLY AS SHE WATCHED DOUGALL GO, but then turned her thoughts to the idea she'd come up with: marrying Aulay Buchanan. Saidh had painted a picture of her brother as a rather tragic figure. According to her he was a good, strong man and fair leader . . . Rather like Dougall, she thought. But Aulay had been shamed and tossed aside by a heartless, selfish betrothed who had judged him by his looks alone.

Murine had not met Aulay and had no idea how bad the scar was that had offended his betrothed so, but if he was anything like Dougall . . . Besides, if there was one thing she'd learned in this life, it was not to judge anything by looks alone. After all, Montrose was a handsome man in looks, but ugly as sin to his very soul underneath. Since her mother had claimed he looked like a younger version of his father and she knew how that man had abused her mother, Murine would say he had been the same. She was quite sure that Aulay was just the opposite, scarred and ugly on the outside but with a heart as fine and kind as Dougall's. She would pick that over a man like her half brother any day. And she would definitely choose it over her brother's plans for her. Or even the nunnery.

Murine just wasn't sure how she would manage a feat like convincing Aulay that marrying her was to his benefit. She had little enough to offer him, just kindness and gratitude for saving her from the fate her brother had intended for her. She could definitely promise that she would be a good wife to him, and that she would be a good mother to any offspring they had as well. But would that be enough?

And what about Saidh? How would she feel about such an arrangement? What if she wanted more for her brother? It had seemed clear that Saidh adored her brothers. She'd also made it clear she was glad Aulay's betrothed had refused to marry him. She'd thought someone so shallow would be a faithless and uncaring wife and that he deserved better. Would she think Murine good enough for her brother?

She needed to talk to Saidh, Murine decided firmly and glanced around, wondering how long it would be before they left. Seeing that the clearing was empty except for herself made her frown slightly. Dougall had refused to leave her alone lest she faint and hurt herself since finding out who she was, yet she was now all alone.

Strange, she thought and then gave a start as Alick suddenly appeared beside her. Not so alone after all, she thought, as she returned the smile he offered her and peered curiously at the skin of liquid he held in his hands like an offering.

"Here," he said holding it out toward her. "I mixed up a tincture fer ye that Rory sent with us. It should help ease the ache in yer head."

Recognizing the name Rory as that of the brother Saidh had claimed was a healer, Murine accepted the bulging skin, and asked curiously, "What's in it?"

Alick shrugged and admitted wryly, "I ha'e no idea. A bunch o' weeds and sech that smell pretty bad. I mixed it in with whiskey to try to make it taste better, but ye may want to plug yer nose and just down it quickly. That always helps me when I ha'e to take Rory's tinctures."

Murine grimaced, and then did as he suggested; she plugged her nose and downed as much of the tincture as she could in one go. It was an awkward business. She had to plug her nose with thumb and finger, while holding the mouth of the skin to her lips with only her other three fingers. Still, she managed to gulp several mouthfuls before having to stop to take a breath. That was when the heat from the whiskey hit her. It burned down her throat and slammed into her stomach with a vengeance that left her gasping and then coughing violently.

Alick quickly grabbed the skin to keep her from dropping it, then set about pounding on her back until the coughing fit ended. He waited for her to catch her breath, and then offered the skin again. "Ye'll need more than that to get the full benefits."

Murine hesitated, but the coughing fit had turned the dull ache in her head into an agony, and in the end, she took the skin and lifted it to her lips again.

"WHOA!"

Dougall glanced up with surprise as two hands caught him in the chest and brought his charge through the woods to an abrupt halt. Realizing that he'd nearly crashed into Conran, he muttered an apology and started to go around him, but Conran stepped into his path.

"What's about?" he asked, eyes narrowed. "Ye look ready to kill someone."

Dougall opened his mouth, then narrowed his eyes and asked, "Where's Geordie? I thought the two o' ye were going fer a swim."

"He's swimming, but . . ." Conran hesitated, and then simply said, "I changed me mind."

Dougall's mouth tightened. He didn't need to be a mind reader to know that Conran had changed his mind because he'd decided he should stick close enough to keep an eye on Dougall and Murine and make sure Dougall didn't behave inappropriately, or threaten her virtue in any way. It was a bit insulting, but Dougall let that go for now and growled what was uppermost in his mind, "Murine's thinking to marry Aulay."

Conran blinked at this announcement. "What? Why would ye think that? She's ne'er e'en met him."

Dougall ran a frustrated hand through his hair and then quickly recounted their conversation, ending with "I'm sure she was about to ask if I thought Aulay would be interested in marrying her."

"Aye," Conran agreed, and then added regretfully, "And he probably would marry her. Out o' gratitude fer her saving Saidh if nothing else. The only thing that might prevent him from doing it is his worries on his scar, but he'd convince himself that saving her from her brother's intentions would make up for it."

Dougall cursed and turned his head away. Conran was verifying exactly what he'd thought himself. Aulay hadn't shown any interest in marriage since his betrothed had humiliated him. He wouldn't talk about it, but they all knew that bitch had scarred Aulay more emotionally than the scar that had cleaved his face. Aulay was sure the scar made him unmarriageable, that no woman would willingly marry a man as ugly as he. He'd seemed to resign himself to a solitary life. But Murine's situation might change everything. Aulay would feel the same gratitude and appreciation for Murine's saving Saidh that they all did, and he'd feel pity for her situation. He'd also think her having to live with what he considered his monstrosity would be better than having her own brother whore her out to his friends and acquaintances. Aye, Aulay would marry Murine, Dougall was sure, and the very idea made him feel like his head was going to explode.

"What are ye going to do?" Conran asked.

Dougall glanced to him with confusion. "About what?"

Conran rolled his eyes. "Dougall, ye're me brother. I ken ye. Ye like the lass. More than like her even. Ye should tell her that and marry her yerself."

Dougall was silent for a moment, considering the suggestion, and then he said reluctantly, "But Murine might be Aulay's only chance at having a good woman to wife. Murine would be a loving wife and a fine mother to his children."

"Dougall," Conran said heavily. "Aulay has no' e'en met Murine. 'Tis no' as if he's in love with her too."

He stiffened at the suggestion. "I'm no' in love with Murine."

"Mayhap not, but ye're halfway there," Conran said dryly and then added firmly, "And do no' try to tell me ye're not. Ye're usually a quiet, grumpy bastard, but no' since we stumbled upon Murine. I've ne'er seen ye smile so much ere this, and ye actually talk to the woman, stringing whole sentences together rather than just grunting on occasion as ye usually do. And ye're hovering over her like a mother with her first bairn," Conran added firmly. "Ye like the lass. Do ye really want to hand her over to Aulay?"

Dougall frowned at the question. The very idea of standing back and watching Aulay wed Murine made him want to hit someone. But . . .

"How the hell should I know?" he burst out in frustration. "I've considered marrying her, but I barely ken the lass. We only met her two days ago and she's been unconscious most o' that time. Hell, I ha'e no' e'en kissed her," he muttered with disgust and then glared at Conran. "Thanks to you."

"Me?" Conran asked with surprise. "How is it me fault ye ha'e no kissed the lass?"

Dougall peered at him with disbelief. "Ye're the one who said me doing so would make her believe I think as little o' her as her brother."

"Oh, aye," he said wryly and then shrugged. "But I did no' mean kissing. Anyway, forget what I said. Ye're considering marrying the lass. Yer intentions are honorable here. Just do no' take it too far ere ye're sure ye want to marry her, else ye'll ha'e no choice in the matter."

"Aye," Dougall muttered, wondering just how far he considered to be too far.

"And I'm thinking ye may want to avoid stopping at Buchanan," Conran added. "It may be better to travel straight on to MacDonnell. That way ye can avoid Aulay meeting her until ye've made up yer mind as to whether ye want her or no'."

Dougall nodded slowly, and then shook his head and pointed out, "Once we get her to MacDonnell, Saidh'll claim all her time and I'll no' get the chance to know her better," he said with frustration and Conran frowned at the truth of those words.

They were both silent for a minute and then Conran said,

"I'm thinking this latest head wound is serious enough that we mayhap should camp here another day or two to give her the chance to heal. Especially since 'tis no' her first head wound."

Dougall glanced at him sharply. "A day or two here?"

"Aye," he said solemnly, and then grinned and added, "I'd give ye a week if I could, but suspect stopping so long would make the lads suspicious. Especially when we are so close to home."

"Aye," Dougall agreed quietly. He considered the matter briefly, then nodded. "We'll camp here tonight and tomorrow night."

"Where are ye going?" Conran asked with surprise when Dougall suddenly moved around him and started away, but not back toward camp.

"I'm going to catch some more game. Having plenty o' food on hand'll keep the lads from complaining. And then I'm going to take a swim to clear me head," Dougall muttered. Dougall rarely rushed headlong into anything. If battle couldn't be avoided, he made a plan. It seemed to him that wooing Murine deserved a plan too. After all, this was the rest of their lives he was to be deciding on.

Chapter 7

$\mathcal{D}$OUGALL HEARD THE LAUGHTER LONG BEFORE HE REACHED their campsite. The sound made him smile slightly as he walked. Murine's tinkling laughter was easily heard among the lower-pitched guffaws of his brothers. It made him wonder if Conran had mentioned their decision to camp here a night or two to allow her to recover from her latest head wound, or not.

"She didn't!" Murine was gasping when Dougall stepped into the clearing.

Curious to know what they were talking about, Dougall paused at the tree line and waited as Alick nodded and said gleefully. "Aye, she did. Saidh put her boots to Aulay, Conran and Dougall and had them rolling on the ground, clutching their bollocks and howling like babies."

"She did the same to you," Conran pointed out dryly.

"Aye, she did," Alick admitted unashamed. "And then she had Geordie in a headlock and was twisting Rory's ear until I thought sure it would pop right off." He shook his head and said with admiration, "She's a scrapper is our Saidh."

"Aye, well she's had to be with the seven o' us fer brothers. We'd ha'e trod all over her if she were no'," Geordie pointed out with affection.

"Aye. That's true enough," Alick agreed and then smiled at Murine and admitted, "That's why 'tis a wonder to me that ye and Saidh are friends."

Dougall frowned. He wasn't at all surprised that Saidh and

Murine were friends. They were both brave and sometimes stubborn women as Murine had proven when she'd refused to eat ere bathing. Besides, the comment almost sounded like an insult, though he couldn't say whether it was an insult to Saidh or Murine. Apparently Murine thought so too, because she sat up a little straighter on the log she was perched on and demanded, "Why?"

"Now, do no' take offense," Alick said quickly. "I'm no' meaning insult. 'Tis jest that our Saidh is . . . well, she's strong, but . . ."

"But I am weak and stupid?" Murine suggested when he hesitated, and Dougall narrowed his gaze on her. Not only did she sound annoyed, she was slurring her words a bit. She was also swaying on her log as if dancing to slow music.

"Oh nay," Alick said quickly. "Ye're far from weak or stupid."

Murine looked mildly soothed by the words and slouched back on her perch, but asked, "Then why are ye surprised we'd be friends?"

"Ye're a true lady," Alick said after a moment. "And our Saidh is . . . not," he finished weakly.

"Oh, pffft." Murine waved one hand a bit wildly. "Saidh's maybe a little rough-and-tumble, but she's still 's much a lady as me." An evil grin coming to her face, Murine added, "Ye'd best be nice to me, Alick Buchanan, else I'll tell Saidh ye said that just so I can see her twist yer ear."

"Oh, nay, ye'd no' do that," Alick said on a laugh, and then concern slowly dawned on his face and he asked, "Would ye?"

Murine leaned back on a peal of laughter and would have fallen off her log if Dougall hadn't moved up just then and put out a hand to brace her back. When she didn't even seem to notice or look around, but continued to giggle at Alick, Dougall glanced to Conran and arched an eyebrow in question.

"Alick gave her one o' Rory's tinctures to help with her aching head," he explained and then grinned and added, "But apparently it was pretty foul, so he mixed it with whiskey. A lot o' whiskey," he said with emphasis. "Murine's feeling no pain."

"Ahhh," Dougall said dryly, and then glanced to Murine when she swiveled on her log to see him and gasped.

"There ye are!" she exclaimed, swaying back away from him. "We were beginning to think ye'd fallen into the river and drowned. I e'en wanted to come find ye, but the lads did no' think 'twas a good idea."

Dougall found a smile tugging at his lips. She was more relaxed than he'd ever seen her, smiling widely, her eyes clear of the worry and sadness that always seemed to cloud them . . . and she'd worried about him. He liked this Murine even more than the one he'd come to know during their trip so far.

"Where were ye?"

His mouth widened further at the slurred demand. She spoke as if she had a right to know and as if she cared and he liked that too.

"I was hunting more game," he said and held up the pheasants he'd scared up.

"Ohhhh," she breathed, her eyes widening on the birds. She reached out to run her fingers lightly down the speckled feathers and admitted, "I like pheasant better than rabbit. Especially the way you boys cooked them yester eve. What was that spice ye rubbed on it ere putting it o'er the fire? It was lovely."

Dougall had no idea. Alick had dressed the birds for cooking, probably with some wild herbs he'd found in the woods, but it had been good, so he held the pheasants out to his younger brother now, saying, "Ye'll have to ask Alick that. 'Twas his efforts ye enjoyed."

Murine swung around unsteadily on her seat to grin at Alick as he stood to take the game. "Then ye must tell me, Alick. 'Twas delicious."

Alick actually blushed at the praise as he took the pheasants, but merely said, "I'll tell ye later. Ye'll be more likely to remember then."

Dougall smiled wryly at the words, suspecting they were true. Murine was definitely feeling no pain just now. He doubted she'd remember much of anything of this day come morn. The thought made him eye her consideringly and then he asked, "Would ye like to take another swim while we're here?"

Murine looked surprised at the question. "I thought we'd be on our way once ye returned."

When Dougall glanced to Conran in question, he shrugged, "I thought it best ye explain that we're staying another night."

"We are?" Murine asked and frowned. "But—"

"Come," Dougall suggested, catching her under the arm and urging her to her feet. "I'll explain on our way to the waterfall."

"I do like the waterfall," Murine announced, apparently already forgetting her concern that they were staying. "'Tis so pretty."

"Aye," Dougall agreed, leading her away from the campfire and ignoring the looks his brothers were giving him. Conran looked knowing and approving, but Alick and Geordie were eyeing him with a suspicion and concern that was rather annoying. They should know Murine was safe with him. He didn't plan on harming or ruining the lass. However, it had occurred to Dougall that if Murine wasn't likely to remember this day's events come morning, he should be able to kiss her without fear she'd think he saw her as a lightskirt. That way he could see if they might suit each other in that manner. It would help him make his decision as to whether he should marry her or not, and it would allow him to do so in a way that wouldn't hurt her feelings or leave her feeling abused. He just had to be careful about it. So far the woman's very presence stirred him like no other. If it turned out, as he suspected, that her kisses affected him even more, than he would have to stomp down on his urges and not overstep. He didn't want to force her into marrying him. He just wanted a little more assurance that he could deal happily with her. He also wanted to be sure she was not cold and unresponsive in that area.

While he was hunting, Dougall had acknowledged that Conran was partially right regarding his feelings for Murine.

He wouldn't say he was half in love with her already, but he definitely liked and respected the woman. Her courage was admirable, she seemed intelligent, and when she'd told them of her family history the day before, he'd been as enthralled as his brothers. Her laughter was captivating, and the mischievous grin that had claimed her when she'd told them her father had killed her mother's first husband had been delightful. In those ways, she was all he could have wanted in a wife. Now he wanted to be sure that they matched in the more physical way. That she was not repulsed by the act. So he'd kiss her and maybe caress her a little to test her response and then he'd return quickly to the fire with her to ensure that was all that happened. At least that's what he told himself as he walked Murine through the woods to the waterfall.

"And then he threw me in!"

Dougall blinked and tuned back in to Murine's words. She'd been chattering away happily as they walked, but he'd been distracted by his own thoughts and hadn't a clue what she was talking about.

"Who threw ye in what?" he asked with a frown.

"Dougall Buchanan!" Murine cried with dismay and then released a huff of exasperation. "Ye were no' listening to me at all, were ye?"

"Nay," he admitted, finding himself smiling at her put out attitude. She was just so damned cute at the moment. It made him realize how much her situation had affected her personality and he wanted to see her without the worry that hung over her like a cloud. "My apologies, I was distracted."

"Hmm." She pursed her lips and stumbled over a branch, staying upright only because he held her up. "Well, I was saying that I always liked to swim. Me brothers and me often swam in the loch at Carmichael. At least we did after the time me brother Peter got annoyed at me and tossed me into the loch. Ere that I was not allowed to swim with me brothers, I was supposed to be a little lady. But when Peter tossed me in . . ."

She grimaced. "I sank like a stone, gulping half the loch water before he realized what he'd done and jumped in to pull me out. Well, Da decided then and there that 'twas more important I knew how to swim than how to sew a stitch. He overrode Ma's concern and ordered me brothers to teach me to swim and we spent many fine afternoons by the loch."

Her smile turned sad then at the thought of her brothers and Dougall frowned, knowing she was thinking of how they died. To distract her, he asked, "And why was yer brother so annoyed with ye?"

"I've no idea," she assured him, nose in the air, then grinned and admitted, "He claimed it was because I took his wooden warrior Da had carved for him and got it all muddy playing with me dolls with it."

"And did ye?"

"Aye," she admitted on a laugh. "I was pretending the wooden warrior was me betrothed come to fight off a mud monster to save me dolls." She chuckled and shook her head. "I do no' think Peter ever managed to get all the mud off his warrior. It was ground right into the wood grain in places."

Dougall smiled, preferring this happy laughing woman to the one he'd come to know. He determined then to do what he could to always see her happy and laughing.

"Oh," Murine murmured as they broke into the clearing. "I'd forgotten how pretty it is here."

"Aye," Dougall agreed, but didn't bother to look at the setting. His gaze was on Murine as he thought about his reason for bringing her to the clearing. He was debating on the best way to approach kissing her without alarming her when he realized she was yanking her gown up to tug it off over her head. It seemed when full of Rory's tincture, the lass forgot her shyness of the previous day. Although it was probably the whiskey that had that effect, he thought absently, as he noted that her chemise had got caught in the cloth and risen enough on one side to reveal the rounded half moon of one delectable butt cheek. Mouth watering, Dougall reached out to catch at the cloth and tug the shift back into place to hide that temptation. He then tried to help her tug the gown off over her head when she appeared to get tangled in the material. The woman was weaving like a banner in a stiff breeze, blinded by the cloth around her head and raised arms, and it took a bit of effort to remove the cloth. It was an ordeal that would have been made easier had she thought to undo the ties first, he was sure.

"There!" she exclaimed with relief once he'd freed her of the cloth. "That's better."

Turning away from him then, she moved eagerly to the water's edge and began to wade in.

"Oh! It's cold! Oh!" she gasped, and the fact seemed to make her rush more quickly forward. In the next moment her head disappeared under the water's surface and Dougall tossed her gown aside and quickly removed the pin to loose his tartan as he rushed forward to rescue her. The tartan fell away at the edge of the water, and Dougall was hurrying into the cold water when her head suddenly popped to the surface on gasps and complaints of the cold.

She hadn't tumbled into the water, he realized, pausing, but had submersed herself in the hopes of adjusting and warming more quickly. She had also moved away from the waterfall rather than toward it, seeking out the deeper water so that she needn't squat or kneel to remain submerged.

Dougall considered turning back to shore to let her swim alone, but the water was already up to his waist, soaking the material of his shirt. There was a stiff breeze today and it would be a cold wait on shore with the damp cloth and that wind, he thought. In fact, he was already going cold from the water. Grimacing, he eased forward and squatted slightly so that the water reached his neck, hoping to warm up more quickly.

He would just keep his distance, Dougall decided moving to the side away from Murine as he eased farther out in the water. Kissing her while she was dressed and on shore was one thing, but kissing her while she was soaking wet and wearing a chemise so thin it went see-through in the water was another entirely. A man had only so much control and Dougall was unwilling to test his too far with this woman.

Knowing it would help him adjust to the water temperature more quickly, Dougall dove under the water, coming up several feet farther out in the river. When he surfaced again a moment later, a sharp squawk reached his ears and he blinked his eyes open to see Murine mere inches away just as she began to smack at him. She must have moved in his direction without realizing he was there while he was under the surface and his sudden appearance had obviously startled her. The woman's eyes were wide with shock and fear and she was batting at him in a panic.

"'Tis me," Dougall muttered, catching her hands and holding them to end her attack on his face.

"Oh." Murine stopped struggling in his hold and eyed him with amazement. "When did ye get here?"

"I brought ye here," he reminded her dryly, releasing her hands and stepping back as he slicked the wet hair back from his face.

"Aye, I ken that," she said with a put-upon sigh. Her arms rose instinctively to cross over her wet chest under water and she moved backward, putting a little more space between them. "But I thought ye still ashore."

"And I thought ye were floundering when ye went under the water so rushed in to save ye," he admitted dryly.

For some reason that seemed to amuse her and she tilted her head and said, "To save me again, ye mean."

Dougall smiled faintly and nodded. "Aye. Again."

"Saidh was right, ye're a fine man Dougall Buchanan," Murine said solemnly. He was still blinking over that pronouncement when she grinned and added, "I never imagined when Saidh was telling me all those tales about ye and yer brothers that one day I'd get to meet ye all."

She hadn't met them all yet, but he didn't want her thinking of Aulay and her possible plans to marry the man, so didn't point that out. Instead, he found himself moving closer to her in the water.

"Are ye warming up?" he asked.

Murine wrinkled her nose and hugged herself in the water. There were goose bumps on her shoulders above the water's surface and she was beginning to shiver. She was definitely cold, but said, "A bit. 'Tis colder today. But still nice," she added quickly as if afraid he would suggest they get out.

Dougall didn't comment; he merely caught her arm under the water and drew her nearer. When her eyes widened with something like alarm, he changed his plans mid move and turned her in the water, then drew her closer so that her back rested against his chest and his body spooned hers as he had when they'd slept.

"What are ye doing?" Murine asked. Her voice was a bit breathless, but she wasn't trying to push him away. Dougall thought that a good sign.

"Trying to warm ye up a bit," he muttered, his voice going a bit gruff as her body slid against his in the water.

"Oh," she breathed and relaxed against him, her arms crossing over his when he slid them around her waist to hold her in place. They were both silent for a minute, and then Murine murmured, "This is nice. Ye're very warm."

"Aye," Dougall murmured, deliberately letting his breath blow against her ear and noting her reaction when she shivered a little and tilted her head slightly, making her ear more accessible and baring her neck to him. Unable to resist what he suspected was an unconscious offering, Dougall pressed a light kiss to her neck, then another to her earlobe and felt Murine tremble in his arms as her breath caught in her throat on a little gasp.

"Dougall?" she said uncertainly, her voice breathless and husky. His name had never sounded so sexy to his ears and

Dougall couldn't resist nibbling at the lobe he'd just kissed, sucking it between his lips to bite lightly at the plump skin as his arms tightened around her, pressing her more firmly against him so that her behind rubbed against the growing hardness between them.

"Oh." She pressed on his arms to tighten their embrace as her legs floated back and around his now, her heels digging into the backs of his legs as she tried to get closer still.

When he let the lobe slip from his lips, Murine turned her head restlessly, seeking, and Dougall answered the unconscious request and covered her mouth with his own. It was an awkward angle and wholly unsatisfying until he released his embrace to clasp her by the waist and quickly turn her in the water. The moment she faced him, he covered her mouth again, relieved when she didn't protest, but opened for him like a flower to the sun, accepting his tongue when he thrust it forward. She gasped and moaned at the intrusion, but didn't push him away or try to stop him. Instead, she tentatively clasped his shoulders and hung on as he taught her to kiss. It was obvious she had little experience, but she was a fast learner and what had started out as a questing kiss quickly turned into a passionate embrace. Dougall released her waist to reach for one breast, squeezing it as he explored her mouth, but the wet cloth was cloaking it. Growling in his throat, he released his hold on her altogether so that he could tug at the material, trying to get it out of the way. In the end, he had to push the clinging material up to get to her breasts. The moment he'd done so, he broke their kiss and pulled back slightly to peer at the bounty he'd revealed.

Gasping for breath, Murine had to clutch his shoulders harder and wrap her legs around his hips to keep the position he'd raised her to, but Dougall hardly noticed as he peered at her soft, sweet breasts. Muttering the word *beautiful*, he lowered his head to claim one rosy nipple, suckling the cold hard bud into his mouth to warm with his tongue.

Murine cried out and bucked against him at the caress, the action rubbing her hot core over his erection in the warming water and Dougall groaned, then let go of her wet chemise to grasp her bottom and urge her up and down against his length again. The damp cloth immediately dropped to cover his head, but Dougall didn't care. He suckled eagerly at her nipple, swirling his tongue over and over the little bud as he raised and lowered her along his length, driving them both crazy with the intimate caress until Murine tugged the cloth off his head and pulled at his hair and one ear in demand.

Releasing her nipple, he raised his head to answer the call and claimed her mouth again. This time, though, she was less quiescent in the kiss, her own tongue sliding out eagerly to meet his before she began to suck on his tongue, little mewls of excitement slipping from her throat as she did.

Dougall couldn't say if it was her excited sounds or the fact that she was sucking on his tongue and it was making him imagine her sucking on something else that did it, but his excitement level ratcheted up sharply and he responded as enthusiastically, raising her bottom a little higher than he'd meant. His erection broke loose from between them with the action, eased forward and hit her pelvic bone hard as he brought her down again.

The jolt wasn't as painful as it was shocking. It made him realize just how reckless he was being. She was wearing nothing but the shift, its hem now floating in the water around them along with the bottom of his shirt. There was nothing to block the way. One slip and he could take her innocence without even intending to, he thought and froze, holding her still with her lower body a little away from his.

"Dougall," Murine moaned in protest when he broke their kiss. She tried to shift against him again, but he held her still, trying to catch his breath and regain control of himself.

"Hush," he murmured and turned sharply toward shore, intending to get them out of the water and set her away from him.

He realized what a stupid idea that was when the supporting water fell away and she, probably afraid he would drop her, tightened her legs to keep herself up. Dougall stopped walking and dropped his head to her chest with a groan as her body slid against his again.

This had really been a bad idea, he acknowledged and took a couple of deep breaths, before saying, "I'm going to set ye down, lass."

"But I don' wan' ye to," she protested. "This feels good. I like it."

The words made his determination falter. If it weren't for the way she slurred her words, he might have taken her there and then. However, there was a definite slur to her words. Murine was in no state to think clearly on this. He had to think for both of them, and while he'd pretty much decided he was indeed going to marry Lady Murine Carmichael and bed her well and repeatedly, he would not have her waking in the morning and accusing him of treating her like the whore her brother had tried to turn her into.

"I like it too, lass, but—"

"Then why are ye stopping? Did I do something wrong? Tell me what to do and I'll—" Her words died on a gasp as he suddenly dropped her into the water. It was a desperate bid to save them both. She was a tasty little bundle and Dougall could not fight himself and her too.

Leaving her to flounder back to her feet in the shallow water, he moved quickly back to shore, grabbed his tartan, laid it out, and knelt to begin pleating it with his back to the water. He didn't do more than glance over his shoulder once to be sure she got out of the water safely, but then immediately turned his full attention forward again. He would give her time to dress and then escort her back to camp . . . and then he would not allow himself to be alone with her until they reached Buchanan and were safely married. He would not have her thinking he saw her through her brother's eyes.

MURINE STEPPED OUT OF THE WATER AND WRAPPED HER ARMS around herself as she peered uncertainly at Dougall's stiff back where he knelt pleating his tartan. She wasn't sure what to do. It had all felt so wonderful to her, but now he seemed angry and she didn't know what to do to fix it. She supposed she'd behaved badly. Actually, she supposed she'd acted as much a lightskirt as her brother could want and Dougall probably thought . . .

Closing her eyes, she turned to face the water, her mind suddenly awhirl with thoughts. Dear God, Dougall probably thought her little more than a whore. He probably thought she sold herself at every turn for Montrose's gain. No wonder he had dropped her in disgust.

Glancing around, she spotted her gown where she'd dropped it before going into the water. Murine hurried over and grabbed it up, then hesitated. She could not put it on over her dripping wet chemise, but was sobering quickly and could not bring herself to strip here. In fact, she was suddenly desperate to escape Dougall and the disgust she was sure to see in his eyes.

She would hurry back to camp alone, change either in the cover of the trees or behind the horses and her bull, then lie down and pretend to be sleeping when Dougall returned to camp. And then she would avoid him for the rest of the trip, she thought as she left him working over his tartan and slipped out of the clearing.

Murine didn't know what she would do come morning, continue on to MacDonnell to talk to Saidh, she supposed. Although she began to wonder if she should bother. Perhaps she should just go straight to an abbey and see if they would take her without dower. Certainly, she was not likely to marry. Her brief consideration of offering herself in marriage to Aulay was now impossible. She could hardly marry him after what she'd done with Dougall. Not that Aulay would want to marry her once Dougall told him of her loose morals anyway.

But the possibility of marrying anyone else didn't seem

viable either. To let someone else, anyone else do the things to her that Dougall had done—Murine gave her head a brief shake. She couldn't believe she'd let him do those things. It all had seemed—

Murine grimaced, her fingers twitching on the material of her gown as she walked. She wanted to think that it had all seemed normal and natural, but the truth was she hadn't been thinking at all. Her mind had been consumed by the sensations he'd stirred in her and the growing need that had seemed to well up out of nowhere. All she'd been aware of was the passion overwhelming her. It was only now, when he wasn't kissing and caressing her, that she was thinking at all, and now the fire and desire that had claimed her seemed somehow dirty and cheap.

Murine breathed out a shaky sigh as she acknowledged that, then glanced around sharply as a branch snapped behind her. Dougall must have finished with his tartan and headed after her. Determined to avoid him, she broke into a run and didn't slow until she came out by the horses on the edge of their camp.

Spotting the men sitting, chatting and laughing by the fire where the pheasants were roasting, Murine slipped through the horses until they made a curtain between herself and the camp, then quickly stripped off her shift and tugged on her gown. Leaving the shift to dry over a branch, she then straightened her shoulders and made her way out from the horses.

The men all fell silent at her approach. It was Conran who, after studying her expression, asked, "Is all well, lass?"

Murine forced a smile. "Fine. I just do no' feel well. I think I need a lie-down."

"Oh," Conran said softly, but was looking concerned now. Not wanting his concern or kindness, Murine didn't say anything else, but simply lay down and closed her eyes to begin feigning sleep as she'd planned.

"ARE YE DONE, LASS?" DOUGALL ASKED, TRYING NOT TO SOUND impatient. He'd finished donning his tartan several moments ago, but had then merely crossed his arms with his back firmly to Murine to allow her privacy. He'd expected her to strip her chemise, don her gown and then give him some indication that she was decent and ready to go, but she appeared to be taking her time. And she wasn't responding to his question. Frowning, he shifted where he stood and said, "Murine?"

He didn't wait more than a heartbeat for an answer before turning. His gaze slid over the empty clearing with disbelief, and then he cursed and strode into the woods, headed for camp at a jog. He was halfway back when he spotted movement ahead. He almost called out to Murine then, but didn't and merely picked up his pace a bit. When the figure he was following suddenly burst into a run, he thought she must have heard his approach and also burst into a run to give chase.

They were nearly to camp when she suddenly veered off to the left and went racing away. Dougall automatically followed, frowning as he did. Where the devil was she going? With her tendency to faint, the damned woman shouldn't even have headed back to camp on her own, but to go haring off into the woods on her own . . .

Dougall pushed that thought aside and concentrated on picking up speed. He hadn't expected her to put much effort into her run so had been taking it easy up until then, expecting her to slow to a stop relatively quickly. But she hadn't and the distance between them had grown. He would lose her if he didn't—

Even as he had the thought, the distant figure before him dodged around a large tree and vanished from sight. Dougall put on another burst of speed as he heard a horse whinny in greeting. It was followed a heartbeat later by the unmistakable drum of horse hooves racing away. By the time Dougall reached and ran around the tree himself, there was nothing to see but a couple of hoofprints in the dirt.

Cursing, he whirled and raced back toward camp, his mind trying to sort out how and when Murine had managed to sneak one of the horses away to that spot, and why she would flee. If she was upset about what had happened between them at the waterfall . . .

Well, surely his putting an end to what was happening when he had, proved his intentions were honorable toward her and she had nothing to fear? he thought. Besides, the horse had already been waiting for her there, which meant she must have planned to flee before they'd even gone to the clearing. What the devil was—

His thoughts and footsteps skidded to a halt as he reached the clearing and spotted Murine apparently sleeping by the fire.

"Dougall?"

He forced his gaze away from Murine and glanced to Conran. His confusion must have shown in his expression, however, because his brother frowned and stood to join him at the edge of the camp where he'd stopped so abruptly.

"Is something amiss?" Conran asked, glancing from him to Murine.

"How long has she been here?" he asked rather than answer the question.

Conran raised an eyebrow and turned to peer at Murine. "Not long. A few minutes mayhap. Why?"

"She—I thought—" His voice died away as his gaze returned to Murine and he took in the bright yellow gown she wore. The same yellow gown she'd worn to the waterfall. She'd traded her ripped gown for this one while he'd been off hunting pheasant earlier, he recalled. But the figure he'd been chasing in the woods had been dressed in dark clothes. It hadn't been Murine at all. The realization made him frown. Whom had he been following in the woods? And if Murine had been back only moments, she couldn't have been far ahead of the person he'd been following. Had the individual been following her?

"You thought what?" Conran prompted when he didn't continue.

Dougall sucked in a deep breath and shook his head. What

he'd thought didn't matter, but it bothered him that someone had been so near their camp. Someone with a horse tethered far enough away that it wasn't likely to be detected by anyone in their group, but close enough to reach quickly if necessary. Dougall had learned long ago to listen to his instincts and they were squawking at him just then. They were reminding him of the string of deaths in Murine's family the last three years, and that when last she'd been injured, she'd claimed something had hit her in the head as she turned. They'd all assumed she was confused after fainting and hitting her head, but she'd insisted she hadn't fainted at all. What if she hadn't? What if she had been hit?

"Pack up," he ordered abruptly. "We continue on to Buchanan."

"At this hour?" Conran asked with surprise, following when Dougall walked toward the horses. "The day is half over. We would not reach Buchanan until well into night. Mayhap not until morn if there is no moon and we are forced to move at a walk after the sun sets."

Dougall stopped, his mouth tightening as he reconsidered. It would be a much longer and more arduous journey if they left now rather than wait for morn. On the other hand, the hair on the nape of his neck was practically crawling with warning. He had a bad feeling that something was amiss and that they needed to get Murine behind the safety of Buchanan's walls as quickly as possible.

Letting his breath out, he glanced to Murine, then caught Conran's elbow to urge him toward the horses. He didn't want to explain anywhere Murine might overhear. He was determined to see her happy and smiling, not worried and full of fear. He would worry for her.

MURINE LISTENED TO THE MEN'S VOICES FADE AS THEY MOVED away and swallowed miserably. It seemed Dougall was so disgusted with her behavior that he couldn't wait to get her to Buchanan and out of his hair. No doubt once there, he'd hand her over to Aulay to arrange an escort for her to MacDonnell . . . after telling him how she'd behaved, of course. It was probably what he'd dragged Conran away to tell him now, she fretted. And Conran, in turn, would no doubt tell Geordie and Alick, she thought unhappily. How could she face any of them once they all knew she'd acted as cheaply as her brother had portrayed her?

Shame writhing through her, she opened her eyes just long enough to cast a quick, furtive glance toward the two men still seated by the fire before closing them again. Murine liked Geordie and Alick. She liked all of them and was already squirming at the idea of their condemnation once they learned just how loose she could be.

Perhaps she should just get on Henry and ride away, Murine thought. It could not be that far to MacDonnell from here. A ride of a day to reach Buchanan and half a day to continue on to MacDonnell, the men had said. Surely if she continued in the direction they'd been heading she would find her way there?

Murine grimaced. She had a lousy sense of direction. On top of that, she hadn't been paying attention to where they were headed before this. She hadn't thought she'd need to. In truth, she supposed she didn't really need to now. The men had promised to see her safely to their sister, and she felt sure they could be trusted to do so. It just meant she'd have to suffer the shame of their censoring looks for the rest of the journey.

"Murine?"

Recognizing Conran's voice, Murine stiffened and forced her eyes open to find him crouched next to her. His expression held neither censure nor disgust, however, but there *was* a certain tenseness to him that hadn't been there before.

"Ye'd best get up and ready yerself. We're leaving," Conran said quietly.

Murine considered asking why, but was afraid she wouldn't like the answer, or that he'd avoid her eyes and give a polite lie. Instead, she merely nodded solemnly and sat up, noting that Dougall was talking quietly to Geordie and Alick by the fire.

Much to her relief, Conran distracted her then by offering her a hand to help her rise.

"Do ye need to tend to personal matters ere we go?" Conran asked once she was on her feet.

Murine shook her head silently.

"Fine, fine," he said and then glanced around as the other men moved toward the horses. He offered a crooked smile. "Ye'll be riding with me this time."

Murine had to work hard to keep from flinching. She shouldn't be surprised that Dougall no longer wanted her on his horse, but still it hurt. Lifting her chin, she said stiffly, "I'll ride Henry, thank ye."

"Ye'll ride with Conran."

Murine stiffened, but didn't glance around at Dougall's voice. "I—"

"We have to ride fast while there is still light. Your cow is slow and ye'll just slow him further with yer weight. Ye'll ride with Conran until nightfall." He paused briefly and then added, "Ye can ride the mare after that if ye insist on riding by yerself. We'll have to ride slow then anyway."

"The mare?" she asked, startled into glancing at him.

Dougall nodded and offered a tight smile. "She's yours now."

Murine merely stared at him as a rushing began to fill her ears. Her brother had offered her services in exchange for both horses. It seemed that despite Dougall's not actually breaching her maidenhead, their little encounter by the waterfall had earned her the mare. Or perhaps it was simply a down payment and he expected more from her for the animal. Before she could refuse the horse or say anything at all, Dougall turned away to head to the fire and quickly set about putting it out.

"Are ye all right? Is something amiss?" Conran asked, sounding genuinely concerned.

Murine shook her head stiffly and allowed him to lead her to the horses, reminding herself that she'd brought this all on herself.

Chapter 8

"Tell us how 'tis possible to travel to Sinclair to meet a prospective husband and yet end up good friends with the other lasses who were there for the same purpose."

That question from Geordie had Dougall glancing toward where Murine sat in Conran's lap, but he just as quickly glanced away. He didn't like seeing her so cozy with his brother, and if he didn't trust himself not to behave inappropriately, she wouldn't be there. But after his lapse at the waterfall, it had seemed best to avoid getting too close to Murine until he could make her his own. So she rode with Conran . . . and it was driving him mad.

"Aye, by rights they should ha'e been yer opponents," Alick put in now. "And yet the bunch o' ye ended up being friends and even with the bride herself." He shook his head. "It seems so unlikely."

"I did no' see them as opponents," Murine said quietly and the sound of her voice drew Dougall's gaze back to her. It was the first time she'd responded with more than a one-word answer to his brothers' efforts to draw her out. Murine had been oddly quiet during the past two hours since they'd broken camp. A fact that his brothers had obviously noted and had been trying to rectify with constant questions and comments. It seemed they were finally making some headway.

"How could ye no' see them as opponents?" Alick asked with exaggerated dismay. "Ye were all vying for the same man's attention."

"There was no vying," she said dryly. "He was already married when he arrived."

"Aye. It must ha'e been a shock and disappointment to all ye lasses when the Sinclair arrived with a bride in tow," Geordie commented.

"It was a surprise, aye, but no' so much a disappointment," Murine assured them. "When I saw all the lasses there I did no' expect he'd choose me anyway."

Dougall frowned and glanced sharply toward Murine at that comment. The woman obviously undervalued herself if she thought that was true. Any man with eyes in his head would have been drawn to her, but it was Alick who gave an outraged squawk and said, "What nonsense! Had he no' already married Lady Joan, 'tis sure I am he would ha'e married ye. In fact, he no doubt regretted marrying the English wench once he met ye."

Murine smiled crookedly at the claim and pointed out, "Yer sister was one o' the women there."

"Oh. Aye." Alick frowned, probably worrying Saidh might catch wind of his comments, Dougall thought with amusement. Still, his younger brother straightened in the saddle and risked Saidh's wrath by saying, "But I'd pick ye o'er Saidh any day."

"O' course ye would, she's yer sister," Murine pointed out dryly. "However, ye did no' see the other women there with us. There were much prettier lasses than me there." Before any of the men could protest, she added, "Mind ye, not all o' them were as pretty in personality as they were in looks."

"Like the one who tried to kill Saidh and Lady Joan?" Geordie suggested dryly. "From what Saidh said, she was a terrible bitch."

"I do no' care for that term. However in this case I'd ha'e to agree. She was a terrible bitch," Murine said primly and Dougall's brothers chuckled.

"I can understand ye and Saidh becoming friends, but it does seem a stretch that ye both befriended Sinclair's bride too," Conran commented when the laughter died away.

"Ye forgot Edith. She is a good friend now too," Murine pointed out and then continued, "As for Jo . . ." She hesitated and then shrugged helplessly. "We could no' help it. Jo is lovely and smart and charming and so very generous. Why, do ye ken, her uncle gave her scads of cloth as a wedding gift and she let all of us choose material for our own gowns from it. And that despite kenning we had all come there in the hopes of winning her husband." Murine shook her head, apparently marveling over that herself, and then stilled and raised a hand to the wound at her temple as if the action had caused it to throb.

"Is yer head troubling ye again, lass?" Conran asked before Dougall could.

"Nay, I'm fine," Murine said with a forced smile, allowing her hand to drop away from her head.

The woman couldn't lie worth beans, Dougall decided. It seemed obvious that the tincture Alick had given her was wearing off. In fact, he suspected it had probably done so hours ago. That might explain her odd silence during the first part of the ride, he thought.

Frowning with concern now, Dougall glanced along the trail ahead, briefly taking note of where they were and what was along the path between here and Buchanan. They'd left so late that he'd planned for them to eat their sup in the saddle as they rode, but he wouldn't have Murine in pain. If they stopped to eat the evening meal, Alick could mix up some more of that tincture Rory had given him and then they could continue on their way after Murine had downed it and gained some relief.

"There's a pretty meadow o' wildflowers ahead," Conran announced and when Dougall glanced to him in question, he added, "If ye're looking fer a place to stop to eat, I mean. There's a nice brook beside the meadow fer the horses to drink from too."

Dougall nodded, but then narrowed his eyes when he noted the knowing grin that claimed his brother's face. Before Dougall could ponder it too deeply, Murine turned sharply so that she could glance between him and Conran.

"Stop?" she asked with alarm. "Nay! Ye said 'twould be quite late ere we reached Buchanan as it is. Stopping would just delay us further."

"Aye, but yer head is paining ye," he said gruffly. "Ye need another o' Alick's tinctures."

Murine looked briefly torn, but then shook her head, wincing even as she did. The small move obviously pained her, but her expression remained firm as she said, "Nay. I'll be fine. I can have more tincture when we reach Buchanan. I'll survive until then."

Before Dougall could respond, Alick urged his mount closer and said, "There's no need to wait. I feared ye'd need more so when Dougall told us we were heading out after all I made a full batch o' me tincture just in case. Here ye are."

"Thank ye, Alick," Murine murmured, smiling her relief. It was the first smile she'd worn since the waterfall, and it was aimed firmly at his younger brother, Dougall noted with displeasure as he watched Murine reach for the skin of tincture. She nearly tipped herself out of Conran's lap with the action, but Conran caught her by the waist to save her from the tumble. While Dougall appreciated it, he couldn't help the way his whole body tensed in reaction. Nor could he help feeling that he wanted to punch his brother, hard. He did not like to see another man's hands on the woman. Even his brother's.

And wasn't that a damned telling reaction? Dougall grimaced as that thought slid through his mind. He didn't need any proof that he cared for the woman and was jealous of any attention his brothers gave her. He'd already decided to marry the wench. There was not much more proof that could be as convincing as that, surely?

Shaking his head at himself, Dougall watched Murine settle back in Conran's arms with the skin of tincture Alick had given her. She was quick about opening and lifting it to her lips, and then she eagerly gulped it down. That more than anything told him just how much her head was paining her. It also made him glance to Alick and ask with concern, "Should she take so much o' it in one sitting?"

"Oh, 'tis fine," Alick assured him cheerfully. "There is nothing in there that can harm her. Well, except for the whiskey mayhap. She wouldn't want to down it all in one sitting, but if she sips it throughout the ride she should be fine." When Dougall raised one dubious eyebrow, he shrugged and added, "Well, plum fou, but fine otherwise."

Shaking his head, Dougall glanced back to Murine, relieved when she lowered the skin with a little sigh of disappointment. He suspected she'd hoped the tincture would take immediate effect. Conran must have thought the same thing, because he reminded her gently, "It took near on to half an hour to begin to ease the pain when Alick gave it to ye earlier."

"Aye," Murine agreed on a sigh. Lips twisting wryly, she then admitted, "But I was hoping if I took twice as much, it might work twice as fast."

That surprised a small laugh from Conran, but he shook his head at that reasoning. "I do no' think it works that way."

"Nay," she agreed, sounding sad.

Smiling sympathetically, he suggested, "Why do ye no' settle yerself against me and rest fer a bit?"

Murine peered at him uncertainly for a moment, appearing tempted by the offer, but then she merely shook her head and tipped the skin to her lips again.

Dougall's mouth tightened at the exchange, but he remained silent and simply watched Murine as she continued to gulp down the liquid. She was a determined little thing. He knew from experience that Rory's tinctures were the vilest tasting creations possible, and judging by her expression this was no exception. But she kept at it, apparently determined to take in as much of the tincture as she could stomach.

Recalling how soused she'd been earlier and how it had loosened her inhibitions by the waterfall then, Dougall found himself grateful that she wasn't riding with him. At least that's what he told himself, but he couldn't help noticing that the more she drank, the more she seemed to slump against Conran. And the more she did that, the harder Dougall's teeth ground together. It wasn't that Dougall didn't trust Conran with Murine, but he still didn't like Murine being that close to him.

His thoughts broke off when Murine gasped as she nearly dropped the skin. Conran caught it for her, but when she slurred a "thank ye" and reached to take it, Dougall leaned over and plucked it from his brother's hand.

"Hey," Murine protested.

"Ye've had enough," Dougall said grimly as he recapped the skin. He then tossed it back to Alick before returning his gaze to her, his eyebrows rising when he saw that rather than glare at him with annoyance for his high-handed actions, she'd slumped against Conran and was already drifting off to sleep.

Dougall eyed her with a frown, then glanced to Alick. "What the devil is in that tincture?"

"Some burdock, coriander and coltsfoot to stave off fever, chamomile for headache, valerian, yarrow and some simpler's joy for pain." He shrugged. "Rory mentioned a couple other things I can't recall."

"And the whiskey?" Dougall suggested.

"Oh, nay, I just poured the mix in the whiskey to cover the taste. 'Tis a vile mixture," Alick said with a grimace. Brightening, he added, "But it appears to have helped with the pain too."

Dougall rolled his eyes and then glanced back to Murine. She appeared to have fallen asleep in Conran's arms. The whiskey was probably behind that, he thought, and aye, she appeared to be feeling no pain now, but he suspected the whiskey would cause her some pain later.

Sighing, he reached out to pluck her from Conran's lap to his own, then took a moment to settle her so that her side was against his chest and he could better see her face. That way he would know when she woke.

Dougall was aware that Conran was watching him silently, but didn't return his gaze or explain his actions. He was the one who had requested Conran take her up on his own horse in the first place. He could now decide she was better off with him if he liked. Besides, he'd already told Conran of his decision to marry Murine. She was his now, so ignoring his brother's questioning look, he simply urged his horse to a faster pace, determined to cover as much ground as possible before the sun set and darkness made the ride more treacherous and forced them to slow.

MURINE JOLTED AWAKE, SUCKING IN A SHARP BREATH AS SHE was punched violently in the back. She whirled then to peer over her shoulder to see who had hit her, and then stared with confusion at Conran Buchanan. Last she knew, she'd been riding with the man, but now she was sitting sideways in—

She turned back to look at the man who presently had one arm around her upper back and found herself blinking up at Dougall. How had she ended up riding with him again? Murine wondered over that, then glanced around again at a bark of sound from Conran. The man had been looking forward when she'd first glanced around, but her moving must have drawn his gaze. He was now staring at her back and with something akin to horror. Murine lowered her gaze and caught a glimpse of the fletching of an arrow that appeared to be protruding from her lower back and then Conran barked out a warning.

The sound caught Dougall's ear and he automatically started to slow to glance around. The moment he did, Conran bellowed, "Faster, Dougall, faster! We're under attack!"

He followed that up by leaning over to slap Dougall's stallion firmly on the rump and the beast immediately burst into a charge that made Dougall curse and take a firmer grip on the reins. His arms automatically tightened around her as he did and the action must have nudged the arrow in her back, because the odd numbness that had followed the punching sensation suddenly gave way to searing pain.

Crying out, Murine grabbed at Dougall's linen shirt and tartan, using her hold on it to pull herself around and try to shift to a position that might ease the pain. There was no such position, however. Or, if there was, she couldn't find it, and gave up the task to merely bury her face in the cloth on his chest, trying to stifle the scream that was attempting to rip its way out of her throat. She'd stayed like that for several minutes before she became aware that the drum of the horses' hooves around her had become a staccato tap.

Raising her head, Murine saw that it was dawn and they were crossing a drawbridge. Twisting her head to peer ahead of them, she glimpsed the curtain walls of a castle just as they rode through them and into a bailey.

Buchanan, she thought with relief. She must have slept through the better part of the ride. Murine turned her face back to Dougall's chest and buried it there again. While she was relieved to have arrived, that didn't ease the pain burning in her back. It did mean that it could be tended to soon though.

Murine grimaced at the thought, knowing she would suffer a lot more pain as they tried to remove the arrow before she gained any relief . . . and yet she was still awake. Where was her habit of fainting when it would be useful? she wondered and then raised her head to glance around again at the sound of male voices hailing them.

Dougall had ridden straight to the stairs to the keep rather than the stables, she saw as he reined in. A whole mess of men had spilled out of the building and were rushing down the stairs toward them, and every last one of them looked concerned, she noted. Several of them also looked very alike, all tall and broad with long dark hair and similar facial features like the men she had traveled with. She knew Saidh had seven brothers, so three of the men rushing toward them were probably the brothers Aulay, Rory and Niels she had yet to meet. The others must be cousins or otherwise related, she thought.

One of the men, one with his hair not quite covering a scar that halved his handsome face like a dividing line, moved in front of the others to peer over her with concern, his mouth tightening as his gaze moved to her back and the arrow protruding from it. The man who could only be Saidh's eldest brother, Aulay, then glanced over his shoulder and ordered, "Ye'd best fetch yer weeds, Rory."

Rory was just a touch smaller than his eldest brother. He was also unscarred and while he too had long hair, he wore it tied back in a loose ponytail behind his head. Nodding, the younger man turned to rush up the stairs and back into the keep.

Aulay then turned back to Dougall, and raised his arms. "Pass her down."

Dougall released the reins and started to shift Murine in his arms until she faced him and dangled off the side of the horse, but then he caught her alarmed expression and paused. There was just no way he could pass her to the other man without the risk of bumping the arrow. At this angle, Aulay would have difficulty taking her without doing so, and did Dougall turn her to face his brother to make sure the arrow wasn't in Aulay's way when he took her, the arrow would most like be bumped by Dougall himself.

Cursing, he eased her back into his lap, shifted one hand under her legs and the other to rest high on her back where it was least likely to jostle her injury, then quickly shifted his leg over his mount and slid off to land lightly on his feet still holding her. Despite how light the landing was, Murine had to bite her lip to keep from crying out as the small jolt sent pain shooting through her back.

"I'm sorry, lass," Dougall said gruffly, pressing her closer as if to shield her from the pain as he started to move.

Murine didn't glance around to see, but was quite sure he was carrying her up the stairs to the keep entrance. A moment later she felt a slight breeze as someone rushed past them and she heard a squeak that she guessed would be the door opening. When she opened her eyes a moment later, Dougall was carrying her into the castle and she blinked to try to adjust to the darker interior.

"Who is she?" Aulay asked once the door closed behind them, leaving most of their welcoming party still outside.

"Lady Murine Carmichael, soon to be Lady Murine Buchanan, me wife," Dougall said grimly.

Murine stiffened and then leaned back slightly to turn wide shocked eyes up to his face. "Yer wife?" she asked in a confused whisper.

"Aye," he growled and pressed her head back to his shoulder, muttering, "Rest."

"But ye're no' in the market fer a wife," Murine murmured with confusion.

Dougall's eyebrows rose at that comment, but before he could respond, someone asked, "Not the Murine who is Saidh's friend?"

"Aye, Niels," Dougall said grimly. "The verra lass."

"What happened?" Aulay asked next.

"She apparently has been shot with an arrow," Dougall said dryly.

For some reason that struck Murine as funny and she released a little gasping laugh that truly sounded more like a grunt or snort.

It made Dougall slow and glance worriedly down at her. "Are ye all right, lass?"

"Ye mean other than being shot with an arrow?" she whispered with a crooked smile.

Dougall's lips twitched with appreciation at the echo of her words, but he merely continued walking, carrying her the last few steps to the stairs and starting up them with her.

"She has no' fainted."

Murine lifted her head with surprise at that comment from

Alick. She'd thought him still outside. But then she hadn't looked around much. Now she did and saw that Geordie and Conran were there too, along with Aulay and another man who could only be Niels.

"Aye, ye're right, she hasna," Conran agreed grimly, following them up the stairs. He shook his head. "More's the pity."

"What?" Murine scowled at him over Dougall's shoulder. "All the four o' ye ha'e done is harp on about me fainting, and now that ye've fed me up and filled me full o' yer tinctures I'm no' doing it and ye think 'tis a *pity*?"

"Now, lass," Conran said soothingly. "I just meant 'twould be easier fer ye were ye in one o' yer faints jest now."

"Aye," Dougall muttered and then paused as he reached the top of the stairs and frowned down at her as he suggested, "Mayhap ye should try and faint."

When Murine merely gaped at him, Aulay murmured, "Saidh's room, I think, Dougall. Rory is no doubt waiting for her there."

Dougall scowled at his brother and turned left off the stairs. "My room. I told ye I'm marrying her."

"Aye, but ye're no' married yet," Aulay argued. "And as she is not only Saidh's friend, but the woman who saved our dear sister's life, she deserves me protection. So, to preserve her honor, she stays in Saidh's room until the wedding."

Dougall scowled, but he also stopped walking. After a brief pause he turned back and headed in the opposite direction. As he carried her past the stairs they'd just come up, he muttered irritably, "I did no' say I would be in me room with her ere the wedding."

"Nay, I ken," Aulay said with a shrug. "But—"

"And I, too, am concerned with her honor," he groused. "Jest ask Conny. He kens."

"Aye," Conran backed him up at once. "Why, he even made me take her on me horse with me when we started this last stretch o' the journey home because he feared he could no' control himself did she ride with him."

Murine's eyes had drifted shut, but popped open again at this news. *That* was why Dougall had made her ride with Conran when they'd set out this last time? Not because he'd been disgusted by her behavior, but because he hadn't trusted himself with her? The idea was a new and wonderful one, doing much to ease her shame.

"But why has she no' fainted? She's always fainting, yet she's taken an arrow and still wide awake," Alick complained, apparently fixated on the subject.

"As she said, we've been plying her with food and tinctures," Conran pointed out. "Mayhap the combination is working to build her humors and prevent the fainting."

"We should ha'e held off on the food and tinctures then," Geordie decided gloomily as Dougall turned into a room at the end of the hall. "She's going to suffer for it."

Murine grimaced, quite sure he was right. This really would be one of the very rare times where fainting would have stood her in good stead. She would have preferred to be unconscious for what was to come.

"Set her on the bed."

Murine glanced around at that brisk order and peered at Rory Buchanan. As Aulay had suggested, the man had obviously expected her to be brought here from the start. She supposed Saidh's room was probably the only one not occupied at the moment. With seven brothers and Saidh, it was doubtful if there were any spare bedchambers for guests at Buchanan, she thought and then blinked in surprise and felt a blush rise up on her cheeks when instead of setting her on the bed, Dougall sat on the edge of it with her still in his arms, then adjusted his hold so that she sat sideways on his lap.

There was a moment of silence, and then Rory cleared his throat and said, "Dougall, I said set her on the bed, no'—"

"I thought it might be helpful if I held Murine for ye. To help keep her still while ye work," Dougall interrupted.

"Murine?" Rory asked with surprise and then moved closer to peer at her face more closely. "Murine Carmichael? Saidh's friend?"

"Aye," she murmured, recalling that he'd run ahead to "get his weeds" before Dougall had announced her name.

"'Tis a true pleasure to meet ye," Rory said solemnly. "Saidh told us o' all about ye and the other lasses she befriended at Sinclair." He grinned. "Ye're the sweet, smart, brave friend who faints?"

"Brave?" Murine asked with surprise; she'd never thought of herself that way and couldn't imagine why Saidh would.

"She told us how ye saved her and Jo," Aulay said, eyeing her with gentle appreciation. "Thank ye fer that."

"Aye." Niels moved closer, gaining her attention. "From what she said, were it no' fer you, they'd both be dead and our Saidh would ha'e been labeled a murderess as well. Thank ye fer saving both her life and her reputation."

"Oh, well . . ." Murine blushed and tried to wave away their thanks, hard to do with Dougall's arms wrapped around her. Still, she said, "She would ha'e done the same fer me had our places been reversed."

"Aye, she would have," Aulay agreed solemnly. "But yer places were no' reversed. So thank ye. Ye're our most welcome guest."

Murine smiled crookedly at the sincere words, and then gave a start when Dougall snapped, "Leave off and get out o' here, the lot o' ye. She needs tending and Rory can no' do that with ye crowding her like a bunch o' crows o'er a carcass."

Murine winced at the description, but Dougall's brothers merely grinned at his outburst. It was Aulay who raised his eyebrows and commented with a grin, "Feeling a little possessive, are we, brother?"

Murine could have sworn she actually heard Dougall growl

deep in his throat, but before she could be sure, Rory suddenly barked, "Out! I want every last one o' ye out o' here now. You too, Dougall. Ye can go growl and brawl below. I need to tend to this young woman ere she bleeds to death. So out!"

The younger brothers all immediately headed for the door. Only Aulay and Dougall remained unmoving at first, but then Aulay nodded solemnly, and eyed Dougall with determination as he announced, "Very well. We will all go below, won't we, Dougall?"

Dougall opened his mouth in what Murine suspected would have been a refusal, but Rory beat him to speech, saying firmly, "Good. Because I'm no' tending to her until e'ery last one o' ye leaves this room."

Dougall closed his mouth with a snap, then stood, set Murine gently on the edge of the bed, and then took her chin in hand and offered what she suspected was supposed to be a smile, but came out as more of a grimace as he said, "I'll be below, lass. Send fer me do ye need me."

Eyes wide, Murine nodded, and then blinked in surprise when he pressed a kiss to her forehead before straightening and turning to leave. She watched him cross the room, bewilderment the only thing she was experiencing just then. The man had said he wasn't in the market for a wife, something she'd reminded herself of several times since finding herself traveling with them. That knowledge firmly in mind, she'd spent the last afternoon and night feeling ashamed of her own behavior by the waterfall and thinking this man was disgusted by her. Now, he announced he was marrying her and that he'd made her ride with Conran because he didn't trust himself around her? Incredible.

"I still do no' understand why she's no' fainted yet," Alick muttered from the hallway as Aulay led Dougall from the room.

"Neither do I," Murine breathed on a sigh.

The sound of the door closing drew her attention and she

watched warily as Rory moved toward her, his expression solemn and apologetic. He hadn't done anything to need to apologize for yet, but she knew enough about removing arrows and cleaning wounds to know that he soon would. This was one hell of a time for her tendency to faint to abandon her, she decided.

"HER BROTHER REALLY OFFERED HER TO YE IN TRADE FOR THE horses?" Niels asked with a combination of disbelief and disgust.

Dougall nodded as he took a drink from the ale a servant had set before him. He'd been explaining how they'd encountered Murine since reaching the great hall.

The moment they'd settled at the trestle table, Aulay had started in with his questions. Dougall was answering, but his mind was on the room above stairs where Murine was no doubt suffering the agonies of hell as Rory worked to remove the arrow from her back. He knew from experience that his brother would either have to force the arrow out through the front of her chest or pull it out the way it had gone in. Either option was painful, but pushing through would have been a quick, hard pain, while pulling it out would take much longer and be an agony to suffer. Murine should be screaming her head off, but there wasn't a sound coming from above stairs.

Perhaps she'd fainted, he thought hopefully.

"Aye, Danvries suggested he keep her until he felt the horses were paid for and then return her," Conran said when Dougall was slow to answer Niels's question. "When Dougall refused, he asked us just to wait then, said he had a friend who would be willing to pay to spend time with his sister and he could then pay for the horses."

"Bastard," Aulay muttered.

"Aye," Niels agreed. "Bloody *English* bastard." He emphasized the word *English* as if that were even more of an insult, and to them it was. They had no love for the English.

After a pause as everyone took a drink, Aulay frowned and asked, "So ye accepted his offer to save her from being passed on to the neighbor?"

Dougall slammed his drink down, the metal cup clanging on the tabletop as he turned on his brother. The thought that Aulay could believe he would behave so dishonorably, or that Murine would go along with such a thing infuriated him. "Of course I did no'."

Aulay held up a soothing hand and said reasonably, "Yet ye've brought her home."

Dougall relaxed at that, realizing how it could be miscon-strued. Breathing out slowly, he nodded and quickly explained about their encountering her as they'd left Danvries land.

"So ye brought her with ye to keep her safe?" Aulay asked, and when Dougall nodded grimly, asked, "And plan to marry her to prevent her brother being able to use her so shame-fully?"

"O' course," he muttered, but glanced toward the floor above as he spoke the lie. He wasn't just marrying Murine to save her from her brother. Dougall was not that self-sacrificing. In the normal course of events, he would have done all he could for the lass to help keep her safe. She had saved his sister's life after all, but marriage was an extreme step.

"Poor lass," Aulay muttered, and then added, "She's lucky ye're willing to marry her."

Dougall merely grunted and continued to stare at the floor above. How long had it been since they'd left the room?

"He's the lucky one," Geordie contradicted. "I would ha'e married her meself had Conran no' made it clear Dougall was interested in her."

"And me," Alick assured him.

Dougall scowled at both men for their comments, not liking the idea of either brother marrying Murine. But then he noted that Aulay was watching him closely, and forced his gaze back to the floor above.

"So she was riding with ye," Aulay commented. "But how did she end up with an arrow in her back?"

That made Dougall frown again. He hadn't really had the time to give that consideration. Glancing to Conran, who had been riding to the side and behind him when they'd left the woods and started into the clearing around the castle, he raised his eyebrows. "What happened? Did ye see who shot her?"

"Nay," Conran said, his voice tight with his own anger. "We were riding along fine, broke from the woods and then Murine gave a start in yer lap and glanced around and I saw she had an arrow sticking out o' her back." He shook his head with displeasure at the memory and then added, "I did look back to see where the arrow came from, but did no' see anyone."

"I did no' see anyone either," Alick said when Dougall glanced to him. "They must ha'e been in the cover o' the woods."

"Aye," Geordie agreed. "'Tis lucky we were so close to the gates when it happened."

"So who would want to kill ye?" Aulay asked.

Dougall glanced to him with surprise. "Me?"

"Aye," he said quietly, and then pointed out. "She was riding with ye, it could ha'e been meant fer you and hit her by accident. I hardly think Murine could have made enemies who would wish her dead. 'Sides, from what ye've said, no one kens where she is."

"Her brother could ha'e caught up to us," Alick pointed out. "Mayhap he is the one who shot her with the arrow."

Dougall shook his head at the suggestion. "There is no profit for Danvries in shooting her. He can hardly trade time with her for coin if she's a corpse."

"Oh, aye," Alick agreed with a frown.

"Then Aulay's right," Conran said, looking troubled. "The arrow could ha'e been meant fer ye."

"So?" Aulay raised his eyebrows. "Who wants ye dead?"

Dougall started to shake his head, unaware of anyone who might dislike him that much, but paused, his head shooting up as if someone had socked him in the chin when a sudden shriek reached them from above stairs.

"YE CAN BREATHE AGAIN, LASS. 'TIS DONE."

Murine let her breath out on a small sob and buried her face in the furs she'd bunched under her face as Rory had worked on removing the arrow. It had been as bad as she'd expected and it had taken a great effort of will not to scream and thrash as he'd worked. Only the thought that doing so would make it take longer and prolong her suffering had kept her still, but her entire body had trembled with the effort as she'd struggled against the pain.

Thank God it was over, she thought and then stiffened, a startled shriek of agony slipping from her lips as he poured something cold on the wound that then seemed to burst into flame. At least it felt as if it were burning the skin off her back. It took a moment for her to realize he must have poured something on to clean the wound. That always hurt like the devil.

"Sorry," Rory murmured, sounding sincere in his apology. "I should ha'e given ye warning."

Murine just shook her head and panted for breath as the pain began to recede.

"I'm going to put a salve on now. It should numb the—" His words broke off as the door suddenly burst open to allow Dougall to stumble in with Aulay, Conran, Niels and Geordie all hanging off him, trying to hold him back. Alick brought up the rear, following them into the room as Dougall crossed half the distance to the bed before his brother's efforts managed to bring him to a halt.

"What's happened?" he growled, his eyes locked on Murine and staying there. "Are ye all right?"

"Aye. I was just startled," she breathed and offered a weak smile. Murine was very aware that she was lying there with her back completely bare. Rory had cut away the material of her gown to work on removing the arrow. That made two gowns ruined, and the only two she'd brought with her, she thought wearily.

When Rory ignored Dougall and the others and began to apply a soothing salve to her wound, she closed her eyes and pillowed her head on her arms. The salve stung at first despite his light touch, but that sting quickly fled, leaving nothing. He'd started to say something about the salve and numbing before Dougall had burst in. It worked very well.

Once the worst of the pain faded, Murine opened her eyes and lifted her head to see that Dougall and his brothers all stood, staring with a sort of horrified fascination as Rory treated her wound. It made suspicion rise within her. The original wound had probably been smallish, the size of the arrowhead that had pierced her, but Rory had had to dig it out. She'd seen the arrow spoon he'd used, but she'd also caught a glimpse of a knife and suspected he'd had to enlarge the wound to fit the spoon in. She hadn't really been able to tell. The pain had pretty much been horrible from start to finish.

"How bad is it?" she asked now with concern.

Still working, Rory was behind her where she couldn't see him, but Dougall and his other five brothers all immediately shifted their gazes to her face. For a moment, no one spoke, and then Dougall cleared his throat, shook off the hold Aulay, Conran, Niels and Geordie still had on him like a dog shaking off fleas, then crossed the room toward her, saying, "'Tis no' so bad, lass."

He was a horrible liar, Murine thought wryly as he stopped next to the bed and his gaze skated to her back again. He actually winced before turning a weak smile her way and adding, "No' bad at all."

"All right, ye've seen she's alive and well and I'm no' torturing her," Rory said quietly. "Now get out and leave us be so I can bind her wound."

Dougall scowled at Rory, but then turned back to offer Murine a smile and said, "I'll wait in the hall until he's done."

"Ye can wait there as long as ye like, but ye're no' coming back in here tonight," Rory said firmly. "She lost a lot of blood and needs to rest now. I won't have ye disturbing her."

"I—" Dougall began, but that was as far as he got before his brothers set upon him again and began to drag him from the room. Murine didn't know if his brothers had been as eager to see that she was all right as he had been and had been fighting themselves as well as him when they'd tried to stop him earlier, or if now that his worry was eased he had less fight in him, but whatever the case, they managed to drag him from the room quickly enough.

"He'll be back the minute I step out of the room," Rory said dryly once the door had closed behind the men.

Murine smiled faintly at the prediction. "Ye don't sound terrible upset about it."

"I'm not," Rory acknowledged, and then explained, "I plan to dose ye with a sleeping powder and wait till it takes effect ere I leave. Whether he returns or no', he'll no' disturb ye."

Murine didn't even consider asking him not to give her the mentioned sleeping powder. She was exhausted and didn't think she'd need it to drift off to sleep, but did suspect she'd need it to stay in that state.

Chapter 9

$\mathcal{D}$OUGALL TORE HIS GAZE FROM MURINE'S SLEEPING FACE and glanced to the door when it opened, but when he saw it was just Aulay he shifted his gaze back to Murine. She had been sleeping when Rory had finally let him in and, much to his frustration, hadn't stirred at all in the two hours since then. While Dougall knew sleep was the best thing for her just then, he really wished she'd wake up, if only for a couple minutes so that they could talk. He was very aware that while he'd announced on his arrival that he was going to marry her, he hadn't yet actually discussed the matter with her to see if she would be willing to marry him.

Part of Dougall assured him she would be grateful to be safe from her brother in the bonds of marriage. But another part was reminding him that she might have been thinking she should marry Aulay, the eldest brother, the one with the castle and title. Her response to him by the waterfall might have been nothing more than the whiskey-laden tincture she'd downed. He needed to talk to her and find out what she wanted. Or, perhaps it was better to say, who she wanted.

"Dougall?" Aulay said quietly, taking the seat across the bed from him that Rory had vacated only moments ago.

"Hmm?" he grunted, not bothering to tear his gaze from Murine.

"The lads and I were talking, and we're a bit concerned—"

"I told ye, there's no one I can think o' who would wish me dead and might have shot the arrow," Dougall growled with irritation. Aulay and the others had questioned him ad nauseam on the subject as they'd waited in the hall for Rory to finish binding Murine's wound.

"Aye, I ken. That's not what we're worrying about right now though. What I was going to say is, we're a bit concerned about Danvries," Aulay explained quietly.

That caught Dougall's attention and he tore his gaze away from Murine to frown at Aulay. "What do ye mean?"

"Well, he's probably searching for Murine," Aulay pointed out solemnly.

"Aye," Dougall acknowledged.

"How long do ye think it'll be before he looks here? She and Saidh are friends after all," he pointed out.

"Saidh does no' live here anymore," Dougall pointed out.

"Aye, but he may not ken that," Aulay said solemnly. "Besides, you boys were at Danvries when she went missing. That in itself—"

"We had nothing to do with her leaving. I told ye she fled on her own and we merely came upon her on the road," Dougall argued at once.

"But he may not ken that either," Aulay pointed out. "If he arrives ere ye marry her, he'll likely refuse to allow the marriage and take her back."

"We can no' let him get her back," Dougall said grimly, his gaze moving over Murine. She looked so pale and weak in the bed. Mouth tightening, he stood up. There was no profit in it for Danvries if Murine married him. The only chance they had was if they were married before he caught up to them. "I'll have Alick fetch the priest. We'll be married at once."

He started around the bed, but Aulay stepped in front of him, forcing him to a halt. "She's not conscious and apparently Rory gave her a sleeping powder. She could remain asleep all day and through the night as well."

"Then I'll say her I dos for her," Dougall growled, trying to step around him.

"Father MacKenna won't marry ye to an unconscious woman, Dougall," Aulay said grimly, shifting to continue blocking his way.

"If we explain the circumstances—"

"He'll say it must be God's will," Aulay interrupted firmly.

Dougall frowned, knowing what he said was true. Father MacKenna was very devout. He wouldn't marry them unless Murine was awake and alert enough that he was satisfied she knew what was about. Unfortunately, that wasn't likely to be any time soon. And Danvries was probably on his way here even now. In fact, he could be at the gate any minute.

"It's all right," Aulay said now, drawing Dougall's attention from his thoughts. "The boys and I came up with an idea."

"Tell me," Dougall growled.

DOUGALL WAS STIRRING THE TINCTURE RORY HAD GIVEN HIM into some cider when the cottage door opened and Conran leaned in to say, "The boys are saddled up. We're heading out now."

He nodded absently, and then glanced at his brother, "Ask Rory for more of this tincture to build her strength. I'm mixing up the last of it right now."

Conran raised his eyebrows. "Already? He gave ye an awful lot of it. Surely 'tis no' all gone already?"

"Well, it is," Dougall said grimly.

Conran frowned and then stepped inside, pushed the door closed and moved to join him by the table. Peering down at the chunky liquid Dougall was stirring, he pursed his lips and then asked, "Is it supposed to be so . . . thick?"

Dougall scowled at the concoction, but admitted, "I've been doubling the amount of tincture in the cider and then doubling it again since yester eve."

"Ah," Conran murmured and then asked, "Is that wise?"

"It should no' hurt her. It's suppose to build her strength and help her heal," Dougall said with a frown, then growled with frustration, and blurted, "She's been asleep for four days, Conny. I've had to shake her to wake her enough to even drink the tinctures. I needs must build up her strength somehow. She was overly thin to begin with, now she's wasting away before me eyes."

"Aye." Conran clapped a hand on his shoulder and squeezed briefly. "I'll bring back more and see if Rory will come check on her himself."

"Thank ye," Dougall muttered.

Nodding, Conran turned and moved away to head outside again. Dougall stood still, listening until he heard the sounds of the others riding away from the cottage, then grimaced and set the tincture-filled cider on the table and walked over to sit in the chair next to the bed where Murine rested.

She'd been sleeping for the four days since he and his brothers had brought her here to the family hunting cottage. At first she'd slept because of the sleeping powder Rory had insisted they give her. But Dougall had stopped giving that to her after the second day and yet still she slept like the dead. The last time he'd managed to wake her, he'd asked her how the pain was. She'd mumbled that it was much better, downed the tincture he'd given her and fallen right back to sleep. And when he'd changed the bandage last night, he'd been able to see that it was healing well. Yet still she was hard to wake and couldn't seem to stay awake for more than the time it took to drink the tinctures he gave her.

Dougall was really beginning to worry . . . and not just about her health, although that was constantly preying on his mind. Aside from that, though, he was also concerned that the longer she remained asleep, the higher the chance was that her brother would find them and end any possibility of their marrying . . .

which led to another worry plaguing him. Dougall still didn't know if Murine was willing to marry him. Did she want to? What if she didn't?

Sighing, he sat back in his seat and then frowned as he noted the slight chill in the air. It had been threatening a storm when he'd stepped outside earlier that morning to head for a swim in the nearby loch. Now, two hours later, rather than warm up, the day must have cooled further. Nestled in the woods as it was, the cottage was sheltered from sunlight and the room was cold enough that a fire wouldn't go amiss.

Standing, he moved to the fire pit, only to frown when he noted that there were only a couple of logs stacked next to it. They needed more firewood, for cooking as well as to warm the cottage. He glanced to Murine, but she was sleeping peacefully, showing no sign of stirring. It would take only a minute to run out and grab a couple of logs, he thought as he headed out the door.

MURINE STIRRED SLEEPILY AND SHIFTED ONTO HER SIDE, GRImacing when the bed coverings slipped down off her shoulder, and cool air crept over her in its place. It was chilly this morning, she thought.

Waking up enough to tug the linens and furs back up, she huddled under them briefly and then opened her eyes. Murine blinked in confusion as she took in the alien surroundings. Rather than her bedchamber at Danvries, or even at Carmichael, she found herself peering around a large room with tables and benches, several barrels and chests for storage and a fire pit to cook over. There were also a handful of wooden chairs by a fireplace at the opposite end of the room from the bed she was in and a set of stairs leading up to a second level.

Not recognizing anything, Murine frowned and started to sit up, only to pause with a wince when the action pulled on the skin of her back, sending a sharp pain through her that immediately reminded her what had happened if not where she was. The pain was nothing like the agony she'd experienced when first injured, or even as bad as that she'd suffered for the day or two afterward, but the wound was definitely making its presence known.

Letting out the breath she'd sucked in when the pain first struck, Murine moved more cautiously, easing her way upward with care until she managed to sit up on the side of the bed with her bare feet on the cold wood of the floor. Relaxing a little then, she glanced around again. She was in a hunting lodge. At least that was her guess. It was similar to her father's own hunting lodge. Well, her cousin's now, she acknowledged sadly. At any rate, the walls were decorated with the mounted heads of beasts no doubt caught by the hunters who used this lodge; hart, boar and wolves all stared down at her from every angle.

Now that she realized she was in a hunting lodge, Murine had a vague recollection of a dreadful ride on horseback. She'd woken in agony to find herself once again in Dougall's arms on his mount, and he'd said something about taking her to the Buchanan hunting lodge to keep her safe from her brother until she healed as he'd urged her to drink from a skin of liquid. She didn't remember much more than that, other than a rather jumbled collection of memories of waking in this room ere this and Dougall feeding her one vile concoction after another and speaking to her in low soothing tones. It was all quite fuzzy, but the recollection made Murine realize that she was hungry and thirsty, and she glanced around for Dougall, expecting him to appear with a cider that tasted slightly off.

When he didn't magically appear as he had each time she'd woken since Rory had removed the arrow, Murine bit her lip and listened for any telltale sound that might reveal to her whether he was even in the lodge somewhere. Glancing at the steps, she wondered if perhaps he wasn't above stairs, but there wasn't a sound. Surely he was here? He didn't just ride out with her, put her to bed and ride away leaving her to fend for herself?

The question made Murine grimace to herself. Why shouldn't he do just that? Dougall wasn't responsible for her. They weren't kin. And she was the one who had run away from her home and her brother. True, it had been to protect her virtue, but that was not his trouble to worry about.

"Right," Murine whispered and forced herself slowly to her feet. Much to her dismay, her legs began to shake the moment she put weight on them. Dear God, she was as weak as a babe. The realization was a bit alarming and made her wonder how long she'd slept.

The bed was a four-poster with a cloth top and curtains around the sides that were presently open. Worried about falling, Murine grasped the post next to her at the head of the bed and waited for her legs to remember their use, but a chill running up her calves drew her attention to what she was wearing. Her feet were bare, the rest of her covered to her wrists and nearly to her ankles by a thin sleep shirt that wasn't preventing the draft in the room from running over her feet and up her legs under the light cloth.

Spotting what she thought might be one of her leather slippers peeking out from under the bed, Murine eased down to her knees to grab it, relieved to find it was indeed one of her leather slippers. They must have put them on her to travel from Buchanan and then taken them off when they arrived, Murine thought. She supposed they'd then got knocked under the bed in the interim.

She set the first slipper on the bed, then bent ever so slowly forward until she was on her hands and knees so that she could look under the bed. She'd just spotted the second slipper when she heard a door open. A cold draft skittered across the floor and then there was a click as of a door closing and the draft died. Mindful of her back, Murine slowly eased up to sit on her knees and peered around, but there was no one there.

She'd just decided she'd imagined the door opening when she heard a slight rustle from above stairs. She hadn't even paused to grab the second slipper before straightening and yet had taken so long at the task that whoever had entered had gone above before she'd got upright.

Murine grimaced and briefly considered shouting out to them, but they'd realize soon enough she wasn't above stairs and return below. Besides, she still needed to retrieve her second slipper. She was in the process of doing so, ever so slowly leaning down again to reach under the bed, when a second draft blew across her.

"What the devil are ye doing out o' bed?"

Murine started at that bark from Dougall and unthinkingly jerked upright, both actions making her cry out in pain as her back responded unhappily.

"Dammit, Murine," Dougall's voice was a soft growl as he hurried around the bed to scoop her carefully up. As he set her on the linens and furs she'd just left, he added, "Ye'll rip yer stitches. Ye were sorely injured. Ye must be more careful."

"I was being careful," she said irritably as he turned her so that her back was to him. "It's just that ye startled—Nay!" she cried in shock, hurting herself anew by spinning around to grab at the back of her nightshirt as he jerked it up.

"Settle yerself," he muttered, catching her hand and forcing her forward to lie on her stomach, which certainly eased the pain but did nothing for her embarrassment as he pulled her nightshirt up to her shoulders so that he could examine her wound. Very aware that her bare behind was now on display, along with nearly everything above and below it, Murine buried her face in the linens and groaned with dismay. It had been one thing for Rory to see her bare back while tending her wound. It was another thing entirely for Dougall to—

Her mental whine ended abruptly as a thought occurred to her and she turned her head, trying to glare at him over her shoulder as she barked, "Who took off me gown and put me in this nightshirt?"

"Rory called in a couple maids to change ye when he finished binding ye," Dougall answered absently, and then muttered, "Ye're no' bleeding through the bandage, but I'll need to remove yer wrappings to be sure . . ."

When his voice trailed off, Murine glanced over her shoulder to see what was wrong and noted that his gaze had found and apparently been halted by the sight of her naked bottom. He was gaping at it with fixed fascination. When he suddenly licked his lips as if gazing upon a tasty pastie and then started to bend down as if intending to take a bite, Murine snatched up as much of the linens and furs beside her as she could and dragged them across her bottom and legs to hide them.

Dougall immediately blinked and straightened. "Sorry," he muttered, dropping the hem of her shift. Turning away, he growled, "I'll fetch fresh bindings."

Murine opened her mouth to say she didn't want him to change her bandages, but then let her mouth close on a sigh. Her bottom was covered now and she truly did not want to go through this again. It was better to let him do it now and get it over with, she decided and simply turned her no doubt red face into the furs and waited for it to be over.

She listened silently as Dougall moved around the large room, but when he seemed to take an extremely long time, she turned her head and opened her eyes to see what he was doing. She found him at the fireplace. As she watched, he finished stacking logs over a collection of moss and bark and then used a fire steel to light the kindling. When he then straightened and moved to a bag on one of the tables to fetch the bindings and salves he intended to use on her, Murine closed her eyes and waited for the heat from the fire to begin to warm her.

"How long ago did ye wake?" Dougall asked as he approached the bed with everything he would need to tend her.

"Just moments ago," Murine said quietly, and asked, "We're at yer family's hunting lodge?"

"Aye," he murmured as he set the items he'd collected on the bedside table.

"Is Henry—?"

"Safe and sound at Buchanan," he assured her and then settled on the side of the bed, announcing, "I need to cut yer old bindings away. I'm going to ease yer nightgown up to yer shoulders to get it out of the way first, though."

Murine merely nodded and then held her breath as he eased the thin cloth up her back. She was safely covered by the furs and linens from the waist down; still, it felt odd letting him see her naked back like this, she thought and grimaced when he held the material up by the back of her neck with one hand as he examined the wound. After a hesitation, she tugged the cloth over her head so it was only covering her arms and the tops of the shoulders, but the rest of the material was now gathered under her chin. It freed him from having to hold it.

"I'm going to start cutting," Dougall announced. "Don't move, else I might cut ye by accident."

Murine murmured her agreement and held still as she felt the cold metal of his blade against her skin. A heartbeat later it was done and she felt the cloth slip down to gather on the bed at her sides. After a moment of silence while he examined her back, she asked, "Are the stitches—?"

"They appear to be fine," he answered before she could finish the question. "I'm going to put some salve on. Rory gave me two, one to help ye heal and one to numb ye."

Murine nodded silently again and waited for the shock of cold salve against her skin, but it took a moment and when he did begin to smooth it on her back it was warm and his touch so gentle it barely hurt more than a twinge. She could only think that he'd heated it between his hands first, and was surprised at his thoughtfulness.

"Now the numbing one," he announced and another moment passed before his warm slippery fingers slid over her back again. He wasn't doing anything Rory hadn't done the day she was injured, yet Murine found herself responding to Dougall's light caress in a way she hadn't experienced with Rory.

"Better?" he asked after a moment.

"Aye," Murine whispered.

A moment of silence passed and then Dougall cleared his throat and said, "Ye'll need to sit up so I can bind yer wound again."

Murine stilled. Despite clearing his throat, his voice had been husky and oddly seductive when he spoke, and now the oddest tingles were running through her at the thought of sitting up. She almost slipped her nightshift back over her head, but knew that would mean holding it up and out of the way while he wrapped the bandages around her front and back, and she was quite sure that holding her arms up would pull on the skin of her back and hurt just then.

"Lass, I've done this several times already while ye slept. There's nothing to be embarrassed about," he said solemnly.

Murine sighed and let him help her sit up, appreciative when he wrapped the linens and furs around her waist from behind, preserving at least some of her dignity. She wouldn't have been able to do it herself; she was too busy making sure the material of her gown remained pressed against her breasts.

Once she was upright, Dougall simply set to work binding her wound, wrapping the cloth around her lower waist again and again, moving higher with each wrap around.

"Does it need to be so high?" Murine asked, her voice a little breathless as he passed the cloth around her front just under her breasts. She had eased the cloth of her nightgown up a bit to get it out of the way. The cloth covered only the top half of her breasts now and she bit her lip as one of Dougall's hands accidentally bumped the bottom of one round globe.

"I'm no' sure," Dougall admitted, his voice a husky whisper by her ear as he reached his hands around her again to pass the wrapping from one hand to the other. "'Tis how Rory did it. Mayhap the more skin ye hold tight, the less the chance ye'll rip a stitch."

"Mayhap," she agreed weakly, her body reacting to his

breath on her ear and the feel of the soft skin on top of his hand rubbing on the sensitive under curve of her breast again on this go-round. How much more wrapping was there? Murine wondered wildly as his hands slid behind her and then started around the front again.

"Dougall?" she said weakly and then bit her lip and closed her eyes as his hands stopped just under her breasts, his skin touching hers.

"Aye?" His own voice was a deep growl now, one she remembered from the waterfall, and that memory set fire to the tinder that his innocent actions had laid inside her. Murine shook her head weakly, then turned to press a kiss to the side of his face as she inhaled his scent.

Dougall immediately turned his own head to claim her lips as he dropped the bindings. At least Murine thought he must have released the cloth he'd been wrapping around her, because his hands were suddenly up under the gown she held in front of her and covering her breasts with no cloth between her flesh and his.

Murine first sighed into his mouth with relief when he began to kiss her, then followed that up with a moan as he began to pluck at her nipples with his thumbs and forefingers while still cupping the bottoms of her breasts with his palms. The sensation had her pushing in two different directions at once. She was twisting her head farther back so that he could deepen the kiss, while pressing her breasts forward into his caress. It put a bit of a strain on her neck and Murine was at first relieved when Dougall broke their kiss to switch to nibbling and kissing her neck and ear while he eagerly kneaded her breasts. But after a moment, she wanted his kisses again and tugged one arm free of the nightgown to reach back for his head even as she tried to turn enough to reach his lips again. The moment she started to try, Dougall released her and stood up.

For one moment, Murine feared he was going to put an end to things again as he had at the waterfall, but then he settled himself in front of her on the bed and caught her by the arms. He started to pull her forward and back into his embrace, but paused with her halfway there. Following his gaze, she saw that her gown dangled from one arm, leaving her bare to his view. His gaze stayed fixed there briefly, then rose to her face for a moment before slipping back to her breasts. He reminded her of a little boy trying to choose which pastry to pick from a tray. In the end, he was a greedy lad and went for all of it. Cupping both of her breasts, he pressed a kiss to each, then closed his hands over them as he lifted his head to claim her lips again.

Murine pressed forward into his caress and kissed him back eagerly. When his tongue invaded her mouth, she welcomed it and inched forward on her knees, desperate to get closer to him. She was vaguely aware of the linens and furs slipping and then dropping down to pool around her knees, but didn't really register what it meant, even when Dougall suddenly clasped one cheek of her bottom to urge her to rise up on her knees.

The action broke their kiss, but it also allowed him to trail his lips down to the breast he was no longer caressing and claim it. Murine gasped and clutched at his upper arms as he drew the better part of her breast into his mouth, sucking almost violently, before letting it slide out until only the nipple remained. He then set about nipping at it lightly while running his tongue over the tip.

"Oh, Dougall," Murine groaned, and then gasped with surprise when something brushed between her legs. Eyes blinking open, she glanced down, but all she could see was Dougall's mouth ministering to one breast and his hand at the other. She couldn't see his second hand, but was definitely feeling it as it brushed across her core again. Murine instinctively tried to close her legs, but his knees had somehow got between hers and now held them open, and then he caressed her again, more firmly, his fingers gliding across her wet flesh and milking a cry of mingled need and excitement from her.

Dougall released the nipple he'd been teasing and tipped his head up even as the hand that had been at her breast slid around her neck and up behind her head to pull her down for a kiss. Murine responded almost desperately to his kiss, her hips bucking under his touch, and then they both stilled as a crash sounded from above stairs. In the next moment, Dougall was off the bed, barking "Stay here" and rushing up the stairs.

Breathing heavily, Murine stared blankly after him and then slowly eased back to her haunches. It wasn't until she heard Dougall crossing the upper floor that she realized she was sitting there naked. Biting her lip, she quickly snatched up her nightgown that had somehow got pulled from her arm and lay pooled on the bed next to her. She recalled tugging it off her one arm, but had no idea how it had got off the other. Murine didn't ponder the matter, but merely pulled it on over her head, then brushed it down into place and slid to the edge of the bed.

She was debating getting up to follow Dougall and be sure all was well when she heard a crash from above. Swallowing, she shifted nervously and glanced around for a weapon as the sound was followed by a second crash. She'd barely begun to look, though, when footsteps moved back across the creaky upper floorboards. It was a great relief when Dougall appeared at the top of the stairs and started down.

"What was it?" she asked with a frown, noting his irritated expression.

Dougall shook his head as he stepped off the stairs. "One o' me brothers must ha'e left the shutters open above stairs. The wind was blowing them about so I closed them," he explained, and then paused as he saw that she was dressed.

Murine glanced at herself self-consciously, unsure what to do or say. She had only dressed because she'd worried there was someone above stairs. Now that she knew there wasn't, however, she would have liked to continue doing what they'd been doing before interrupted. Unfortunately, she didn't know how to let him know that. Or even if she should. He had told

Aulay that they were to be married, but did that mean they could or should do the things they'd been doing? Would he think her a lightskirt if she—

"Ye're probably hungry."

Murine glanced up at his gruff voice to see that he'd turned his back and was moving to the pot simmering over the cooking pit and she sighed, knowing they wouldn't continue with the pleasure he'd been teaching her. Telling herself it was for the best, Murine got cautiously to her feet and when she found them a little less shaky than the first time she'd got up, moved slowly to the table.

Dougall turned from the fire with a trencher of what appeared to be a thick and hearty soup, then paused when he saw her seated at the table. A frown flickered across his face and she thought he would give her hell for getting out of bed, but the next moment the frown was gone and he crossed to set the trencher in front of her, then returned for a second one for himself. He then fetched spoons and two mugs of cider as well before sitting down next to her.

"It smells good," she murmured as she dipped her spoon in the soup. "Did you make it?"

Dougall smiled crookedly and nodded. "The lads hunted and cleaned the meat, but I did the rest."

"The lads?" she asked curiously.

"Geordie, Alick and Conran," he explained. "They came here with us."

Murine nodded, and glanced around, wondering where they were. They couldn't have been upstairs or one of them would have closed the shutters before Dougall could have got up there.

"They rode back to Buchanan fer supplies," Dougall announced now. "And to see if your brother showed up there."

"Oh," Murine murmured and, not even wanting to think of her brother, picked up her drink to take a sip. A heartbeat later she was spitting it back out and coughing up clumps of weed that had lodged in her throat.

"Damn!" Dougall jumped up and rushed around the table, but when Murine saw him raise his hand as if to slap her back, she squealed in alarm through her coughing and held up a hand to stop him. Dougall immediately froze. Fortunately, Murine had coughed up the worst of it by then and her coughing eased. She took a moment to catch her breath and then glanced to him with wide eyes.

"What the devil is in me cider?"

"One o' Rory's tinctures. 'Tis supposed to help build up yer strength," he explained, reaching for his own cider and offering it to her.

Murine took the drink and sipped cautiously, but needn't have bothered. His drink was weed free. It was also much more tasty than her vile drink.

"I guess I overdid the tincture," Dougall muttered and then explained, "I was a bit worried. Ye seemed to be sleeping a lot."

Murine relaxed and offered him a smile. "Thank ye fer seeing to me while I've been recovering."

"It was nothing," Dougall growled and moved back to reclaim his seat.

When he immediately began to eat his soup, Murine turned her attention to eating her own. It really was very good. It seemed Alick was not the only Buchanan man who knew how to cook, but Murine was enjoying it too much and was suddenly so starved she didn't take the time to tell him so. As much as she enjoyed it, and as hungry as she was when she started the soup, Murine barely finished half of it before she had to set her spoon down.

"Ye don't like it?" he asked with a frown.

"Oh, nay!" she assured him, and then frowned as she realized that could be misconstrued and said, "Aye, I like it very much. 'Tis just that I'm full already." She glanced down at the remainder of her soup and added, "I actually ate to the point o' making meself uncomfortable it tasted so good." She peered at him and said, "Ye're a very good cook. Who taught ye?"

Finished with his own soup, Dougall pulled her half-full trencher before himself and picked up his spoon before answering, "Me parents. Ma and Saidh would often come to the lodge with us when Da brought me and me brothers hunting. We never brought servants though. Ma would cook what we caught and we'd all help with the meal and cleanup. It was family time," he explained with a small smile of remembrance. Scooping up a spoonful of soup, he added, "When she passed, Da took over the cooking and taught Aulay and me some more." He swallowed the spoonful of soup and added, "He said kenning how to cook a hearty meal was often thought a servant's business, but there are few servants traveling with ye in battle and it behooved a man to ken how to sustain himself."

Murine nodded and then smiled slightly and pointed out, "Ye didn't mention yer mother teaching Saidh to cook."

"She tried," Dougall said dryly and then assured her, "Our Saidh is no' verra good at it. She's no' got the patience."

"Ah," Murine said with a chuckle and watched him finish her soup.

Pushing the second trencher away, he hesitated and then stood, saying reluctantly, "I should probably put ye back in bed and let ye rest. Ye're most like tired."

Murine was tired, but noting his reluctance, and recalling his expression when he'd said she'd slept a lot, she shook her head at once. "Nay. I'm fine."

"Really?" Dougall asked with surprise.

"Aye. Besides, I think I must ha'e been abed too long. I'm a tad sore in spots other than me back."

"Oh." Dougall looked as if he weren't sure whether to allow his happiness that she wasn't tired show through, or show concern for her sore spots. Both emotions battled on his face briefly.

Murine saved him from making the decision by asking, "I do no' suppose ye ha'e a chess game here?"

"Aye." Dougall smiled. "Ye play?"

Murine nodded. "Me father and I used to play of a night."

Smiling at this news, Dougall moved to a chest under the stairs and knelt to open it. A moment later he was returning to the table with a chessboard and a bag that it turned out held finely carved chess pieces. Leaving Murine to admire the little carved men, Dougall quickly fetched them both more cider and then returned to help her set up the board. Within moments they were deep in the game.

"Did yer mother play chess?"

Murine glanced up with surprise at that question from Dougall, but then shook her head and turned her gaze back to the board as he made his move. "Nay. She never cared for the game."

"Hmm." Dougall sat back to wait for her to take her turn.

As she moved her rook out, Murine asked. "Did your mother? Play chess, I mean?"

"Aye." Dougall smiled. "We have two boards and used to hold little competitions, four playing, and then two playing the winners and so on."

Murine smiled at the thought, imagining Saidh, Dougall and his brothers all much younger, playing chess with their parents. Frowning, she glanced up and asked, "Saidh has never talked much about yer mother. How old were ye when she died?"

"She only died four or so years ago," he said quietly.

"Oh, I'm sorry. I shouldn't have asked. I—"

"Lass," he interrupted gently. "It's been four years. The loss of her still hurts, but she was a good mother and deserves to be remembered and talked about."

"Oh," Murine breathed, thinking that was possibly the wisest, most wonderful thing she'd ever heard. Clearing her throat, she changed the subject somewhat by asking something she'd been curious about since Alick had offered her Rory's tincture and explained that he was the healer in the family. "Did Rory tend yer mother when she fell ill?"

"Nay, Saidh did," Dougall said solemnly, and then grimaced and added, "Not that there was a lot o' time to tend her. And Saidh didn't really ken how to help her. None of us did."

"Not even Rory?"

"Rory?" He looked surprised at the question and then shook his head. "Up until then Rory had no interest in healing. But he was close to our mother, and took her loss hard. Her death is what turned his interests that way." He frowned at the memory. "We sent for all the best-known healers. None of them kenned what to do. In the end we all just stood by and watched her die. All of us feeling helpless and useless." He shifted as if shrugging away the unhappy memory, and then said, "I suspect Rory took up learning about healing so that he need never feel that way again."

"I see," Murine murmured and stifled a yawn behind her hand.

Dougall smiled faintly and added, "Rory's a bit of a man possessed when he's interested in something. He spent the better part of two and a half years traveling all over England and Scotland to learn from the best healers. Now people send for him when there is a tricky case or injury."

Murine smiled faintly at Dougall's pride in his brother and watched him make his next move. Fighting off another yawn that tried to overtake her, she asked, "Did your father fall at the same time?"

"Nay." Dougall's expression closed up, and his words were a little curt when he said, "He died in battle."

"I'm sorry," Murine murmured, making her own move and shifting her bishop. Apparently the father's death was still too raw for him to discuss as he could his mother's.

"'Tis all right," Dougall muttered and huffed out a little sigh before saying, "Our da died in the same battle that scarred Aulay."

"Oh," she said with understanding, and she did understand. Saidh had told her that Aulay was terribly self-conscious about the scar that halved his face. She supposed, that being the case, he would hardly welcome his brothers talking about their father and the battle that had taken his life as well as Aulay's good looks and self-confidence. Dougall verified her thoughts as he took his next move.

"Aulay has struggled with his scar since that battle. He does no' like to talk about it and we all honor his wishes rather than make him . . ."

"Miserable?" she suggested gently when he paused.

"Aye," he admitted. "Talking about it puts him in a foul mood for days, so we all just don't talk about it. Check," he added with a slow smile before adding, "And mate I think."

Murine glanced down to the board with a start, her eyes widening as she saw that it was, indeed, checkmate.

"Ye're a good player," Dougall complimented.

Murine grinned at the claim and shook her head. "Good to beat."

"I had an unfair advantage, ye're tired," he said apologetically. "Ye started yawning halfway in."

She opened her mouth to protest, but had to stop to cover it as another yawn stretched her jaws. Once the yawn had ended, she grimaced and said, "Aye. Fine. I'll sleep. But only fer an hour or so. Then I'll let ye beat me at chess again. Or we could play nine men's morris if ye have the game."

"We do," he assured her, and then teased, "And I'll look forward to trouncing ye at that too."

Murine scowled at him for the comment. She'd half expected him to scoop her up and carry her to the bed when he stood. Since he hadn't, however, and didn't appear to be intending to, she slid her legs over the bench and stood up. She then glanced down with surprise as her bindings unwound and dropped onto her feet.

Dougall cursed softly and then grimaced. "I never finished with yer bindings."

It wasn't really a question, so Murine didn't bother to agree. He'd stopped before doing anything to ensure the end remained in place. In fact, she wasn't sure they'd been at the end of the bandage when he'd dropped it to cover her breasts. That thought had a decidedly warming effect on Murine as she recalled the feel of his hands on her excited flesh.

Dougall glanced to the binding and then the bed, but shook his head as if in answer to a question before announcing, "'Tis best I bind ye here at the table. There is something I need talk to ye about."

Murine's eyebrows rose slightly as she wondered what one had to do with the other. He could talk to her while binding her on the bed too. Or perhaps the bed was too tempting for him to risk it, she thought suddenly. Murine didn't ask if that were the case, however, but glanced down at the gown she wore. He would either have to lift it up, or lower it to her waist to replace the wrapping. And while he'd already seen her breasts and bottom, he hadn't seen her front below the waist and she wasn't ready to bare it to him so cavalierly, so when he bent to pick up the binding, she quickly shrugged her shoulders out of her gown and let it drop to rest at her waist, held there by her hips and one hand.

Dougall straightened and then froze as he saw what she'd done. His eyes widened, and then glazed over slightly as he stared at her naked chest. It was not a dissimilar reaction to the one he'd had the first time he'd seen her breasts, but this time Murine was not in the same state she had been then. This time, she was actually a bit uncomfortable and embarrassed. At least she was until Dougall suddenly dropped to his knees, caught her by the waist and drew her forward so that he could latch on to one of the nipples she'd bared.

Murine bit down on her lower lip and caught at his shoulders as he began to suckle, her body immediately responding to the caress. Both of her nipples were promptly hard pebbles on her chest, she saw as he released the first breast to pay attention to the second one.

It was all a tad abrupt and even overwhelming. He had not primed her with kisses, and Murine found herself longing for those kisses even as she moaned over what he was doing.

When Dougall's hands left her waist to cover both cheeks of her bottom and squeeze eagerly, her gown slipped down to drape over his hands, the front dropping below her belly button. He couldn't have possibly seen that from his position at her breasts, and yet the moment it did, his mouth started a heated trail down her belly and then paused at her hip before he ran his tongue along the line of skin just above the cloth of her gown.

Murine gasped and grabbed his head now, her hips doing a little shimmy in reaction to the sensation that was part ticklish and part excitement as his tongue teased her. When his hands shifted just a bit lower, the cloth dropped with it and his mouth followed, burning a trail.

"Dougall," she cried uncertainly. Her legs were suddenly shaking madly and she wasn't sure she could remain upright. She was holding him now as much to keep her feet as to urge him on. It was something of a relief when his hands shifted to catch her by the waist and lift her. She lost the gown altogether then, but at least he'd removed the risk of her falling, she thought, then blinked her eyes open with surprise when she felt hard wood beneath her bottom.

He'd bypassed the bench and set her on the edge of the table, she realized just as he settled on the bench before her and ducked his head between her legs to taste her. Shock and embarrassment struck her first, but were quickly nudged aside by the crash of excitement that followed. Dear God, he was— she—"Oh God!" she cried, clutching at his head again as he bent to his meal.

Murine wasn't sure what the devil he was doing, but Dougall was definitely driving her mad as he laved and nibbled and suckled by turn, using his tongue, teeth and lips to search out every last drop of passion in her. When his hands slid up between them to knead her breasts, she gave up holding his head and grabbed at them, squeezing them encouragingly, half aware that somehow her legs had wrapped themselves around his back and her heels were digging in, urging him on too.

When he withdrew one hand, she let it go, and then bucked on the tabletop as it slid between her legs to join his mouth in pleasuring her. She felt his fingers run lightly over her skin beside his madly working mouth and then they dipped below it and she felt something pressing into her.

"Aye!" Murine cried, her hips shifting on the wooden surface, trying to meet the pressure. But the pressure eased briefly before it surged back, this time pushing a little farther. Sobbing her need, Murine dropped her hands to the tabletop and pushed with her whole body this time, crying out as the dam of excitement inside her burst just ere something else broke and she felt pain. Murine was quite sure she knew what had happened, he'd pushed through her maidenhead, but it was much less painful than she'd expected, just the tiniest twinge, hardly felt above the roaring wave of release she experienced.

She was still riding that wave when Dougall straightened between her legs, clasped her hips and slid into her. This was not quite the same as when he'd pressed his finger into her. This was much bigger and for a moment she feared he would not fit, but much to her surprise her body managed to accommodate him. Still, they both went briefly still as her body encased his.

Dougall shifted his hands to her face then and tipped her head back so he could kiss her. If she'd thought his kisses carnal and exciting before, they were nothing next to the hungry devouring she experienced this time, and then he shifted his hips back, withdrawing slightly from her body before surging back in even as his tongue withdrew and thrust into her mouth.

Murine breathed a long groan into his mouth as all the tension that her body had just released suddenly sprang back into place. He was driving her back to that cliff edge again, and she was going willingly, her legs wrapping around him, her heels digging into his behind to urge him on, her hands clutching at his sides, nails scoring him as she tried to make him move faster and harder. Dougall resisted the silent demand at first, his movements almost leisurely, but just when she thought he would drive her mad, he growled into her mouth and began to thrust more swiftly. When he tore his mouth away on a triumphant roar, Murine was there with him, her cry joining his as her body convulsed around him.

Chapter 10

$\mathcal{D}$OUGALL BREATHED OUT A LITTLE SIGH AND OPENED HIS eyes, his gaze moving over the lodge. It was a place full of good memories for him . . . and now he'd added another. He didn't think he'd soon forget this one. Murine was . . . asleep, he realized as his eyes drifted down to her. Damn, he'd worn the poor lass out. Here she was recovering from a wound that might have killed her, and he—

His thoughts died as he thought of her wound. He immediately tipped his head to try to get a look at it. Fortunately the lass was shorter than he. She'd also ducked her head against his chest and he was actually able to see the wound in question from his position. A little breath of relief slipped from his lips when he saw that it appeared to be fine.

Dougall briefly considered putting her bindings back on as he'd intended to do before she'd so unceremoniously let her gown drop, but then changed his mind. Doing so would wake her and he'd fair worn her out. Besides, the air would do the wound some good, he told himself. It absolutely had nothing to do with the fact that he wasn't looking forward to having to apologize to her for taking her maidenhead.

When he finally did apologize, it would probably be good if he could put some sincerity into it. The problem was, he wasn't feeling at all sorry. Doing so ensured that there was no question but that she'd have to marry him now, and Dougall was hoping her eager response to him meant that she wouldn't mind too much about that. He certainly saw it as a good sign for their life together. The woman was a wildcat, easily excited and very enthusiastic. He knew without looking that she'd scratched the hell out of him. He could feel the blood trickling down his sides.

Moving slowly and carefully, Dougall slipped his hands beneath her bottom and lifted her off the table. He briefly considered kicking the bench behind him out of the way, but then decided against it, unwilling to risk waking Murine. So, instead, he eased slowly to the side to get out from between it and the table and then turned in a slow circle to face the bed before starting to walk. By the third step he decided that waking Murine might not be a bad thing after all. He was still inside her, and the friction as he walked was certainly waking parts of him he'd thought sleeping.

They were halfway to the bed when Murine moaned sleepily and tightened her legs around his hips. Another step and she rubbed her face against his chest, then closed her lips on the nipple nearest her mouth. That made Dougall pause. No one had ever even touched his nipples. He'd never thought doing so would even affect him, but her nipping and suckling at it now was definitely having an effect, he realized and took another step.

Murine groaned as their bodies rubbed together, and then nipped at his nipple before releasing it to raise her head in search of his lips.

Dougall smiled faintly when he saw how swollen they were already from his kisses, then lowered his head to cover her mouth with his own as he took the next step. When her tongue slid out and pushed between his lips, he almost fell to his knees with surprise. While Murine had always responded eagerly to his kisses, this was the first sign of aggression she'd shown and his heart nearly flew out of his chest with excitement at the action.

Oh, aye, she would make a fine wife indeed, he decided and strode the rest of the way to the bed more quickly. Once there, rather than set her down, Dougall settled on the bed himself, arranging her in his lap as he went before breaking their kiss. He then lay back, holding her arms to urge her to remain upright as he did.

Murine blinked at him, awake, but obviously confused at this new position, and he smiled, his voice a husky growl as he instructed, "Ride me, lass. Pleasure yerself on me body. Ye can go as fast or as—" His words died on a sharply indrawn breath as she suddenly shifted her hips above him.

"How?" she demanded in a sharp whisper. "Tell me what to—"

Now it was Murine's turn to gasp in air as he slid one hand down between where they were joined and began to caress her. Murine didn't ask for further instruction. Clutching the arm of the hand he had at her waist, she began to move her body into his caresses, her hips rising and falling, rotating and sliding back and forth by turn.

Dougall tried to control her movement with both his caress and the hand he had at her waist, but it was like trying to herd a wild horse. She wasn't interested in his guidance, she was doing exactly as he'd suggested and using his body as she chased the excitement he was stirring. The problem was that what she was doing was working too well. His excitement was growing by leaps and bounds and Dougall very much feared he was going to reach the end of the race before she did if she didn't stop.

In a desperate bid to make her do so, he left off caressing her and grasped both of her hips, but she merely leaned forward, changing her angle enough that she was caressing herself on his body. That was even worse for him and Dougall changed tactics, trying to think of unpleasant things to stave off his mounting excitement. Unfortunately, her breasts were bobbing directly over his face and it was difficult to think of anything unpleasant with that view.

Dougall was just about to resort to viciously biting his own tongue to prevent his body finding release when Murine sud-

denly began to thrash above him, her body squeezing and puls-
ing hard around his staff as she cried out her pleasure. Relieved
beyond measure, Dougall immediately took over steering this
ride and pumped up into her hard a bare two times before the
release he'd been trying to avoid rode over him like the king
and his court stampeding the table at a feast. When it ended,
he found Murine slumped atop him, already fast asleep again.

Chuckling softly to himself, he slipped his arms around her,
careful to avoid her wound, and then simply lay there, holding
her as she slept.

MURINE YAWNED SLEEPILY AND SHIFTED IN BED, FROWNING
when her knee bumped into something extremely hard. Blinking her eyes open, she stared at her "bed." What her knee had
bumped was a rather large upraised knee, and her bed was
Dougall's body. Murine lay with her hip and one leg on the bed
and her head and upper body across his chest. Her other leg
was splayed over one of his. It was a most indelicate position.

Eyes shooting upward, she peered at his face in the early afternoon light. She wasn't positive from this angle, but thought
he might be asleep. That was something at least. How embarrassing would it have been had he been awake and watching
her drool all over his tartan? And she'd definitely been doing
that, she decided as she felt the dampness beneath her cheek.
The thought made her frown. The man hadn't even removed
his clothes while she was completely naked. How fair was that?

"Lass?"

Murine stiffened and raised her head again, eyeing him
warily. She wasn't sure why, but something about his tone put
her on the alert. She had the feeling that he was about to tell her
something unpleasant.

"I'm sorry, lass, I meant to talk to ye earlier, but then—" He
grimaced and then said almost apologetically, "Ye realize this
means we ha'e to marry."

Murine peered at him uncertainly. It wasn't because, despite

his words, he didn't sound the least bit apologetic, or even because she felt sure she'd heard a note of gloating in his voice. It
was the words themselves.

"I thought we were to marry anyway? Ye told Aulay—"

"Ye remember that?" Dougall asked with surprise.

"Aye," she murmured and wondered if she wasn't supposed
to. Had he not meant it at the time?

"I thought ye might ha'e been in shock and missed it," he
admitted with a wry smile.

"Oh," Murine murmured and lowered her head, unsure what
to think now. Had he said it because he hadn't expected her to
remember? Had he not meant it at all? Dear God, had she—?

"I am sorry," he repeated and she didn't need to look to see
that he was frowning. "I realize that I may not be all ye wanted."

Startled, she raised her head. "What do ye mean?"

"Well, Aulay's the eldest. He inherited the title and castle,"
Dougall pointed out, then shrugged and said, "Not that we'll
need live in a hovel. Between me mercenary work, acting as
Aulay's first, and me horse breeding, I've saved a good deal of
coin over the years. I'll build us a fine home. But it'll take some
time, and we may ha'e to stay here or with Aulay while our
home is being built."

Murine tilted her head and frowned at him. "Ye think I care
about that?" She didn't give him the chance to answer, but continued, "Ye think me so light o' character that I would choose a
title and castle over the man?"

"Many women would," he pointed out gently.

"Aye," she agreed grimly, pushing herself up to her hands
and knees and then easing back to sit on her haunches as she
spat, "But those women did no' spend a year under the thumb
o' a brother who delighted in tormenting her with all she'd lost,
and who would sell her to the first man who came along with
something he wanted."

Clucking with disgust, Murine shifted off the bed and scur-
ried over to grab up her nightgown and drag it on. "I have lived

in a castle with a man of title, Dougall, and I was miserable there. The dwelling does no' make the home. The people in it do. I—"

She broke off with surprise when he was suddenly in front of her, grasping her hands.

"I'm sorry," he said for the third time, but this time sounded sincere. "I did no' mean to offend ye."

"Well ye did," Murine said quietly. "Honestly, Dougall. Today in this cottage . . ." She waved around at their surroundings and shrugged unhappily. "This was the happiest day o' me life to date." Peering at him earnestly, she added, "And that's including all me years growing up at Carmichael with me family who I loved dearly. I had a happy childhood, and mayhap the last years and losing all those I loved has colored me memories, but none of them seem as shiny to me as simply playing chess and talking with ye and . . ."

Blushing, she trailed off.

Dougall smiled faintly, and suggested, "And playing bed games with me?"

"We were no' in the bed the second time," she pointed out dryly, but didn't fight him when he pulled her to rest against his chest.

"Ye mean the first time," he corrected.

"Nay. The first time we were on the bed and ye ran above stairs to close the shutters," Murine mumbled into his chest.

"Oh. Aye," he murmured, rubbing her bottom through her gown rather than risk rubbing her back, miscalculating and hitting her injury. "I was no' counting that time. We did no' carry it through to the end then."

She shrugged in his arms, squeezing a little closer until her breasts were plastered to his chest and the apex of her thighs was pressing against his pelvis. Still, it was only when she tipped her head back and slid her hands up and around his neck to pull his face down for a kiss that he realized he was exciting her with his caress. And that he had stirred some in-

terest in himself with the action too. Christ! He couldn't even
be near the lass without wanting her. He should have known
that touching her so intimately would lead to—

"Nay, Murine," Dougall breathed, pausing before his mouth
touched hers. Removing the hand that had been squeezing her
bottom, he caught her arms and dragged them down. "Ye'll
pull yer stitches reaching like that. And ye'll be sore do we do
it again. If ye're not already," he added with a frown and asked.
"How do ye feel? Are ye tender?"

"A little," she admitted. "But I still want ye."

Dougall stared blankly, stunned that she'd admit as much.
He had no doubts that Murine had been a virgin ere today.
Hell, she hadn't even known how to kiss at first, but she was
a quick learner and seemed to have little shame when it came
to the bedding. God bless her parents for raising her to be that
way and not turning her into one of the cold, timid prudes he
had occasionally encountered in the past, Dougall thought suddenly.

"Please, Dougall?" She shifted against him, and then rose
up on tiptoe to press a kiss to his neck. He was tempted, more
than tempted, but he didn't want her sore and needing a week
to recover.

"Are ye thirsty?" he asked suddenly, hoping to distract her
long enough for her to tire again.

Murine pulled back to blink at him. "Thirsty?"

"Aye. I'm thirsty," he announced. "Go sit yourself on the bed
and I'll fetch us some cider. Then mayhap we'll . . ." He let his
voice trail away.

A big grin on her face, Murine turned and skipped back to
the bed.

She was actually skipping for God's sake! Dougall thought
with amazement. Like a child who'd been promised a boon.
He should really just follow her to the bed, bend her over it and
give her a good seeing to. Lord knew his body was crying out
for him to do so . . . again.

Giving his head a shake, Dougall turned abruptly and moved to the mantel. He'd moved the tincture-laced cider there when he'd cleared the table to play chess after they'd had their soup. Now he grabbed it and took a moment to pour half of it into a new container, and then dilute it with fresh cider before pouring himself one as well. He carried both back to the bed.

"Here ye go," he said, handing her the cider laced with Rory's tincture. He raised his own drink to take a swallow as he waited for her to take the other one, then nearly choked on the liquid when she released her hold on the linens and furs she'd pulled up to her chest and he saw that she'd removed her gown. How had he missed that her shoulders were naked? he wondered as he watched her take several swallows of her drink. She wrinkled her nose slightly after the third and complained, "'Tis bitter."

"There is still some of Rory's tincture in it," Dougall explained solemnly. "He said it would build yer strength. Drink up so I can remove the mugs and join ye."

It was all he had to say; she downed the rest of her drink in two large gulps and then smiled as she handed him the empty container.

Dougall carried the empty mugs to the table and set them down, then turned back to the bed.

"Do ye ken ye've seen all o' me, but have yet to remove even yer tartan?" Murine pointed out and while there was a definite naughtiness to her expression, there wasn't a sign of weariness.

It seemed her earlier exhaustion had fled. Dougall was trying to decide if that was a good thing or bad when her words suddenly registered and he glanced down. She was right of course, at the table he'd merely lifted the hem of his tartan, and then they'd still been joined as he'd carried her to the bed.

"'Tis most unfair," Murine added.

In truth, he supposed it was. Holding her gaze, Dougall reached for the pendant at his shoulder and removed it. His tartan immediately dropped away. Leaving it where it fell, he stepped out of it and crossed halfway to the bed before stopping and tugging his shirt off over his head.

"Oh, Dougall," Murine breathed, easing to her knees and crawling on them to the end of the bed, leaving the linens and furs behind.

"Aye?" he asked, looking her over one more time for any signs of weariness before drawing closer to the bed.

"Ye ha'e the most beautiful chest," she murmured.

He couldn't help noticing, though, that it wasn't his chest that held her attention. She was looking farther south than that. He wasn't terribly surprised. This was probably the first time she'd got a good look at a male body. Dougall was quite sure she'd caught a glimpse here and there so had had some idea what to expect to see on her wedding night. It was difficult not to in the close confines of a castle where there was precious little privacy. But he was quite sure she'd never had one she could inspect more thoroughly, as she was doing now, staring at his suddenly growing member. His cock obviously thought itself a flower and her eyes the sun, Dougall acknowledged and sighed to himself. He really didn't want to chance bedding her again and perhaps doing her harm.

Spotting her hand moving toward him, Dougall shifted out of reach and moved to sit on the bedside instead. Murine immediately followed, settling next to him.

"We ha'e to be careful," he lectured solemnly.

She nodded at once though he suspected she wasn't paying him much attention. At least not his words.

Catching her chin in hand he raised it and said, "We must go slow and gentle to protect against rubbing ye raw."

"Aye, Dougall," Murine whispered solemnly and rested her head on his chest as sweet as ye please while her hand drifted down his stomach toward his groin. He held his breath until it stopped on his leg without touching him, then let his breath out slowly. For a minute he'd feared she'd agree and then race headlong into it. Murine had a distressing tendency to do that, he noticed. She'd rushed in and saved Saidh and Jo when their lives had been under threat, she'd rushed upstairs and packed a bag to flee her brother at Danvries and she'd rushed—

Dougall's thoughts died as a soft snore reached his ears. Stiffening, he tucked his head down to stare at the top of Murine's head, then twisted slightly to get a look at her face. He didn't know whether to be relieved or groan with despair when he saw that she was sleeping against his chest like . . . well, like someone who was recovering from a terrible wound and in need of sleep for healing.

Shaking his head, Dougall eased out from beside her and guided her to lie on the bed on her stomach. He then gently tugged the linens and furs up to cover her to her waist before straightening. It was only then he realized he hadn't put her bandages back on. He didn't want to risk irritating the wound by covering her fully with the furs, but she might catch a chill without it.

More of Rory's numbing salve would do the trick, he decided and grabbed it off the bedside table where he'd left it earlier. He took some out of the jar and rubbed it between his hands briefly to warm it, then spread it gently over her wound. Once satisfied she wouldn't suffer any pain, he tugged the linens up to cover her and straightened. Then he just stood there staring down at her. Murine Carmichael. Soon to be Murine Buchanan. She was going to be his wife, he thought with a grin.

Chapter 11

DOUGALL HEARD THE HORSES AS THEY ENTERED THE CLEARing around the cottage. Blinking his eyes open, he straightened away from where he'd been leaning against the headboard of the bed and slid his feet to the floor. He had been awake most of the night, first to watch over Murine, and then fretting about his brothers when they hadn't returned by nightfall. He wasn't sure what time he'd given up and sat in the bed next to Murine, but he'd fallen asleep sitting up. Judging from the light drifting through the cracks in the shutters, it was mid to late morning now. Standing, he quickly crossed the cottage to the door and slid out to greet his brothers with a scowl.

"What the devil took ye so long?" he snapped as they reined in and began to dismount.

"Danvries was at Buchanan," Conran announced as if that said it all, and in a way it did. It certainly excused any delay in their returning.

"Did he see ye?" Dougall asked with a frown, accepting the bag Conran unhitched from his saddle and handed to him.

"Nay," Conran assured him. "The men on the wall saw us approaching. One o' them rode out to warn us off. We camped in the woods until he and his party left this morning and then continued on to the castle."

"Good thing we did too," Alick put in, unhitching a bag from his own saddle and approaching. "Aulay had told him that we hadn't returned yet. He would ha'e recognized the lie and demanded to ken where ye and Murine were had we ridden in while he was there."

"Which is why Aulay had the men watch for us and sent someone to warn us off," Geordie pointed out dryly, joining them with a bag of his own. Turning his attention to Dougall, he added, "Aulay told him that Saidh had married the Mac-Donnell. Danvries said he would check there next, but to send word when we returned if Murine was with us."

Dougall snorted at the thought. They'd send word to Danvries when hell froze over. He didn't even intend to send word that they were married once the deed was done. As far as he was concerned, Danvries was no longer a part of Murine's life. She was his now.

"Is Murine awake yet?" Alick asked, clutching his bag. "We brought her dresses."

"She was still asleep when I came out," Dougall murmured and then glanced from bag to bag. "If Alick's bag has dresses, what is in the other two?"

"Dresses," Geordie and Conran said as one. When Dougall goggled from them to the large sacks, Conran shrugged and said, "Well we didn't know what Murine would like. We decided to just bring them all and let her choose."

"What about the bread and cheese and wine ye were supposed to fetch back?" Dougall asked with disbelief. It was a rare day indeed that his brothers forgot about their bellies. "We can hunt up meat, but ye'll soon grow tired o' a diet o' meat alone."

"It's all coming," Conran said soothingly. "A cart is following with all of that."

"And the rest of the dresses," Geordie put in with amusement. When Dougall peered at him blankly, he shrugged and pointed out, "Well, between those Saidh left behind and Mother's wardrobe, there were a lot of gowns. We couldn't carry them all ourselves and the food too."

"We rode most of the way with the wagon, but trotted ahead

once we got close to the cottage so that Murine could dress before the men get here with the cart and help carry everything in," Alick added, moving past him toward the cottage.

"Has the lass woke up at all for more than a minute or so, or has she slept through our absence?" Conran asked, following when Dougall hurried after Alick.

"She woke," Dougall said at once. "We ate, played chess and . . . other games," he finished vaguely.

"Well, that's good to hear," Conran said.

Dougall merely grunted and hurried into the cottage. He glanced around then until he spotted Alick by the bedside peering down at a still sleeping Murine.

"She looks better," he announced in a loud whisper. "She has some color in her cheeks now."

"Aye," Dougall murmured, pausing beside the younger man and smiling as he noted that Alick was right. "The exercise appears to be doing her some good."

"Walking to the table, sitting up fer a game or two, and walking back to the bed is hardly exercise," Conran said with amusement as he joined them at her bedside.

Dougall didn't think he moved a muscle at Conran's words, but he must have flinched, or done something else to give himself away, because in the next moment Conran was sucking in a sharp breath.

"Never say it!" he cried with dismay. "No' with the lass so wounded and ailing?"

"What?" Dougall asked with feigned innocence.

"Ye did!" Conran accused. "Ye dirty devil! Could ye no' at least ha'e given her the time to heal first?"

"What did he do?" Alick asked with concern.

"He tupped our Murine," Geordie said dryly, apparently able to follow what Alick couldn't.

"He didn't," Alick said at once. "She would no' ha'e let him. They're no' married yet."

"Mayhap she was still sleeping," Conran snarled, and staggered back several steps when Dougall hauled off and slammed a fist into his face. The moment he regained his balance, Conran charged Dougall. And then all hell broke loose.

IT WAS A CRASH THAT WOKE MURINE. BLINKING HER EYES open, she winced as various aches and pains struck her. Most were from sleeping, unmoving, on her stomach for days on end. But the worst pain came from the wound on her back. She needed more of Rory's numbing salve.

Murine barely had that thought when another crash caught her attention. Frowning, she twisted her head to peer around, and then paused, her eyes widening incredulously at she stared at the four men rolling around on the cottage floor, fists flying as they crashed into various pieces of furniture. Chairs went tumbling as they rolled toward the fire, then they headed the other way sending the trestle table toppling.

"What the devil," she muttered and eased to her hands and knees, then shifted to sit on the bed to stare at them. And that's all she did; stare. Murine had no idea what to do about a situation like this. Life at Carmichael had never been this . . . well . . . rowdy. Her brothers had never fought in the castle. They'd never really fought, period. If they had a disagreement, their father made them take it to the yard and had them wrestle each other and every other soldier in the castle until they'd worked out their anger. They never would have rolled around, crashing into furniture and breaking it. Her mother would have snatched them all bald had they tried it. Including her father. It wasn't that her mother had ruled her father. She hadn't; he had definitely been the leader in the couple. But she did rule the house, and with an iron fist. This sort of behavior would not have been acceptable.

Although, Murine admitted as she watched the men tumble back toward the chairs by the fireplace again, it was rather entertaining to watch. Or would be if you didn't happen to care for one of them very much and the others quite a lot, and didn't want to see any of them hurt. Honestly, they were like to kill themselves with this nonsense, she thought, and then glanced to the door when someone pounded at it. Her gaze swung to the men again, but they didn't appear to have heard the pounding over their own curses and the racket they were making, so Murine heaved a sigh and slid off the bed. She was most relieved to find the shakiness of the day before completely gone as she crossed the floor. Truly, it had been quite unsettling to feel so weak. Worse even than the fainting business that now seemed to be cleared up, she thought as she opened the door to Niels Buchanan.

"Er . . . Lady Carmichael." Niels's gaze slid uncertainly over her nightgown before fixing on her face and staying determinedly there.

"My apologies for my state of dress. I fear I have nothing to wear," Murine murmured, fighting to keep from covering herself up with her hands. Really, while she knew it was wholly inappropriate to answer the door as she was, it was not as if she had a dress to wear. Besides, the nightgown with its high collar and long sleeves covered more than her gowns would have anyway. Unfortunately, telling herself that didn't prevent the blush that she could feel blooming on her skin.

"Did me brothers no' give ye the dresses?" Niels asked with a frown as an older man stepped into view behind him.

"Dresses?" Murine asked with interest.

"Aye." The older man nodded. "They rode ahead with them so Dougall could give them to ye and see ye dressed ere we arrived. So ye would no' feel uncomfortable around all us men."

"Oh," Murine murmured and turned to glance to Dougall and the three brothers she knew best as another crash sounded. They'd slammed into one of the chests stationed around the room, she saw, and watched the foursome roll toward the bed as she explained, "I just woke up to find them like this. I guess they forgot about the dresses."

The older man stepped up beside Niels and peered into the room at the brothers. Shaking his head, he said, "Ye'll ha'e to forgive me nephews. They're good lads most o' the time, but can be idiots on occasion."

"Nephews?" Murine asked with surprise, turning back to the man.

"Aye. I'm Acair Buchanan. Youngest brother of the father to these lads," he announced, waving toward the pile of men rolling around the floor, cursing up a storm and fists still flying. "I was away when ye arrived at Buchanan with the lads. So when I heard Dougall was fixing to marry ye, I decided to travel out with Niels here to deliver the supplies and meet ye."

"Oh, how nice," Murine said sincerely. "'Tis lovely to meet Dougall's family."

"Soon to be yer family too, lass," Acair said solemnly.

"Aye." Murine smiled as she said that. She had family again. Or would once she and Dougall married.

"I think I see the sacks the lads brought," Acair said gently, prompting her out of her silence. "Two o' 'em at least. Lying just there by the bed."

Murine turned to glance back into the room and this time spotted them at once. They were lying on the floor next to the bed as he'd said. It was a wonder she hadn't tripped over them on the way to the door. Not that she would have stopped to see what was in them with someone pounding at the door.

"Ye'd best let Niels get them, lass," Acair said, catching her arm to stop her when she started away from the door to fetch the bags. "The lads might knock ye down if ye try yerself."

"Oh. All right," Murine murmured as Niels immediately started to make his way through the room, managing to avoid the rolling mass of male fury by dodging this way and that a time or two. Niels grabbed both bags by the bed, turned to head back to the door, then dodged to the right to avoid his brothers again and apparently spotted the third bag and sidestepped to grab it too before hustling to the door.

"Here ye go," he said, sounding a tad breathless as he held out the sacks.

"Thank ye." She smiled at him as she took the bags, surprised at how heavy they were. They must be crammed full of gowns to be so heavy, she thought with a frown, then glanced into the cottage and eyed the stairs. "I'll just go above stairs and change—"

"Here." Acair took the bags Niels had just given her. Holding them in one hand, he took her elbow in the other. "I'd best escort ye, lass, so those fools do no' take ye out on yer way by." Glancing to Niels he suggested, "Why do ye no' start getting buckets o' water from the well. I'm thinking we'll need at least four."

Niels nodded and rushed outside.

Before Murine could ask what the water was for, Acair began to usher her across the room to the stairs, and she was loath to distract him. Crossing the room was something like a dance. Acair rushed her the first couple of steps, paused and drew her to an abrupt halt to avoid flailing legs as the men flew past, then hurried her two steps to the left and forward before pausing again as Alick flew past them to crash against the far wall and tumble to the floor. They watched the youngest Buchanan shake himself, pull himself to his feet and then dive back into the battle, then the uncle hustled her the last few steps to the stairs.

They were able to move more slowly then, but, much to her dismay, Murine found herself already a little out of breath by that point. It was a reminder that she was still recovering from her injury. This was only her second time out of bed.

Noticing her winded state, rather than send her on her way, Acair took the bags she carried and urged her ahead of him up the stairs, saying, "I'll see these up there for ye. Take yer time with the stairs. Ye're still recovering."

"Thank ye," Murine repeated and started up the stairs, moving as quickly as she could, which wasn't quick at all. By the time she reached the top, all she wanted was to sit down . . . and some cool air. Not necessarily in that order. Her heart was racing; she was out of breath and even sweating from the small effort it had taken to mount the stairs, which just seemed pitiful to her.

Acair stepped onto the landing and moved around her to open the door to the upper room. He walked in, set the sacks on the large bed, then turned, bowed to her and headed for the door, saying, "While ye change, I'll help Niels fetch more water. I'm thinking it might take more than the four buckets I originally thought to douse the fire in me nephews' bellies."

Murine opened her mouth to thank him yet again, but he held up his hand to stop her.

"Lass, do ye thank me again, I'll be insulted. Ye're soon to be family, and this was little enough to do fer ye. Take yer time up here. I ken from experience me nephews are slow to cool once their temper is up. It may take as many as eight trips to the well to sort them out."

Murine smiled faintly, and nodded as she watched him close the door, then moved the few steps necessary to reach the bed and sank to sit on the side of it. Good Lord, she was pathetic, Murine thought, pressing a hand to her chest as she waited for her heart to stop pounding so fiercely. It was going as wild as it had the day before under the influence of Dougall's caresses. The only difference was that then she hadn't wanted to stop. Her heart could have pounded its way out of her chest and she'd not have wanted to stop. It had all felt so good.

Murine shivered at the memory, and then crossed to the window and opened the shutters to find some fresh air. The cottage was warm thanks to the fire below, but it was positively stifling up here and she was already sweating from mounting the stairs.

A dark, gray day met her once the shutters opened, but Murine didn't care. She merely tipped her head up, leaned out a bit and sucked in the cool, refreshing air. Then she leaned on the window ledge to allow the air to rush over her for a moment more. Once her heartbeat had stopped its mad racing and she felt a little less sweaty, Murine started to turn back to the room, but paused as she spotted a bit of cloth caught in a crack between a couple of the stones on the rock ledge. Curious, she managed to tug it out of the spot where it had been wedged so that she could examine it. It was still damp from the rainstorm they'd apparently had. She must have slept through that, Murine thought. She hadn't heard a sound.

Turning the cloth over in her hand, she started back to the bed. The cloth was thick, expensive and jagged as if it had got caught in the crevice and torn off. It was not worn and frayed as if it had been there for ages. She could only guess that one of Dougall's brothers must have sat on the ledge to get fresh air, and torn his tartan when he got back up. Although it didn't match the tartans that she'd seen Dougall's brothers wear, nor Dougall's either. The bit of cloth was made with yellow, green and red threads. Dougall was wearing a blue and green tartan from the same material Aulay and Niels had been wearing at Buchanan. The others had tartans made with blue and red and black threads. Different batches of cloths she guessed. But then, mayhap one of them had changed their tartan after arriving here. She hadn't really noted what the boys were wearing as they'd rolled around on the floor.

Murine paused at the bed and tossed the bit of cloth next to the sacks Acair had set there and then opened the first bag, the cloth soon forgotten. It didn't really matter whose it was. It wasn't like she could sew it back in place. With the pleats they put in the cloth to don it, they probably hadn't even noticed the piece missing.

As she had guessed, there were several gowns crammed into each sack. It meant that each one was a mess of wrinkles as Murine pulled them out. She tugged all the gowns out of each bag, then examined them quickly before choosing the least wrinkled one, which was still terribly wrinkled. But there was nothing she could do about that, so Murine simply tugged off her nightgown and donned the dark blue gown that was the best of the lot. She then carried the others over to the window and hung them from the shutters, hoping the damp air would help remove the worst of the wrinkles in them.

Leaving the room then, Murine moved to the top of the stairs and glanced around the room below. It appeared Acair had managed to calm his nephews. At least they weren't rolling around on the floor below anymore. Actually, they weren't even there. The room was completely empty.

No doubt they were outside, unloading the supplies Acair had mentioned, Murine supposed, and grasped the railing to start down the stairs. She'd only managed the first step when the door burst open and Dougall entered. His brothers, uncle and the other man who had brought the supplies followed him in. Each of them was carrying a crate, a sack or a barrel, and Murine paused, her eyes going wide. Good Lord, how long did they think to be here? she wondered and started to step down to the next step, but froze when Dougall spotted her and barked, "Stop."

Still carrying the chest he had perched on his shoulder, Dougall jogged up the steps and urged her back onto the landing. He then led her back into the bedchamber.

"There are more gowns in here fer ye to choose from," he announced as he set the chest at the foot of the bed.

"Oh," Murine moved toward the chest, thinking he wanted her to go through them now, but he caught her arm to halt her when she moved toward it.

"Ye can look at them later," he announced, ushering her back out to the landing.

She peered at him with a combination of irritation and confusion. "Then why did ye stop me from going below?"

Dougall scooped her up into his arms, careful to avoid her injury, then started down the stairs with her, saying, "Because ye were wavering like a candle flame in a breeze. Ye're still too weak fer managing stairs. I'll no' ha'e ye toppling down them and breaking yer neck."

Murine merely grimaced, aware that she had been shaky on her legs as she'd started down the stairs. It was really a bit of a relief that she hadn't had to manage them on her own, she thought as Dougall carried her to the table and set her on the end of one of the benches there.

"Here ye go, lass," Acair said gruffly, setting a mug on the table before her almost before Dougall had finished setting her down. "Drink up. 'Tis cider. 'Twill build yer humors."

"Here, Murine, ye should ha'e soup too," Alick announced, setting a trencher of the steaming soup before her. "This'll help build yer strength as well."

"And mayhap some cheese," Conran announced, cutting some off a large round he pulled from a sack.

"And bread," Geordie added, slamming down a loaf beside her and digging out his knife.

"An apple." Niels set it in front of her soup.

"And if ye eat all that, ye can have one o' Cook's pasties," Dougall announced, settling on the bench beside her to dig through a sack he'd retrieved. He withdrew another, smaller sack, from it and opened it to reveal the promised pasties.

Murine glanced at all the offerings. Her gaze then narrowed as it slid over the faces of each man. "What is amiss?"

The forced smiles each man was offering immediately slid from their faces to be replaced with grimaces, and defeated sighs as every man looked to Dougall. The silent message was that it was his place to tell her what was what.

Dougall muttered what she suspected was a curse under his breath, and then shifted unhappily in his seat and shook his head. "Ye should eat first. Then we'll talk."

"But I want to know," she protested with a frown.

He shook his head. "Upset affects yer appetite and ye need to build yer strength. Eat and then I'll explain."

"How can I eat while fretting over what ye ha'e to tell me?"

she argued. "'Tis better to know what is wrong, than to worry over what might be wrong. Me worries may be ten times worse than the truth."

"Eat, Murine. Ye—"

"Yer brother arrived at Buchanan yesterday," Acair announced.

"Dammit, Uncle," Dougall snapped.

"'Tis better to tell her," Acair said with a shrug. "Ye were jest getting her upset with yer arguments."

"He's right," Murine said soothingly, patting Dougall's arm as she spoke. "Besides, this is not such upsetting news. This was to be expected. Montrose kens Saidh is a friend and does not ken she's married. Of course he would come to Buchanan in search of me." She paused and reconsidered briefly, then admitted, "Well, actually, he might ken she's married and living at MacDonnell if he's been waylaying me messages and reading them."

"Aye," Conran agreed with a frown. "I'm sure Saidh would have written ye with the grand news."

"Which means he stopped at Buchanan because he suspects us o' helping ye escape," Alick said with dismay.

"O' course, he does," Murine said calmly, picking up her spoon to dip it in her soup. "If ye hadn't, I most like would no' ha'e made it out o' England alive. He and his men would ha'e found me body on the side o' the road, a victim to bandits or other ne'er-do-wells."

"And yet ye risked fleeing Danvries anyway," Dougall said quietly. "Despite thinking ye'd die in the attempt."

Murine shrugged. "Well, I was hoping I would no' end up dead. But I suspected I probably would," she admitted. "That's why I wouldn't let me maid come with me. Me dead was one thing, but I wasn't going to be responsible for her death too." Pausing, she lowered her spoon and turned to Dougall to say. "Which reminds me, we must send for Beth the moment we're married, Dougall. The English were terrible to her at Danvries, and I'm not entirely sure my brother might not have taken his anger over me escape out on her."

"Aye," Dougall agreed on a sigh, but then added, "But that is the second part o' what we ha'e to tell ye."

"Oh?" She set her spoon down to give him her full attention.

"Conny and the boys were supposed to bring the priest back along with the supplies."

Murine glanced around at the men in the room. "I see no priest."

"The boys had to camp out in the woods surrounding Buchanan while they waited for yer brother to leave. When he did this morning, they rode in to gather the supplies and fetch the priest, but . . ." Dougall grimaced. "The priest is missing."

Her eyebrows flew up. "Missing? Are ye sure he has no' just gone to tend to someone in need? Our priest at Carmichael was often called upon to tend to the sick or dying."

"Aye, but we asked around and no one kens o' anyone in such a state," Alick argued, and then scowled and added, "'Sides, 'tis most suspicious that he disappeared just when yer brother and his men left."

"Ye think Montrose took yer priest?" she asked with surprise. "Why would he do something like that?"

"So Dougall can no' marry ye," Alick said as if that should be obvious.

Shaking her head with bewilderment, she pointed out, "But he does no' ken we were going to marry. And I doubt he would have guessed we might. He offered me to Dougall and Dougall refused."

"He did no' offer ye in marriage," Dougall said grimly, and then waved all of that away and said, "We'll sort out what happened to the priest later." Taking her hands he added apologetically, "But the fact is that while I intended we marry right away, we can no' do so without a priest."

"Oh," Murine said with understanding. They'd thought she'd

be upset by the delay. Smiling crookedly, she said, "'Tis all right, Dougall. We can wait."

Her words made him scowl. "'Tis no' all right. I want to marry ye, dammit."

She blinked and then blushed at the words, but patted his hand. "And so ye shall. I'm sure the priest will show up."

"Murine, ye do no' understand," Dougall said with a frown.

"What do I not understand?" she asked with confusion.

"We will ha'e to *wait*." His gaze dropped over her body and his hand tightened on hers as he stressed the word *wait*, and Murine suddenly understood. His brothers had been with them from the start until last night, and it sounded like they hadn't intended to be away then. They probably wouldn't be left alone again. Dougall meant that the heady taste she'd had of passion last night had been all there would be until they were properly wed and he didn't like that at all.

For some reason, his distress made her much more accepting of the matter. Smiling crookedly, she squeezed his hand back. "'Tis all right. I'm sure 'twill no' be long. If we have to wait for the priest, we have to wait."

Dougall scowled at her easy acceptance and pointed out sharply, "The longer we wait, the greater the risk yer brother will find ye and prevent our marrying altogether."

Murine stiffened at that suggestion. "But he has already checked at Buchanan. Surely he will not return?"

"Ye think once he checks and finds out ye're no' at MacDonnell, Drummond or Sinclair, he will no' head right back to Buchanan?" Dougall asked solemnly. "We were in the area when ye made yer escape, and he was told we'd yet to arrive home despite the fact that we left ahead of them."

"Aye," she agreed with concern, but then brightened and pointed out, "But 'twill take a while for him to check at MacDonnell, Drummond and Sinclair. MacDonnell may be close, but Sinclair is a good distance north, and Drummond is almost as far east. On top of that, traveling with such a large party will slow him down. Surely the priest will turn up ere he can visit each place?"

"Murine, he does no' have to visit each place himself," he said solemnly. "He can set up camp and send small, fast-moving parties to each of the holds to ask after ye. He can also send out several lone men to ask at the castles along the route to see if anyone saw ye or us in our travels."

"Oh dear," Murine breathed. He didn't have to explain to her that while they had not seen anyone on their journey that did not guarantee they themselves had not been seen. In fact, it was almost a certainty that they had. At Carmichael there were always men watching the roads and the land borders of the property for trouble. Sometimes they were hidden in the branches of a tree, unseen by travelers as they kept an eye out. Sometimes they were traveling the road, but rushed their horses into the woods with their thickets to hide themselves to let the travelers pass without needing to address them. But every laird knew who crossed or passed his land. Someone would have seen the Buchanan lads travel past with a lass and a bull, and Montrose would learn that. If he hadn't already, she realized. He might have already stopped to ask those questions.

"If he doesn't know already, Montrose could find out all that he needs to as soon as tomorrow night or the morning after at the latest," Dougall said now, verifying her own thoughts.

"And then he'd return to Buchanan," she realized unhappily.

"Aye." He nodded, his expression grim. "We need to marry quickly to protect ye."

"Oh," she said weakly.

"Now, there's no need to fret overmuch," Acair said when Dougall fell silent. "Aulay has already sent several men out to find and bring back a priest. But in the meantime, ye need to stay here."

"And it might be best do ye stay inside," Conran suggested, and when she glanced to him with a frown, he added, "Just in case he sends men to scout our land and one o' them stumbles across the cottage."

"Oh. Aye." Frowning, Murine turned to her soup, scooped up a spoonful and quickly slid it into her mouth. As the men had feared, their news had affected her appetite. She was no longer hungry, but it was sounding more and more like she might need her strength back as quickly as possible. There might be trouble ahead.

She was scooping up a second spoonful of soup when the door opened. Everyone turned to look as Rory entered, his "bag o' weeds" in hand.

He raised an eyebrow at their expressions, and explained, "Aulay thought I'd best come check on Murine's wound." He glanced to Dougall and added, "And then mayhap I should stay a bit. Just in case."

Murine turned silently back to her soup, and thought, *Correction, there was definitely trouble ahead*. At least the Buchanans must think there would be if they believed she needed seven men guarding her here in this little cottage in the middle of nowhere. She supposed she shouldn't be surprised.

Murine had been relieved and very happy when she realized that Dougall had meant it when he'd told Aulay he planned to marry her. She liked Dougall, a lot. She respected his strength and intelligence and appreciated his kindness . . . and truly, the things the man made her feel with his kisses and caresses . . . Aye, she was a lucky woman and had thought her troubles over.

Obviously, she'd been far too optimistic. Anyone with half a thought in their head would have considered the sorrow and tragedy of the last three or four years of her life, and realized it wasn't going to be that easy.

Chapter 12

*M*URINE SHIFTED RESTLESSLY ONTO HER SIDE, RELIEVED TO find she could do so without her back complaining. She was sick unto death of sleeping on her stomach, and doing so was actually giving her aches and pains she did not appreciate. Sighing, she tucked one arm under her head and peered around the dark room. When Dougall had stressed the bit about waiting, she'd thought it cute and even flattering that he seemed so distressed by the idea of not having access to bedding her until they were properly wed. Now she was finding it much less so.

They'd spent the afternoon and evening talking and laughing with his brothers and uncle, playing chess and nine-men's morris. But the whole time, Dougall had been at her side, his arm and leg occasionally brushing against hers, his chest at her back as he leaned behind her to pass something to one of the other men or to accept a drink or whatnot that one of them passed to him.

By the end of the night, all she'd been able to think about was that at least they could share a good-night kiss. He was after all going to be sleeping in the hall outside the door of the upper bedchamber, so no doubt would walk her above stairs. Surely he'd get the chance to kiss her then, she'd thought and had been craving that kiss ever since. Her body had been longing for it, crying out for the opportunity to press itself against his as his mouth explored hers.

However, that kiss had never come.

The moment she'd announced her desire to retire, Dougall had popped to his feet as if he'd been waiting forever to hear the words. However, his uncle had also risen, announcing that he'd join Dougall on the floor outside her room to help guard her in case of an attack.

Dougall had looked like he wanted to hit someone at this news. As for Murine, she'd just wanted to cry. This waiting business was utter hell.

Sighing, she rolled back onto her stomach and then turned onto her other side so that she faced the door. For a while after she'd retired there had been the sound of laughter and deep voices from below. While Dougall and his uncle had bedded down at the same time as she, the others had apparently remained awake for a while. Now there was only silence though. Everyone appeared to be sleeping except her. She was lying there restless, wide awake and thirsty.

Murine grimaced at the last thought. She'd sipped all day at the tincture-laced cider Dougall had put out for her on first rising. She would have refused it altogether and requested undosed cider except that while checking and redressing her wound, Rory had commented that his tincture appeared to be doing her good, and that she was much farther ahead in healing than he'd expected. She'd decided she would drink the vile thing, but it was a nasty brew and it had taken her all day to get it down.

Now her mouth was so dry she doubted she could spit if her life depended on it. She wouldn't even mind accepting a drink dosed with the vile tincture at this point. Hell, she'd even welcome sleeping powder being added to it. That seemed preferable to lying there wide awake and aching for Dougall. Truly, the man was like pastry, so yummy that she wanted to gorge herself on him.

Muttering under her breath, she tossed the linens and furs aside and sat up in bed, then got to her feet to cross to the door. She considered dressing first, but every last one of the men had seen her in her nightgown. Besides, she suspected Dougall would be in a similar state to her own, wide awake, restless and wanting. If so, he'd no doubt insist on fetching the drink for her anyway so that he could dose it again with the strengthening tincture. Well, she thought, unless he wanted to risk slipping into the bedchamber with her while the others slept.

Murine supposed she should be shocked at her own thoughts and loose behavior, and she was sure she would be later. But right now she kept remembering the feel of his hands on her and the taste of him as he'd kissed her and she didn't give an owl's hoot that the church said 'twas wrong to enjoy such acts. She wanted Dougall, and God had made her this way so it couldn't be a sin.

Opening the door as soundlessly as she could, Murine peered out into the hall but couldn't see a darned thing. The fire below was dying and the dim light it gave off didn't reach up here. She wasn't even sure where Dougall and Acair were lying. After a hesitation, she took a step out into the hall, stopping abruptly as she accidentally kicked someone.

"Sorry," she whispered.

When a snore was her answer, Murine grimaced. She recognized that snore from the journey to Buchanan. So much for Dougall lying out here yearning for her, she thought grimly as a second snore answered from somewhere to her right. Both men were dead to the world. Judging by the various snuffles and snores coming from below, it seemed she was the only one awake.

Clucking under her tongue, Murine lifted her foot again, this time feeling around with her toes until she found a bit of floor to step on. Dougall must be lying on his back directly across the threshold of the door, she decided as she tiptoed over him. She had to take a large step to get past him. Sighing her relief once she'd managed the task, Murine moved cautiously toward where she thought the top step was. She moved with her hands stretched out before her in search of the railing, and her toes leading the way, feeling for floor before she stepped. Fortunately, she managed to find the top of the stairs without incident.

Breathing out a little sigh of relief then, she moved cautiously down the steps, her gaze seeking out the men stretched out on the main floor. Conran, Geordie and Niels had the bed, Conran and Geordie sleeping with their heads at one end and Niels in the middle with his head at the other end to make room for them all. Rory was curled up on furs on one of the trestle tables and Alick had done the same on another. It seemed none of them had been eager to sleep on the cold stone floor. She couldn't blame them when there were no rushes to keep the cold from creeping into the bones. At least the floor upstairs where Acair and Dougall were sleeping was wood and not stone.

Murine made it down the stairs without incident and was fetching herself some cider from the fresh casket the boys had brought back with them when she thought she heard something outside. She stilled briefly and then straightened, peering toward the shuttered windows as she listened. A moment passed and she was about to return to her chore when the nearer shutters crashed open and something afire flew into the room and smashed on the stone floor by the trestle tables, fire splashing outward like liquid from a spilled drink.

Even as Murine sucked in a startled breath, two more missiles flew through the window, one landing in front of the fireplace, the other extremely close to the bed. Dropping the half-full mug of cider, Murine shrieked, "Fire!" at the top of her lungs.

Rory was on the table nearest her and sat up as if she'd stabbed him. He took one wild-eyed look around, and then bounded into action, tossing aside his furs and rolling to the floor. But even as she breathed her relief at that, she was noting that no one else had moved at all.

The first ball of fire had crashed under Alick's table and

spilled outward beneath it, but the man was still sleeping, a sausage roasting over the pit. Murine rushed to the end of the table where the fire had not reached and grabbed his ankles, shaking him violently. "Wake up! Alick! Wake up!"

"Get out of here, Murine," Rory barked, pulling her away from the table and pushing her toward the door. "I'll get him."

Murine didn't argue, she merely rushed to the bed that was starting to catch fire, and slapped at Geordie's face, shouting at him to wake up. When he didn't stir, she leaned over and slapped Conran next.

"They've been dosed with something," Rory growled, suddenly beside her. She glanced around to see that Alick was off the table and the cottage door was open. Rory must have got his youngest brother out and come back, she realized.

"See if ye can wake Dougall and Acair," Rory ordered, dragging Conran off the bed.

Nodding, Murine whirled and rushed for the stairs. She hadn't gone there first because the three men in the bed had been in more peril, but now she raced up the stairs. Panic was making her heart race, and she couldn't help noticing that she was feeling none of the exhaustion that just walking up these same steps hours ago had raised in her.

The fire spreading below added a lot of light to the situation, and this time, Murine had no trouble making out who was who and where the men lay. Dougall had fallen asleep in front of the door. Acair was a couple feet to the left of him on the landing. She tried to wake Dougall first, slapping him viciously several times, but then gave up to do the same to his uncle. Much to her relief, while Dougall hadn't stirred at all, Acair opened his eyes and mumbled with confusion.

"Wake up," she ordered, tugging on the man's hand. If she could get him up, he could help her with Dougall, she thought, pulling at him in an effort to get him to sit up.

"What's about, lass?" he slurred, his eyes trying to drift shut.

"Ye ha'e to get up," she growled, and reached out to twist his ear, hoping the pain would help. It seemed to. At least he let out a roar and sat up abruptly at the action.

"Damn, woman, what the devil?" He was still slurring, but was at least, somewhat alert now so Murine continued to pull at him.

"Ye ha'e to get up. Fire!" she added, shrieking it into his face.

"Fire?" Acair started to struggle to his feet, and managed to do so with her help, but he had to lean on her heavily to remain upright. There was no way he was going to be any help with Dougall, she realized unhappily, but ushered him to the stairs. She then paused, staring at the room below with dismay.

In the few minutes she'd been above stairs, the fire had spread below. Flames were licking at the bottom of the stairs now, and the trestle tables were both pyres burning brightly, as were the chairs by the fire and even the bed. The bed was empty now though, she saw with relief. Rory must have got his brothers out.

Murine barely had the thought when Dougall's brother dashed back in through the cottage door and came to a dead halt as he peered at the burning stairs and then up at her. A struggle took place on his face, and then he shook his head and moved along the floor below the stairs until he was past the part that was burning.

"Leave him and jump, Murine. I'll catch ye," he ordered, a wealth of emotions in his voice. She heard grief, regret and determination in the tone. He was making the only sensible choice. Trying to save the only one he thought he could.

Well, to hell with that, she thought grimly and didn't even take the time to think about it, but stepped out from under Acair Buchanan's arm and gave him a shove that sent him tumbling.

Much to her relief, the man crumpled and rolled down the stairs like a Shrovetide football before unrolling and coming to a halt on his back just past the fire at the base of the stairs. Murine couldn't see any obvious injuries on him. There were no limbs at odd angles, or bloody wounds on his head, but he was definitely not conscious anymore.

"Get him out o' here," she yelled at Rory as he rushed to his uncle. "I'll get Dougall out the bedchamber window."

Not waiting for a response, she rushed back to Dougall then. He and Acair had brought up furs to sleep on. Murine bent to grab hold of his now by the end by his feet. She then dragged his legs away from the wall and toward the stairs, turning his body so that his head slid toward the door. As she straightened from the effort, Murine glanced toward the stairs and briefly considered sending him down the stairs on his fur. But in the short few moments it had taken her to shift him around, the fire had moved fast, reaching halfway up the stairs. She didn't want to risk his stopping and getting caught in the fire.

Mouth tightening, she hurried around to his head and grabbed the fur there to start dragging Dougall into the bed-chamber. The wooden slats were hot under her feet, warmed by the fire below. They didn't have much time, she realized a bit frantically, and drew on her reserves of energy to move more quickly as she dragged Dougall across the floor to the window.

It was only once there that she considered the problem of how to get him out the window. Dougall was a big man with wide shoulders and lots of heavy muscles. Before this she'd appreciated that about him, but in that moment she would have been happier were he smaller like Alick, who hadn't quite grown into manhood yet.

Straightening her shoulders, she opened the shutters and peered out into the darkness. If Rory was there, she couldn't see him. Leaving the shutters open, she hurried back to Dougall's feet and grabbed the edge of the fur there again, to turn him so that he faced the window feet first. She then dropped his feet and raced back to kneel by his head.

Leaning forward, Murine pressed her hands to his shoulders and pushed forward, moving his upper body toward the window now, and forcing his legs to bend. His knees started out rising, as his butt moved forward, but then fell to the side so that he lay somewhat twisted at the waist, his back and shoulders flat on the floor, his hips and legs turned to the side in a bent position.

Murine straightened then and moved over to grab him about the knees and lift his legs up onto the window ledge. They were much heavier than she'd expected. Still she managed to hook his legs over the ledge, so that his feet dangled out the window. Murine then paused to consider her next move. She'd thought to get herself behind him, raise his shoulders to lean against her chest and then force him up and out the window, but she was having serious doubts over being able to manage that. Unfortunately, she didn't have any other ideas and there was precious little time to come up with one.

Gritting her teeth, she knelt behind his head, scooted forward until her knees were on either side of his ears, then lifted his head with her hands and quickly closed her knees beneath it. She then started easing forward on her knees, lifting his shoulders onto them as she went, which forced his head upward against her stomach. She continued doing that until she had the man folded like linen cloth, his chest pressed against his upper legs where they hung down from the ledge, and his head lolling back on her shoulder.

She'd rather hoped that his butt would be off the ground at this point and she'd be able to push him up and out of the window, but his legs were long and his behind was still on the floor, which was almost unbearably hot now. She was beginning to feel like meat in a skillet.

Forcing herself to calm down and consider the situation, Murine eyed the window and Dougall's position. She needed leverage to get him up to the ledge. Alternately, she needed enough weight on the other side to pull him over and out, and she needed one or the other quickly.

The idea when it came was a mad one, she was sure. However, it was also the only one she had . . . and she needed material to do it. Murine glanced back toward the bed and the linens there and sighed to herself. She'd just wasted several minutes getting Dougall to this position and now was going to have let him lie flat again. But there was nothing else for it.

Grinding her teeth, she scuttled back from him and eased his head back to the floor, then rushed over to the bed. A glance out the door as she tore the linens off the bed showed her that the flames had reached the top of the stairs.

The room was also filling with smoke, she noted, and rushed over to slam the door closed, before hurrying to the window again. The air was better there, fresh air coming in to push back the smoke. Dropping the bottom linen on the floor, Murine stepped on it to give her feet a break from the rising heat of the wood, and began to rip the top linen into strips the length of the linen and a good six inches wide that she quickly tied together. The swath of makeshift rope it created was much longer than she thought she'd need, so she stopped then and quickly tied one end of the linen rope around Dougall's chest under his arms. She then glanced to the shutters. Both looked sturdy enough, but Murine gave each a tug just to test them. When the one on the right shifted a bit at her tug, she turned her attention to the shutter on the left and slung the free end of the linen over it.

Murine didn't stop to think about what she was doing then. She was too afraid she'd talk herself out of it. So, she climbed up on the ledge, pulled the free end of the makeshift rope under the shutter and tied that end around her chest under her arms.

Murine then turned to peer at Dougall, sent up a silent prayer that this would work and stepped back off the ledge. She fell easily at first, then felt a slight jerk around her chest as the rope pulled tight. She continued to fall then though, her momentum dragging Dougall up off the floor of the bed chamber and toward the top of the shutter. She saw him pulled out of the window and up the shutter to the top and then they both jerked to a halt and she cried out in pain as the makeshift rope cinched around her chest and dug into the skin under her arms.

Sucking in a deep breath, Murine glanced down to see how far she was from the ground. Her eyes widened with dismay, though, when she saw that it wasn't ground beneath her, but water. How had she failed to make note of the fact that there was a moat around the damned hunting lodge when she'd looked out the window earlier? she wondered. But knew the answer. She hadn't looked out at all during daylight other than to note that the sky was gray and threatening. She'd never looked down. And it had been too dark to make out anything from the window when she'd peered out moments ago.

Had she known there was water . . . Well, she hadn't had a choice, she would have done the exact same thing. But at least then she would have been aware that getting Dougall out the window was not the only obstacle. Now she had to worry about dragging his unconscious body out of the water. If they ever actually got into the water and didn't just dangle there from the shutters like—

Her thoughts died as she heard a cracking sound from above, and then the shutter tore away from the wall, and she was falling again.

Murine glanced up as she hit the water and immediately recognized her next problem; Dougall was going to land on top of her. He was hurtling toward her feet first.

DOUGALL TURNED ON HIS BACK, AND STRETCHED THEN yawned mightily as he began to shake off the claws of sleep that seemed to be cloying at him.

"Finally."

Dougall blinked his eyes open and stared blankly at his elder brother Aulay as several realizations struck him. First, while he'd gone to sleep on a hard bed of furs on the floor in the hall at the hunting lodge, he was waking in a bed. Second, it was his own bed in his own bedchamber at Buchanan.

"What the hell!" he muttered, sitting up, then glanced sharply to Aulay. "Murine?"

"She's fine," his brother assured him quickly. "She's sleeping in Saidh's room. Rory's watching over her."

Dougall relaxed a little at this knowledge, but then asked with confusion, "What happened? How did we get here?"

"Ye drank poisoned cider," Aulay said dryly and when Dougall just peered at him blankly, asked, "Ye recall the cider the lads brought to the lodge with the supplies?"

"Aye," Dougall said slowly. "We forgot to unload it. We all went out and grabbed something. The casket of cider was left behind though. I saw it as I turned away, but assumed someone else had grabbed it when I got done carrying the chest o' gowns upstairs fer Murine. Apparently no one had though. When the original casket we'd brought with us the first day ran out, we realized no one had fetched in the casket and Geordie went out to get it."

"Aye, well someone dosed it with something between the lads' arrival and when Geordie fetched the cider in," Aulay announced. "At least, that's what Rory thinks. He said he and Murine were the only ones who didn't drink from it?"

"Aye, ye ken he does no' like cider, and Murine was nursing a cider from the first casket all day. She didn't care for the tincture I mixed in it, but was determined to get it down."

"Aye, well, her not liking the tincture saved all yer lives," Aulay said solemnly. "Murine was awake when the fire pots came flying through the lower windows. She woke Rory, but they couldn't wake any o' the rest o' ye. Rory had to cart Alick, Geordie, Niels and Conran out. Then she got Uncle Acair down the stairs and he carted him out as well."

"Got me down the stairs?"

Dougall glanced to the door at that amused question to see his uncle limping into the room.

"The way I hear it, she tossed me down the stairs like a sack o' potatoes," Acair said on a laugh.

Dougall raised his eyebrows. "Ye don't sound too upset about it."

"Aye, well, she saved me life, did she no'?" Acair said solemnly, settling on the edge of his bed. "Rory came running in from getting yer brothers out, saw Murine standing at the top o' the burning stairs with me hanging off her like a drunk on Sunday and ye unconscious on the floor. He says he knew he could no' save us all and told her to leave us both and jump over the rail and he'd catch her. But she would no' leave us. He says she sent me flying down the stairs, and left him to get me out while she dragged yer sorry arse out o' the hall, and across the bedchamber to the window."

"And Rory climbed in through the window to pull me out," Dougall guessed.

Acair snorted at the suggestion. "The hell he did. She got ye out herself," he announced and then nodded firmly when Dougall's eyes widened in surprise. "Made rope out of a bed linen, used the shutter to set up a pulley affair, tied one end o' her rope to you, and one end to herself, then jumped out the window like a bride on the eve of an unwanted wedding. Her weight pulled ye up and out the window and then ye both crashed into the moat when the shutter gave way. Damned near killed her when ye landed on top o' her too," he added grimly. "Fortunately, Rory had finished getting me out by then and rushed around the moat, getting there just in time to help get ye both out o' the water."

"Damn," Dougall breathed.

"Aye," Acair nodded solemnly. "Ye've got yerself a fine woman there, Dougall Buchanan. Smart as a whip, that one. Brave too. And if ye don't get her before a priest ere her brother catches up with her, I think I just might ha'e to beat ye senseless." His mouth tightened. "Right after I kill that wastrel brother of hers."

Nodding, Dougall tossed aside the furs covering him and got up out of the bed, only to pause and ask, "How did we get here though?"

"Murine and Rory piled the lot o' ye in the supply cart and brought ye back to Buchanan," Aulay answered, standing as well. He shook his head and added, "After all she'd been through I worried she'd reopened her wound, but Rory says while she split a couple stitches she came out much better than she should. He said this won't set her back much in healing."

"Thank God," Dougall growled and headed for the door, announcing, "We can no' risk staying here."

"Nay. Danvries could return," Aulay agreed. "But ye can no' stay at the lodge. Rory says 'tis ruined."

Dougall was frowning over that news as he stepped into the hall.

Following, Aulay added, "I sent a couple men to MacDonnell this morning, with instructions to return the minute Danvries leaves. I'm thinking ye should head there when they return and have the priest at MacDonnell marry ye. The sooner that's done, the better all the way around."

Dougall paused in the hallway and turned to his brother. "Ye think he drugged the cider and set the fire?"

"Nay," Aulay said firmly. "It just does no' make sense fer him to kill her when he planned to make money from her. But ye came damned close to dying last night and if nothing else, yer marrying her will see Murine safe if the next attack kills ye."

Dougall merely turned and continued on toward Saidh's room. He still couldn't think of anyone who would want to kill him. But the arrow couldn't have been meant for Murine. As Aulay had said, it made no sense for Danvries to want her dead and he couldn't imagine she'd made any enemies. Except maybe . . .

Pausing abruptly, he turned to face Aulay. "That woman who tried to kill our Saidh and Lady Sinclair?"

"Aye?" Aulay paused too, his brows pulling together in a frown as he tried to sort out what Dougall was thinking.

"What happened to her?" he asked.

"I don't know," Aulay admitted.

"She would ha'e been executed," Uncle Acair announced, catching up to them.

Dougall noticed again that the older man was limping. There was no sign that he'd broken anything in the tumble down the stairs Murine had sent him on, but he must have twisted an ankle or something, he thought and then shifted his attention from the man's gait to his face as his uncle added, "Or banished to a nunnery if her family was powerful enough to keep her alive."

Dougall nodded slowly. That made sense, he thought and then pointed out, "If she was no' executed, she could be seeking revenge on Murine for foiling her plan. Or her family might be seeking it for her."

"Possible," his uncle murmured thoughtfully. "Her actions must ha'e been a great stain on the family name when she was caught."

"I'll look into it," Aulay said quietly.

"Thank ye," Dougall muttered and then jerked around to catch Alick by the arm and pull him to a halt when he tried to rush past them. The door to Saidh's room was the only one left at this end of the hall, so he knew where the lad had been headed, but still barked, "Where do ye think ye're going?"

"To give Murine me shirt," Alick answered, tugging at his arm.

"Yer shirt?" Dougall peered down at the soft linen in the boy's hands, then back to his face. "Why the devil would she want one o' yer shirts?"

"Because all o' Saidh's and Mother's gowns that we gave her went up in flames when the lodge burned," Alick pointed out with a grimace. "The only thing we left behind here were a pair o' braies Saidh likes to wear under her gowns. Murine's going to wear those, but she's got no dress to wear o'er them so"—he raised the hand holding the shirt and shrugged—"she needs something to cover the top o' her."

"God's teeth," Dougall muttered, jerking the shirt from Alick's hand and turning to continue on to the door to Saidh's room.

There was no damned way his woman was running about in braies and a shirt. No way on God's green earth.

They'd sort out something else . . . and quickly. Because Murine was obviously awake, and his instinct was telling him to bundle her up and get her out of there. He'd rather camp in the MacDonnell woods and approach the castle where his sister and her husband lived the minute Danvries left than wait to hear from the men Aulay had sent. He wanted the wedding done and Murine safe as soon as possible.

Chapter 13

$\mathcal{D}$OUGALL WATCHED MURINE RAISE HERSELF SLIGHTLY ON the mare she was riding, astride, to tug at the bottom of her braies as if they were crawling into places only he should be, and had to swallow the sudden rush of liquid in his mouth. He'd have been more than happy to tug at the braies for her, and not just to stop their crawling. He'd like to drag them right off, pull her onto his lap and slide into her warm, moist—

"I'm surprised ye let Murine wear the braies," Aulay said, interrupting his lascivious thoughts.

"I can no' *let* her do anything. She's no' me wife yet," Dougall growled. They were the exact words Murine had said to him when he'd reached her room and announced she couldn't wear the braies, that they'd have to find something else. She'd followed that up by announcing that there *was* nothing else, and there was no time for her to sew anything since she was quite sure they didn't want to remain at Buchanan any longer than necessary and risk her brother returning to find her there.

Dougall hadn't been able to argue with any of it, especially the part about remaining at Buchanan. He himself had wanted her away from there as soon as possible. So, he'd tossed her the linen shirt, turned on his heel and marched out to order his horse readied. By the time Murine was dressed and came below, his horse, as well as seven others, had been waiting at the base of the keep steps. Six were each of his brothers' mounts, the seventh was the mare he'd gifted Murine with when he'd decided to marry her. He'd learned then that Aulay had decided that the whole family should travel to MacDonnell. All of his brothers wanted to attend the wedding. They also wanted to see their sister, Saidh.

Understanding this, Uncle Acair had offered to remain behind and look after Buchanan until Aulay's return. While their uncle hadn't broken anything in the tumble he'd taken down the stairs, and he was sorry to miss the wedding himself, he'd also apparently gained several bumps and bruises that would have made riding extremely uncomfortable.

Dougall was glad to have his brothers along to help keep Murine safe, but was less happy about her riding her own mount. While she hadn't shown signs of fainting since before she'd been shot with the arrow, she'd also spent most of that time asleep. Now, on top of everything else, he had to worry about her fainting and falling off her horse.

And that was the only reason his eyes hadn't left her braies-clad bottom since they'd departed Buchanan two hours ago, he assured himself and then almost snorted aloud at his own lie. Damn, she looked fine in those braies. Too fine. They made him want to lay her down, strip them off and bite her on the arse . . . and that was not an urge he'd ever experienced before with anyone. But it was just one of the ideas of what he'd like to do to her that had rolled through his mind during this ride.

Dougall was toying with some of those ideas when Geordie, Niels and Alick came charging around the bend ahead, racing toward them. Dougall immediately dug his heels into his horse to urge him to a run, aware that Aulay was doing the same. They quickly caught up with Murine where she rode with Conran and Rory on either side. They'd spaced themselves out that way on purpose. Since they expected trouble to come from ahead, they'd had Geordie, Niels and Alick ride out in front of the group to watch for approaching parties. Conran and Rory had stayed with Murine to guard her, and Aulay and Dougall had ridden a good distance behind. At least they'd started out a good distance behind, but Dougall had found himself reducing the distance with every mile they'd passed, finding himself drawn to the woman like a bee to a flower.

"What is it?" he barked when his brothers reached them and reined in. He scanned the road ahead tensely as he waited for the answer, mentally preparing himself to drag Murine off her horse to his own and race off into the woods with her if the lads had bad news.

"Our boys are on the road ahead, riding this way," Geordie announced.

Dougall relaxed a bit in the saddle.

"Danvries must have left MacDonnell," Aulay commented.

Dougall nodded. Aulay had told him that he'd sent men ahead to find out if Danvries was still at MacDonnell. If he was, they'd been ordered to wait until Murine's brother and his party left, and then ride back with that news. If they were returning, Danvries must have left MacDonnell, no doubt headed north toward Sinclair. Unless he was heading south and the Buchanan men were just riding ahead of them, trying to reach Buchanan with a warning ere Danvries could get there.

That last thought made Dougall frown and he asked, "Did ye talk to them?"

"Nay. They were still a good distance away when we turned back to bring ye the news," Niels admitted. "We thought we'd do that ere riding to meet them."

Dougall nodded. "You and Alick ride ahead now and make sure they're no' bringing news that Danvries is headed this way. Signal us if he is, so we can get Murine off the road."

The two men immediately turned their horses and raced back the way they'd come. Dougall then urged his horse up between Conran's mount and Murine's mare. Hooking his arm around her waist, he dragged her from her horse and onto his lap.

"Just in case," he murmured by way of explanation as he watched his brothers ride away.

Murine didn't comment and simply slipped her arms around

his waist and shifted about to find a more comfortable position. Dougall glanced down then and found himself peering straight down the shirt she wore. While Alick was the smallest of the brothers, he was still quite a bit larger than Murine and the neckline was presently gaping, allowing him a perfect view of at least two thirds of the top of each breast. The only thing hidden from him were her nipples.

It was a damned fine sight, Dougall decided, fighting the urge to tug the cloth down and lavish the rounded globes with attention.

"Are ye still mad at me?"

Dougall blinked and glanced blankly to Murine's face at her question.

"Fer insisting on wearing the braies when ye did no' want me to," she explained.

"Oh." He shrugged, and admitted, "I was. But I've found I quite enjoy the view."

Murine's eyes widened and then she blushed at his words and ducked her head with shyness or embarrassment. Sadly, the action blocked his view of her breasts.

"There's Geordie."

Dougall jerked his gaze to the road ahead to see his brother ride into view and rein in to give him the signal for the all-clear. Danvries had not headed south. They could ride straight to MacDonnell.

"Looks like the sup will be a wedding feast," Aulay said, and then added with a grin, "And judging by the way ye were looking down Murine's top, it's no' a moment too soon."

When Murine turned her face into his chest with a moan of embarrassment, Dougall suggested his brother do something that was physically impossible and put his spurs to his horse. He was eager to get Murine to MacDonnell and get her wedded.

"TRULY?" MURINE ASKED, WATCHING SAIDH CLOSELY. THEY had arrived a little more than two hours ago. There had been greetings and quick explanations and then Saidh had rushed Murine above stairs to her bedchamber to "prepare" her for the wedding. She'd been bathed and powdered, and now Saidh's maid, Joyce, was fussing with her hair while Saidh searched through her chest of gowns for one Murine could wear.

"Truly, what?" Saidh asked distractedly, holding up a gown, considering it, then tossing it aside.

"Ye do no' mind? About Dougall marrying me?"

"Murine," Saidh drew out her name with exasperation, dropped the gown she'd just picked up and crossed the room to clasp her by the arms. "I truly am glad that ye're marrying Dougall," she assured her solemnly, then smiled wryly and admitted, "It ne'er occurred to me until Dougall announced he was wedding ye, but I think the two o' ye are perfect for each other. I should ha'e dragged ye home to him that first time we met."

Murine let her breath out on a relieved little sigh, and pulled away from Joyce's fussing to hug her friend. "Thank goodness."

"I do no' ken why ye'd think I would no' be pleased," Saidh commented, hugging her back. "Ye've become a dear friend. I'm happy ye and Dougall found each other."

Murine's eyes opened and she frowned at the words and stepped back to remind her, "I ha'e no dower, Saidh. Does he marry me, he gets only me."

"And that is a lot," Saidh assured her firmly. Releasing her then, she turned to walk back across the room. Bending to continue her sorting of gowns, she added, "Dowers are quickly spent and soon forgotten. The bride is not and ye will be a fine wife to Dougall. He's lucky to ha'e ye."

Murine sagged with relief at these words. She'd been concerned that Saidh might think Dougall deserved a bride with a dower, not a bride with a brother who not only gambled away her dower, but then tried to whore her out like a—

"Do ye ken?" Saidh said suddenly, interrupting her thoughts and Murine glanced over as her friend turned from the chest to stare at her briefly before pointing out, "We'll be sisters."

Murine blinked at the announcement and then a slow smile blossomed on her face. "Aye, we will."

"Me best friend and me sister," Saidh said with a smile and shook her head as she turned back to her chest. "I ne'er imagined for a minute the day we arrived at Sinclair that I would gain so much and it would all turn out so well."

"Neither did I," Murine murmured and realized that it *had* all turned out well. She'd learned on arriving that Saidh had never received the messages she'd sent to her. She'd also learned that Saidh had sent her several as well. None of which had reached her. Montrose had obviously been blocking the messages both ways. And probably any messages to and from Jo and Edith too. They were all still her friends. And now, she was about to marry Dougall and not just gain a wonderful husband, but Saidh for sister, six wonderful brothers, and countless cousins, aunts and uncles.

The thought of the number of relatives she was gaining was rather dizzying. On the ride here, Conran and Rory had been discussing how disappointed their extended family would be at missing Dougall's wedding. Rory had even suggested that perhaps they should hold a belated wedding feast for the whole family at some later date after everything was cleared up and they were sure she was safe. Curious, Murine had asked about their family and the men had started listing off the Buchanans . . . and there were many. The Buchanans were a prolific lot. She was gaining a large family and while it couldn't make up for the loss of her parents and brothers, it would go a long way toward helping soothe the hurt.

At the moment, her future looked very bright indeed.

So long as Montrose didn't arrive before they could exchange vows, she thought a little anxiously.

And so long as whoever had shot her with an arrow, and then drugged the cider and set the hunting lodge on fire didn't attack again and hurt or kill any of her new family.

Perhaps everything was not as settled as she'd hoped, Murine now thought with a frown.

"Here!" Saidh straightened from the chest and held up a golden gown with satisfaction. "This will look perfect on ye. Do ye like it?" she asked, turning the gown so Murine could get a better look.

"Aye," she whispered, reaching out to touch it when Saidh brought it closer. The gown was beautiful.

"'Twill bring out the gold in yer hair," Saidh murmured, glancing to her head and then smiled and added, "Ye've out-done yerself, Joyce. Her hair looks perfect."

"Thank ye, m'lady," Joyce murmured as she stepped away. "Shall we get her dressed then?"

"I'll help her with that," Saidh said quickly. "Why do ye no' go see if ye can help below? I want a few minutes to talk to Murine alone . . . about the night ahead," she added meaning-fully.

"Ah. O' course," Joyce murmured, and then squeezing Mu-rine's arm she said, "Ye make a beautiful bride," before slipping from the room.

Murine watched her go, then turned reluctantly back to Saidh, wondering if she dare tell her that there was no talk nec-essary. Before she could decide, a knock sounded at the door and Saidh tossed the gold gown over the end of the bed and rushed to answer the summons. Murine watched her accept a tray from the woman in the hall with a thank-you, then push the door closed with her foot as she turned back into the room.

"Here we are," Saidh said cheerfully, carrying the tray to a table by the fire. "Ye go ahead and start dressing, and I'll pour us both some wine, then help ye with the stays," she suggested.

Nodding, Murine dropped the linen Joyce had wrapped around her after her bath and picked up the gown Saidh had set on the end of the bed. By the time she pulled on the gown and crossed the room to Saidh, the drinks were poured and waiting and Saidh had taken two other items from the tray and appeared to be contemplating them solemnly.

"Oh, good," Saidh said, noting her arrival. Setting down the loaf of bread and carrot she'd been considering, Saidh hurried to help her with her stays, then stepped back to look her over. Smiling, she said, "Perfect."

Murine grinned and relaxed a bit, then glanced to the loaf of bread and carrot and asked, "What's this?" The bread might have been meant as a snack to have with the wine, she supposed, but had no idea why the servants would send up a knobby, dirty carrot, so fresh from the ground there was still dirt clinging to it.

"Sit down," Saidh instructed, moving to the table to collect their wine.

Murine dutifully sat down, accepted her wine when Saidh held one out to her, then sipped at it, when Saidh raised her own drink to her lips. Much to her surprise, rather than sip at her own wine, Saidh downed the liquid in one long gulp, then set her goblet down with a little grimace.

"All right," Saidh murmured, picking up the loaf of bread and the carrot and turning to her. Holding the loaf up, she announced, "This is you."

Murine's eyebrows rose and she murmured uncertainly, "It is?"

Saidh frowned and peered at the loaf, then turned to set it on the table, pulled a *sgian-dubh* from her waist and sliced it in half. She then sliced a slit down the center of the loaf as well before setting down her *sgian-dubh* and turning back to Murine with them.

"*This* is you," she said, holding up the altered bread so the crusty side was against her hand and the soft center with the slit faced Murine. Raising the carrot, she added, "And this is Dougall."

"Oh," Murine breathed, suddenly understanding what Saidh was doing. Shaking her head, she murmured, "Saidh, I—"

"Do no' interrupt, Muri," Saidh admonished, using the nickname the other women had taken to using when they were all together. "This is difficult enough."

"Sorry," Murine murmured.

Saidh nodded, sighed, considered her props, and then stuck the carrot down the neckline of her gown between her breasts and moved back to the table to pour herself another goblet of wine. After downing that one as quickly as the first, she turned back to move in front of Murine again.

"Right. This is you, and this is—oh hell," she muttered, realizing she held the empty goblet instead of the carrot. The carrot was still in her décolletage. Saidh hurriedly set the empty goblet on the table, retrieved the carrot from her gown, then positioned herself in front of Murine and started again. "This is you, and this is Dougall."

She turned the loaf of bread so the open side with the slit faced the carrot, then proceeded to push the larger end of the carrot into the slit of the bread. "And this," she said, withdrawing and pushing the carrot back into the bread, "is what will happen tonight."

Murine stared at what Saidh was doing with the bread and carrot and thought to herself that this was the most pitiful thing she had ever seen. Had she not already been bedded by Dougall, she would most likely be horrified and dismayed at this display. Good Lord.

"But it's much nicer than this looks," Saidh assured her, continuing to thrust the carrot into the bread. She was missing the slit entirely, and mashing the bread with each push. "He'll kiss ye and such first, and ye'll get all excited and feel like punching him hard in the face." She jammed the carrot into the bread this time as if the carrot was her fist and the loaf his face. "But then ye'll feel like a little explosion has gone off in yer body and 'twill be so nice."

Much to Murine's relief, Saidh stopped beating up the bread with the carrot then and gave a little sigh. Whether it signified her relief that she had finished the explanations she'd felt she should give, or Saidh was thinking of how nice the release felt, Murine wasn't sure. She was still caught on the part about wanting to punch him hard in the face. Murine had never experienced quite that desire with Dougall yet. Mayhap he wasn't doing it right.

"Understand?" Saidh asked, eyeing her hopefully.

"Er . . . uh huh." Murine nodded quickly.

"Oh, thank God," Saidh muttered, tossing her props on the table and then dropping into the seat across from Murine's. She then eyed her barely touched goblet of wine and asked, "Are ye going to drink that?"

"Nay," Murine said with amusement, offering it to her. The whole ordeal had obviously distressed Saidh much more than her, she decided and thought it might be a good thing if Saidh had all sons and no daughters with Greer. The woman would never survive a house full of daughters.

"As I told Saidh, I knew Beathan Carmichael, and I find it hard to believe he'd leave Murine's care and future in the hands o' Montrose Danvries. He had little respect for his wife's son."

Murine glanced up from the chicken she was eating at that comment from Saidh's husband. The wedding had gone off without a hitch. The MacDonnell priest had been happy to preside over the wedding, and there had been no sudden arrival of Montrose to put an end to things. She was married and safe from his machinations, or at least she would be once they'd officially consummated their marriage.

That being the case, Murine had been happy to settle down to the wedding feast and enjoy the meal, and without the usual bride's fear of the night to come. She already knew what to expect, and not because of Saidh's odd visual presentation.

Murine was seated beside Saidh with their husbands on either side of them, Dougall next to Murine and Greer next to

Saidh. Dougall's brothers had then taken up seats on either side of the men and the conversation had been light and filled with congratulations and well wishes as the food was carried out. Murine had let it drift around her as she ate, but now lifted her head at that comment from Greer.

"I was thinking the same thing," Dougall responded solemnly.

"Well, it bothered me enough that I've had an ear out on the matter and I've learned a couple o' interesting things," Greer informed him.

Dougall stiffened with interest. "What ha'e ye learned?"

"Murine's cousin, Connor, is the second son o' the Barclay and her father's sister," Greer announced, and then added, "The Barclay died a couple years back, leaving all to the eldest son."

Dougall shrugged, appearing disappointed. "That's no unusual. 'Tis common for the eldest to inherit the title and land. Aulay got Buchanan and became laird when our father died."

"Aye, but I bet yer father left something to each o' ye other boys," Greer said solemnly.

"Aye, we each got a parcel o' land and some coin," Conran said from Dougall's other side.

"Well, Barclay left Connor no' even a farthing. It seems he was sure his wife was unfaithful and Connor was no' his son."

Dougall raised his eyebrows at that and looked thoughtful.

"I also learned that less than a year after the father's death, the brother banished Connor from Barclay. The rumor is there were some unexplained deaths and accidents around the new laird that nearly took his life. He apparently suspected his brother but could no' prove anything."

"So he banished him," Dougall murmured.

"Aye." Greer nodded and then cautioned, "'Tis just rumor though, I have a man looking into it, but it's no' been verified yet."

Dougall nodded his understanding, and picked up a chicken leg. Murine turned her own attention back to her food as he bit into the drumstick.

"There's more," Saidh announced when Greer turned his attention back to his own food. "Edith wrote me. She'd just returned from court with her family and says yer cousin Connor was there when she first arrived. She said a friend o' yer father's was there. Laird MacIntyre, I think it was."

"Aye, Laird MacIntyre and me father were dear friends," Murine verified with a smile at the thought of the man. He'd been a large part of her life while growing up.

"Well, Edith wrote that Laird MacIntyre cornered Connor at court and confronted him in front of everyone about his getting the castle and title while ye were shuttled off to yer brother's in England. He said, 'Beatie would ne'er do that to wee Murine.' He did no' believe it fer a minute, and was demanding to see the will to make sure it was no' a forgery or something."

"Ye ne'er told me that!" Greer exclaimed suddenly.

Saidh turned to offer him an apology. "I ken, I'm sorry. But that was the letter the messenger brought just as me brothers and Murine rode in. I did no' get the chance to read it until after I finished helping her dress." She shrugged apologetically. "And then I did no' get the chance to tell ye what with the wedding and everything."

"Oh." Greer squeezed her hand and bent to press a kiss to her forehead. Then he straightened and asked. "Did Connor produce the will?"

Saidh shook her head. "He said he would hardly bring it to court. It was at Carmichael, and MacIntyre was welcome to visit him there if he wanted to look at it," Saidh answered and then turned to Murine and said, "Ye've no' seen the will, ha'e ye?"

She shook her head.

"Were ye no' there for the reading after he died?" Dougall asked with a frown.

"Nay," Murine said quietly. "I was at Sinclair when father died. Montrose showed up there, broke the news of father's death, and took me directly to England. I have no' been to Carmichael since I left for Sinclair. But," she added as everyone fell silent. "I doubt the will is forged. Connor was the beneficiary and he had never been to Carmichael ere he got the news he'd inherited the castle and title," she pointed out

"But Danvries was," Greer said quietly. "I was told he arrived just before yer father died."

Murine nodded. "I gather he went to Carmichael in the hopes that Mother would give him more coin. She'd given him some in the past when he'd gambled too deep," she explained.

"But yer mother was dead by then," Saidh pointed out.

"Aye, but he didn't know that," Murine said, then grimaced and explained. "So much happened in such a short time. First me brothers died, then Mother was ill, and then Father got sick as well." Murine paused and then admitted with embarrassment, "In truth, I did no' even think to write Montrose to let him know. I don't think Father did either." Feeling guilty that she could forget to write her half brother and let him know that their mother was dead, she tried to explain. "Montrose was not really a part of our life. He lived in England and showed up at Carmichael perhaps a handful of times over the last ten years, and then it was usually to beg a favor or money from Mother."

"And she gave it to him?" Aulay asked curiously.

Murine nodded.

"What did yer father think o' that?" Dougall asked quietly.

Murine smiled crookedly. "He hated it. The only fights they ever had were about it. He used to berate her fer giving it to him, saying Montrose should learn to stand on his own two feet."

"Which makes it even stranger that yer father would leave ye in his care," Dougall pointed out grimly.

"Aye," Greer agreed.

It was Aulay who said, "I'm thinkin' MacIntyre had it right and ye might want to see this will, lass. Something does no' smell right here."

Murine frowned, but before she could protest, Greer asked, "Ye say Connor was never at Carmichael, but Danvries showed up just ere yer father died?" When Murine nodded, he glanced to Saidh and back before saying, "Saidh told me that the death of yer father came as something o' a shock? That he had been recuperating when ye left fer Sinclair?"

"Aye," she murmured. "He was well on the mend. I would no' ha'e left had that no' been the case."

"Murine told us that on the journey to Buchanan," Alick announced. "What of it?"

Greer opened his mouth, then closed it and bent to whisper something in Saidh's ear. Her eyebrows rose, but then she stood and glanced at Murine as she announced, "I'm thinking it's time to get ye ready for the bedding."

Murine blinked up at her in surprise and then felt a blush heat her face as the men all began to cheer in agreement. Sticking out her tongue at the lot of them, she got to her feet and caught Saidh's arm to drag her away from the table as quickly as possible.

Honestly, she hadn't been at all worried about the bedding, but that was because she'd only been thinking about the bedding itself, and not the bedding ceremony that preceded it. Now Murine was beginning to realize how embarrassing it might be. Good Lord, having so many male relatives might turn out to be much less enjoyable than she'd expected.

DOUGALL WATCHED SAIDH AND MURINE RUSH UPSTAIRS, waited until the bedchamber door closed behind them and then turned to peer at Greer. "Ye wanted Saidh to take Murine above stairs because ye did no' want me wife to ken that ye're thinking her half brother may ha'e killed her father."

"Aye," he admitted with regret, and then pointed out, "Ye have to admit, 'tis odd that Murine's father appeared to be recovering when she left for Sinclair, but then died abruptly just days later *after* Danvries got there."

"And then a will was produced that basically cut Murine off from everything but her dower," Aulay said thoughtfully.

"But Danvries did no' benefit from her father's death," Dougall pointed out. "Connor did. If Danvries was going to kill the man and switch out the will, would he no' have switched it fer one that profited him more?"

"Danvries got control of her dower," Greer pointed out.

It was Conran who snorted at that. "Her dower was Waverly Place, a manor house. A nice manor house," he conceded, "But nothing compared to Carmichael. And from the little we know of the man, Montrose is a greedy bugger. If he was going to kill her father and switch the man's will for another, he would have made sure the forged will left everything to him."

Dougall nodded, but his mind was turning over new possibilities and after a moment he said, "Mayhap it did in the end." When the others peered at him in question, he pointed out, "If he was in cahoots with Connor, he might ha'e got much more than the dower, just not in the will."

"That's more than possible," Greer agreed, nodding slowly. "And ye have to admit, if that's what happened, 'twas a damned clever scheme."

"Aye," Aulay agreed. "Danvries switches the will and helps Beathan to his grave, but is never suspected because Connor is the only one who appears to gain from the death. And Connor gains but is never suspected because he was nowhere near Carmichael Castle or Beathan ere the will was read."

Conran frowned, then turned to Dougall and said, "I'm thinkin' we need to take Murine to see this will."

The other men all nodded in agreement.

Chapter 14

$\mathcal{M}$URINE STRETCHED SLEEPILY AND TURNED ONTO HER SIDE with a little yawn.

"Good morn, wife."

Blinking her eyes open at that husky voice, she peered at the man lying on his side facing her. Dougall. Her husband. Yesterday they'd been wedded, and last night she'd definitely been bedded . . . several times. The memory made her smile and acknowledge, if only to herself, that it had made the embarrassment of the bedding ceremony almost worthwhile. Almost. Good Lord, those Buchanan lads liked to tease. Murine didn't think she'd ever forget their hoots, hollers and the ribald comments as they'd lifted the linen to put Dougall in bed next to her and got a glimpse of her lying there naked. Murine had wanted the bed to open up and swallow her.

"What are ye thinking about?" Dougall asked softly, reaching out to run his fingers lightly across her cheek.

"About last night," Murine admitted with a crooked smile.

"Oh?" he asked with interest, easing a little closer in bed and letting his fingers trail down along her neck now. "And what were ye thinking about last night?"

"That it almost made it worth putting up with yer brothers' teasing during the bedding ceremony," she admitted.

"Almost?" Dougall asked with feigned offense. "Then I did something wrong. Mayhap I should try again."

"Mayhap ye should," she agreed just before his mouth covered hers. He'd barely begun to kiss her when pounding sounded at the door.

"We've come fer the sheets!" Aulay bellowed through the wooden door and pounded again.

Dougall groaned with disgust and rolled away to get to his feet, bellowing, "Hang on to yer swords. I'm coming."

Snatching up his tartan from the floor, he tossed it to her, suggesting, "Wrap that around yerself, love. They won't wait long." Then he bent to grab his shirt and began to tug it on as he walked to the door.

Murine stared after him briefly, held still by his calling her love, then quickly scrambled off the bed and wrapped the tartan around herself as she realized he was about to open the door.

"Ah, good, ye both survived the night," Aulay said with amusement, stepping into the room and to the side as Alick, Conran, Geordie and Niels moved toward the bed. His gaze slid over Dougall in naught but his shirt, which barely covered his more interesting bits, and one eyebrow quirked upward. "I'd ha'e expected ye to be up and dressed by now. The rest o' the castle is up enjoying breaking their fast."

"I felt like a bit o' a lie-in," Dougall said dryly.

Murine smiled faintly at the claim and then glanced to the small splotch of dried blood on the bottom linen the other men were removing from the bed. Dougall had cut his own hand to produce the blood and she wondered guiltily if it looked anything like the proof of innocence should. There had been no blood last night. Dougall had taken her innocence in the hunting lodge. Actually, she hadn't been sure there had been any blood at the lodge since they hadn't been in the bed when he took it, but Dougall had assured her he'd carried the proof of her innocence on his body. She'd taken him at his word, glad he would never doubt her innocence ere him. It was something she'd fretted over; what if her eagerness with him made him think she was more experienced than she was? What if he thought he was not the first man her brother had offered her to? And that mayhap someone else had taken her innocence? He'd reassured her that was not the case. He knew she was innocent.

Aulay and Dougall fell silent as their brothers carried the bloodied sheet past, and then Aulay said quietly, "Greer said to hang it from the rail along the landing so Montrose sees it first thing when he arrives." He waited for Dougall's grim nod, then glanced to Murine and said, "Saidh's been waiting fer ye to wake. She's got a selection o' dresses fer ye to borrow. I'll let her ken she can bring them along to ye now."

"Thank ye," Murine whispered with a frown as he turned to walk out of the room. The moment the door closed behind him, she turned to Dougall. "What did he mean? Montrose is no' coming here, is he? He left just ere we arrived. Why would he return so soon?"

Dougall grimaced, and crossed the room quickly to her side. Taking her arm, he urged her to sit on the side of the bed with him, and admitted, "Because he was invited."

"What?" she gasped with horror. "But why? He—"

"Aulay asked Greer to send a messenger after him with an invitation to our wedding," Dougall admitted and Murine goggled at him.

"Why would he do that?" she asked with horror. "If Montrose had got here before we were married, he would have—"

"The men didn't leave until the ceremony was finished," Dougall said quickly.

Murine stared at him blankly, and then simply said, "What?"

Dougall sighed, and explained, "We planned it all after ye left the table last night. The wedding was well over then. We decided 'twas best to send the invitation so that he kens we're married and stops hunting ye. So, we sent a couple men after his party with the invitation."

"To a wedding that was already done," she said dryly.

"Aye. The men were to claim they left around mid morning

to head out after him with the invitation, but one of their horses threw a shoe on the road, and they were delayed."

"Oh," Murine said weakly and then grimaced and asked, "Do ye really think he'll come here at all? I mean, if he kens he's too late to stop the wedding . . ." she said hopefully.

"He'll come," Dougall said dryly. "He'll want to be sure. He'll probably also bluster about and try to claim it should be annulled and such, saying I stole ye."

"Ye did no' steal me," she said with outrage.

"Aye, but he may claim I did in a bid to make me pay him coin to cover his gambling losses," Dougall pointed out quietly.

Murine scowled at the thought. "Well, don't give him any. Father was right, Mother should no' have given him a farthing. He never cared about her. He never cared about any of us," she said bitterly, thinking of how he'd tried to sell her for horses.

Dougall took in her expression, then pulled her into a quick embrace, his voice gruff as he said. "Aye, well now ye've a husband and six brothers and even a sister who do care, and each of us would give our life fer ye, lass. I swear it."

Murine smiled faintly, and squeezed him tight, whispering, "As I would fer all o' ye."

A short laugh slipped from Dougall, and he pulled back to eye her wryly. "Aye. Ye proved that when the lodge was afire." Brushing her hair back from her face, he added, "Me brothers were most impressed that ye stayed to try to help wake them and get me and Uncle Acair out and did no' just get yerself outside to safety when Rory ordered ye to."

"Well, I could hardly leave ye all to burn," she pointed out dryly.

"A lot o' lasses would ha'e," he said solemnly.

Before Murine could respond, another knock sounded at the door.

"That'll be Saidh," Dougall said, getting up. He paused then, though, his gaze sliding from the door to the tartan she still had wrapped around her. Standing, Murine removed it and

handed it over, then grabbed the top linen that was in a crumpled heap on the foot of the bed and wrapped it around herself
toga style in the tartan's place.

"Ye go ahead and pleat yer tartan, I'll get the door," she suggested.

"Thank ye, love," Dougall murmured and caught her arm to
draw her closer so he could press a quick kiss to her lips.

When he released her, Murine watched him kneel and spread
out the plaid, then turned to continue to the door, a smile curving her lips. This marriage business was quite nice so far, she
thought with a happy little sigh that died along with her smile
as she opened the door and saw the sheet over the railing. It
reminded her that Montrose would soon arrive, and she wasn't
sure what he would do. Or *could* do for that matter. She suddenly wasn't so sure that Dougall's marrying her had saved
her. Could Montrose have the marriage annulled? He was her
guardian after all. He might be able to argue that it should be
annulled because they hadn't had his permission and approval.

"I recognize that look."

Murine tore her gaze from the sheet to glance at Saidh, who
was waiting on the doorstep.

"Ye're fretting again," Saidh accused, and then caught Murine's arm and dragged her out into the hall, lecturing, "Come
along. We'll have none of that."

"Where are we going?" Murine asked with alarm, her hand
tightening on the linen she was holding together around her
chest as Saidh ushered her up the hall.

"To my room," she announced, then explained, "I decided
'twould be easier to bring ye to the gowns than to bring them
to ye."

"Oh," Murine sighed, grateful when they reached the next
door and Saidh ushered her inside.

Closing the door, Saidh urged her toward the bed where
several gowns were laid out and said, "Now, stop yer fretting,

Murine. Ye and Dougall are married. Montrose can no' do a thing about it."

Murine nodded and tried to remove the anxiety from her expression, but she wasn't at all sure Saidh was right about Montrose not being able to do anything about her marriage. And she was quite sure she wouldn't stop fretting about it until he arrived and did his worst.

"She'll make herself ill with worry."

Dougall grunted at Greer's comment and tore his gaze from where Murine sat by the fire with Saidh, sewing. The pair were silent as they worked, both of them noticeably tense in their seats, their gazes sliding toward the door with a frequency that suggested they expected it to burst open any minute.

Turning back to the table where he, Conran, Geordie, Alick and Greer were all gathered, he picked up his ale and took a long swallow before admitting, "All this waiting is beginning to fray on my nerves too."

"Aye," Conran said grimly. "It has been near a week. I expected the bastard to show up the morning after the wedding."

"We all did," Greer said dryly, and then shook his head. "Mayhap he decided there was nothing to do and returned to Danvries."

Dougall shook his head. "When he did no' show up here the second morning, I had Aulay send some men to watch Danvries Castle. They've been sending back daily reports and while most o' the men who rode out with Danvries to search for Murine returned two days ago, Danvries and six o' his men still ha'e not."

"Then mayhap he stopped at a friend's keep, or rode to London to gamble," Alick suggested.

"Mayhap," Dougall muttered, and then shrugged and said, "Whatever the case, it looks like he does no' intend to come here after Murine, so . . ." He turned to Greer and said, "We thank ye fer yer hospitality and patience with us, but we'll be getting out o' yer hair the day after tomorrow."

Greer's eyebrows rose and he glanced to the women by the fire. "Have ye told Murine?"

"Nay," Dougall admitted with a grimace. That was a chore he was not looking forward to.

Greer frowned. "Surely did Murine ken ye no longer expect Danvries to show up here, she would relax a bit."

"Aye," Dougall acknowledged.

"Then why have ye no' told her?" Greer asked reasonably.

"Because he's worried how she'll react when she learns where we are taking her next," Geordie growled before Dougall could respond.

"Carmichael?" Greer asked at once.

Dougall nodded. "MacIntyre wants to accompany us. His messenger returned with the news this morning. We are riding out to meet up with him the day after tomorrow and then will travel to Carmichael to demand to see the will." He smiled apologetically and added, "That is why we have to trouble ye with our presence for the added day."

Greer waved that away and picked up his own ale, only to set it back down untouched as he asked, "Is that why Aulay rode out with Niels and Rory this morning?"

"Aye," Alick said with a grin. "They're rounding up our soldiers."

"MacIntyre's bringing an army, and so are we," Dougall said, and then explained, "Just as a show of force. We want to ensure Murine's cousin shows us the will."

"Well," Greer said with a slow grin. "If it's force ye want, I'd be happy to bring me men along for the journey." Before Dougall could respond, he added, "She's my family too now, Buchanan. But more importantly, Murine saved Saidh's life and reputation at Sinclair. Had she not, I wouldn't now have my lovely wife. I *will* return the favor and stand up for her now she needs it."

"Well then, I guess ye're coming," Dougall said wryly.

"Damned right I am," Greer agreed and then got up abruptly.

"Where are ye going?" Dougall asked with surprise.

"To send a messenger to Sinclair," Greer explained. "He'll want to help too. Ye'll like him, by the by."

"Well, damn," Conran murmured as they watched Greer hurry away. "If Sinclair brings men too that'll be four armies riding up on Carmichael. Connor's going to piss himself when he sees us coming."

"Aye," Dougall agreed with a grin and got to his feet. "It's time I told Murine what we're planning."

"Good luck," Conran said quietly.

Nodding, Dougall turned and started toward the women by the fire.

"HE MUST NO' BE COMING."

Murine glanced up from her sewing at that frustrated comment from Saidh and raised her eyebrows.

"Yer brother," Saidh explained. "Surely if he was coming, he'd have been here by now?"

Murine sighed and set her sewing in her lap. She'd thought that herself several times, but the men were all so tense she suspected they had news they were keeping from her and Saidh. Like perhaps her brother was rounding up support and planned to lay siege to MacDonnell and demand her return so that he could have the marriage annulled.

Rather than say that, however, she offered, "I'm so sorry, Saidh. I ken we have overstayed our welcome, and—"

"Murine Buchanan," Saidh snapped, looking offended. "Ye can just stop what ye're saying right there and shut yer mouth. Ye have not overstayed yer welcome. We're happy to have ye here." She frowned and then added, "I just wish we were no' all so tense and worried and could enjoy the visit. This constant worry about what might be going on is exhausting."

"Aye, 'tis," Murine agreed with a sigh. The past week had

been wearying. The days were spent stuck in the keep, trying to distract themselves from the ever-present worry that Montrose might ride up any moment and throw her life into chaos. Though the nights were not quite as bad. Dougall was usually able to distract her with his kisses and caresses, but afterward, she found herself lying awake, worrying. And she knew Dougall did too.

"I'm fair sick o' being stuck indoors too," Saidh announced suddenly, shifting restlessly in her chair. "I could do with a good hard ride about now."

"So could I," Murine admitted.

"Then I shall take ye for one."

Both women glanced around with surprise at that announcement as Dougall paused by Murine's chair.

"Where's Greer?" Saidh asked, glancing toward the table where Conran, Geordie and Alick were sitting talking.

"He went to find a messenger. He should return directly," Dougall assured her, then smiled down at Murine and asked, "Ride?"

"Aye," she breathed with relief and set her sewing on the table next to her chair as she stood up. Noting that Saidh hadn't stood, she raised her eyebrows. "Are ye no' coming?"

Saidh hesitated, her glance shifting past her to Dougall before she shook her head. "I think I'll wait fer Greer."

"Mayhap we should too," Murine said, glancing to Dougall. "Then we could all go."

Saidh chuckled at the effect that suggestion had on Dougall's expression and shook her head. "I suspect me brother wants some time alone with ye, Muri. Go on. Greer will be along soon and I shall demand he take me for a ride too."

When Murine hesitated, feeling guilty at the idea of leaving Saidh behind when she'd been stuck indoors as well, Dougall scooped her up in his arms and turned to stride toward the door.

"Have fun," Saidh called with a grin.

Murine just shook her head and looped her arms around Dougall's neck. It wasn't until the keep doors closed behind them and he started down the stairs with her that Murine asked, "Does this mean we can stop worrying about Montrose coming to take me away?"

"There was never any chance of his taking ye away," Dougall assured her grimly as he stepped off the stairs and started across the bailey. "I'd ha'e challenged him to a wager of battle and killed him first."

"Like me father did to save me mother," Murine murmured.

"Exactly like that," he assured her, and then as he entered the stables, added, "But, aye, we no longer expect yer brother to come after ye."

"Half brother," she corrected, finding it irked her to have to admit even that much of a relationship to the man.

"Half brother," he agreed, setting her down outside the stall that held his horse. "Wait here."

Murine stepped back and then moved to lean against the stall rail as he walked over to collect his saddle. He was inside the stall, saddling his mount when she asked, "Is that why Aulay, Niels and Rory left this morning? Because ye'd all decided Montrose wasn't coming?"

Dougall paused briefly in what he was doing, and then continued as he said, "Part of the reason."

"What is the other part?"

Dougall was silent as he finished saddling his mount, then led the animal out of the stall and caught her hand in passing. After leading both her and the horse out of the stable, he quickly mounted, then leaned down to lift her up before him.

"I can ride, Dougall," she said quietly as he urged the horse to move.

"I ken. Ye rode most o' the way here from Buchanan," he reminded her. "I just like it when ye ride with me."

"Oh." She smiled faintly, pleased that he liked to ride with her. "I like riding with ye too."

"Do ye?" he asked, brushing a kiss by her ear as they passed under the gate and started across the drawbridge.

"Aye. I liked riding astride too, though."

"Did ye?" he asked with interest, and then said, "Here, take the reins."

Murine took them and then released a startled gasp when he suddenly caught her at the waist and lifted her several inches.

"Swing yer leg over," he ordered. "Ye can ride astride with me."

Murine swung her leg over at once and he eased her down onto the horse's back.

"Ye're wearing braies under yer gown," he commented with amusement.

Murine glanced down to see that her position had raised her skirts enough to reveal the dark braies beneath. Flushing, she shrugged. "I've worn them every day since the wedding, taking them off just before the sup. I thought I should be prepared."

"Prepared for what?" he asked.

"For anything," she said dryly. "In case ye ha'e no' noticed, me laird, I ha'e ruined quite a few gowns since fleeing me brother's castle."

"Aye, I had noticed," he said on a chuckle. "And I'm thinking I may ha'e to step up me horse breeding to keep ye in gowns."

"Or ye could just keep me naked," she suggested, leaning back against his chest.

"Could I?" he asked with interest, nuzzling her neck. "Ye would no' mind?"

"Nay," she breathed, squirming her bottom against him as he nipped at her earlobe. "Not if ye were naked too."

"Better and better," he growled, then caught her chin and turned her face back and up so that he could kiss her.

Murine sighed and then moaned into his mouth as excitement immediately burst to life within her. But then she pulled back and gasped, "Mayhap ye should take the reins. I fear I might drop them."

"Nay. I'm busy," Dougall argued and promptly let his hands slide up to cup her breasts.

Murine squeaked in surprise and glanced around, relieved to see that they had reached the woods surrounding MacDonnell and the men on the wall couldn't see what he was doing. Taking advantage of the way she'd turned her head, Dougall kissed her again, his hands continuing to knead her breasts for a moment as he thrust his tongue into her.

When she moaned and kissed him back, he began to tug fretfully at the neckline of her gown. He didn't have to tug much. Saidh was a little bigger than her and the tops of the gowns she'd given her were all a little loose on Murine. They'd spent the last several days altering the gowns, but this was one that hadn't yet been taken in. Within moments he had her breasts free and was squeezing and caressing them without the cloth between them.

Breaking their kiss now, Dougall muttered, "Muri?"

"Aye?" she moaned, arching into his touch.

"I like it when ye ride astride too."

Murine gave a breathless chuckle, but didn't point out they weren't exactly riding anymore. She'd lost her grip on the reins a moment ago and his mount had immediately slowed to a stop.

"Husband," she said breathlessly, "Mayhap we should—oh," she gasped, her body jerking with surprise as one of his hands suddenly dropped from her breast to cup her between the legs.

"Whoa," Dougall growled when his mount sidled nervously at her action. Releasing her other breast, he grabbed up the reins lying in her lap and took control again, of both of them. The hand between her legs was still there. His fingers now pressing firmly against the cloth beneath them, and moving up and then down, caressing her through the material.

"Dougall," she gasped weakly, grabbing for his hands to try to stop him.

"If ye were no' wearing braies, I'd turn ye around to straddle me, tug yer skirt out o' the way and—"

"Oh God," Murine gasped, interrupting him as her excitement jumped up several levels from the combination of what he was doing and the image he was putting in her head. She now really wished she wasn't wearing those braies. And she was suddenly desperate to have him inside her.

"Husband, please," she begged, twisting her head against his shoulder, her nails now digging into the hand between her legs.

"Please what, Muri?" he breathed by her ear, urging the horse to move faster even as his fingers moved faster against her.

"Stop the horse. I need ye," she admitted on a groan.

"Soon," he assured her, and then ordered, "Touch yer breasts fer me, lass. I can't."

Murine licked her lips uncertainly, but raised her hands to cup her own breasts.

"Oh, aye, that's it, love. Squeeze 'em," he instructed. The hand between her legs withdrew briefly to drag her skirt up, and then returned to touching her, this time with only the thin material of the braies in the way as he began to rub at her core again. Murine groaned and kneaded her breasts almost painfully as her hips moved involuntarily under his caress, her bottom rubbing against the hardness she could feel growing between them, and then he was reining in and she blinked her eyes open to see that they'd reached a clearing by a loch.

Murine had barely noted that when they were at a complete stop and Dougall was lifting her out of his lap to set her on the ground next to his mount. She grabbed at the stirrup to steady herself, then stepped back to get out of the way as he dismounted. Once on his feet, Dougall immediately caught her by the arms and pulled her forward for a kiss. It was hard and demanding and she responded in kind, vaguely aware that he was backing her away from the horse.

She barely felt the bark of a tree press into her back before Dougall broke the kiss and dropped to one knee to catch the bottom of her skirt and flip it out of the way. It flew up and then dropped down over his head and shoulders and she stared down wide-eyed as she felt his hands begin to work at the ties of her braies.

"Should I—" She'd been about to ask if she should hold her skirt up, but lost the thread of the question as he started pressing kisses to the flesh revealed as he tugged her braies down. His lips slid over her hip, down her leg and then he caught her behind one knee, urging her to raise her leg. The moment she did, he tugged her braies off over her foot. He then did the same with her other leg. She saw them go flying out from under the skirt and then Dougall pulled back, straightened and caught the top of her gown and began to push that down over her shoulders.

Murine began to help then, pushing the material off her arms so that it hung about her waist. She then reached for the pin of his tartan as he gave the gown the last shove needed to send it to the ground to pool around her feet. Murine unsnapped his pin and his tartan dropped away. Dougall immediately jerked his shirt off over his head, tossed it aside and then pulled her into his arms.

Murine sighed with pleasure as his warm body pressed against hers. She raised her head for his kiss and he started to lower his head, then paused abruptly.

"Yer back?" he asked with concern. "Did I hurt ye when I pressed ye against the tree?"

She shook her head quickly. "'Tis fine. Rory says he'll take the stitches out tomorrow."

"Thank God," Dougall muttered and then swept her legs out from under her, and dropped to a knee as he lowered her to lie on their discarded clothes. He didn't cover her then and slide into her as she'd expected, but settled on his side next to her and began to kiss her as his hand glided over her body, running across her stomach, and then up to toy with first one breast and then the other.

Murine moaned into his mouth, and then clutched at his

shoulders, trying to pull him over her. But Dougall resisted, instead sliding his hand down over her belly and pelvis to dip between her legs. Murine tore her mouth away on a gasp and cried out. Hips bucking and back arching, she clawed at him now, desperate for him to fill her and assuage this terrible need he was building in her.

"Dougall." His name was almost a sob.

"Whist, love," he chided, his fingers sliding across her slick skin and moving in circles around the nub of her excitement. "Don't fash. Relax and enjoy it."

She could just have punched him, and the thought made her eyes pop open. She suddenly understood what Saidh had been talking about. Until now, Murine had always been upright, riding him to prevent causing her back wound to pain her. It had left her in control as she'd sought her pleasure. This time Dougall was in control, and he was driving her crazy with his teasing caresses.

She tried to shift then, hoping to push him on his back and mount him, but Dougall merely tossed one leg over hers, pinning her in place with it and his chest.

Murine growled in frustration, her head thrashing on the ground. Then, desperate to bring an end to her torment, she managed to work her hand down and find his erection. She closed her hand around him, and then hesitated. She wasn't sure what she was supposed to do, but the way Dougall briefly stilled when her hand closed around him suggested to her that she was on the right track. When his fingers began to move against her flesh again, she instinctively eased her own hand down his length, imitating what happened when he joined with her.

Dougall immediately sucked air in through his teeth, and growled, "Leave off, love. I want to pleasure ye."

"I want ye in me," she countered and slid her hand up his length now.

He ground his teeth together, but then merely lowered his

head to claim her lips. When she opened her mouth for him, he thrust his tongue inside, at the same time pushing a finger inside her body.

Murine cried out into his mouth, her body arching so far she feared she'd break her own back. When his finger then started to retract, she raised the one knee she could and planted her foot flat on the ground to push her hips up to meet the next thrust. This time a second finger joined the first, filling her almost as completely as he did when he made love to her. But this time he didn't pull back out, but kept his fingers imbedded in her, pressing firmly as his thumb began to run back and forth and around the nub that was the core of her excitement.

Murine's body seemed almost to vibrate with tension for a moment and then she screamed into his mouth and bucked and thrust as her release finally exploded over her in mind-numbing waves. Only then did Dougall withdraw his hand and shift over her to join his body with hers. Murine gave a half gasp, half groan as he filled her, and then wrapped her arms and legs around him as he began to rock in and out of her.

At first she thought she was done and would simply hold him and wait for him to find his pleasure, but she was mistaken. Within moments he had her crying out and clawing at him again. Only this time when she found her release, she was not alone and Dougall's shout joined hers as he held himself still, planted deep within her, then he sagged on his arms briefly before shifting and rolling to his side and then his back, taking her with him to lie on his warm body.

Murine nestled into him, her eyes just closing when he said, "Wife?"

She blinked her eyes reluctantly back open, but was too exhausted to lift her head to look at him and merely mumbled a sleepy "Mmm?"

He hesitated and then said, "We leave the day after tomorrow."

Murine merely nodded and closed her eyes again, supposing they would return to Buchanan until Dougall had built a home for them. They'd talked about it just the other night. He'd inherited land and a good sum of money when his parents died. All the boys had. And he'd added to it with his horse breeding and some mercenary work he'd apparently done before his father's death. When put together with what coin he'd saved from acting as Aulay's first the last several years, Dougall apparently had more than enough money to build them a fine home.

She didn't care. She would have been happy living with him at Buchanan for the rest of their lives, or even in a small cottage. So long as they were together, she didn't care where they lived.

"For Carmichael," Dougall added, and Murine stiffened.

They both remained still for a minute, and then she sat up abruptly and stared at his solemn face.

Sitting up as well now, Dougall took her hands. "Laird MacIntyre wants to see the will, and I think ye need to as well."

"I don't," she denied, pulling her hands from his. "I ken what it says and that's enough."

"It isn't," he insisted, catching her hands again. "Murine, I would wager me life that the will is a forgery. Yer father would no' leave all to a nephew he'd never met and—"

"I told ye, me fainting made him fear the people would no' accept me to—"

"I ken ye think that, but I think ye're wrong," he said firmly. "And whether he would leave ye in charge o' Carmichael or no', he certainly would no' ha'e left ye in Danvries' care." He frowned. "Murine, yer father killed Montrose's father in a wager o' battle rather than leave yer mother, *a complete stranger to him*, in the man's care. He would then hardly leave you, his own daughter and only remaining child, in the hands of the man's son. Especially when that son was as weak and cruel as his father ever was."

Murine swallowed and lowered her head. That had hurt her more than anything. She had not minded so much that the castle and title had been left to her cousin Connor. While women often inherited both titles and property in Scotland, she knew it was rarely done in England. What had bothered her was that she had been left in Montrose's care when her father had always seemed to detest the man. And she, too, hadn't believed it when Montrose had first told her . . . not until he'd explained that her father apparently felt her habit of fainting made her weak and in need of care.

"Me fainting," she began unhappily.

"Does no' make ye any less the brave, strong woman I've come to know ye are," Dougall said firmly.

Murine waved that away. Of course he saw her as strong now. She hadn't fainted since the journey to Buchanan, she thought, and said as much to Dougall. "Ye've forgotten how I was before ye and yer brothers started making me eat and filling me with tinctures."

"How were ye?" he asked solemnly.

"I was forever fainting," she pointed out with irritation. "I was weak."

"Weak?" he asked with amusement. "Lass, yer fainting did no make ye weak. As far as I can tell it did no' slow ye down at all. Even with yer fainting ye saved me sister and Lady Sinclair from a murderess. And ye fled yer brother, his home and England itself to travel alone to Scotland to preserve yer virtue," he pointed out. "That does no' seem weak to me."

"I did no' travel alone," she pointed out solemnly.

"Nay," he agreed. "But ye started out alone. Ye braved bandits and every other danger of the road to flee." He gave her hands a shake. "Ye're no' weak, Murine. Ye ne'er were, even with yer fainting. And if I can see that, yer father would ha'e too," he said firmly.

Placing a finger under her chin, he raised her face until she met his gaze, and said, "I ken ye think yer father felt ye weak because o' the fainting, and I ken that the possibility that he did hurts ye. But Muri, he was no' a stupid man and surely saw what I do. That ye're beautiful, fine and strong, fainting or no'."

Murine bit her lip and blinked against the tears suddenly crowding her eyes.

When one escaped to race down her cheek, he brushed it away solemnly and said, "We are riding out to meet up with MacIntyre the day after tomorrow, and then riding to Carmichael and demanding to see the will. Ye need to ken that yer father did love and respect ye, and was no' so shamed by yer fainting that he left yer care to a bastard like Montrose."

Realizing he was waiting for her agreement, she let her breath out on a sigh and nodded.

Dougall relaxed and managed a crooked smile. "'Twill all be fine," he assured her, pulling her forward for a hug.

"Will it?" Murine murmured with her cheek against his chest, and pointed out, "Because if the will was switched, it brings up questions about Father's death."

Dougall stiffened and pulled back slowly to meet her gaze and she saw regret there, but he nodded. "Aye, it does."

When Murine merely stared at him, he admitted, "It has always bothered me that yer father was apparently on the mend when ye left, yet dead days later." He shook his head. "I know ye well enough to ken that ye would no' have left Carmichael unless he had been *well* on the mend."

"He was up and about, his breathing mostly clear with just the occasional cough and sniffle," she said solemnly. "He even spent the afternoon below stairs by the fire with me the day before I left."

Dougall nodded again, as if he'd expected as much, and then pointed out, "And Montrose would hardly switch out the wills and risk yer father recovering and discovering the switch."

Chapter 15

MURINE GLANCED UP AT A SIGH FROM SAIDH, AND WATCHED her pace back and forth in front of the fireplace, wringing her hands anxiously. Murine had never thought she'd see the day when Saidh Buchanan, now MacDonnell, would wring her hands like a helpless woman. But she'd been doing it all morning.

Biting her lip, Murine sat back in her seat and tried to think of something to say that might soothe Saidh. However, she'd been doing that all morning, and there was simply nothing that could be said that would help in this situation until it was resolved.

Murine sighed and peered down at her untouched sewing again. She hadn't slept well since Dougall had told her they would be heading to Carmichael today. She'd woken up that morning, exhausted after the second long night where more time had been spent worrying over the coming journey than on actual sleep, only to learn that the journey had been delayed because Greer's squire was missing. It seemed the young lad, named Alpin, had been supposed to return yesterday from a two-week visit home, a trip that had been prescribed in his squiring contract. The lad was expected to arrive by the sup. When he hadn't arrived by bedtime, Greer had begun to worry. When dawn arrived with still no sign, he'd sent men out to ensure the lad and his escort had not encountered trouble on the road. His men had returned quickly with the news that they'd found the escort dead on the road not far from MacDonnell . . . and there was no sign of the boy.

Greer had immediately started a search, and Dougall and his brothers were helping with it.

"I should be out there helping them look," Saidh exploded with sudden frustration.

"Aye, ye should," Murine agreed mildly, turning her gaze back to the sewing that she'd been holding for quite some time, but hadn't sewn a stitch in.

She could feel her friend's indecision and then Saidh threw herself into the chair next to Murine's with a sigh and muttered, "Nay. I should stay here."

Now it was Murine's turn to sigh, although she did so with more exasperation than anything else. Standing up, she set the sewing aside and said, "I ken ye stayed behind to keep an eye on me, Saidh. But I am perfectly safe here in the keep. Besides, I'm tired. I have no' slept well the last two nights for worry about the journey today, and I would like to lie down for a rest, but so long as ye're here, I feel I need sit with ye. Why do you no' go help with the search," she suggested. "That way I can go have a lie-down and stop watching ye pace about like a mother hen."

Saidh couldn't get out of her seat swiftly enough. Bouncing to her feet, she gave Murine a quick hug, then rushed for the door, calling, "I'll wake ye when we find him."

Murine watched her push through the doors, then shook her head and turned to make her way across the great hall and above stairs. Saidh had mentioned Alpin several times over the last week. Murine had figured out pretty quickly that she'd come to care for the boy, but hadn't realized just how much. Today though, she'd come to realize that Saidh pretty much counted the boy as an eighth brother, or even an adopted son. Murine sincerely hoped they found the lad alive and well. She suspected Saidh would be inconsolable otherwise.

The sack holding the gowns Saidh had given her waited on

the bed next to Dougall's bag and Murine grimaced at the sight of them. They seemed to symbolize the trip they were supposed to start that morning, the one that had caused her lack of sleep, and the reason she was so exhausted now. A trip they hadn't ended up taking.

Her mother used to say that worry was a waste, what would happen would happen, and sometimes what you worried about never occurred. Her mother had been a wise woman, Murine acknowledged as she walked to the bed and grabbed Dougall's bag to move it to the floor. She'd just set it down and started to straighten to move her own bag as well when a scuffing sounded behind her.

Murine started to turn, and then cried out as something slammed into her head. She barely had time to recognize the dark embrace of unconsciousness closing around her before it had fully enfolded her.

"Two guards."

Dougall glanced to the man riding beside him. Greer was scowling ferociously, rage, fear and frustration in every line of his body as he muttered those words again. Dougall didn't have to ask what his brother-in-law was talking about. Alpin's father had sent the boy back with an escort of two guards, both of whom were dead, their bodies on the way back to Alpin's father with the message that his son was missing.

"And two lads barely old enough to grow hair on their faces at that," Greer snarled. "What kind o' idiot sends his only son on a journey with but two striplings to guard him?"

Dougall grimaced, but didn't comment. He suspected Greer was just venting his upset and did not really want a response.

Alick was among the men traveling with them, however, and sometimes didn't know when he should comment and when he shouldn't.

"Well, ye did say his father was English," Alick pointed out. "They're no' always the brightest o' people."

"Alick," Dougall growled in warning.

"Well, they're not," Alick insisted. "Grandfather always said it was on account o' inbreeding."

When Greer arched an eyebrow and glanced to Dougall, he immediately shook his head and advised, "Ignore him. He's young."

"What's that got to do with anything?" Alick asked with irritation. "I'm just telling ye what Grandfather said."

"Alick," Dougall began, but then paused as he spotted a woman riding toward them, her dark hair flying in the breeze. "Is that Saidh?"

"Aye," Greer said slowly, concern creeping across his face.

"I thought she was going to stay at the castle with Murine," Alick said with a frown.

Mouth tightening, Dougall spurred his horse forward to meet her, barking, "Where's Murine?" as they met and both reined in.

"She was tired and wanted to lie down so I came to help with the search," Saidh answered quickly.

Dougall nodded, relief flowing through him. For a moment he'd feared she too was out here riding around somewhere.

"Why were ye all headed back to the castle?" Saidh asked as Greer and the others caught up. "Did ye find Alpin?"

"Nay," Greer answered solemnly.

"Then why are ye heading back to the keep?" she asked shortly. "He is out there somewhere, alone and afraid and—" Her words died as Greer pulled her from her horse and into the cradle of his arms on his own mount. "Breathe, love. We are doing all we can. I have the men looking further afield, and have sent a messenger to his father with the news and requesting he let us know if he receives a demand fer coin for the boy's return. In the meantime, we were heading back to the keep to map out the area and try to decide the best course of action."

Saidh sagged against him at this news. "I'm worried about him, Greer."

"Aye, I ken," he said on a sigh, then pressed her head to his chest and urged his horse forward again.

Dougall leaned to the side to grab the reins of Saidh's mare, and then followed the couple, aware that his brothers were on his heels.

Most of the MacDonnell men were out searching for Alpin, so it was something of a surprise to ride into the bailey and find it full of men. Dougall rode up next to Greer and glanced to him in question as they slowed, but his brother-in-law gave a slight shake of his head that said he had no idea who the men were.

"Aulay's back," Alick said suddenly and Dougall relaxed as he spotted his brothers Aulay and Conran standing by the stairs with Greer's first, Bowie, and an older man he didn't recognize.

The plan had been for Aulay, along with the soldiers he'd collected from Buchanan, to ride straight out to where they were to meet MacIntyre rather than take the slight detour to Mac-Donnell. The rest of them were going to ride from MacDonnell to meet the two parties. Of course, once the issue of Greer's squire had popped up, Dougall had sent Conran to meet up with the group and explain the delay. It appeared they'd got the message, Dougall decided as Greer said, "And if I'm no' mistaken, that's Laird MacIntyre with him."

"Perhaps they've come to help with the search," Saidh said hopefully.

"We shall see," Greer said quietly.

Noting the concern in the man's voice, Dougall eyed him briefly, and then peered more carefully over the men by the stairs. This time he noted the grim expressions each wore and felt concern begin to lay claim to him. It was looking to him like if they'd found the boy, it wasn't alive.

Sighing inwardly, he reined in next to Greer and quickly slid off his mount. By the time he turned to help Saidh down, however, she'd already dropped to the ground and started toward Aulay and the other men.

Cursing, Greer pretty much leapt out of the saddle and ran the first several feet to catch up to his wife before she learned whatever news the men had. Dougall held back with Geordie and Alick to allow them a moment's privacy with whatever news they were about to be given. But much to his surprise, when the four men realized Dougall was hanging back, they moved around the couple and approached him.

"Dougall," Aulay said solemnly. "Murine is missing."

"What?" he asked with confusion, his gaze shifting to Saidh as she hurried back.

"Nay," she told them with a frown. "Murine went to lie down ere I left. She's probably still up in her room."

"Nay, she's not," Aulay said solemnly, never moving his gaze from Dougall. "Laird MacIntyre asked to see her the moment we arrived. The servants in the hall said she had gone up to the room you shared, and hadn't returned below. But when Bowie went to knock there was no answer. He opened the door and the room is empty." Pausing then he grabbed Dougall bracingly by the shoulders, before adding unhappily, "There is blood on the bedchamber floor."

For one moment the world seemed to spin around Dougall, and he felt sure he was about to imitate Murine and faint dead away. Then he was moving, pushing through the people who had crowded around and hurdling up the steps into the keep. He heard footsteps behind him as he rushed across the hall and up the stairs, but didn't stop until he burst into the bedchamber he and Murine had shared.

Dougall barely heard the door hit the wall over the rushing in his ears as his gaze slid quickly over the empty room. He noted his bag on the floor. It had been on the bed with Murine's when he'd left that morning, he recalled, and then his eyes found the drops of blood on the floor by the bag. Moving forward, he followed the trail of blood to the wall by the fireplace and paused with confusion.

"The passage."

Dougall turned sharply at those gasped words from Saidh. "What?"

She hesitated, and then glanced to Greer. Her husband grimly glanced around at the crowd that had followed. Aulay, Mac-Intyre, Bowie, Conran, Geordie and Alick were all there, and he sighed, then closed the door before turning back and nodding to Saidh. She immediately moved up next to where Dougall stood and pressed a brick in the wall.

Dougall stiffened as the wall shifted, revealing a dark, narrow passage. He then surged forward only to pause a step inside. The passage led in two directions, left and right, and he had no idea which way he should go. Both ways were in darkness and there were no sounds to indicate someone was in there. Turning back sharply, he asked, "Where does it go?"

Greer's expression was grim. "Ye can use it to get to the other rooms, or down into the gardens behind the kitchen, or down to a cave by the loch."

Dougall nodded abruptly. "I need a torch."

As Alick turned to rush out into the hall, Aulay turned to Greer and asked, "Who all knows about the passage?"

"As far as I ken, just Saidh, me, Bowie and Alpin," Greer said with a frown, and then added, "And now all o' you."

"Alpin? The lad who's missing?" Dougall asked sharply

Greer nodded slowly, his expression thoughtful.

"Alpin would no' have done this," Saidh protested quickly. "He's just a lad. He could no' ha'e forced Murine out of the room."

"Nay," Greer agreed. "But he could have told whoever took Murine about the passage."

"He wouldn't," Saidh said with certainty.

"He could have been made to," Greer said apologetically. "That could explain why he was taken."

Saidh blanched at the thought of how he could have been made to, but rallied and asked, "But how would they ken he knew about it or that it even existed?"

"They may have taken the lad to find out the layout of Mac-Donnell," Aulay pointed out quietly. "As Dougall's squire they'd expect the boy could tell them how many people were here and where Murine was most likely to be."

"And what? Ye think Alpin would just volunteer the information about the passage?" Saidh snapped, and then said staunchly, "He would no' do that."

"Then mayhap they suspected there were passages. Many castles have them. They could have forced him to tell," Greer said, but when Saidh paled, he added quickly, "Or tricked him."

Alick rushed back into the room then with half a dozen torches crushed together between his hands. He nearly dropped the bundle when Dougall grabbed one and tugged it out of the collection, but Conran, Geordie and Greer stepped forward to help.

"Dougall, wait," Aulay caught at his arm as he turned back toward the passage. "Ye do no' ken where they've taken her. We need to consider this and—"

"They'd have taken her to the cave Greer mentioned. The gardens and another room make no sense," Dougall growled, jerking his arm free. Glancing to Greer he asked, "Which way to the cave?"

"They'd hardly stay in the cave," Aulay pointed out. "'Tis the first place we'd look."

Dougall frowned at those words, recognizing the common sense behind them.

MacIntyre spoke up for the first time, pointing out, "But they can't travel far either. There are men everywhere searching for the boy. Someone would have seen." Spearing Greer with a glance he said, "Is there anyplace not far from this cave you mentioned that they might hide?"

"Several," Greer said grimly.

"Then 'tis good we have so many men just now, is it not?" MacIntyre said mildly and then turned to walk to the door, saying, "We'll need to make a list of these several places you mentioned, Greer. But first I need to send my first to collect my soldiers."

"As do I," Aulay murmured, and explained, "We left the men camped on the edge of MacDonnell while we rode in to see whether or not help was needed with the search."

When silence fell briefly and everyone seemed to turn and look at him, Dougall felt his hand tighten painfully around the torch he held. Murine was missing. He needed action. He needed to hunt down the bastards who had taken her, tear them limb from limb, then bring her safely home. Instead they wanted to make lists and send messengers.

Unfortunately, he knew their way had merit, but he felt like he should at least check the cave and not just decide she wasn't there.

"Greer, I'd appreciate it if ye could start making that list," Dougall said finally. "Meantime, I'd like to borrow Bowie to show me the way to the cave. I want to check it at least. Even if they are no' still there, I may find a clue to help figure out where she is."

"A good plan," MacIntyre murmured. Nodding, Greer glanced to his first. Bowie immediately took one of the two torches Alick was still holding and moved past Dougall to lead the way.

MURINE BLINKED HER EYES OPEN TO DARKNESS, BUT STILL IM-mediately closed them with a moan as she became aware of the throbbing in her head.

"Hush. Someone will hear you."

Stilling, she forced her eyes opened again and peered around. She was lying on her side, her wrists bound uncomfortably behind her back, and she was quite sure that had been her half brother's voice. At first, all Murine could see from her position was darkness, but then she was able to make out shadows and shapes in one direction, and noted the figure standing at an opening where some light appeared to be coming from the other side.

"Montrose?" she said uncertainly. The figure shifted, blocking all light briefly before moving toward her and allowing a good deal more light in. Enough to see that she was lying on the damp, dirt floor of a cave.

"I said hush," he growled, pausing in front of her threateningly. "Do I have to gag you?"

Murine glared at his shadowed face. With the dim light that was filtering into the cave behind him, all she could really make out was his silhouette.

"Mayhap ye could use whatever ye were going to gag me with to wipe the blood from me face instead," she suggested dryly. "'Tis dripping into me eye and stings."

"'Tis probably water," he muttered, but knelt before her and pulled her into a sitting position, then dug a bit of cloth from somewhere on his person that he began to use to wipe her face. "I can hear it dripping from the ceiling."

"Mayhap," she allowed. "But it tastes like blood. Some apparently ran into my mouth while I was unconscious from being *hit over the head*," she added heavily.

Murine thought he grimaced, though she couldn't be sure in this light or lack thereof. But his voice held reluctant apology as he muttered, "Sorry about that. 'Twas not the plan. I was waiting in the secret passage when ye entered the room. I was just going to sneak up behind ye and drop a sack over you, then bundle you into the passage. But you started to turn, I panicked, and . . ."

"And you hit me," she finished accusingly, but there wasn't much heat behind her words. Her mind was preoccupied with this secret passage he'd mentioned. Would anyone realize he'd taken her that way? Surely the servants working to clean the great hall had noted her going up to the room and that she hadn't returned. Hopefully they'd say as much if questioned and Greer or Saidh would realize how she'd been smuggled out?

"I said I was sorry," Montrose snapped and gave up cleaning her face. Straightening, he growled, "Now be quiet or I *will* gag you."

He turned to move back to the opening where light was slipping in, filtered by leaves and branches she saw before his body blocked most of that light as he peered out at whatever was out there. Murine remained silent for a moment, but then couldn't resist saying, "Dougall will come for me."

"Eventually," he agreed, not bothering to look around. Then he shrugged, "But he and the MacDonnell men are all out looking for the boy. Your absence will not be noticed for hours."

"The boy?" she asked with surprise. "Do ye mean Alpin? Do ye ken where he is?"

"He is fine," Montrose said impatiently, not looking around. "He is with Connor, awaiting our return."

Murine stilled. "Cousin Connor?"

"Aye," Montrose said absently, frowning at something beyond the leaves.

"So they were right then," Murine said sadly, staring at his dark silhouette as her mind began to race. Montrose and Connor were in cahoots. Had Montrose switched his will for one that left her in his care and then killed her father as well?

"Who were right?" Montrose asked, glancing around and she could hear the frown and worry in his voice. "And about what?"

Murine hesitated, but then shrugged and said, "Dougall, Greer and the others. They all think you switched Father's will for a forged one." She paused as Montrose sucked in a hissing breath, and then added, "And then killed him."

"What?" he squawked with dismay. "I did not kill him."

"I notice ye're no' denying switching the will though," Murine said dryly.

"What if I did?" he snapped. "It's not as if anyone was hurt by it. You made out well enough. You married a Buchanan and they're all rich as sin. They were not left with fallow fields and a castle full of mouths to feed when *their* laird died."

"So ye thought to improve the situation by gambling away what coin ye had?" she asked dryly, and then added, "And when that did no' work, ye went after *my* inheritance. What matter if ye had to push me father into his grave a decade or so early," she added bitterly.

"I told ye, I did no' kill him," Montrose growled, striding across the floor to loom over her. "He was ill. He died of his illness."

"He was recovering," she countered furiously. "All that re-mained of his illness were some sniffles and the fact that he still tired easily. He spent the afternoon before I left playing chess with me in the great hall. Do ye think I'd ha'e left oth-erwise?" she added sharply, and shook her head. "Ye can no' convince me he died of his illness, Monti. I ken better. Besides, I hardly think ye'd have switched the will and then let him live and risk his discovering it."

Of all her words, the last ones seemed to have the most impact and Murine watched narrow-eyed as his head went back as if she'd punched him. But after a moment, he turned away, stammering, "I-I didn't kill him." Voice gaining strength, he added, "I wouldn't kill anyone. Even him, who I hated for stealing Mother."

Murine's mouth tightened at his words. She'd heard the claim many a time this last year when Montrose was in his cups. Her father had killed his father and stolen his mother and was to blame for his having to live with his grandfather, a miserable old bastard who had made his and William's life hell.

She'd tried to tell him that their mother had tried desperately to get their grandfather to release him and William to her, but he wouldn't listen. And, frankly, she was tired of feeling guilty about having her parents while he had been raised by his pa-ternal grandfather. Especially since, while she'd had a wonder-ful childhood, the last several years had been a hell made up of loss and grief, followed by a year of misery and humiliation at the hands of the man before her. She found it hard to feel sorry

for the abuse he'd suffered when he'd turned around and in-
flicted his own abuse on her this last year in the form of insults
and petty cruelties, which had been topped off with his trying
to whore her out.

"Just admit ye killed him and be done with it," she snarled
angrily. "Who else would have done it? Connor and ye are the
only ones who benefited from his death and Connor was no'
there."

"Aye, he was," Montrose said quickly.

Murine peered at him with disbelief. "Connor ne'er even set
foot in Castle Carmichael until after the reading of the will."

"Aye, he did," Montrose insisted. "He rode in as one of my
soldiers the night your father died."

When she didn't look convinced, he snapped, "Do you think
he would have included me in the matter otherwise? He was
the one who came to me. He'd heard about your father being ill
and wanted to switch the wills, but needed a way to enter Carmichael without being noticed. He had a beard and mustache
then, donned braies and mail, tucked his hair up under a cap
and rode in with my men, pretty as you please. No one even
gave him a second look. And no one recognized him when he
later returned in a tartan, his face clean shaven and his long
hair down."

Murine's eyes widened at this. She almost believed him.
But—"Why did he need a way into Carmichael at all if ye were
the one who was to switch the wills?"

"*He* was supposed to switch them himself originally," Montrose said stiffly. "But I convinced him that 'twould be better
did I do it. Were I to get caught in the room, I could claim I just
wanted a word with your father. Were he caught, no excuse
would suffice."

"Well ye did no' do that out o' the kindness o' yer heart,"
Murine said grimly, knowing he'd only take a risk like that if
he had something to gain from it.

"Nay," he admitted stiffly, his nose rising somewhat. "My

having the original will was to ensure he paid me fairly for my aid."

"More fairly than he'd intended and more often," Murine guessed quietly. "Ye've been blackmailing him."

"I owe a great deal of coin to some very powerful lords," Montrose said rather than deny it. "Besides, he owes me. He inherited everything . . . and all because of me."

"Everything except Waverly," Murine pointed out coldly.

"Aye," he acknowledged unhappily. "I made that part of the bargain. The original plan was that he would have your care, but I knew the king was interested in Waverly and hoped he'd forgive a debt I owed him if I signed it over to him instead. I convinced Connor to change the will so that I had your care and charge of your dower."

"And did yer plan work?" she asked. "Did the king forgive your debt?"

Montrose grimaced. "Only part of it."

Murine was silent for a moment, considering what she'd learned, then murmured, "So yer claim is that ye only switched the wills and 'twas Connor who killed father?"

Montrose frowned and looked torn for a moment, but then shook his head. "Nay. Connor is not a killer. I would not have dealings with a killer. Nay. That would ruin me. Yer father must have relapsed," he decided. "His ailment must have returned and hit him harder the second time. Or mayhap his heart just gave out from the strain."

"Connor is not a killer?" Murine asked with disbelief. "What do ye call what he did to Alpin's escort?"

"He did not do anything to the boy's escort," Montrose said with a frown. "He said he grabbed the lad while they were distracted."

"Then why were they found dead on the roadside?" she asked.

She saw his hands squeeze into fists, and then he peered briefly out of the opening again before hurrying over to grab her arm and drag her to her feet. "The way is clear. We can go now."

Once upright, Murine struggled against him, keeping him distracted while she did the only thing she could think to do and quickly tore the lace trim from one sleeve of her borrowed gown. She let it fall to the cave floor as Montrose dragged her toward the opening he'd been standing in front of. Her hope was that they would realize she'd been taken out through the secret passage, and that Dougall would find the lace and know she'd been there. She would leave her entire gown in pieces across the country for him to follow if she had to, and if she could.

Chapter 16

"STOP DAWDLING. WE ARE ALMOST THERE."

Murine grimaced at that news and dropped the bit of cloth she'd managed to tear from her sleeve. "That eager to see me dead, brother?"

"I told you, Connor is not a killer," Montrose growled, jerking her several feet forward.

"Aye, and if ye believe that then ye're lying to yerself," she said as she peered around at where they were. It seemed to her like they'd been walking for hours, but she suspected that was mostly because she *had* been dawdling. Had they ridden on horseback they probably could have covered the distance much more quickly. But they were on foot, and Murine had done everything she could think of to slow their progress, sure that if Connor got his hands on her, she was as good as dead. That thought made her jerk her arm from Montrose and say, "Ye can tell yerself what ye like, but in yer heart, ye ken he killed me father and Alpin's guards, and now ye're delivering me to me death."

"He does not want to kill you. He wants to talk to you," he said impatiently, and then using a more wheedling tone, added, "All you have to do is agree to say you saw the will and knew your father was leaving all to Connor before his death and all will be well."

"Oh, aye," Murine said dryly as he caught her arm and started pulling her forward again. "And what of Alpin?"

"What of him?" Montrose asked shortly.

"He can hardly let him live," she pointed out. "He kidnapped him, killed his escort and—"

"Shut up!" Montrose bellowed suddenly, shaking her by the hold he had on her arm. "Just shut up."

"Why?" she asked softly. "So ye can pretend ye've not sunk so low that ye're willing to be a party to murder?"

Montrose stared at her bleakly, then jerked around when a branch snapped in the trees ahead. A moment later a man stepped into view. Tall, with dirty blond hair and an affable smile, the man glanced from Murine to Montrose, then said, "I was beginning to worry ye'd been caught. Then I heard ye shouting, Monti." He tilted his head. "Everything a'right?"

Montrose stared briefly, then sighed and started forward, pulling Murine behind him. "Aye. My sister was just irritating the hell out of me as usual."

"Ah." The man she supposed was Connor Barclay nodded with understanding. "Siblings can be a trial at times."

"Is that why ye tried to kill yers?" Murine asked sweetly, recalling the rumors Greer had garnered about this man. "Imagine. Had ye succeeded ye'd be the Barclay now. Instead ye failed and were banished. Yer mother must be doubly proud."

If she'd been looking for a response, Murine certainly got that. The man closed the distance between them so quickly she couldn't even try to avoid the fist he slammed into the side of her head.

"Connor!" Montrose barked, catching his arm as he wound up for another blow. "She's annoying I know, but you'll not convince her to help us that way."

Murine cautiously lifted her head and peered up to see the fury disappear from Connor's face as if it had never been there and a crooked smile take its place. "Ye're right, of course. Silly o' me," he said lightly. "I fear I've always had a short temper." Turning back the way he'd come, he added, "Bring her along. There is much to talk about."

Montrose watched the man disappear into the trees and then let his shoulders drop with a little sigh. After a moment, he turned to scowl at her. "Watch your tongue around him. Be nice and sweet and agree with everything he says."

"Ye're afraid of him," she breathed with realization and noted the sudden tic by his eye.

"You saw him. Only a fool would anger him," he said grimly, hauling her to her feet again.

"I'm surprised ye ha'e the courage to blackmail him then," she said quietly.

"Needs must," he said grimly, urging her forward. "Besides, I only do it in writing. I wouldn't dare try it face to face. He'd kill me."

"Connor?" she said with feigned surprise. "Nay. He's no' a killer," she reminded him and kept walking when he paused abruptly. After a moment, he caught up and took her arm again, but they were both silent as he led her out of the trees and walked her across an overgrown field toward what appeared to be an old abandoned barn.

"Close the door and then put her with the boy," Connor ordered when Montrose led Murine into the building a moment later.

The door had been open when they reached it, but now Montrose paused to do as Connor had instructed. It was not a quick task. The door was hanging from one hinge and had to be lifted and shifted into place. It took Montrose several moments to manage it, and Murine took the opportunity to look around.

The lower part of the building was stone; the upper half, though, was wood and the ceiling was thatched. There was a torch stuck into a holder in the wall next to the door and a fire with a pot hung over it at this end of the building. Two barrels had been turned into furniture, one cut in half, the cut end on the ground so the tops could be used for seats. A second barrel had been cut apart as well, made short to serve as a table. There was a skin of what she'd guess was ale or wine on the barrel that served as a table, but that was pretty much it. The rest of the room appeared empty except for a pile of rags in the back right corner.

Finished with the door, Montrose took Murine's arm and urged her to the back corner of the building. It was darker than the front where a lantern and fire burned bright, but more than light enough for her to see that what she'd thought was a pile of rags on the ground was really a small, slim boy rolled up into a ball.

Montrose drew her to a halt beside the boy and Murine peered down with dismay, noting the lad's bruises and abrasions. She then turned a glare on her brother.

Montrose frowned and hissed, "He was not that bad when I left."

"What was that?" Connor asked sharply.

Forcing a smile, Montrose turned to say, "I was merely telling Murine that all would be well if she behaves and agrees to do as we ask."

"Hmm," Connor murmured.

Swallowing, Montrose turned back to Murine and hissed, "Sit down and try not to draw his attention or ire."

"Untie me," she hissed back.

Montrose hesitated, but then shook his head. Pushing down on her shoulder to force her to sit, he said with true regret, "I'm sorry. I daren't."

Murine watched him walk back to Connor with a sigh. She supposed it had been too much to hope that he'd turn on Connor at this point. It was obvious he was terrified of the man. She suspected he was regretting the part he'd played in all of this, but knew he would save his own hide first and at the expense of hers and Alpin's if necessary. Montrose was not much of a man.

A moan from the boy beside her drew her attention, and Murine turned to glance at him with concern. She'd thought him unconscious when she'd first noted his injuries, but if so he was regaining consciousness now.

"Alpin?" she said softly.

Another moan was her answer and then the boy blinked his eyes open and peered fearfully around.

"'Tis all right," she reassured him. "The men are at the other end of the building just now."

"Are you Lady Murine?" he asked, squinting at her through swollen and bruised eyes.

"Aye." She nodded and he closed his eyes unhappily.

"I was hoping they'd no' get ye," he said sadly, and then wiped at the tears suddenly coursing down his face and said, "I'm sorry, m'lady."

"'Tis all right," she said quickly, wishing she could hug the poor creature. "'Twas no' yer fault."

"Aye, 'tis," he muttered. "I tried to be brave and strong like Greer and not tell, but he . . . hurt me something awful."

Murine bit her lip, her gaze sliding over the injuries she could see. There weren't just bruises and abrasions, there were cuts on his skin as well as what she suspected were burns. Alpin hadn't given up the information about the passage easily or quickly.

"How did he ken about the passage to begin with?" Murine asked quietly, glancing toward the men at the other end of the building. Montrose and Connor were talking quietly and she wondered what about, but couldn't hear.

"When he asked me about secret entrances, I said there were none as far as I kenned, and he said Milly told him that there was and that she knew I kenned about it and how to open it," Alpin said wearily.

"Milly?" Murine queried.

"She used to be a maid at MacDonnell, but she was rude to m'lady one too many times in front o' m'laird. After the third warning, he found her a place with our neighbors, the Mac-Kennas."

"I see," Murine murmured. Connor had obviously encountered the woman at some point. Perhaps he'd stopped the night at MacKenna on his way back from court. For all she knew he was good friends with Greer and Saidh's neighbor.

Her gaze slid to Montrose and Connor again and she shook her head, and asked, "Did he just get lucky in taking ye? Surely he did no' ken when ye'd be traveling, or even that ye were away from MacDonnell."

"Aye, he knew," Alpin assured her. "The escort m'laird arranged to take me home to me parents also delivered Milly to the MacKennas. She kenned I was going home and when me father's men would bring me back. I'm pretty sure she would ha'e told him." Alpin grimaced. "She never liked me much."

Murine's mouth tightened. She hadn't a clue what to say to that.

"Do no' worry," Alpin said suddenly, and when Murine raised her eyebrows in question, he assured her, "M'laird'll save us."

"I'm sure he will," she said solemnly. They fell silent for a moment and then Murine glanced toward the men again before commenting almost in a whisper. "Yer hands are tied in front o' ye rather than behind."

"Aye," he admitted, and then she saw him cast a nervous eye toward the men before he said, "If ye turn just a bit, and I turn just a bit, I might be able to untie ye."

"That would be grand," she said, flashing him a smile before she began to shift around in small, careful increments, checking to see if the men were paying them any mind between each movement.

"What do ye think they're talking about?" Alpin asked quietly as she felt his fingers begin to work on the rope around her wrists.

Murine shook her head, and then realized he would be looking at the rope and not her head and said, "I do no' ken."

"Do ye really not ken? Or are ye just saying that rather than worry me?" Alpin asked solemnly and Murine smiled wryly. He was a smart lad.

"I suspect Connor is trying to trick Montrose into revealing where my father's will is."

"When we first met the Englishman at the cave—"

"Ye were at the cave?" she interrupted with surprise.

"Aye. M'laird's men were searching the woods and outbuildings. The cave was safer. But Connor did no' like it in there, so when the men began to move further out, he told the Englishman . . . Danvries?" he said uncertainly.

"Aye, Montrose Danvries," she verified.

"He told Danvries to meet him at the barn after he'd fetched ye."

"I see," Murine said on a sigh.

"Anyway, while we were waiting in there for the men to move on, the Connor fellow kept demanding that Danvries tell him where some will was and to give it to him. He seemed quite angry about it. Why does he care about some old will?"

Murine's mouth twisted and she said, "I suspect aside from everything else, Connor is tired o' blackmail and hopes to be rid of all his problems here today. If he gets the will back, Danvries can't blackmail him with it anymore."

"You and me, we're a part o' those problems ye're thinking he wants to be rid of, aren't we?" Alpin asked solemnly.

"I'm afraid so," she acknowledged.

"And the Englishman is blackmailing him? That's the other problem?" he asked.

"Aye," she whispered.

Alpin worked silently for a minute and then asked, "What will happen if the Englishman gives him the will?"

"I suspect Connor will try to kill you and I, make it look like my brother did it and then probably kill him and take his body away somewhere it would no' be found," she said honestly. There was no sense lying. The boy had already proven himself smart enough to see through it had she tried.

"Aye. I suspect ye're right," Alpin said quietly. After another moment of silence, he asked, "Is yer brother likely to give him the will?"

"Nay," she said with certainty. "Montrose has a healthy sense o' self-preservation."

"Ye mean he's a coward," Alpin suggested.

"That too," Murine said dryly.

"Good," Alpin said staunchly. "He'll keep him talking fer a good while then, and that'll give us a chance to try to escape."

Murine smiled faintly at the brave words and suddenly thought she understood why Saidh was so attached to the boy.

"WHAT IS IT?"

"I'm no' sure." Dougall straightened and turned over the bit of lace he'd spotted on the ground. It had seemed to take forever for he and Bowie to reach this cave at the end of the passage, and they'd arrived only to find it empty except for the bit of lace in his hand. Frowning, he dangled it from his fingers and noted that it was a circle. Eyebrows drawing together, he muttered, "I believe it is the trim from the sleeve o' me wife's gown."

"Really?" Bowie moved closer to peer at it with excitement. "She must have ripped it off and left it behind for us to find. She's leaving us a trail."

"Aye," Dougall closed his fingers over the bit of cloth and raised his torch a little higher to peer around, but everything was dark outside the circle the torch cast. "Where is the exit?"

"Over here." Bowie led him to an arch in the stone with bushes growing high beyond it.

No one would have found the entrance to the cave from outside if they hadn't already known it was there and been searching for it, Dougall thought as he started to push through the bushes.

"Wait!" Bowie caught at his arm. "Shouldn't we tell the others? We might need help getting her back. We do no' ken who has her or how many men they have with them, or how they left here. They may be on horseback and we are on foot."

Dougall frowned, but then nodded. "Aye. Go back, tell them

what we found, then bring men out on horseback. Bring my mount too. In the meantime, I'll look around and see if she's left a trail. If she has I'll follow it, but leave it in place for ye to follow on yer return."

Bowie hesitated, looking as if he wanted to protest his going alone, but then nodded and turned to head back toward the entrance to the passage, saying, "If ye find them, wait for our help. I'll return as quickly as I can."

Dougall merely grunted a response that could be taken as Bowie wished, and ducked out of the cave. If he found Murine and she was in peril, he wasn't going to wait. He wasn't sure he could wait even if she wasn't in immediate peril. It just wasn't in him to stand by and watch the woman he loved suffer pain or torment or even just fear if there was something he could do about it.

Steps slowing to a halt, Dougall stared around the clearing he now stood in. It was on the edge of a loch and looked serene and beautiful. And he'd just described his wife, at least in his own thoughts, as the woman he loved.

Dougall lowered the torch he held. It was still daylight, though the sun was dipping toward the horizon. However the torch was unnecessary.

"I love me wife," he muttered. Damn, that didn't seem a good thing, not with the way trouble followed her. So far Murine had done nothing but faint, take an arrow, and run about in burning buildings rather than see herself safe. Now she'd gone and got herself kidnapped by either her brother or some other villain to boot. If she carried on this way the woman would be in her grave ere she'd seen thirty years. Or he would because his heart had seized up from all the trials she got herself into . . . and still he loved her.

Was not that just perfect, he thought dryly and moved to the edge of the loch to douse his torch in the water. He couldn't go fall in love with a prim miss who would stay where he put her and do what she was told. Nay. Not Dougall Buchanan. He fell

in love with a little hellion who threw grown men down burning stairs and dragged others out bedchamber windows using
a damned bed linen and shutter as a pulley.

The thought of how that must have looked brought a smile to
Dougall's face, as he tossed the torch aside and began to search
the clearing for any bit of cloth his wife might have left behind.
Murine might be a passel of trouble, but she was never boring
and was definitely damned clever, he decided as he spotted a
bit of white on the green grass at the opposite edge of the clearing. It was just a part of the trim this time, he noted, examining
it briefly. Setting it back down for the others to find when they
followed, he started into the woods. He moved slowly, eyes
scanning the ground for the next bit of lace, and hoped like
hell that wherever she'd been taken to wasn't far, else she'd be
naked by the time she got there.

"There," Alpin breathed with relief as Murine felt the
rope fall away from her wrists.

"Good," she murmured, keeping her hands exactly where
they were. "Now give me your hands and let me see if I can
free you."

She felt his wrists bump against her hands, and quickly
explored with her fingers, trying to sort out what was what.
Murine soon decided that it was much harder than she would
have expected to sort out ropes and knots that you couldn't see.
She was frowning in concentration and tugging on a particular
strand of rope, when Connor suddenly pounded the makeshift
barrel table and bellowed, "I want the damned will, Monti. I'm
no' a cow fer ye to milk all the days o' me life."

Murine eyed the pair warily, her fingers moving more
quickly on the rope around Alpin's wrists. Connor obviously
had no intention of even pretending to try to convince her to
support their claim that the switched will was the true one. She
suspected he'd just used that excuse to get Montrose out here
to take her. He'd probably planned all along to find out where

the will was and kill them both. That seemed the smarter plan to her. MacIntyre would hardly push the issue about the will once she was dead.

Murine paused in her efforts to untie Alpin as it occurred to her that the attacks on the way to and at Buchanan might not have been directed at Dougall at all. The men had been sure they were at the time and she'd agreed with them because she hadn't thought there might be anyone out there who would want her dead, but now . . .

She stared at Connor silently, considering that he might have shot her with the arrow. He might also have set the fire at the lodge, she realized and recalled the bit of cloth she'd found on the window ledge. It had been made up of yellow, green and red threads, she recalled and peered at the tartan Connor was wearing. It was made up of yellow, green and red threads.

"M'lady?" Alpin said anxiously.

Recalled to her task, Murine mumbled an apology and began to work again on the rope, but her mind was racing now. Connor must have been at the lodge. He must have been the one who drugged the cider and set the fire. He'd probably come up with the idea to kill her on his way home from court. Surely he would have been in a panic at the possibility that he was about to be discovered, what with MacIntyre demanding to see the will. He would have been trying to find a way out of his problem, and killing her would have been the easy answer.

But how had he known where to find her? Murine wondered with a frown. He shouldn't have known she'd fled Danvries, let alone that she was traveling with the Buchanans. Unless he'd stopped at Danvries first and spoken to Montrose.

Her gaze shifted to her half brother. Montrose was bargaining and wheedling with Connor. She recognized the obsequious expression on his face combined with the calculating glitter in his eyes. It meant he was saying what he thought would appease Connor, while calculating what he could get away with.

She suspected he'd be lucky to get away with his life this time. A man who would burn seven innocent men to death to see that one woman died was not one to be trifled with.

"Ye did it," Alpin hissed and the rope and his hands suddenly pulled away from her busy fingers. "Ye loosened it enough I can get me hands out."

"Don't," Murine instructed at once. "Pretend they're still tight. The rope is in front on ye and we might need them to think we're still bound."

"A' right," Alpin said softly.

Murine hesitated, then started to shift again, this time moving so her back was to the wall, and then easing back to it.

"What are ye doing?" Alpin asked under his breath.

"The bottom o' the wall is made of fieldstone and old. One o' them might be loose," she breathed as she came up against the stone wall.

"Should I—" Alpin began, but paused when she shook her head abruptly.

"Nay. I'll try to find ye one too. But they might notice if we move around too much."

Alpin nodded at that and Murine concentrated on running her hands over the stones behind her back. Much to her surprise, she was quick to find one that shifted under her touch. Concentrating on that stone, she worked it back and forth a bit and then it slid easily out . . . and was followed by several more that just slid down with it. Good Lord, the wall was ready to crumble around them, Murine thought and winced as the stones clacked together. The noise seemed extremely loud to her, but the two men at the other end of the barn didn't seem to notice. At least they didn't look around.

"Here," she whispered, sliding two or three of the large stones toward Alpin.

"Ye've made a hole," Alpin said with hushed excitement.

"How big is it?" she asked worriedly and tried to feel for herself to see. "Could ye get through it?"

"Nay," Alpin said, then peered up from where he lay with a frown. "I'd no' leave ye here alone anyway."

"Ye could go bring back help," she pointed out, though the truth was she'd rather he went and hid somewhere than risk getting caught trying to escape.

"Aye!" Connor snapped suddenly, drawing her attention back to the two men again. "Or mayhap I'll just kill ye and take me chances that ye've hidden it so well no one would ever find it anyway." When Montrose merely stared at him wide-eyed, apparently at a loss for how to respond to that, Connor stood abruptly and started toward the back of the barn, pulling his sword from his waist as he snarled, "I grow tired of this. Surely they've given up the search by now. 'Tis time we take care of these two."

"Nay!" Montrose rushed to follow. "You said you just wanted to convince her to back up the will. I will not be a party to murder."

Connor paused and gave a barking laugh as he turned to face Montrose. "Ye will no' be a party to a murder," he assured him, and then added, "Ye'll be a party to several."

Montrose sagged unhappily. "Ye did kill Beathan."

"Me uncle?" he asked on a laugh. "Of course I did. Did ye think I'd have ye switch the will and risk his discovering it?" He let that sink in and then added, "I killed his sons too."

"Ye killed Colin and Peter?" Murine cried in shock, her hand closing around one of the stones behind her.

Connor turned to sneer at her. "Aye. Although, I suppose taking credit for that is not right since I merely hired mercenaries and bandits to do the actual killing." Scowling he added. "Ye were supposed to die too, leaving Uncle Beatie heirless, but they bungled the job. I killed them for that though, and to keep their mouths from ever flapping." Glaring at Montrose, he continued, "I should ha'e gone ahead and killed ye meself like I planned, but then Monti came to me with that damned idea of his. Switch the will, he says. He'd get control o' ye and yer dower estates and I'd get everything else."

Murine turned a hard gaze on Montrose at this news. The way he avoided her eyes told her Connor was telling the true version of events.

"So I thought, what the hell. That works nicely too. But then I go to switch out the wills and the original is gone. He'd taken it of course, to blackmail me from now till judgment day, the bastard."

Montrose shrugged. "I just wanted to ensure—"

"What about the fire at the Buchanan hunting lodge?" Murine interrupted grimly, not caring one whit what her brother wanted.

"Aye. That was me," Connor admitted without shame. "Killing ye seems the best way to deal with MacIntyre wanting to see the will."

Murine's mouth tightened. "And the arrow—"

"Aye," he interrupted, and then added, "And I hit ye in the head when ye slipped away from camp on yer way to Buchanan. I'd ha'e stabbed ye in the chest then but the Buchanans came rushing out and I had to flee." He scowled at her with displeasure. "Ye've been damned hard to kill, Muri."

"Don't call me that," Murine said sharply, not liking him using the nickname her friends and family had always used.

"Why not?" he snapped. "Everyone at Carmichael does. It's always Muri this and Muri that. Oh how we miss our Muri," he said bitterly. "I am sick unto death of hearing it." Turning sharply he thrust his sword into Montrose. As Monti stared blankly down at the blade that disappeared into his chest, he added, "And I am sick to death of you using that damned will to bleed me dry."

The minute the last word left his lips, Connor withdrew the sword and then watched dispassionately as Montrose wavered briefly, then dropped to his knees before falling facefirst onto the dirt floor.

Caught by surprise, Murine simply gaped down at her half brother and would have been skewered next on Connor's sword if Alpin hadn't suddenly lunged up from where he lay and pushed her to the side. Knocked out of her shock, Murine glanced around wildly as she fell, relieved when she saw that Alpin had managed to avoid the blade even as he saved her. She also saw that Connor was now raising his sword, intending to bring it down on them.

As she hit the ground, Murine recalled the stone she held and immediately rolled onto her back to hurl it at Connor. The melon-sized stone hit him in the forehead and Connor bellowed with pain and rage as he stumbled back a step. But he recovered quickly and stepped forward, raising his sword again and then froze as the tip of a blade suddenly pushed out of his chest.

Blinking, Murine leaned to the side to peer around Connor, and saw Dougall standing behind the man, his sword buried in Connor's back.

"Ye're not m'laird," Alpin said with disappointment and Murine glanced around to see that he'd crawled over beside her to look around Connor and see who had saved them.

"Nay," she said on a relieved laugh. "This is me husband, Dougall."

"Oh, I guess that's all right then," the lad muttered, blushing when she slid an arm around his shoulders and hugged him to her chest.

Murine smiled, then glanced around with a start as Connor crashed to the ground in front of them. Dougall had withdrawn his blade, she saw as he set it aside and moved quickly to drop to one knee in front of her.

"Are ye all right, love?" he asked, his hands sliding over her in search of injuries.

"Aye," she whispered, then glanced to the boy beside her and added, "But Alpin is in a bad way. He needs Rory."

Dougall nodded and immediately turned his attention to the

boy. A frown claimed his expression as he looked him over, and then he scooped him up and stood.

"Do ye have a horse?" Murine asked worriedly as she followed him the length of the barn. "I can walk if ye ha'e only the one. Alpin needs—"

"'Tis all right. I came on foot, but the others were arriving when I rushed in here," Dougall said soothingly.

"The others?" Murine asked and then followed him outside and stopped dead, her jaw dropping open. The sun was setting on the horizon, half hidden by the hills, but there was still more than enough light to see that the field was awash with men on horseback. Murine could even make out the four banners snapping in the early evening breeze.

"I gather we're a little late," Greer said dryly, dismounting and moving quickly toward them.

"That's all right, m'laird. Lady Murine's husband saved us," Alpin said as Greer took him from Dougall.

"Did he now?" Greer asked gruffly, his concern obvious as he took in the boy's various injuries.

"Only after Alpin saved me wife," Dougall said solemnly. "Thank ye fer that, lad."

Alpin shook his head and said miserably, "She would no' ha'e been there at all if no' fer me." Turning an earnest face to Greer, he added, "I tried no' to tell him how to get into the passage, m'laird. I swear I tried ever so hard, but—"

"Hush," Greer growled, carrying him back to his mount. "Ye did well, better than well. We need to get ye back to Saidh now. She's been fretting something awful."

Dougall slipped his arm around Murine and they watched as Greer passed Alpin to his first, Bowie, so he could mount his horse. Once in the saddle, he quickly took the boy back, arranged him carefully in his lap and then broke from the group and rode back toward the castle with several of his men following.

"Danvries and Connor's bodies are inside," Dougall announced as he urged Murine toward where Aulay, MacIntyre and Sinclair were now dismounting.

"I'll have some men collect them," Aulay assured him.

"So, they were in on it together after all," MacIntyre said dryly, and shook his head. Glancing to Murine he asked, "And the will?"

"Fake," she admitted on a sigh. "Montrose kept the original though. I imagine it's somewhere at Danvries."

The old man nodded. "I'll take me men and ride there first thing on the morrow to fetch it. But I ken what it'll say. Beatie would have left everything to you, lass."

Murine merely shrugged unhappily and then blurted, "Connor killed Father, and hired the men who killed Peter and Colin."

MacIntyre closed his eyes and sighed wearily, then shook his head before opening his eyes again. Expression solemn, he said, "Don't let that taint Carmichael fer ye, lass. Remember the good times ye had there, and think on the people there who need ye. Connor was a ruthless bastard, I doubt he showed the clan much care."

Swallowing, Murine nodded and then glanced to Dougall when he touched her shoulder. Alick had brought his mount and Dougall was already on him. Now he leaned down and lifted her up in front of him.

Once she was settled sideways in his lap, Murine glanced back to MacIntyre. "Are ye coming up to the castle?"

"Aye. I'll visit fer a wee bit ere I head back to camp," he said with a smile.

Murine nodded, then glanced to Campbell Sinclair and smiled before asking hopefully, "Is Jo here too?"

"Are ye jesting? I could no' keep her away," he said with a smile. "She's up at the castle showing off little Bearnard. She'll be happy to see ye well and safe."

Murine nodded, then leaned back into Dougall with a sigh as he turned his horse to follow the path Greer had taken back to the castle.

They rode swiftly out of the clearing, but once they'd left the field and the men behind, Dougall suddenly slowed his mount to a standstill. Surprised, Murine straightened and turned to peer at him in question, but he didn't look down at her. Instead he stared over her head at the road ahead as he asked, "Do ye want an annulment?"

"What?" she asked with shock.

Sighing, Dougall finally looked at her and said, "Ye only married me for protection from yer brother. But now ye're safe, and ye're no' longer a dowerless lass. In fact ye're rich. Ye've Carmichael and probably Danvries too, and could marry anyone ye like. If ye want an anul—"

"Nay," she interrupted sharply, and then frowned as confusion filled her mind. "Do ye want to annul our marriage? Is that why ye asked? Ye only married me to save me. Do ye want—"

"Nay," he assured her solemnly, then raised one hand to clasp her cheek and said, "I love ye, Murine."

"Really?" she asked with a smile.

"Aye," he said solemnly. "Ye're reckless and too brave fer yer own good, and 'twill probably take all the coin I would ha'e spent on building a castle to keep ye in gowns, but I love ye."

She laughed at his words, then hugged him tightly and whispered, "I love ye too, husband."

Dougall remained still for a moment, and then pulled back and raised his eyebrows. "That's it?' I love ye too, husband' is all ye have to say?"

Murine hesitated, concern filling her that she'd done something wrong. Perhaps she should say why she loved him, or when she'd realized it. Her worries faded away, however, when she noted the teasing glint in his eyes.

Schooling her expression, she offered, "I love ye too, husband, and I am no' wearing braies under me gown today."

When his eyes widened incredulously, she tilted her head and asked, "Will that do?"

"That'll do, love," he growled and urged his mount to start moving again as he bent to kiss her.

Want more Lynsay Sands?
Keep reading for an excerpt from
her next Argenau family novel,

**IMMORTAL
UNCHAINED**

Coming April 2017
from Avon Books

"$\mathcal{I}$ BEGIN TO THINK THEY ARE GOING TO BE LATE," DOMI-tian murmured, hefting his duffel bag higher on his shoulder so that the microphone hidden in his sleeve would catch his words.

"Perhaps it is a sign." Lucian Argeneau's voice was surprisingly clear. The earpiece they'd given Domitian was so small that it was unseen once inserted, but the sound came through loud and crystal clear. "We should scrap this now and—"

"Still trying to talk me out of going, Uncle?" Domitian asked with amusement, and then suddenly impatient, added, "I do not know why you are so resistant to my doing this. Especially with Uncle Victor, Lucern, Decker, Nicholas, Aunt Eshe, Mirabeau LaRoche and Santo Notte now among the missing. I would think with all of them having been taken—"

"That is precisely why," Lucian interrupted him in a growl. "This is dangerous. We have already lost several hunters, people armed and trained to handle situations like this. You, Domitian, are going in there unarmed, and you are *not* a hunter."

"True, but I was a warrior once. I can handle myself," Domitian argued. "Besides, none of your hunters were invited, I was."

"Yes, but was it because you are a chef and Dressler wants you to work for him? Or because you are an immortal who he wants to add to his collection?"

"I told you. He does not know I am an immortal," Domitian said slowly and firmly, stressing each word. They'd had this conversation several times already, but it seemed they would have it again. "If Dressler knew, he could have taken me at any time. He has been a regular in my restaurant for five years. He obviously does not know."

"Or perhaps he did not wish to kidnap an immortal so close to home," Lucian countered. "It might have led us straight here to Venezuela."

Domitian shifted impatiently at the suggestion. "One immortal missing in Caracas would hardly have brought you here when so many have gone missing in the United States."

"Perhaps. Or perhaps we would have—"

"Is that helicopter headed this way?" Domitian interrupted, raising a hand to shield his eyes from the sun as he watched the vehicle approach. It was flying low and seemed to be headed straight for where he stood at the base of the large dock . . . which was where he'd been directed to wait for his ride. He'd expected a boat, but—

"Are those pontoons?" Lucian asked sharply in his ear.

Domitian knew that Lucian and the others wouldn't have as good a view from the small boat where they waited further along the docks. Aside from that, they were staying out of sight in the small cabin in the bow, which had only tiny windows that were glazed and screened. Their view would be highly obscured compared to his.

"Yes. The helicopter has pontoons," he confirmed, his gaze on the skids with the floatation devices affixed to them. It was fitted out to be an amphibious helicopter so that it could set down on water or land, which made Domitian suspect that this *was* his ride. Apparently he wasn't the only one to think that, he realized, wincing as a loud curse sounded in his ear.

"You are not to get on that helicopter!" Lucian ordered firmly. "Make an excuse. Tell them you have changed your mind. We did not plan for this. The boats out in the bay might lose the helicopter. Do you hear me?"

His thoughts racing, Domitian watched the helicopter slow and begin to drop by the end of the dock. To get onboard or not was the question. If he said he had a fear of flying, Dressler might send a boat for him and then Lucian's men could follow from a safe distance to find the island. Then again, he might not. Dressler might suspect something was afoot and simply cancel the job offer altogether . . . and Domitian couldn't risk that. He had to get on that island. His life mate was there and could be in danger.

"Domitian? Can you hear me?" Lucian barked sharply, and then his voice faded as he asked someone else, "Is this thing working? Why is he not answering?"

"Perhaps the noise from the helicopter is drowning you out," another voice responded. Domitian was pretty sure that voice belonged to the young hunter, Justin Bricker and was grateful for the suggestion. He would pretend it was true and he couldn't hear his uncle. He *was* getting on that helicopter. He might be risking his life doing it, but not getting on risked his chance of any kind of a happy future.

"Dammit! Domitian! Do not get on that helicopter! Domitian?"

Ignoring the voice in his ear, Domitian watched the helicopter set down, not on the water, but on the end of the dock. He then started forward.

"Domitian Argeneau!" Lucian's voice roared in his ear.

"It's Argenis, Uncle. Not Argeneau," Domitian reminded him gently before unobtrusively plucking the earpiece from his ear and tucking it into the front pocket of his tight jeans. It didn't matter what anyone said. He was going, Domitian thought as he watched the back, side door of the helicopter open.

Instinctively ducking, he rushed quickly under the rotors to the entrance. A man in a suit was waiting with his hand out to take his duffle bag. Domitian handed it over with a nod of thanks, and then grasped the doorframe and climbed in. The window seat was the only one available, so he settled into it and pulled the door closed without having to be told.

Domitian then started to turn to get a better look at the other men in the helicopter, but stiffened in surprise as he felt a sudden sharp pain in the side of his neck. He lost consciousness almost at once.